Emperor and Clown

Emperor
and Clown

Book Four of A Man of His Word

Dave Duncan

© Copyright 1991 by D.J. Duncan
First e-reads publication 1999
www.e-reads.com
ISBN 0-7592-3958-4

THE VOICE I HEAR this passing night was heard
In ancient days, by emperor and clown:
Perhaps the self-same song that found a path
Through the sad heart of Ruth, when sick for home,
She stood in tears amid the alien corn;
    The same that oft-times hath
Charmed magic casements, opening on the foam
Of perilous seas, in faery lands forlorn.
                    KEATS, *Ode to a Nightingale*

Table of Contents

Emperor
and Clown

1

Naught availeth

1

Of all the cities of Pandemia, only Hub had no legend or history of its founding. Hub was a legend in its own right, and history was its creation.

Hub had always been. It was the capital of the Impire, the mother of superlatives, the City of the Gods. It sprawled along the shores of Cenmere like a marble cancer.

Alone among all the dwelling places of mankind, only Hub had never known sack or rape or the ravages of war. Forever it had lurked in peace behind the swords of its legions and the sorcery of the Four. Hub was graced by the spoils of a thousand campaigns and nourished on taxes extracted from half the world. Slaves in forgotten millions had died to build it, priceless artworks had crumbled and weathered away in its halls and gardens to make space for more.

It was the best and worst parts of a hundred cities, melted into one. Its finest avenues were wide enough to march a century abreast; its darkest alleys were slits where half a legion could have vanished without trace.

Hub was grandeur. Hub was squalor. Hub gathered all the beauty of the world and offered every vice. Its wealth and population were uncountable. Year in and year out, by ship and wagon, food poured into Hub to feed its teeming mouths, yet the humble starved. Hub exported war and laws and little else but bodies — especially those in summer, when the fevers raged. The rich imported their wine from distant lands, but their servants drank from the same wells as the poor, and they infected their masters.

All roads led to Hub, the imps boasted, and in Hub the greatest ways led to the center, the five hills, the five palaces. The abodes of the wardens, the Red, the White, the Gold, the Blue — beautiful but sinister, these were secret places, masked and buttressed by sorcery, and few went willingly to those. In their midst, highest and greatest, shone the Opal Palace of the imperor, seat of government and all mundane power.

To the Opal Palace came glory and tribute and petitions and ambassadors.

And to the Opal Palace came also, each in its own time, all the problems of the world.

At the center of Pandemia, Shandie thought, *is the Impire. At the center of the Impire is Hub. At the center of Hub is the Opal Palace — although that isn't quite true, because it's too near the lake to be really in the center — and at the center of the Opal Palace is Emine's Rotunda, and at the center of the rotunda is me.*

Am I, he amended hastily.

And that wasn't quite true, either, because the exact center of the great round hall was the throne, and he was standing one step down from the throne, on Grandfather's right.

He must not move. Not a finger. Not a toe. This was a very formal occasion.

And Moms had warned him: Ythbane was running out of patience with Shandie's continual fidgeting at state functions. Princes must know how to behave with dignity, Ythbane said, not twitch and shuffle and pick their noses on the steps of the throne. If he couldn't learn how to stand for a couple of hours, at least he would be stopped from sitting down for the rest of the day. Not that Shandie had *ever* picked his nose on the steps of the throne. He didn't think he really fidgeted enough that any of the audience could see. He didn't think he'd earned his last few beatings, but Ythbane had thought so, and Moms always agreed with anything the consul said. And Grandfather didn't even know who Shandie was now.

Grandfather was on his throne, so he was the center of the rotunda, and the palace, and the city, and the Impire, and the world. From the sound of his breathing, he was asleep again. Moms was on his far side, also on the first step; but she had a chair to sit on.

2

Dad had stood here once, he remembered. Where he was. Moms didn't talk about Dad now, not ever.

Keeping perfectly still would be much easier if you could sit down to do it. Shandie's knees were shaking. His left arm was a torment of fire ants from staying bent, holding up his toga. If his arm fell off, would that be counted as moving?

Ythbane would probably beat him anyway.

He was still sore from last time.

Grandfather snorted and snuffled in his sleep. Lucky Grandfather!

One day I will sit on that throne, and be Imperor Emshandar V.

Then I will kill Ythbane.

That was a wonderful thought.

What else should an imperor do? First, have Ythbane's backside beaten — right there, on the floor of the rotunda, where the fat delegate was still kneeling, reciting his nonsense. In front of the court and the senators. Shandie caught himself about to smile, and didn't.

Then be merciful and cut off his head.

Second, abolish these stupid, stupid togas!

Why should formal occasions require formal court dress, togas and sandals? No one wore them any other time. What was wrong with hose and doublet and shoes? Or even tights, which were the latest craze. Ordinary people never had to wear these *ridiculous*, scratchy, uncomfortable bed sheets. Sane, ordinary people hadn't worn things like these for thousands of years. *Oh, my poor arm!*

Abolish togas, that was certain.

And abolish all these dreadful formal ceremonies!

Why bother with them? Grandfather certainly didn't want them — he'd been weeping when they'd brought him in. The birthday homages had just started, too. They would be going on for weeks. What sort of a way was that to celebrate a birthday, even a seventy-fifth?

A birthday was one day. That's what the word meant. Birth*day*!

Shandie's tenth birthday was just a month away, and he was going to have a one-day birthday. Mostly awful ceremonial, too, but a party with some other boys if he was good, Moms said.

The toga was hot and heavy. Sunlight blazed down from the windows in the high dome, casting his shadow at his feet — but he mustn't look down.

The fat delegate from wherever-it-was came to a stuttering end at last, obviously as relieved as Shandie. He bent forward to place his offering beside the other offerings, then crawled back a pace and touched his face to the floor. Everyone looked up at Grandfather, and Shandie froze. Even his eyes.

Don't blink while Ythbane is watching!

3

Grandfather was supposed to say something then, but all Shandie heard was another half snore.

As a consul, Ythbane stood at the head of the line of toga-clad ministers, nearest to the imperor. Shandie could feel those hateful eyes washing over him, looking for signs of fidgeting, but he stared rigidly across at the empty White Throne and did not breathe. Little tremors crawled over his scalp. If his hair stood on end, would Ythbane call that fidgeting?

Ythbane said loudly, "His Imperial Majesty welcomes the greetings from his loyal city of Shaldokan."

The fat delegate looked confused, but then realized he could begin his withdrawal. He had trouble managing his toga while crawling backward at the same time. Probably he'd never worn one of the stupid things before in his life. Now he was rising and bowing, and so on . . .

The chief herald ponderously consulted his list. "The honored delegate from the loyal city of Shalmik," he proclaimed. This one was a woman, one of only two women today. She was very ugly, but these were northern cities, so maybe she had some goblin blood in her. Goblins had been talked of a lot just lately, although Shandie had almost never heard them mentioned until a few weeks ago. In the spring, a horde of the little green vermin had ambushed and massacred four cohorts of Grandfather's legionaries while they were on diplomatic business — and tortured the prisoners to death! Marshal Ithy had promised Shandie he would punish them severely.

Twenty-four cities had delivered their birthday presents. That left four more to come after the woman. Then there would be some sort of petition — the Nordland ambassador was waiting in the background. A jotunn, of course. He was old, but he still looked strong enough to take on a century single-handed. Maybe his hair had always been that pale color. He would have those creepy jotunn blue eyes, too. Ugly, bleached monsters, Moms said. Imps were the only really handsome people.

Emine's Rotunda was very big. Shandie wondered how many people it would hold, but if he asked Court Teacher he would just make Shandie work it out on his abacus. Circles were tricky — was it times twenty-two, divide by seven, or the other way?

There were at least a hundred senators on the bank of seats around the north side, distinguishable from their guests and other notables by the purple hems on their togas. *They* certainly weren't keeping still. They were talking and reading and some of them were dozing, like Grandfather was.

The southerly seats held lesser people, even commoners, and they were being quieter, but he mustn't look around to see how many there were.

Emine II (q.v.), imperor of the First Dynasty, and legendary founder of the Protocol (q.v.), which brought the powers of sorcery under control by establishing the Council of Four

4

Wardens (q.v.), occult guardians of the Impire . . . Without Court Teacher telling him to, Shandie had memorized a whole page about Emine and recited it for Moms, and she had been pleased and given him a candycake. She had made him repeat it for Ythbane that evening, and even Ythbane had praised him and almost smiled.

They were always pleased when he did bookish things well. They wouldn't let him do military things — things with horses and swords, although those were what he really wanted, because when he grew up he was going to be a *warrior* imperor, like Agraine. He wasn't allowed to do boyish things with other boys hardly at all now. And ceremonial things he hated and usually got beaten after, for fidgeting at. The price of being the heir. Moms said, but it was all Ythbane's idea.

The woman delegate on her knees had forgotten her words. She stopped, turning ashen pale. Shandie felt sorry for her, wondering if the city fathers would order her beaten when she went home to wherever-it-was. The silence dragged on. No one helped, or could help. The line of ministers remained motionless, staring over her at the opposing line, which was made up of heralds and secretaries. Farther away, the large group of delegates-who-had-done-their-speech looked hugely relieved that this wasn't their problem. The small group of delegates-who-haven't-done-it-yet looked terrified.

The woman began all over again from first genuflection, gabbling the words in a shrill voice. The senators in their comfortable chairs were paying no attention.

Those spectator benches went all the way around, except where the four aisles were, of course, but they still left lots of room in the middle. And in the center of that big round floor were the two round steps with Grandfather's throne on top. Today was a north day; northern cities paying homage, the Opal Throne facing north. Halfway between Shandie and the senators, the White Throne stood on a single step. That place belonged to the warden of the north, but it was empty. Shandie had never seen a warden. Not many people had. And nobody ever wanted even to talk about them, even Grandfather, but he at least wasn't scared of them. He was imperor, so he could summon the wardens.

One day I will be imperor and use Emine's buckler to summon the wardens.

Even before Grandfather got old, he had not been frightened of the witch and the warlocks. They couldn't touch him, he'd said; that was in the Protocol. No one could use magic on Shandie, either, because he was family. Not that being heir apparent was much comfort when he was bent over Ythbane's writing table with his pants down. Any magic would be better than that.

The poor woman came to an end at last; eyes turned toward the throne; Shandie stopped breathing again. The pins and needles in his left arm were making his eyes water. If he wriggled his fingers just a little, very slowly, surely no one would notice and tell Ythbane he'd been fidgeting?

Ythbane spoke for Grandfather again; the woman scrabbled away; another delegate came forward to kneel.

Tomorrow would be East's turn — eastern cities bringing greetings, Grandfather seated facing east, toward the Gold Throne. Moms and Shandie, too. The senators would have the eastern seats, facing west. He wondered how the senators chose who came on which day, because that wasn't the whole Senate sitting there.

Not long to go now.

It was awfully hard to keep his knees from shaking, and they did hurt. He tried to imagine the witch of the north suddenly appearing over there on her White Throne, although it wasn't really white, being carved out of ivory. Bright Water was a goblin, and hundreds of years old. He'd heard people muttering that maybe she'd set the goblins on the Pondague legionaries, but he knew that only East would use magic on Grandfather's army. What was the word? He'd seen it in his history book. *Pre-roga-tive! Prerogative* (*q.v.*), whatever (*q.v.*) meant. Bright Water's prerogative was Nordland raiders, but it was silly of the Protocol to put a goblin woman in charge of jotunn sailors. South's was dragons and West's was weather.

If Bright Water ever did appear on her throne, then likely all the warlocks would appear, as well, each on his own throne — Olybino and Zinixo and Lith'rian. An imp, a dwarf, and an elf. That was silly, too. The Protocol should have made all the wardens imps, to protect the Impire properly.

One day, when Shandie got to be Emshandar V, then he would get to read the Protocol (q.v.). Only imperors and wardens ever did.

No sorcerer would ever come to a brain-melting boring meeting like this, though.

They were done! Now another herald was unrolling a scroll. Ythbane nodded. "His Excellency, Ambassador from the Nordland Confederacy . . . "

Ambassador Krushjor came striding forward like a great white bear, followed by a half-dozen other jotnar, all shockingly half naked in helmet, breeches, and boots and nothing else — dumb barbarians showing off their hairy chests and *hey-look-at-that* muscles! Ambassadors were the only people excused formal court dress. They were allowed ethnic costume. It did look silly, though.

Oh, Holy Balance! Shandie realized that he could use some of those muscles himself right then. His left arm was sagging under the weight of the train draped over it. He tried to raise it and couldn't. It wouldn't obey him. It was dead.

But Ythbane couldn't have noticed yet. He was eyeing the jotunn ambassador, and having to lean his head back to do it. The consul was not big for an imp, and the older man was an average-size jotunn. Some of the younger jotnar in the back were even bigger, with bushy gold beards. And muscles! Bet they could hold up a toga for weeks if they ever had to. Moms called the jotnar "murdering monsters."

The senators had fallen silent, as if this were going to be more interesting than . . . Gods! There, up in the back row — how could he not have noticed sooner? Just in time, Shandie remembered not to move. It was Aunt Oro, right in there with the senators! He hadn't seen her in months. She'd been away at Leesoft. His heart jumped, then sank — he wanted to run to her, or at least smile and wave, but of course he mustn't move. He thought maybe he'd twitched a little on seeing her, but Ythbane was still watching the jotunn, so it wouldn't matter.

She'd understand that he must put duty first, and mustn't fidget on formal occasions.

Fancy Aunt Oro in with the senators! But of course she had senatorial rank. Much higher rank, really, because she was *Princess Imperial* Orosea. She even outranked Moms, who was only Princess Uomaya. So Aunt Oro could sit anywhere she wanted, but he'd have expected her to have a chair on the steps of the throne, like Moms. He wondered when she'd returned to court. He hadn't heard a whisper, and he was pretty good at picking up gossip, because he spent a lot of time around grown-ups and they tended to forget he was there.

Surely she wouldn't go back to Leesoft without coming to see him? He wouldn't mind a hug from Aunt Oro. It wouldn't be unmanly to let her hug him just once — it wasn't as if everyone did. Or anyone, really. Of course it would be unmanly to mention the beatings. All boys got beaten, and princes were special and had to be specially beaten. So Ythbane had said last time, making a joke — he'd added a couple of strokes, saying Shandie was being impudent by not laughing.

If Aunt Oro asked any questions, of course, he'd have to tell the truth, and if he was still limping . . .

"*The matter of Krasnegar has already been settled, signed and sealed!*" Ythbane was shouting. Bad sign. He shouted a lot these days. He'd never shouted before Grandfather got old.

Shouting wasn't going to do him much good with the jotunn, though. The big silver beard parted to show big yellow teeth. "With respect, Eminence —" He didn't look respectful. "— the document we initialed was merely a memorandum of agreement. It was always subject to the approval of the Thanes' Moot."

"And you were to send it —"

"It is on its way to Nordland. I respectfully remind your Eminence, though, that Nordland is months away, and the Moot meets only once a year, at midsummer."

The ministers were whispering at Ythbane's back, the secretaries and heralds fretting and shuffling. The jotnar were smirking. Ythbane seemed to

7

swell, all pompous in his toga with a purple hem. "So it will not be ratified until next summer —"

"Isn't that obvious?"

"— but until then —"

"No! Until the news reaches Hub! You do realize that the return journey will also take months?" The pale-skinned old man leered down at the consul, and his manner was so like the one Ythbane himself used on Shandie that Shandie almost disgraced himself by giggling. Ythbane would kill him if he did that.

Ythbane swung around and whispered for a moment with Lord Humaise, and Lord Hithire, and a couple of other new advisors Shandie didn't know; then he turned around to confront the ambassador again, his face dark as a postilion's boot.

"The wording of the memorandum was very specific. Until the Moot's decision is conveyed to his Imperial Majesty's council, both sides shall act as if the agreement has been ratified in formal treaty. The king will remain in —"

"King?"

"Oh . . . what's his name? . . . the former Duke of Kinvale!" Ythbane was snarling. He was ever so mad now, and . . . Oh, *no!* Shandie's dead arm had drooped so low that the train of his toga was starting to slide off it. *God of Children!* What did he do now?

" . . . and you were to nominate a viceroy *pro tem*, subject to . . . " The consul was growing even louder and madder. He would stay mad for days after this. Shandie needed to yawn. His toga was falling off him. He *really* needed to go pee. He wasn't much interested in Krasnegar — he'd overheard a few whispers that it was a sellout, that the Council had settled for a paper triumph and given the kingdom to the jotnar. If that was so, then Shandie would take it back when he was grown up and a warrior imperor, but right now he was too weary to care. Another pleat slid off his hand.

Ythbane had finished, but whatever he'd said had not impressed the big blond bear.

"I am an ambassador, not a plenipotentiary, Eminence, as you know. I never professed to have the power to override the thane's personal rights in this matter. Indeed, if he chooses to press his claim, then the Moot itself would back him as King of Krasnegar. The thanes would never infringe a privilege of one of their own number." He glanced round at his companions, who grinned; then he added, "Not this one's, anyway!"

"Kalkor is a murdering, raping, barbar —"

Now the ambassador swelled, and to much better effect than Ythbane had managed. He stepped closer, his fair face ominously flushed. "Do I report your words to the thane as official Imperial policy, or as your personal opinions?" His bellow reverberated down from the dome.

8

Ythbane fell back a pace. The ministers exchanged worried glances; the jotunn flunkies grinned again.

"Well?" roared the ambassador, still wanting an answer.

"What'th all the sthouting?" a new voice said.

Shandie jumped and looked around before he could stop himself. Grandfather was awake! He was slumped awkwardly in his seat, but he was awake. His right eye was open, the left half closed as always, and he was drooling, as always, but obviously he was having one of his good spells, and Shandie was glad, glad, glad! — they were so rare now! It was as if the old man had gone away, like Aunt Oro, and it made Shandie feel all cozy-nice to see him come back, although it would only be for a few minutes.

And Grandfather had noticed Shandie! He smiled down at him. "You're toga'th come tooth, tholdier," he said quietly. But he was smiling, not angry at all! And Shandie must move to obey an imperial command, whether Ythbane liked it or not. Quickly he gathered up the fallen folds with his right hand, looping them back on his left arm, and he lifted that useless limb back into place and held it there. The pleating was an awful scrimmage, but it would have to do. He smiled briefly, gratefully, up at Grandfather, then turned to stare across at the White Throne again, going as still as a stone pillar again. Pity he'd had no excuse to move his feet a bit.

Ythbane had recovered from his surprise. He bowed to the throne. "A discussion of the Krasnegar matter, your Majesty."

"Thought that wath all thettled?" Grandfather's voice was very slurred nowadays, and quiet, but the words obviously staggered the courtiers. Clearly he still understood more than they had believed.

"Ambassador Krushjor's views of the concordat —"

"Memorandum!" the ambassador roared.

"Whaz 'e want?" the imperor mumbled.

Ythbane scowled. "He demands safe conduct for Thane Kalkor to come here to Hub to negotiate in person on a matter —"

"— he has the best claim to the throne of Krasn —" Krushjor bellowed, much louder than the consul.

"— burning and looting —"

"— thane of Gark, and an honored —"

"— ever dares show his face —"

Then . . . sudden silence, with everyone staring up at the throne behind Shandie's left shoulder. If it wasn't sorcery, then Grandfather must have gestured.

"Kalkor?" the tired old voice whispered.

"Yes, Sire! The same murdering raider who has been killing and looting all through the Summer Seas for months. The Navy's Southern Command has been completely reorganized over the matter, as your Majesty will recall, but too late to stop this Kalkor escaping westward, through Dyre Channel. He sacked three towns in Krul's Bay and is now apparently in, or near to, Uthle. He has the *audacity* to propose that he sail his infamous orca longship up the Ambly River — *all the way to Cenmere!*"

Ministers and secretaries shook their heads in disbelief. Senators rumbled with outrage. Shandie had been reading up on that geography just yesterday: the Nogid Archipelago, and the horrid anthropophagi (q.v.), and the Mosweep Mountains, and trolls . . .

"Worse!" Ythbane added loudly. "He, a notorious pirate, demands to be recognized as sovereign ruler of Gark, as if it were an independent state, so he can negotiate directly with your Imperial Majesty on the matter of Krasnegar. He furthermore demands safe conduct for —"

"Granted!"

Ythbane choked, stared, then said, "Sire?" disbelievingly.

"If he'th here behaving himthelf, then he'th not looting thomewhere elsh."

There was a long, shocked silence, then the consul bowed. "As your Majesty commands." The senators were glaring.

"When he leavth, tell the Navy," Grandfather said wearily.

Smiles flashed among ministers and secretaries and heralds. Ripples of mirth rolled through senatorial ranks. The jotnar scowled angrily. Ythbane even put on his smile face, briefly — which wasn't a smile like anyone else's.

Shandie heard a sort of groan from Grandfather and desperately wanted to turn and look, but he daren't, and besides, he was suddenly feeling awfully sick in his stomach. There was a funny ringing in his head, too.

"Safe conduct for Thane Kalkor and how many men, Ambassador?" the consul inquired with icy politeness.

"Forty-five jotnar and one goblin."

Ythbane had already turned to give orders, but at that he spun back to Krushjor, "Goblin?"

Grandfather was snoring again. The sunlight was fading.

"A goblin," the ambassador said, "male, apparently."

"What's he doing with a goblin?"

"No idea. Perhaps he looted him from somewhere? You ask — I won't! But his letter was very insistent that he will be bringing a goblin with him to Hub."

Suddenly the ringing in Shandie's ears swelled to a roar. The step swayed beneath him. He staggered and heard himself cry out.

As he pitched forward, the last thing he saw was Ythbane's dark eyes watching him.

10

2

Far, far to the east, evening drew near to Arakkaran. Yet white sails still sprinkled the great blue bay, and the bazaars were thronged. Palms danced in the warm and salty winds — winds that wafted odors of dung and ordure in through windows and scents of musk and spices and gardenias along foul alleys. All day, as every day, by ship and camel, mule and wagon, the wealth of the land had flowed into the shining city.

Jotunn sailors had toiled in the docks, while elsewhere a scattering of other folk had plied their trades: impish traders, dwarvish craftsmen, elvish artists, mermaid courtesans, and gnomish cleaners; but these outsiders were very few amid the teeming natives. Tall and ruddy, swathed mostly in flowing robes, the djinns had argued and gossiped as always in their harsh Zarkian dialect; they had bargained and quarreled, laughed and loved like any other people. And if they had also bed and cheated a little more than most — well, anyone who didn't know the rules must be a stranger, so why worry?

At the top of the city stood the palace of the sultan, a place of legendary beauty and blood-chilling reputation; and there, upon a shaded balcony, Princess Kadolan of Krasnegar was quietly going insane.

Almost two days now had passed since her niece had married the sultan, and Kadolan had heard nothing since. Inosolan might as well have vanished from the world. Of course a newly married couple could be expected to treasure their privacy, but this total silence was ominous and unsettling. Inosolan would never treat her aunt this way by choice.

Kadolan was a prisoner in all but name. Her questions went unanswered, the doors were locked and guarded. She was attended by taciturn strangers. She would never have claimed to have friends in Arakkaran, but she did have many acquaintances now among the ladies of the palace; persons she could address by name, share tea and chat with, whiling away a gentle hour or two. She had asked for many, with no result.

Especially she had asked for Mistress Zana. Kadolan had a hunch that Zana's was the most sympathetic ear she was likely to find, but even Zana had failed to return her messages.

Something was horribly wrong. By rights, the palace should be rejoicing. Not only was there a royal wedding and a new Sultana Inosolan to celebrate, but also the death of Rasha. Arakkaran was free of the sorceress who had effectively ruled it for more than a year. That should be a cause for merriment, but instead a miasma of fear filled the air, seeping from marble and tile to cloud the sun's fierce glare.

It must be all imagination, Kadolan told herself repeatedly as she paced, but an insistent inner voice whispered that she had never been prone to such

1 1

morbid fancies before. Although no one outside Krasnegar would have known it, and few there, she was almost seventy years old. After so long a life, she should be able to trust her instincts, and her instincts were shouting that something was very, very wrong.

She had left Inosolan at the door of the royal quarters. Two nights and two days had passed since then.

The days had been hard, filled with bitter loneliness and worry. The nights had been worse, haunted by dreams of Rasha's terrible end. Foolish, foolish woman! Again and again Kadolan had wakened from nightmares of that awful burning skeleton, that fearful, tragic corpse raising its arms to the heavens in a final rending cry of, LOVE! — only to vanish in a final roar of flame.

Four words of power made a sorcerer. Five destroyed.

Master Rap had whispered a word in Rasha's ear, and she had been consumed.

The balcony was high. Over roofs and cloisters Kadolan had a distant view of one of the great courtyards, where brown-clad guards had passed to and fro all day, escorting princes in green or, rarely, groups of black-draped women. Horsemen paraded sometimes. They were too far off for her to make out details, and yet something about the way they all moved had convinced her that they were as troubled as she.

She had erred.

So had Inosolan.

A God had warned Inosolan to trust in love, and she had taken that to mean that she must trust in Azak's love, that in time she would learn to return the love of that giant barbarian she had married.

And then, too late . . .

He was only a stableboy. Kadolan had never even met him until that last night in Krasnegar. She had not exchanged a word with him directly. She did not know him. No one did — he was only a stableboy! Not handsome or charming or educated or cultured, just a commonplace laborer in the palace stables. But he had saved Inosolan from the devious Andor, and when the sorceress had abducted Inosolan, he had shouted, "I am coming!"

How could they have known? Crossing the whole of Pandemia in half a year, fighting his way in through the massed guards of the family men, removing the sorceress by telling her one of his two words of power — even if he had not planned the terrible results.

The God had not meant Azak. The God had meant the stableboy, the childhood friend.

It was all so obvious now.

Too late.

And the boy . . . man . . . Rap?

12

At best he was chained in some awful dungeon somewhere, under peril of the sultan's jealousy. At worst he was already dead, although she feared that death itself might not be the worst.

Even that last awful night in Krasnegar, Kadolan should have realized that a stableboy who knew a word of power was no ordinary churl. And somewhere on his journey he had learned a second word; he had become an adept, a superman. That was an astounding feat in itself, but even two words of power could not save him now.

To and fro . . . to and fro . . . Kadolan paced and paced.

She had been Inosolan's chaperon and counselor. She should have given better advice.

She had tried, she recalled. She had been inclined to trust Rasha, where Inosolan had not. What better things might then have happened? Who now could know? Kadolan had warned against the flight into the desert, which had ended so ignominiously, in defeat and forced return. But Kadolan had not been insistent enough.

So Inosolan was doomed to a life of harem captivity, bearing sons in an alien land. Her kingdom was lost, abandoned by the impire and the wardens to the untender mercies of the Nordland thanes.

And the boy Rap was dead or dying, and that guilt tortured Kadolan worse than anything.

Love or mere loyalty, neither should be so cruelly repaid.

She had never put much stock in magic. She was not a very imaginative person, she knew, and she had never quite believed in the occult — not even when she had sensed the death of Inosolan's mother and gone racing back to Krasnegar, fleeing from Kinvale at three days' notice to catch the last ship before winter. In retrospect, that had been a miraculous premonition, and yet she had refused to believe, she had never told anyone. Holindarn had accepted that her arrival was a merely a fortunate coincidence. Inosolan had been too young to wonder about it at all.

The balcony had grown insufferably hot below the westering sun. Reeling with weariness from her endless pacing, Kadolan tottered indoors and sank into a padded chair.

By the palace standards, her new quarters were almost an insult — old and shabby, absurdly overfurnished with ugly statuary in the style of the XIVth Dynasty, which must be loot from some long-forgotten campaign. It was almost as if she had been locked up in a boxroom until someone figured out what to do with her.

Why, oh, why would Inosolan not answer her messages?

Had they ever reached her?

13

3

Farther down the hillside, in the middle of the city, evening shadows lay cool and blue across Sheik Elkarath's jeweled garden, and the air was fragrant with jasmine and mimosa. The earliest stars twinkled, fountains tinkled.

Master Skarash was definitely tipsy now. He reached for the wine bottle and discovered that it was empty. He tossed it into a hibiscus. How many did that make? What did it matter? What was the cost of a few bottles of wine against the profits to be made from a major business partnership? Opportunities like this came rarely in any merchant's lifetime, and Grandsire was going to be enormously proud of him. Of course the details were still somewhat obscure and extremely complex, and would have to be worked out very carefully in the morning, when both parties were more alert, but there was no doubt that this evening's jollity would reap huge wealth in the future for the House of Elkarath. It would be the first coup of a very long and successful career.

Skarash bellowed loudly for one of his cousins to fetch more wine. He peered blearily at his drinking companion.

"You did say *exclusive* license, sir?"

"Absolutely," said the visitor. "The Imperial court prefers to deal with a single supplier for each commodity — or even several commodities. It saves superfluous bookkeeping, you understand."

Skarash nodded wisely, hiccupped, and shouted again for wine. How wise Grandsire had been to leave him in charge until his return! "How many commomm-odities would you expect?"

"Many! But enough of tedious business. Let us talk of lighter things. I understand you have only recently returned from Ullacarn?"

"Thatsh absholutely correct. How did you learn that?"

"On the same ship as the sultan?"

Skarash nodded again as a shrouded maiden — a cousin or one of his sisters, perhaps — scurried out from the house with more supplies.

"From Ullacarn?" the stranger inquired, smiling. For an imp, he was extraordinarily handsome. Very cultured and likable. And he had the polished accents of a high-class Hubban. Skarash had been listening carefully to those rounded vowels . . . not lately, though.

"Yesh," he found himself explaining, "I went directly. By camel. Not that we traders go directly, you unshersand . . . understand . . . because we wander. Right?"

"Of course," the stranger agreed with another winning smile. "And the sultan?"

"The sultan and Grandsire made a small detour."

"Detour?"

"Through Thume!"

1 4

"No! The Accursed Land? Now you have really intrigued me!"

A little later Skarash found time to wonder if he had been wise to mention that Grandsire was a mage, and now votary to Warlock Olybino himself, but the imp poured out more wine himself and proposed a toast or two, and the conversation continued without significant interruption.

Talk droned; insects hummed.

"But how on earth could even a mage have tracked them down in such a wilderness?"

"Ah!" said Skarash, being mysterious. He really ought to call for some food, to mop up all this liquor slopping around in his insides. Djinns were notoriously susceptible to alcohol and tended to shun it for that reason. He never normally indulged in it himself. "Well, the sorceress had given Grandsire a device to trace the use of magic, you see . . . "

4

"Aunt?"

Kadolan blinked her eyes open. The room was dark. Her head felt thick and a nasty taste in her mouth told her she must have been asleep. Then she made out the shrouded figure standing in the moonlight.

"Inos!"

"Don't get up . . . "

But Kadolan struggled to her feet and reached out, and they came together and hugged.

"Oh, Inos, my dear! I have been so . . . er . . . concerned! Are you all right?"

"All right? Of course, Aunt!" Inosolan broke away and turned toward the window. "Of course I am all right. I am the most cherished, tightly guarded woman in Arakkaran. Perhaps in all of Zark. How could I not be all right?"

Kadolan's heart shattered at the tone. She moved forward, but her touch caused Inosolan to edge away.

"What are you doing all alone, sleeping in a chair, Aunt? Have you dined yet this evening?"

"Tell me, dear!"

"Tell you what?"

"Everything!"

"Really! You want the details of my wedding night?"

Kadolan gulped and said, "Yes, I think maybe I do."

Slowly Inosolan turned to face her. She was swathed from head to floor in some sweeping white stuff. Only her eyes showed. "Why, Aunt! That is not a very ladylike question."

"Don't joke, Inos. There is something wrong."

"Intruders have been breaking into the palace and killing guards."

15

"Inos, please!"

"There is Rap. He is in prison."

"Yes."

"Recause of me. That is wrong — that a faithful friend should suffer for trying to aid me."

"In a few days, when the sultan has had time to repent of his anger . . . "

Inosolan wrung her hands. "Do we have a few days?" Her voice quavered, then steadied. "What are they doing to him, Aunt? Do you know?"

"No, dear. I have asked."

"I dare not. Azak promised no more bloodshed, but he is insanely jealous. I never knew what that phrase meant before. It's a cliché, isn't it, *insanely* jealous? But in this case it's exact. He forbids me even to think of another man. To plead for Rap again would doom him instantly. And what he did in the Great Hall . . . "

"We shall do what we can, dear."

"Little enough, I fear."

Silence fell, and the two stared at each other in the diffuse glow of the moon beyond the windows while Kadolan heard the pounding of her heart. "There is more, isn't there?" she said.

Inosolan nodded. "I never could deceive you, could I?" Then she raised a hand and removed her veil.

Oh, Gods! Kadolan closed her eyes. No! No!

"Rasha died too soon," Inosolan said.

"She had not removed the curse!"

"No, she hadn't. She'd said she would, but she hadn't got around to it. He was going to kiss me."

Even in that spectral glow, the marks were plain. Two fingers on one cheek . . . the print of thumb on the other. And the chin! Burned into the flesh.

How frail was beauty! How fleeting!

Gone now. Gone! Hideous, scabbing wounds!

Shocked, stunned, Kade staggered back and tumbled into her chair. She stared up at Inosolan in shivering, impotent horror.

"The pain is bearable," Inosolan said. "I can live with that."

But the marriage . . .

Oh, Gods! The marriage?

"He still cannot touch a woman," Inosolan said bitterly, "Not even his wife."

The room seemed to blur, and Kade wasn't sure if that meant she was about to faint or if her eyes were just flooded with tears. "What can we do?" She had not dreamed that things could get worse, but they had — Inosolan condemned to a chaste marriage, doomed to lose even Azak's one-sided love, for he would surely turn against a woman he craved and could never possess.

"There is only one thing we can do," Inosolan said in a futile attempt to sound calm. "What we tried to do before — we must go and seek occult aid."

"Master Rap?"

"No, no! He is only an adept. It will take a full sorcerer to cancel a spell."

"Sorcerer?" Kade was too horrified to think properly.

"The Four, the wardens. A curse set upon a monarch is political sorcery, so they should be willing to remove it. And heal my face, I hope."

Kade took a few deep breaths, but her brain was dead as flagstones. "Well, I have always enjoyed sailing, and a visit to Hub at last —"

"No."

"No?"

"You are not coming. He will not allow it. I have come to say farewell, Aunt. And Gods bless." The usually musical voice was flat and cold as a winter pond. "And . . . and thank you for everything."

"But when?"

Somewhere a door creaked, and boots clacked slowly on the tiles in the corridor. Kade struggled to rise and failed.

Inosolan came and bent to kiss her cheek. "It will be days before the court realizes he is gone," she whispered quickly. "Officially we shall be touring the countryside. That will hold for a week or two. After that . . . well, the Gods will provide. And Prince Kar, of course, will be in charge here."

Hub? "You can't go veiled in Hub!"

"I can't *not*!"

Oh, Holy Balance! May the Good preserve us — Inosolan had lost everything now, even her beauty.

The boots were almost at the door. Only one man had unimpeded access to any room in the palace.

"Remember Rap," Inosolan breathed. "Do what you can. He'll be safe with Azak gone, I'm sure. There is a fast ship," she added, a little louder, "headed west, and a carriage waits. He thinks we can just reach Qoble before the passes close. Wish me luck, Aunt. Wish us luck?"

"But the war?" Kadolan cried. "Isn't the Impire massing troops in Ullacarn?" Zark was about to be invaded. A djinn sultan journeying to the enemy's capital . . .

"Just one more risk to take," Inosolan said brightly. "It will be a most interesting journey. Gods be with you, Aunt. We'll be all right. We'll be back by spring — my husband and I . . . look after yourself."

The door swung open , and a tall shadow stood there, its jewels faintly shining.

17

"Gods be with you both," Kade said, and watched Inosolan glide silently away, like a wraith, following Azak into the darkness.

5

However much Andor might be enjoying himself out in the sheik's pleasance, back in the dingy kitchen quarters of the rambling mansion, the chairs were hard and the hot air rancid with scents of long-dead cooking. Gnats and moths twirled around the smelly lamps and held races on the low ceiling. Gathmor crossed his ankles the other way and eased his back. The bulky djinn on the other side of the table scowled at him briefly and went back to scratching his armpits. He had not spoken a word to Gathmor all evening, which was fine by Gathmor; from the smell of him the oaf was a camel driver by trade, now being used as watchdog to make sure the jotunn behaved himself. Gathmor would like very much to see him try. He'd observed many others wander through the scullery during his long wait; he'd take on any two of them cheerfully.

The women, on the other hand . . . Even wrapped like corpses, they moved like elves, and there was something challenging in all that concealment and the swirl of cloth as they hurried past on their master's business. It really caught a man's imagination; made him watch the folds shift for a hint of how much lay beneath, and where. The flame-red eyes . . . After all, Wanmie must have died in Kalkor's massacre, and in some ways that was beginning to feel like a long time ago. In some ways. Not that she'd have grudged him a nibble or two at another table, once in a while, had he ever wanted that. He was very tempted to try speaking to the next shrouded maiden who came through — and not just to rouse the camel driver, either.

He'd had as much boredom as he could stand. He'd been in this squalid pesthole for four or five hours, capping two days of useless talk and argument and mostly waiting around. Waiting for Thinal, or Darad. And now Andor. Or being a common porter — sometimes a man would do for a shipmate what he wouldn't dream of doing for himself.

A large youth stuck his head round the door. "You! Your master wants you."

Gathmor smiled and said softly, "Did I hear you correctly?" The camel driver brightened and glanced at the youth. For a moment the evening began to look interesting.

"Your *friend?*" the youth said, scowling.

" 'Employer' would do," Gathmor admitted, and heaved himself to his feet. "Lead on, Valiant." Turning red faces redder was the best fun he'd found in Zark so far. It wasn't much.

18

He swung his bundle up on his back and followed. Common porter! When he reached the door, he saw that Andor was as good as dismasted. So the sailor took the proffered lantern in one hand and a firm grip on the imp's arm with the other, and steered him out into the night before the cheerfully wine-scented farewells were finished. The door thumped shut behind them; bars and chains rattled behind it, and the night was hot.

It was also dark. He'd been rash, Gathmor realized, going outdoors before he'd got his night eyes back; he wasn't used to these landlubber games. He pulled Andor back into the doorway again, raising the lantern high to peer at all the shadows. Andor hiccuped discreetly.

There were a lot of shadows, but most of them were too small to conceal anything. The walls were very high, but moonlight played its magic in places, and some windows still glowed here and there. A few households kept lamps burning above their doors.

"Uphill or downhill?" Gathmor said, when he was satisfied that there were no footpads close.

"Uphill, downhill, in my lady's chamber . . . "

"Call Sagorn!"

Andor sniggered. "I think I'm too drunk to remember how. Gods, but that kid was a trader! I couldn't get a thing out of him sober. Ooops, I think I'm going to call the gnomes."

"Do it, then, or bring Sagorn now and do it next year."

Andor reeled into a corner, but there were some things even Andor could not do elegantly. Gathmor studied the shadows and the narrow moonstruck sky roofing the canyon and tried not to listen. Serve the sleazy twister right!

He was getting very tired of the whole bunch of them. In the last two days he'd been working with all five — one at a time, of course — and Evil knew how confusing it was. He'd no sooner get one straightened out than he'd be dealing with another and having to start all over.

"Awright!" he said when silence returned. "Tell me what you found out, or else call Sagorn and let me have his ideas firsthand."

"You boneheaded Nordland blackguard!" Andor gagged a few more times, but nothing more happened. "I still think we're wasting our time. Why don't we go back down —"

"Don't try it!" Gathmor snarled. "It didn't work the last time and it won't now."

Andor could probably still talk him into leaving Arakkaran and abandoning his shipmate. He'd done so two days ago, and they'd sailed on the dawn breeze. But only Jalon could work the pipes to summon real winds, and when Andor had called Jalon, Jalon had simply waited until Gathmor recovered his wits and stopped threatening. Then they'd come back to Arakkaran. Andor's charm was irresistible, but it wore off. Jalon was a jotunn, and a real man inside, despite his puny exterior.

Andor started to speak, groaned briefly, and vanished.

Sagorn stood in his place, pale face and silver hair shining bright in the light of the lantern. He sighed approvingly. "Nicely done, sailor."

"What did he learn?"

"Ah!" For a moment the old man stood in silence, pondering or perhaps merely rummaging through Andor's memories. "Uphill," he said, and began striding into the dark. Adjusting the bundle on his back, Gathmor moved to his side, and the shadows danced away at their approach, only to sneak in softly behind again.

"What did Andor find out?"

"I never thought I should be grateful to a gnome," Sagorn remarked. "But Dragonward Ishist outshines any doctor I have ever heard of. He must be the equal of —"

"You're going to need medical help again very shortly, you know."

The scholar chuckled dryly and slowed his pace. He had begun to puff already. "We could use Ishist right now, couldn't we? If what we heard about gangrene is true, then the faun hasn't long to live. His healing powers must be failing."

Gathmor shuddered. Before noon Thinal had gone over the palace wall again, so that Andor could interview a couple more guards. The trouble was that then he'd called Darad to ensure their silence, and all the others were becoming understandably alarmed by the sudden epidemic of anemia in their profession.

"And Darad saw Princess Kadolan on a balcony," Sagorn remarked. "That's important, although none of the others realized."

The alley entered a tiny square, and Gathmor peered around nervously. "Last warning — don't play games with me, Sagorn."

The old man snorted. He was wheezing now, but obviously headed back to the palace. How long could their luck last?

"Is there a solution?" Gathmor demanded.

"Certainly."

"*There is?*"

"Certainly. I have known it since Jalon called me yesterday. I just didn't want to raise your hopes by mentioning it."

Gathmor promised himself revenge on this scraggy old bookworm — someday, somehow. "Raise them now."

"More magic! Rap is merely an adept. His powers have kept him alive this long, despite his injuries, but since he can no longer speak to talk his guards into —"

"I am only an ignorant sailor!" Gathmor shouted. "But I am not stupid. I know all this." The old windbag always used too many words, but he seemed to be dragging this story out deliberately.

20

"Will you tell the world? Keep your voice down! Now, do you want to hear or not?"

"What is the answer?"

The two jotnar emerged onto a wide road, better lit by the moon. There was no wheeled traffic in these early-morning hours, but a band of men went by on the far side with lanterns and suspicious glances, guarding a fat merchant encased within them like a yolk.

Sagorn was laboring, puffing harder. "More power! If we can learn another word, then I will be an adept, also, and so will Andor, or Thinal, or Jalon, or even Darad. I admit that the thought of Darad as an adept is . . . " He sensed Gathmor's fury and broke off. "That is the answer! Another word of power."

What madness was this? "And where exactly do you propose finding one of those now, after failing for a hundred years?"

Sagorn chuckled dryly. "I know exactly where."

"Where?"

"The girl has one."

"Rap's princess? She does? You're serious?"

"Absolutely! One of Inisso's words has been handed down in her family. Her father passed it to her on his deathbed. It was perhaps the reason the sorceress abducted her. But I couldn't be sure . . . She does not seem to have had fair fortune, and even a single word normally brings good luck."

"Now you're sure?" Gathmor was certain he was overlooking something in this argument.

"Yes, I am. That was why we have been cultivating Master Skarash all afternoon. He was one of her companions in the desert."

"One word? A genius? What's her skill, then? What's she good at?"

Sagorn sniffed disparagingly. "That seems to be still a mystery. At least the djinn boy told Andor he didn't know. He may not have been informed, of course, but at one point in their adventures, she was definitely exercising some sort of power. It was how his grandfather was able to find her again."

"Grandfather?"

"Elkarath himself. He's a mage. But he isn't here. He's still in Ullacarn, working for Warlock Olybino now. Forget him. We must find Inos and persuade her to share her word of power with me. Or with one of my associates. Then we can save Rap!"

"How?"

Sagorn paused to rest, leaning against a high stone wall — the wall of the palace grounds, in fact. He took a moment to catch his breath and wipe his brow. "The faun is no fighter, but with two words he held off the whole palace guard. Imagine Darad with two words! Another word will bring many new skills, of course, but it must also strengthen the skills we've got now.

Gods — Thinal will be able to walk out the door with the sultan's throne under his arm."

"Listen!" Gathmor swung around to stare toward the corner. There were gates to one of the palace yards just around there, and he could hear . . . Yes! Horses.

He doused the lantern, but the two of them were still far too conspicuous in the moon-washed street. "Come on!" After grabbing the old man's wrist, he began to run across the road, feeling the straps of his bundle dig into his shoulders at every step. There was a dark alleyway on the far side, but farther uphill, closer to the approaching cavalry. The hoofbeats were very near now. Djinns were insanely suspicious folk, even in daylight.

He had no sense of change, but suddenly the wrist he held was different. He let go, and Thinal hurtled out in front, heading for cover like a rabbit, with Andor's overlarge garments flapping around him. No hero, Thinal. Ladened by his pack and the dead lantern, Gathmor couldn't keep up with him. He watched the little thief vanish into the shadows, heard the hooves grow louder, and saw the leaders wheel around the corner just as he reached the alley also and plunged into the welcome darkness.

It was not an alley, merely an oversized alcove, and he was brought up short by a high, solid fence. Of Thinal there was no sign whatsoever.

Cursing fluently, Gathmor dropped the lantern, swung his pack down to the ground, and began fumbling with the ties — there was a sword inside. But he knew he'd been seen, and one man couldn't hold off an army. He was a fist-and-boots man, anyhow — he'd never used a sword in his life. He stopped, gasping for breath, knowing it was useless. A prowler near the palace at this time of the morning, running away . . . he was a dead man! Sweat trickled icily down his ribs.

The horses never broke stride. A dozen cantered by his patch of darkness, then a coach, rumbling and bouncing, and a solitary giant of a man on a black stallion, and finally another twenty or so horsemen, riding on inky shadows in the moonlight.

And they were gone. Their clamor died away down the hill, and the silence of the night returned, broken only by his own hard breathing.

Gathmor jumped as another man dropped nimbly at his side, Thinal coming down from above, having scaled a sheer wall in his inimitable style.

"Funny time of day to be going for an outing," the thief remarked in a puzzled tone.

Jalon scowled at him. Of all the five he knew Thinal least. The kid'd been busy, these last two days, but he did his work alone. Gathmor had caught glimpses of him, but they'd exchanged few words. Slight and foxy, the young imp was also nondescript and unmemorable.

"Come on, then," he snapped. "I need my stuff."

Common porter! Snarling, Gathmor set to work on the pack. Then he paused. "What's the old man's plan, exactly?"

"Kadolan," Thinal said, stripping off Andor's fancy robes. "Darad saw her on a balcony. He doesn't think, of course."

"So I gathered. Why her?"

"Hurry! Because no one can possibly get close enough to Inos to have a private chat, right? No man, anyway. You know how djinns guard their women." Stripped bare now, he pushed Gathmor's hands away and the bundle yielded swiftly to his thieving fingers. "But I may be able to get to her aunt — she won't be so well guarded."

"And then what?"

Thinal began emptying the pack, tipping out all the miscellaneous garments and equipment the team had collected for their nefarious exploits. He found the shorts he wanted and pulled them on, dancing round on one foot at a time, then he went hunting for his shoes. Burglars disliked floppy robes.

"Then Jalon."

"Jalon?" Gathmor didn't think he was usually so stupid. The occult gang was deliberately trying to confuse him. Sagorn was a schemer and Thinal a sharpie. He was only an honest sailor.

Thinal pulled the sword from the pack and hung it on his back. It was a fine dwarvish blade, but the hilt was so distinctive that it might as well have had *Stolen from the Palace of Arakkaran* written all over it. Once inside the grounds, he could call Darad to use it anytime there was need of violence. He peered up at Gathmor. "Then . . . then we'll improvise. Got a better plan?"

"No," the sailor admitted angrily. "But you have. Out with it!"

"Inos tells Jalon her word. As adepts, we rescue Rap . . . Don't wait around. This may take all day, or even longer. Look for us . . . " He paused, thinking. "The North Star Saloon, dawn and dusk and noon? If none of us shows in two days we're dead. All right?"

"Why Jalon? And shouldn't you find a shadier stretch of wall to climb?"

"Not at this time of night. No one around."

Gathmor opened his mouth to argue, but it was too late. Leaving the sailor standing in the scattered mess of clothing, the kid sprinted across the empty street and seemed to flow straight up the wall on the far side. In moments he had vanished over the top.

Gathmor waited for sounds of discovery, and there were none.

He sighed and bent to stuff all the clothes back in the sack.

Then he straightened.

Wait a minute!

Rap was dying — chained to the floor, all his bones broken, his tongue burned out, gangrene . . . Even if Darad or Thinal had become adepts, they wouldn't be sorcerers. They might rescue Rap, but they couldn't cure those awful injuries!

But did Inosolan know that Rap had been broken like that? If she thought he was just locked up in a cell, then she might very well believe the gang's story and hand over her word of power — and it wouldn't do Rap a damned bit of good!

The stillness of the night was shattered by an explosion of jotunn curses.

Of course they'd duped him!

They would dupe the girl!

And Rap would still die.

6

"Shandie! Shandie! Oh, my poor baby! Shandie!"

The voice came from a long way away, a very long way. It sounded much louder than it could possibly be, because that was Aunt Oro's voice, and she had a very soft voice, always, and she never shouted.

He was lying facedown. Because.

He was asleep, really. The room was dark, the bed soft. Sleep.

"Shandie!"

He smiled. He was glad she had come, and hoped she would see his smile in the dark and know he was glad, but he was much too much asleep to say anything. The world was all very woozy, and if he tried to wake up then he would feel his sore butt, and he didn't want that.

"Shandie! Speak to me!

He mumbled, tried to say he would see her tomorrow. Didn't think it came out right, because his mouth was all woozy, too. Moms had given him the medicine. To take the pain away.

More than usual medicine, 'cos it had been a very big beating. He'd been a very bad boy. He couldn't remember just how, but he had. Ythbane had been very, very disappointed in him.

Sleep . . .

"And what are you doing in my bedroom?"

That was Moms this time. She was shouting. Oh, dear, Moms was angry.

"I'm visiting my nephew! And what is a nine-year-old doing still sleeping in his mother's bedroom, may I ask?"

That was Aunt Oro again, but it didn't sound like Aunt Oro, who was sweet and cuddly and never, never shouted. 'Cept she was shouting now.

So was Moms. "He's my son and I'll decide where he sleeps. And I'll thank you —"

"What's the matter with him? What have you doped him with?"

"Just a mild sedat —"

"Mild? He's dead to the world! Laudanum? It must be laudanum! You give your own son *laudanum?*"

"Mind your own business!"

"This is my business!"

He was starting to cry. He could feel tears. He didn't like all this shouting, and he wanted to sit up and tell them to stop shouting over him, but he couldn't even lift his head, 'cause it weighed ever so much and was so woozy. Dark. Woozy. Sleepy.

"It is not your business!"

"Yes it is! He's my nephew, and heir to the throne. And who did *this?*"

Ouch!

"See?" Aunt Oro, shouting louder. "This sheet is stuck to him. Caked blood! No bandages, even?"

"Too swollen. Just compresses."

"Who did it?"

"He was disciplined."

"Disciplined? You call this discipline? I call it flogging."

"He disgraced himself today."

Yes. Now Shandie remembered. He hadn't just fidgeted. He'd fallen down and interrupted the ceremony and shamed himself before the full court. Of course he'd had to be beaten for that.

"He *fainted!* I saw. Grown men faint when they have to stand too long. Shut up and listen to me, Uomaya! Hear me out. I saw. He fainted like a soldier on parade."

"They get punished —"

"He's only a child! He shouldn't even have been there. Certainly not made to stand all that time! Of course he fainted!"

"And I will see my child reared as I choose. I repeat, it is none of your business . . . "

"And I say it is . . . "

The voices came and went; louder, softer. Like waves on Cenmere. Rock me to sleep . . .

"This book? What sort of book is this for a boy of his age? *Encyclopedia Hubbana?* Is that all he gets to read?"

He did love Aunt Oro, but did wish she would go away now, stop shouting, let him'n'Moms go to sleep. The voices faded . . . then came back loud again.

"There'll have to be a regency declared, won't —"

"Oh, so that's what brings you back to Hub? Think that you can get yourself made regent, do you —"

"Who else? You, I suppose? Daughter of a common soldier? Gods! Who else? Not that slug Ythbane? Eeech! The rumors are he dyes his hair. Does he?"

"How the Evil should I know?"

"How indeed?"

Moms screamed then, so loud that Shandie almost wakened. The fires of Ythbane's switch burned hot again; he heard himself groan.

"Quiet!" Aunt Oro said. "You'll waken the boy. Now listen to me, Uomaya! I don't care who shares that fine bed of yours. I don't care if he does have a blue tint to him. But I won't let either one of you be regent, nor both together. Shandie's a minor; I'm next in line. You've been trying to cut me out. Gods know I don't *want* the job, but I've got a duty. What's wrong with Father, anyway? Is that your doing, too? What are you doping *him* with?"

"Don't be ridiculous! He's old —"

"He wasn't old a few months ago! Not like that. I heard the rumors, so I came back and —"

"Well, it's none of my doing. And it isn't poison, because we've changed his attendants several times, so it's just some sort of old-age sickness. And it can't be sorcery, not on him."

"What do the wardens say?"

Please! Shandie thought. *Oh, please go away and let me sleep, please. When you wake me, then it hurts.*

"Wardens?" Moms laughed. "You think I talk to witches and warlocks? They must know, but they haven't spoken."

Aunt Oro groaned. "And of course they won't do anything."

"They *can't* do anything. That's the Protocol, dearie. Family's exempt. No magic cures for us."

The voices sank lower. Shandie sank away into dark wooziness again . . . and was roused by another voice.

"Your Imperial Highness! An unexpected honor!"

The consul!

Angry. Oh, dear.

Shandie discovered he was weeping again, into the sheet. He hadn't been bad again, had he? No more, please, no more!

"Consul Ythbane! Are you responsible for this torture?"

"That is not your affair, Highness."

"Yes it is! Why wasn't I informed of my father's illness?"

"We didn't think you'd be interested. You bury yourself out in the country all the time, breeding horses. The council saw no point in worrying you."

"And you're trying to ram through a regency for yourself, aren't you? You and Uomaya? Don't think I haven't heard."

Shandie had never heard Aunt Oro be angry like this before.

"Heard what?"

"That you're lovers."

"Watch your tongue, woman!"

Aunt Oro gasped. "*You* dare threaten *me?* It is *you* who must beware. Why else would you be in the princess's quarters in the middle of the night? You've been waiting until the old man's completely incapable, and then you're planning to marry her and —"

"And the opposition has summoned you. I expected this, of course." Ythbane's voice was getting deeper, which was a bad sign, but quieter, which was nicer. "Well, let me give you a warning, Princess Orosea. Your dear husband — how is his clock collection?"

"Fine . . . I mean, what on earth has Lee's clock collection got to do with anything?"

"They're dwarvish, aren't they? Most of them? He trades with dwarves. Dwarves make the best clocks."

"So?"

Aunt Oro had stopped shouting. Nicer.

"The Dark River border is alight again. Open war may have begun already. Trading with Dwanishian agents will be taken as evidence of treason."

Mumble.

"But I do! Lots of witnesses. Documents. So here are my terms, Highness! You leave Hub by morning, or a Bill of Attainder will be laid before the Assembly at noon."

Mumble. Weeping? Who was weeping?

Moms laughing. Good.

"I shall also have some documents for you to sign before you depart. Within the hour."

Mumbles.

Soft mumbles.

Whispers. Quiet. Dark. Sleep . . .

* * *

Naught availeth:
>   Say not the struggle naught availeth,
>   The labour and the wounds are vain,
>   The enemy faints *not*, nor faileth,
>   And as things have been, things remain.
> Clough, *Say Not the Struggle Naught Availeth*

27

2

Darkling way

1

"Who's there?"

Kadolan twisted her head as far round as she could — which wasn't very far these days. She overbalanced and grabbed at the bed for support. She had been praying.

Again a faint sound on the balcony, a flicker of movement in the moonlight . . . A burglar? In the palace of Arakkaran, with its innumerable guards? Inos had mentioned intruders —

"Princess? Highness? My pardon if I frightened you."

Her leaping heart took wing altogether, and she gasped with the pain of it. "Doctor Sagorn?"

"It is I," said the soft, dry voice. "I fear my entry was unorthodox."

Kadolan thought of how high that balcony was, and remembered a ruby brooch, and understood. The thief . . . whatever his name was . . . Sagorn gave her no time to catch her breath.

"My garb is not very seemly, ma'am," he said. "Perhaps I may scout for a robe of some sort? I apologize for waking you so suddenly."

She did not sleep on the floor, but in an embarrassing situation like this, a true gentleman would always imply he had seen much less than he had. "How extremely kind of you to come, Doctor. Please do go into that room there, and I shall be with you in a moment."

He murmured, and she heard a shuffling, cautious tread. Then she levered herself up from her knees and fumbled to find her housecoat. She allowed a few moments for her unconventional visitor to make himself decent, and for her heart to finish its slow descent from the heights, and for a quick adjustment of her nightcap over her curlers.

Then she went in. He was a blurred dark shade in a chair, with specter-pale shanks connecting it to the floor. Something that was probably a sheathed sword lay at his feet. She settled herself carefully in a chair opposite.

"Lights may be inadvisable," she said cautiously.

"Indeed they may! I regret disturbing your sleep like this."

"I was not sleeping." She would not mention nightmares of incandescent sorceresses. "I was invoking the God of Love."

After a thoughtful pause, Sagorn said, "Why Them?"

"Because it must have been They who appeared to Inos. I can't think why none of us realized. *Trust in love,* They said."

He sighed. "How true! And Inosolan did not, did she?"

"She did not realize! We believed that you were all dead — that the imps had killed you."

"And the faun, also, obviously."

"Yes. May I offer some refreshment, Doctor? There is usually some fruit and —"

He raised a pale blur of a hand — her night vision had never been good, and now it was terrible. "That is not necessary."

"So how did you escape from Inisso's chamber, Doctor? And how on earth did you manage to bring Master Rap here, all the way from Krasnegar in so short a time?"

Sagorn chuckled dryly, an oddly nostalgic sound. "I did not bring him. He brought me."

Ah! Sudden relief! "Then he is not only a seer, he is a sorcerer?"

"Just an adept, ma'am. He knows two words of power."

"His own . . . and you told him yours?"

Pause. "Yes, I did."

"That was extremely generous of you."

"It seemed advisable at the time," he murmured, and she wished she could make out his expression.

For a moment neither spoke — there was just so much to say! Kadolan's head was whirling as she became aware of all the possibilities.

29

"You are good friends, then, you and Master Rap?"

"Fellow travelers on a strange road. But I have come to appreciate Master Rap. Even for a faun he is . . . 'tenacious' would be the politest term. He is steadfast and honorable. I owe him much."

Detecting curious undertones, Kadolan waited for more, but apparently there was not to be more.

"So to what do I owe the pleasure of this visit, Doctor?" Formality was always the safer path in emotional moments.

He threw back his head and guffawed. "Kade, you are a wonder! You do recall . . . but I suppose this is no time for reminiscences."

"Hardly," she murmured. "If the guards find you, you may have enough time to write your entire life story."

"Or no time at all?"

"Exactly."

How long ago had it been — thirty years? Longer . . . she happily married in Kinvale, her brother passing through on his travels with his mentor Sagorn. Good times, but long ago, and she would not allow him to promote a passing encounter into a friendship that had never been. Sagorn had been much older than she in those days, and more a tutor than a friend to Holindarn. Keep it formal.

"Well, now," he said. "The boy is now in jail, I understand."

"That is true. He is lucky to be alive."

He chuckled. "Then age must rescue youth. You and I must organize his escape before the sultan changes his mind."

Had there been an odd timbre to that remark also? Since her eyesight had started failing, Kadolan had come to depend much more on nuances of tone than she ever had in her youth. She felt a twinge of caution, as if some young swain at Kinvale had overstated the value of his estates or boasted of his prospects in the military. Her hunches in such matters were usually reliable. Men trusted words more than women did, as a rule, and hence were less mindful of how they were spoken.

"But of course!" she said eagerly. "How do you propose we go about it, though? The sultan gave orders that he was to be most strictly guarded."

"Quite! I have seen palaces in my time, but never one so like an armed camp. I do not believe that a rescue is humanly possible . . . mundanely possible!"

Carefully Kadolan said, "So?"

"It would seem that the God's caution to Inos referred to the stableboy. Not Andor, certainly. Nor, I suspect, the sultan."

"Is Master Rap in love with my niece?"

Another of his dry chuckles . . . "Ha! He has fought his way past warlocks and sorcerers and dragons, out of jails and castles, jungles and pirate ships, through storm and shipwreck to reach her side. And I think in return he would happily serve her as ostler for the rest of his days."

Kadolan tried to swallow the nasty knot in her throat. Just as she had feared — a stableboy! And a faun! The Gods had strange ideas sometimes. How could she have known?

"Then we must do everything we can for him. Explain your plan, please."

"I propose that Inosolan make amends for her failure to trust in love."

That startled her. "Inos? A single word from her to the sultan would —"

"No!" Sagorn said sharply. "A word to me."

"Oh!" Now Kadolan saw, and her distrust swelled up like a summer thunderhead. Dawn was coming. The sage's face was a little less of a vague paleness. She could see his eyes now. "Her word of power, you mean, Doctor?"

"Exactly. The sultan took precautions against an adept escaping. He ordered that the prisoner must not be allowed to speak, and must be watched at all times, and so on. He did not consider the possibility of another adept attempting a rescue, and I am confident that an extrication could be effected by an adept. We — my associates and myself, that is — know at present only a single word, and we reduced our power when we shared it with Master Rap . . . not that we grudge the sacrifice, of course. No regrets! To be truthful, the loss was not as severe as I would have expected. Perhaps our word is known by many people, so sharing it with one more made little difference. But a second word is certainly requisite for the venture I have proposed."

Kadolan sat and thought for a while, hoping to hear some more before she explained the problem.

"And if he dies in jail," Sagorn said, his voice a little harder, "then what we gave away will be returned to us."

"So you hope to go to Inos —"

"I think Jalon may be the answer here, ma'am. He is a skilled mimic, of course, and quite expert at female impersonation. Zarkian costume could hardly be more suited to the purpose. If you were to invite your niece to your quarters to hear a remarkable *female* singer, then I doubt that the sultan would object." He waited for reaction, then added testily, "And after that, you will have to arrange a private interview, of course. That should be possible, I think."

Kadolan took a deep breath. "Sharing the words is always risky, is it not? You yourself explained that to us. Of course your own integrity is beyond question, Doctor, but if Inosolan shares her word with you, then can you guarantee your associates' good behavior afterward? Or would she fare like the woman in . . . Fal Dornin, I think it was?"

He sighed. "She is well guarded here, ma'am."

That was not much of an answer.

"It is the only possible solution!" he insisted.

The first breath of morning twitched the drapes with a hint of impatience. Time was slipping away.

She cut the knot. "It is impossible. The sultan and sultana are not in residence."

Sagorn released a long hiss of breath. "When do you anticipate their return?"

"At least two weeks," she said cautiously. That was true.

Silence. She saw him rub his cheek. The sky was growing brighter beyond the arched windows. Dawn came swiftly here.

"Too late. Doctor?"

"Yes." There was a note of defeat in that voice, and Kadolan did not like the implications.

"Have you any word of Master Rap's condition?" she asked.

The lanky form seemed to sink deeper into the chair. "Not good, ma'am. Not good at all."

Hmm! He had not mentioned that sooner, and she wondered why. It would have added urgency to the request.

Give him a word of power, indeed!

"In any case, would it not have been better strategy for Inos to have passed her word directly to Master Rap? A mage could not be held captive; even Prince Kar said so. And more in keeping with the tenor of the God's command, too?"

Sagorn uttered a sort of hollow chuckle. "The point would seem to be moot. And just how could the sultana have ever visited that dungeon without the sultan finding out and stopping her?"

There was another answer, though. Kadolan's prayers had been heard.

"Could you visit that cell, Doctor?"

"Me, ma'am?"

"You and your . . . invisible companions."

His pale eyes glittered in the feeble wisps of dawn light. "Why do you ask?"

Aware that she was fencing with a celebrated mind, and must certainly lose the match very shortly, Kadolan said, "You could take a message?"

"Possibly, at the risk of all our lives. What message would be worth it?"

"A very confidential one."

She did not need dawn to be aware of his suspicion. "I wish you to take me now to see Master Rap," she said firmly, and was surprised at how firm that was, considering the way her insides were behaving. "We had better go at once, as daylight is not far off."

Sagorn stayed still as a crouching leopard for long seconds. Then he said, "I never could understand how so powerful a sorcerer, a former warlock, could have known but three words."

It was hopeless. "Doctor?" she said blankly. "We must hurry if —"

"Inisso gave one word to each of his three sons."

"That is the legend." She began to rise.

"The words now known by Inosolan and Kalkor and Angilki. But the fourth descended in the female line?"

Hopeless! Kadolan sighed and sat back again.

"Do tell," he said coldly.

"Yes," she admitted. "The kings have never known of it. When our mother died, Holindarn was still a bachelor, so she passed it to me. But always it belonged to Krasnegar — so that there would be another available if it were needed, I suppose. When he married Evanaire, then of course I told her."

"'Of course,' you say? Few would!"

The ancient secret was out. Kadolan had laid herself open to murder now. "I don't think it can be a very powerful word, Doctor. Evanaire was a marvelously popular person, but she had always been a sweet girl. And I am no worker of miracles. Never have been. Just a useless aristocratic parasite."

"And the finest chaperon and trainer of young ladies in the Impire!" He thumped the arm of the chair, raising a puff of dust. "I should have guessed! The missing fourth word!"

"I never believed in it . . . but I did feel something when Evanaire died. The very day."

"Of course you would — your power had increased! And your niece needed your talent!" He was suddenly excited, the scholar slaying a mystery. "And it was not Inos whom Elkarath detected working magic in Thume — it was you! Your occult power at work when your ward was in danger!"

"Gracious!" She had not thought of that. "How did you ever hear about that?"

"The missing fourth word!" he said again . . . gloatingly?

She hauled herself to her feet. "Missing no longer. I wish to share it with Master Rap."

Still Sagorn remained in his chair. "How ironic! When the imps were breaking down the door and Inosolan and I were arguing about telling the boy our words to make him a mage — there you were with a fourth word, and could have made him a full sorcerer!" He cocked his head quizzically. "Would you have done so, had he been willing?"

"Probably." She had not been required to decide then. "Had I thought that Krasnegar needed it. I truly fear it may not be strong enough to do any real good, but . . . who knows? Let us go and try to give it to him now."

Sagorn stared up at her unwinkingly. He had draped a woman's robe over himself, and did not seem to be wearing very much under it; his scrawny arms were bare. "You are either a very brave woman or a very foolish one, Kadolan. You are suggesting something that is absolutely impossible."

"What happened to your devoted friendship for Master Rap?"

"Tell me the word, and I will get him out of that cell. I swear!"

"No, Doctor. I shall tell it to the stableboy or no one."

Tension crackled in his voice. "Why, for the Gods' sake?"

"Because I think you are sent. You are the answer to my prayers." Suddenly the strain won, and her temper flared, as it had done perhaps three times in her adult life. She shouted. "Now, which is it to be? Do you help me, or do I yell for the guard and turn you in?"

His jaw dropped. "This is utter madness, Kade!"

"I mean it! I shall scream for the guards."

"But I cannot take you myself! I should certainly have to call Andor to help, and anything he can't handle will need Darad. They will know what I know, and Gods know what they will do."

She nodded. "It will be a very interesting journey. Try to find something to fit in that closet there. There are some ancient masculine garments. Now, if you will excuse me for a moment, Doctor?"

Heart thundering wildly, she headed back to her bedroom.

2

Kadolan had not dressed herself faster in fifty years, yet all the time she was doing so, she was thinking of Sagorn's warning about Darad. Sir Andor, of course, might very well try to charm her into babbling her word of power to him now that he knew of it, but the words themselves were supposedly proof against magic, and Andor without occult amplification she thought she could rebuff.

Come to think of it, last year his talent had challenged hers head-on at Kinvale, and she had held the field.

But Darad! When that monstrous man had attempted to abduct Inosolan, it had been Kadolan who had thrown the burning oil on his back. All the other injuries and indignities he had suffered thereafter had stemmed from that, and she could not believe that the slow-witted jotunn killer would be prone to ready forgiveness. If Sagorn needed to call Darad, then her little expedition was going to sink without trace, and she with it.

She hesitated at the door. "I am ready, Doctor."

"Would that wrapping a turban were as easy as bandaging!" he said. "Have you any small implements?"

"What sort of implements?"

"Little knives or hat pins."

"Hat pins, Doctor? In Zark? Really!" But she went and fumbled among her things, and remembered the tray by the bed, which yielded a fruit knife. Then she jumped as Sagorn strode in, bedecked in the loose garments and flowing cloak of Zarkian nobility. They were dark, but the light would not yet admit what color — green, probably. There was a strong odor of must about them and his turban was crooked, but anyone close enough to question such details would have much more pressing queries about his pallid jotunn face.

She bobbed a curtsy. "I congratulate you on your tailor. Doctor."

He chuckled. "I couldn't have asked for better, could I? If words of power bring good luck, then perhaps these are a good sign. Our luck is holding."

He accepted the little knife, and a few pins, and a buttonhook. He declined a shoehorn and a belt buckle.

"Lead on, Highness," he said. "And may your God of Love be with a pair of old fools."

Kadolan found that remark in very poor taste, and decided he must be nervous. She led the way down the corridor, being as quiet as possible. She was somewhat nervous herself, truth be told. She tried to remember that she was doing this for Inosolan, who surely deserved a little luck at last.

Three words made a mage. A mage could cure wounds and sickness, and burn scars, certainly. If only she could have more faith in her own word of power! Even if all the words had started off equal — whenever and wherever they had started off — then some must have become greatly weakened since, diluted by too many sharings. Perhaps they even wore out from too much use, and the one she knew was centuries old, one of Inisso's.

The corridors were stuffy, bitter-scented with dust, and still hot from the day. Massive XIVth Dynasty statues stood in rows along the walls — too valuable to throw away, too ugly to be wanted.

She tiptoed past the room where four maids slept, and another where the housekeeper snored. Then her feet brought her to the outside door, and a thin slit of light showed below it. This was as far afield as she had been since Inosolan's wedding night.

Sagorn went close to the door and very gently tried it. Then he stooped to whisper in her ear.

"Locked or bolted?"

"Locked, I think," she breathed back.

"Guards outside?"

"Likely."

She thought he would give up then and turn back, but he merely nodded. He was barely visible, for the window was small and the little vestibule dark. It smelled strongly of beeswax.

"Thinal, then. Hold this sword handy." Sagorn drew the blade, and she took it gingerly and stood close as . . .

As the figure beside her seemed to collapse to half size, and there was the imp youth she had seen once in Inisso's chamber of puissance. As then he was comically bundled in vastly oversized clothes. He put up a hand to straighten the turban, which had slipped sideways during the transformation. His dark eyes were little higher than hers, and near, and they glittered. For a moment he just seemed to be studying her, as if trying to find traces of magic in her. Without looking, he reached in a pocket and brought out the fruit knife. It glittered also.

"Princess?" His voice was so soft that he seemed to convey the words without any sound at all. "Princess Kadolan! What's for me that I help you give away a word of power when there's needier bodies to hand?"

Kadolan's scalp pricked at his revelation of the occult. Sagorn had guessed her secret, and whatever he knew, all the others knew also, including this little felon. She held the sword, but she had no illusions of being able to hold him off if he tried to take it away from her. He was a fraction of her age, doubtless well versed in back-alley athletics. He could probably best her with nothing but the fruit knife. She had not been prepared for Thinal.

"Well?" he said, still soft as gossamer. "What's my gain if I risk my life for you?"

Did he want her to offer him payment? He could steal all the wealth he might ever want. Her tongue felt dry. "Not for me. For Inosolan."

"I give no spit for Inosolan! Would she risk her life for me?"

Kadolan could not think of a plausible reply.

Then his teeth gleamed also.

"You need me!" He sounded surprised. "Even if you could twist me to call any of the others, they'd be useless. Only I can climb from the balcony. Only I can open this door! You all need me!" He grinned more widely.

"'What do you want?"

"The word. Now! Then I'll go tell Rap."

"You expect me to trust you?"

"You got no choice, lady!" Even that minuscule whisper was filled with brazen glee. How often had this guttersnipe ever felt important to anyone, or had power to bargain?

"No. I tell the word to Rap or to no one. It is too frail a word to divide further."

He shrugged, maybe. "Then I'm gone. The whole idea is moonshine anyway. It's dawn already." He headed back toward the corridor.

"Stop!" Kadolan said, as loud as she dared. "Or I scream!" She raised a fist as if to thump on the door, hoping a cat burglar could see better in the dark than she could.

He stopped and turned.

"Guards?" she said. "There are guards just outside. I will call them."

"Stupid old baggage!" He took a pace toward her, and she half expected to feel Darad's hands on her throat.

36

"What about Rap?" she said desperately. "So Inos wouldn't risk her life for you — would he? For a friend?" It was the wildest guess of her life.

"Of course not! Well, not unless . . . " His voice changed. "But I suppose he's just about crazy enough to . . . In Noom, when Gathmor . . . If . . . Oh, crap! You would have to say that, wouldn't you?" Thinal stepped past her to the door, did something with the fruit knife, and the lock clicked . . .

Andor snatched the sword from Kade's grasp and thew open the door, reeled through into brilliant lamplight, and stopped, swaying and blinking. Kade followed — and recoiled.

The anteroom contained two guards, true. There were many weapons and clothes scattered around the floor, and also cushions. Also the guards themselves. And also four women. All six were asleep, all unclothed. The air stank like a wine shop.

Andor hiccuped, staggered, and . . .

Sagorn slid the sword awkwardly back into the scabbard. Kadolan followed him across the room, trying to keep her eyes averted from the remains of the orgy, but that was impossible. There were very few places safe to put feet, and she had to hold her skirts high lest they trail on the tangle of bodies and limbs. She breathed a sigh of relief as the door closed behind her.

"Fortunate that Thinal did not call your bluff," Sagorn remarked, steadying her arm on the stairs — or perhaps letting him steady her; two old fools, stumbling down a league of unlighted steps in a palace like an armed camp.

"I had noticed some of the maids yawning a lot."

"West."

"Beg pardon?"

"We just turned west. I am keeping track."

"Oh, that's nice."

Eventually they ran out of staircases, and a short exploration brought them to kitchen quarters, large and echoing and smelling of rank meat. Junior drudges snored in corners and under tables. Soon they would be roused to perform the first duties, but they would be unlikely to question well-dressed persons, and even less likely to raise an alarm. The intruders picked their way through the shadows from one guttering lantern to another, from window to window. Things scuttled along the skirting — rats, maybe, or worse. Kadolan wondered about snakes and scorpions, not sure if she wanted more light here or less. Cockroaches like terriers! If any of the castle kitchens had looked like this in Krasnegar, Mistress Aganimi would have hurled herself from the battlements.

Then a door that obviously led to the exterior.

"Cover your face, ma'am," Sagorn said. "There may well be a way to the jail that does not require going outside, but I can't take a week to find it. Walk behind me."

He shot back the bolts, and the hinges creaked . . .

3

The Palace of Palms was a city in itself. Some of the buildings were interconnected, others stood apart in parkland. It had streets and alleys, wide courtyards and shady cloisters, its many levels connected by ramps and wide stairways. Sagorn stayed close to walls, as much as he could; he headed east, and generally downhill. He seemed to know roughly where he was going. The sky was starting to turn blue overhead, and above the lip of the sea it held a reddish stain like washed blood.

Twice he pushed Kade into doorways as patrols went by in the distance. There must be guards on high places who might see. It was madness, total madness.

At last he brought her to an alley and stopped. He wiped his face with a thin, pale hand. For a minute he seemed to lack breath.

"This is the building! How to get in, though?"

The stonework looked older than most, but Kadolan doubted that even Thinal could scale it, and the windows were all barred, even on the topmost, third story.

"We shall have to find a door," she said, and set off along the alley. His footsteps followed. She found a door. It was very small, and very solid, with a small peephole but no handle or keyhole.

"Bolt hole," Sagorn muttered. "Back exit. Not an entrance."

That one looked hopeless. Kadolan continued her progress. Maddeningly, the buildings on the other side had several doors, most raised a couple of cubits above ground level, as if for unloading wagons. One of them was ajar, too. She wondered if the cellars might connect belowground, but as Sagorn had said, they did not have a week to explore. The alley led to a courtyard. She peered cautiously around the corner, along to the main entrance, an imposing archway with guards posted. She backed hurriedly.

"It will have to do!" she said firmly, and retraced her steps to the obscure little door they had found earlier. She stopped a few paces back from it and racked her brains.

"Even Darad can't break that down!" Sagorn protested. His deep-grooved face was gray with worry. "If he had an ax and an hour and no interruptions . . . "

Kadolan's heart was fluttering like a butterfly, and she felt light-headed. Somewhere she had cast herself adrift; she was reckless with a victory-or-death sensation she had never known before. It must be her jotunn blood showing, a trait from some ancient berserker ancestor. She wondered if she might have a seizure before the problem was resolved, and discovered that she did not care. She was staking everything now.

"I can't go back, can I? Let's knock and see what happens."

He closed his eyes and shuddered. "Then I must call Darad."

"Andor? If I knock, and someone comes, then Andor could talk him into opening the door."

Sagorn shook his head wearily. "Andor is drunk."

"Drunk? Sir Andor?" That did not sound like the cultured young gentleman she had known in Kinvale.

"It was in a good cause." Sagorn leaned against the wall and rubbed his eyes. "Andor is drunk. Thinal is dazzled by his own importance and dizzy from lack of sleep. Jalon, of course, would be totally useless in an escapade such as this." He shook his head. "And you and I're both too old for such nonsense. It is hopeless!"

"Rubbish!" Kadolan said. "Listen! If that is a sort-of-secret way out, then it may also be a sort-of-secret way in, may it not? These djinns are all half crazy with intrigue . . . spies and double agents, coming to report? There may very well be a doorman within earshot, waiting to let them in. Now you call Sir Andor . . . No?"

"It will lead to swordplay. Even sober, Andor is only an amateur swordsman."

"You called him earlier."

"Thinal called him. He didn't think. It will have to be Darad, whichever one of us calls him."

"Not Darad!"

Darad had killed a woman for half a word.

Baffled silence and angry glares.

"You are the thinker, Doctor! Think!"

Sagorn sighed. "Listen, Kade, Darad might be all right. Especially if you talk to him about Rap! Darad likes Rap now."

She found that hard to believe. The faun had set his dog on Darad, and his tame goblin, too. He had smashed chairs on Darad. But if it had to be Darad, it had to be Darad.

"Very well. Go ahead! I'll risk it."

Sagorn gave her a disbelieving look. "Very well. Gods be with you, my dear."

Impudence!

Then the green clothes ballooned, and stitches ripped, and the giant was there.

Clenching fists, she raised her head to see the scars and tattoos, the battered nose and an enormous wolf-like grin. "Good morning, Master Darad," she said faintly.

An earthquake of silent laughter shook his monstrous form. He leered. "And good day to you, lady. Need my help now, do you?"

39

She fell back a step. "I am truly sorry that I hurt you when you were in Krasnegar. My loyalty to my niece, you understand — "

A guttural chuckle stopped her. "Jotunn blood?"

"Er? Oh, yes. Our family is about half imp and half jotunn."

"Jotnar breed good warriors," he agreed. "Shows in Rap, too."

Ah! "I want to visit Master Rap. He is in serious trouble."

A nightmare scowl replaced the leer. "Yes. To make him a mage, right? Filthy djinns! And time is short, right? Good man, the faun. Must hurry. Well, you knock, and see what happens!" The jotunn ripped off his cloak and dropped it. He drew his sword in a flash of steel that made her jump; then he stepped back against the wall beside the door.

Shivering, Kade checked that her yashmak was in place. She placed herself in front of the peephole and rapped on the wood. She wondered if that puny noise would be audible at all inside. She kept her eyes down — blue eyes, not red djinn eyes. She could see Darad's feet, his toes protruding from the remains of Sagorn's boots. She could see the sword. Dawn breezes ruffled her robe and brought soothing scents of morning, of grass and flowers. There were still songbirds in the world, too, and not far off.

She counted fifty heartbeats. Then she raised her hand to knock again, and a voice spoke from the grille. "The cricket sings low."

Password? Merciful Gods, what would be the reply to that?

"I have a message from the Big Man."

"The password?"

"I was not told the password!" she cried, still not looking up. She remembered the lionslayers — "Women are not told the passwords."

"Women don't bring messages from the sultan."

"Then his message will not arrive, and he will want to know why."

The man grunted. After a long, nerve-wrenching silence, she heard a bolt being drawn. The hinges swung in well-oiled silence.

Kadolan was hurled aside and almost fell as Darad spun around the jamb, slammed the door wide, and vanished into the dark interior. She heard a bone-cracking thump and a muffled cry. She followed, through the entrance, into a small, dark chamber. There was a chair in one corner, stairs opposite, a body on the floor, and a dark giant standing over it, topped by a gap-tooth wolfish grin.

"Good so far!" Darad rumbled. "Shut the door. Right. You stay close now!"

"Wait!"

A body on the floor!

She had killed a man.

Where was the good in that, to offset the obvious evil? The thought was appalling, and even worse was the certainty that she could not halt what she

40

had started, and more bloodshed must follow. Ignoring her command to wait, the warrior went leaping up the stairs, sword in hand.

"Stop!" she cried, and hurried after him. She heard crashes and a shriek that became a ghastly bubbling noise as she emerged into another room. Light streamed through a barred window onto three bodies and Darad gloating over them. Killer and floor and furniture were splattered with brilliant red. She had never seen so much blood.

This was a talent for fighting magnified to genius by a word of power.

One of the men on the floor began to groan, and move. Darad casually chopped off his head.

Kadolan spun away from the sight, thrusting knuckles into her mouth to stifle a rising scream. The room began to sway, but she was granted no time for hysterics or fainting. The door flew open and a brown-clad man burst in and stopped, staring down aghast at the slaughter. Darad crossed the room in a blur, grabbed the newcomer by his tunic, hauling him forward and slamming him back against the stonework . . . once . . . twice. Then he dropped him.

They listened. Silence.

The jotunn leered at Kadolan's expression. "Only djinns!" he said, sheathing his bloody sword. "Come here. You listen good."

He stopped and raised the man he had stunned, pushed him against the wall again, and this time held him there with no visible effort. He slapped his victim's face a few times to rouse him, then pulled the man's own dagger from his belt and held the point before his eyes.

"You know where the faun is?"

The guard was barely more than a boy, one of the family men. He sported a pink mustache, but his beardless cheeks had turned a sickly pale mauve. His turban had fallen off, loosing torrents of ginger curls, and all the knives and swords and blades hung on his person were going to do him no good at all. He made some incoherent gibbering noises.

The point of the dagger went into his left nostril. Ruby eyes bulged and his neck seemed to stretch.

"You know where the faun is? Else you no good to me, djinn."

"Yethir."

"Tell me how to go there."

"Ug . . . ug . . . "

"Tell or die!"

"Go right. Second left. Right. Downstairs all the way."

"That's all?"

"Yethir!" Suddenly he screamed: "*I swear it!*"

"Good!" Darad cut his throat and dropped him. He said, "Come, lady, shut the door," and shot out into the hallway.

41

Kade reeled after him, closing the door. Darad was already only a fading drumbeat of footsteps, and he apparently did not need her assistance with the simple directions.

He met only one more man on the way. Kade heard an oath, but by the time she turned the corner, the wide corridor was empty. She hurried along the trail of blood, wondering if Darad was taking the corpse to use as a shield, or if he was just expecting to hide evidence. Many of the stains must be dribbles from Darad himself, for he had bathed in it.

Left . . . right . . . She came to a dark opening, access to a spiral stair. Faint muffled thumps of boots came from below. She ran on to the next corner and stretched on tiptoe to remove a lamp from its hook. Then she came back to explore the stairs.

They were narrow and uneven and tricky, the only handhold a thick rope hanging by the newel, winding down into the unknown. She was grateful for it, though, thinking that a broken leg now would not help the cause at all. Darad must be far ahead of her, committing Gods-knew what sort of atrocities on her behalf. Shadows danced for her lamp. She almost tripped on a body, and lost more time clambering by it to continue her descent. It was probably the one Darad had been dragging.

She emerged into a dark and extremely fetid cellar, and the feeble lamp showed nothing but floor anywhere. She listened and heard nothing but a faint dripping . . . only water, hopefully . . . and an echoing hollowness that suggested a large space. Then she thought to examine the floor and found a few spots of blood. Of course they led to another opening, another stair, right by the one she had just left. Even Darad had found that.

The second stair was narrower and steeper, and carved from solid rock. There was no rope to cling to, either. Up in the real world, night had ended. Here it never would, but her lamp was already guttering and its supply of oil might be timed to run out just after dawn. The air was indescribably thick and fetid. She shivered convulsively, and she would have fled anywhere in the world had she been able to think how to go about it. Five men dead already! Somehow the jotunn's command to follow seemed to be the only option open to her, and her feet continued to obey without any further instructions from her.

Then a monster reared up out of the dark in front of her — pale eyes glaring in a blood-covered ogreish face . . . white canine teeth like fangs . . . Great scarlet hands reached for her, snatched her lantern away, and extinguished it. Shocked and blinded, she overbalanced and would most certainly have fallen had the giant not taken her bodily in those gory hands. He carried her as he backed down to the foot of the steps.

Breathless and giddy, Kadolan found herself in a bare room like a cave, its rock-carved roof low enough to be oppressive even for her, while Darad was

42

forced to stoop. She saw no furniture, only some ominous chains heaped in one corner and corroded staples set into the walls. Somewhere she could hear voices.

There were a few doors set in the side walls, all closed and very likely hiding nothing but empty cells. Even for a dungeon this place had a very unused feel to it.

The end wall, facing the stair, held two doorways, side by side. One door was open, showing the cell beyond it utter black and presumably empty; but the other door was closed, and light was streaming from a barred grille in that closed door. This was horribly reminiscent of a chapel, the bright window and the dark. But the voices also were coming from the illuminated cell.

The air was nauseating. She wondered how anyone could stand it, and was glad she could not identify all the mingled stenches. Yet she thought she registered a slight breeze, and of course this sewer would become a deathtrap very soon if it had no ventilation at all.

Untroubled by heat or stink or religious symbolism, Darad was standing, listening, and literally scratching his head. Beyond the door dice rattled, and some men laughed. Master Rap must be in there. Azak had ordered that the prisoner was to be guarded at all times.

Perhaps Azak had also given orders that the prisoner was to be killed at the first sign of a rescue attempt. Most certainly the door would be bolted on the inside. It would not be opened to strangers, nor without this empty space being inspected through the grille. Those were obvious precautions.

There seemed to be at least four or five men in there. How many could one jotunn killer handle at a time? How could the intruders persuade the defenders to open the door? How long before someone found the shambles upstairs and the guards arrived in force?

Kade leaned weakly against the wall and wondered why she had ever expected to outwit Azak at his own game. The sultans of Arakkaran had been practicing this sort of iniquity for centuries; he had probably imbibed a skill for it with his mother's milk.

Darad turned to glance at her, and she could just see the hideous expression on his bloody face. He had drawn his sword again and didn't know what to do with it. She was in command.

"Andor," she whispered.

There was a pause, and then the man holding the sword was Andor. He almost dropped it, and the point struck the floor with a clink that sounded terrifyingly loud. Andor staggered, then recovered. He had not been heard; the gaming and laughter continued.

He stared down in horror at his sodden garments, and then scowled at Kade. "Now you know how it feels to have Darad's memories."

43

"How do we get in there?" she responded urgently.

Time was desperately short. There was a trail of blood, there were bodies . . . there was certainly no time to wonder how they were ever going to get *out*.

Andor belched and wiped his mouth with his free hand, pulling a face. He blinked at the solitary square of light. "Haven't the foggiesh," he whispered.

"Can you talk them into opening the door?"

"How many?"

"At least four."

He shook his head, and swayed. "Too many. Just one, maybe. But they'll cluster near the door for a sshtrnger — stranger. Beshides, 'm not at my best today. Take too long."

He blinked fondly at Kadolan and smiled a sheepish grin that called up all her mother instincts to understand and forgive.

She suppressed them. "Then call Doctor Sagorn and see if he has any bright ideas."

"At least he's sober," Andor agreed solemnly, and vanished with a final circumspect hiccup.

Sagorn snapped, "Come!" Moving awkwardly, as if trying to avoid the touch of wet cloth, he led the way across the cave and ducked into the empty cell. Kadolan followed, wishing she was going to the light, not the dark — to the Good, not the Evil. Even she almost had to duck for the low doorway. The place was rank, a kennel, and the putrid, ammoniacal stench told her what it was being used for. But it was dark, and they could not be seen from the grille.

"How do we get in there?" she repeated. "Or separate them?"

"I don't know! Warfare is not my skill. I think we just wait and trust our luck. Be quiet and let me think."

Kade stood and trembled, and knew that she was doing no useful thinking at all. All those deaths to save one man! And likely two more deaths would follow when she and her varying companion were discovered. It was terribly wrong. She had sinned dreadfully. She was serving the Evil.

A clatter of metal from the other door sent more icy tremors through her. Hinges creaked. Sagorn grunted and pulled her back, away from the faint gray rectangle of the doorway. Then the man holding her arm was Darad again.

"Have one for me, too, Arg!" a voice called, and there was laughter.

"You hold your own, Kuth!" a clearer voice shouted, out in the dark antechamber. The hinge creaked as the man closed the door behind him. "I couldn't handle anything that size!"

There was another chorus of laughter and shouted agreements from Kuth. The door slammed and the bolt scraped. Arg brought no lantern, so there was only one place he could be going.

44

His shape darkened the entrance. He stopped and spread his feet. Darad waited until he was in full stream before he moved. Kade had already closed her eyes. When she opened them, the giant was dragging the body away from the doorway.

And was Sagorn again.

He stared down at the latest corpse. "That was unexpected," he muttered. "Does it help?"

"I can't see how, except that it feels like luck. Two people with words of power ought to be twice as lucky, I'd think," he muttered. "And right now anything would help . . . Ah!" He released a long sigh of inspiration.

"What — " Kadolan said.

"Just watch. Here!" He pulled a dagger from his belt — a dagger that might still be warm from cutting a boy's throat. "Even Darad may need assistance this time."

The handle was sticky. Kade accepted it reluctantly, unable to conceive that she would ever bring herself to use it. She opened her mouth to say so, and discovered she was facing yet another man — a shorter one, but not Thinal. Pale jotunn hair shone in the darkness. She should have recognized him, but she guessed first.

"Jalon?"

As Andor had, the minstrel looked down at his bloodstained clothes and he shuddered even harder. His teeth chattered briefly. She knew Master Jalon to be a gentle, sensitive person, a dreamer. Never a killer.

"Why you?" she demanded. She could not take very much more of this. No more at all! She chewed knuckles again, fighting down a crazy urge to scream. She was a princess and at least half jotunn and she must behave accordingly. But perspiration was pouring from her, and the foul air was making her head thump, and she had never done anything more violent in her life than fly a hawk.

Inos! She was doing this for Inos! The thought seemed to steady her.

But Jalon also was teetering on the brink of panic. His teeth clattered again briefly, ending with a click as he clenched his jaw. Then he began to whimper. "I can't! He's crazy! Impossible!"

Kadolan had no idea what plan Sagorn's brilliance had devised. She knew only that a hundred family men would be pouring down those stairs any minute. There was just no time! She tried the argument that had worked so miraculously on Thinal.

"Please, Master Jalon! Try! For Rap's sake?"

The whimpering stopped in a gulp.

"Yes. For Rap! You're right!" The minstrel brought himself under control with an effort that Kadolan heard more than saw. He put his head out of the

45

doorway, cleared his throat quietly, and then shouted. She almost dropped her dagger from shock.

"Hey! Kuth! Look at this!"

It was a Zarkian accent. It was the voice of the dead man. It was perfect mimicry.

A muffled query . . . then a clearer one, as someone inside came to the grille. "Who's that?"

Jalon moved back a step. "It's Arg, stupid. Who else would it be? Come and see this, for Gods' sake."

"See what?" The unseen Kuth was suspicious.

A lesser artist might have overdone it; Jalon knew when to stop. He went away, by becoming Darad, who crouched low, sword at the ready.

The bolt scraped. The hinges groaned. Kuth put his turbaned head out. "Come on, Arg — you know the rules. Five in here always. You want me to go see something, then you gotta come here and — "

Darad went. Gritting her teeth and brandishing her dagger, Kadolan followed — out one door, in at the other, and *don't fall over the corpse*, into the painful brilliance of the lamplit cell. The heat and stench struck her like a flood of boiling sewage, the stink of men and oil smoke, and excrement, and also a sweet rank rottenness that was worst of all.

The gamblers had been sitting on a rug at the far end of the room. Three were still scrambling to their feet, drawing their swords. Another had perhaps been already upright, for he was charging forward as Kade came in, and she saw Darad's blade twist into his belly. It didn't kill him, but the sound he made showed that it hurt. And right in front of Kade, where she must be careful not to trip over it, was . . .

That was where the awful smell was coming from. Naked, spread out like a chained butterfly, swollen, twisted, blackened flesh rotting alive . . . Could he possibly be still alive? Mercifully unconscious, of course.

Then she saw that Darad was backing. The cellar was just wide enough for three men abreast, and three men were what he faced. They all had scimitars. Two had drawn daggers also. They stepped over their screaming, writhing companion and continued to advance in line abreast. They were all stooping because of the low headroom, and Darad's size was a handicap now.

In the romances Kadolan had read in her younger days, more action-related than those she preferred in her maturity, heroes were always taking on three or four villains at once. They held one off with a sword, another with a chair, and likely put the rest out of the fight with a kick. Rap had used chairs against Darad.

There were no chairs in this cell. There was a rug, with some cushions, and there were two dying men on the floor, one of them fastened there. And one swordsman could not handle three unless he took them by surprise.

Kadolan remembered that she was carrying a dagger.

A dagger was very little use against a sword, and Darad was back almost as far as Rap, with nowhere else to go. She changed her grip, stepped to the left, and threw the dagger with all her strength at the man on that side. She would never have gotten in a second blow with it, anyway.

Even if the family men had registered that she had a blade, they might not have guessed that she would throw it, or could do so under that roof. At that range she could not miss, and yet she almost did. The blade struck the man's shoulder and fell, but it distracted him, which was all the assistance Darad needed. He battered the center man's sword aside, feinted at the Right-hand face, lunged before Center could restore his guard, slitting his sword arm from wrist to elbow. Then he parried Right-hand's attack and riposted with a cut across the face. The wounds gave his opponents pause. Left-hand was still clutching his shoulder; Darad ran a sword into his heart and then took him by the belt. As the other two lunged simultaneously, he used the body as a shield against Center, while he parried Right-hand with his blade. Then he threw the body at Center and riposted under Right-hand's guard. The rest was just a matter of tidying loose ends.

Satisfied he had won, Kadolan turned her face away. Out beyond the doorway, on the far side of the anteroom, the stairway entrance glowed bright. Someone was coming!

She slammed the door shut — *boom!* — and struggled with the great bolt until it grudgingly scraped home. Through the grille she heard boots on the stairs.

Then she turned and dropped to her knees beside the prisoner and whispered, "Master Rap?"

Darkling way:
　　She hurried at his words, beset with fears,
　　For there were sleeping dragons all around,
　　At glaring watch, perhaps, with ready spears.
　　Down the wide stairs a darkling way they found;
　　In all the house was heard no human sound.
　　　　　　　　　　　Keats, *The Eve of St. Agnes*

47

3

Best-laid scheme

1

The aurora had faded, the lights, the blazing stars. The trumpets and meadowlarks had fallen silent, the dark returned.

Darkness and silence — deeper now, because he could hold the pain away altogether instead of only partly. Lately he hadn't been able to do very much about the pain, because his will had been sapped by weakness and creeping death. Now he could banish all feeling, shut out everything. That was good. Much better.

Now he could make himself die.

Ironic, that! She'd told him a word of power. He'd recognized the feeling, the glory. So he was a mage. A mage ought to be able to make himself die. Sink down. Deeper. Darker. Colder. Peace.

She was Princess Kadolan, Inos's aunt. He wished she would stop shouting in his ear like this.

He wished whoever was doing all that hammering would stop, too.

Sagorn, also, fretting and pacing. Let the old scoundrel think his way out of this one.

He squashed out his hearing, closing his ears. Peace. He couldn't see, of course, after what they'd done to his eyes; but he didn't need eyes. And the princess's pleading kept sliding through, also. Annoying.

All those djinns outside the door, with swords and axes, it was almost like being back in Krasnegar, with the imps trying to break their way into the chamber at the top of the tower, except this was a cellar under a cellar. A cave, not a tower. Other end of the world. Everything upside-down. Funny. That was what all the noise was. He could stop that.

But why bother?

That was what Inos's aunt was shouting about. To make him stop the djinns. Telling him he had power now.

Power wasn't the problem.

Will was the problem.

He didn't want to.

Inos was married. Married by her own choice. She'd been angry with him when he broke up the wedding. Not that it had been all his fault. Lith'rian had planted the idea — he could see that now. Big joke to an elf, that. Probably that was why. He ought to resent that and want revenge on the warlock. But who could ever get revenge on a warlock? And it didn't matter all that much. He would snuff himself out like a candle-flame and then he wouldn't have to care anymore.

Care about Inos.

Why shouldn't she marry if she wanted to? Big, chunky fellow. Rich. Royal. Good-looking. Everything a queen would want. Everything he wasn't. Lost her kingdom, didn't matter. She'd found another. A bigger, better, brighter place. So Inos was happy and didn't need him, had never needed him. He needn't have bothered coming.

Poor old Krasnegar.

But he could still feel the ax blows, even if he had corked his ears and turned his hearing off. Nuisance. Annoying. Disturbed a man when he was busy dying. Could stop the djinns if he wanted. Too much effort.

All that way he'd come, and he needn't have bothered.

How did a mage snuff himself? Oddly difficult.

Words didn't want to be lost? No, one of them didn't. The other two were shared and didn't mind. Interesting — his mother's word was all his own, then.

Could make Sagorn open the door, though. That might be easiest. Just a command to the old man to pull the bolt, and then they'd all be quiet and let him die in peace. Not long. The old rascal wouldn't like it.

Too bad about Inos's aunt. Nice person. Well thought of in the castle. Polite to the staff. Real lady. Pity to see her here, all frantic and dirty. Maybe best just to pull the roof down and kill them all. Or snap the bolt himself and let the djinns in.

Now what was she screaming about? Inos?

Inos hurt?

He'd missed the thought. Could pry for it. Bad manners. Not nice thing to do, poke in someone's mind. Ask her to repeat that? Yes, he'd do that.

Couldn't talk with his tongue all cooked. Heal his tongue, then? Not hard. Turn his hearing on again, take the corks out?

Too much bother.

Door wasn't going to last much longer. Then they'd all let him have some peace.

Inos. Happy. Husband and kingdom and children. Good. Want Inos to be happy.

Hurt? Injured?

Ask her to say that bit again? She'd stopped shouting. Weeping? Poor lady. What about Inos? Inos hurt?

Have to cure his tongue. Uncork his ears.

So.

"What about Inos?" he asked. "Hurt?"

A sort of gasping noise from Princess Kadolan . . .

"Her face has been burned, Master Rap. It's going to be terribly scarred. She isn't beautiful anymore."

That was very bad! Terrible! *Anger!*

He cured his eyes and opened them, so she would know he was listening. Too late, the door was falling.

Take away the door. Put a wall of rock there. Good, that had stopped the djinns — let's see them knock holes in that!

Rap frowned up at Princess Kadolan. "Tell me about Inos," he said.

2

For a few minutes, Kadolan just stood and watched the miracles happen. Then she realized that she was no longer looking at a broken, rotting carcass. It was almost back to being a young man, and he was wearing nothing but caked blood. She turned away, only to find that Sagorn was also staring, completely spellbound. She nudged him and gestured; he scowled; she insisted.

They walked to the far end, stepping carefully over the sprawled corpses until they reached the rug, still sprinkled with dice and coins. He gave her a hand and steadied her as she settled herself on a cushion. Then he sat beside her, but he faced himself toward the mage. Two old fools . . . but maybe they'd win out yet.

The doorway was filled by a wall of masonry, black like the walls of Inisso's castle, and quite unlike the adjoining local rock, which was reddish.

The family men had been balked for a while, but their quarry was entombed, and the flickering lamps were steadily fouling the air. There was no obvious way out of this crypt, yet she kept telling herself not to worry, because the sorcery was on their side now. Things were going to be different.

Sagorn coughed repeatedly. Once he frowned and looked up, and when she followed his gaze, she saw a tiny aperture in the rocky roof. She had felt a faint draft earlier and guessed that there must be some ventilation, yet a child could not climb through that small chimney. Still, it was better than nothing. It might explain why the guards had sat at this end of the room, or perhaps the prisoner had been put by the door so they would look him over every time they came and went. It didn't matter. She was too weary to care.

"Ought to put out the lamps," Sagorn muttered. "Just leave one." But he did not move. His face was haggard, the clefts in it deeper than ever, and his skimpy hair was plastered in white streaks. The blood on his garments had dried, but his hands and the folds of his neck were blood-streaked. Kadolan must look as bad herself. It had been a very close-run thing. Reaction was setting in, and she felt older than the witch of the north.

Then Sagorn exclaimed in wonder and she turned to see that the faun was sitting up and had his hands free. He pulled the rusty fetters off his ankles as if they were made of taffy. He glanced at his audience; Kadolan averted her eyes again quickly.

In a moment, though, he came walking over, and he was fully dressed — boots and long pants and a long-sleeved shirt, the sort of rustic homespun garments a stableboy would wear in Krasnegar. He was clean, and the stubble had gone from his face; but he still had the idiotic tattoos around his eyes, and his brown hair was tangled like a gorsebush.

Rasha had changed her appearance to suit her mood. Kadolan felt confident that Master Rap would regard that sort of deception as beneath his self-respect. He must have power in plenty, or he could not have achieved the wonders she had already witnessed, but he would not tamper with the truth. She might soon have to admit that the Gods knew what They were doing.

He bowed clumsily to her. "I am greatly in your debt, ma'am." He stammered and blushed. "A woman . . . lady . . . having the spunk . . . I mean —"

"It was the least I could do, Master Rap. I feel responsible for much of what has happened."

His eyes widened. They were clear gray eyes, very innocent looking, but she sensed that he was using more than a mundane self-control to keep his face from revealing his thoughts. His calm was uncanny — no man could recover so quickly from such an ordeal. "You, ma'am?"

51

She nodded wearily. "I'd rather not go into it now."

"Of course, ma'am." He frowned and waved a hand at one of the bodies. "How many died altogether?"

She glanced at Sagorn, who said, "Eleven."

Rap pulled a face. "God of Mercy! I'm not worth that!"

Could he be serious? "You don't think they deserved it? After what they did to you?"

He shrugged. "It wouldn't be the ones who deserved it who died, would it? The Gods are rarely so tidy. And besides, I started it! I killed three, they told me. And wounded more. I can't blame them too much for wanting to get even." He shook his head sorrowfully.

He seemed to be sincere — but who could tell with a mage? She did not know this boy. She must just remember that Inosolan had chosen him as her friend, and unconsciously as more than friend; and the Gods had confirmed her judgment. Who was Kadolan to question now?

"Can you get us out of here, Master Rap?"

"I have no idea! I haven't been a mage long enough to know what I can do." A faint hint of smile tugged at the corners of his big mouth — whatever Inos had seen in him, she had not chosen him for his looks.

He frowned and glanced around. "The djinns are bringing sledges. Persistent lot, aren't they? I suppose I can put the door back and make them stand aside to let us pass . . . This is rather like the night we had the imps after us, isn't it?" His eyes strayed to Sagorn, whom he had been ignoring. "And this time I did become a mage!"

Sagorn smiled cynically, but he could not conceal his dislike. "This time you had no choice."

Rap ignored the barb; he looked upward. "I think — I can stretch that air hole. Would you mind climbing a ladder, your Highness?"

"I'll climb a greasy pole if it will get me to a bathtub."

He twitched, instantly apologetic. "I can remove the blood, ma'am. If you want."

"I'd rather do it with hot water, thank you."

He nodded, then stared at the hole in the roof again, for longer. It widened imperceptibly until it was a shaft, and there was a bronze ladder stretching down to the rug.

"I'll go first," he said. "I need to work on the top a bit more." He went scrambling up the rungs and disappeared.

Kadolan looked at Sagorn, who was scowling but failing to conceal his amazement.

"An efficient young man!" she said.

The sage nodded. "Oh quite! A very efficient young man. A very stubborn one, too."

"What does that mean?" She struggled to rise, feeling her weariness like a wagonload of marble on her shoulders.

"I mean that Master Rap always does exactly what he wants to do, and no one can ever talk him out of it. And now no one can stop him, either."

3

The original chimney had been much too narrow to have been dug by mundane hands. Obviously it was the work of some long-ago sorcerer, who had modified a natural cave to make the dungeons, just as Rap was now modifying the wormhole into a manhole. The rock wasn't too hard to do, because it was just reshaping; the bronze ladder was really difficult. After a couple of fathoms of that, he switched to spruce, and wood was much easier to produce, somehow.

He'd wondered how it felt to do magic, and now he knew. He couldn't have explained it, though. Can a man explain how he saw, or how he made his muscles work in the right order when he was running? Describe *green*. Or *pretty*. Stop your heart for a minute. Magic was like those. It just was. It was possible, so he could do it. Just wanting . . .

Well . . . he could do some things, and now he was trying to do an evil lot of things all at once, and he hadn't even had a chance to practice with some simple lessons. Basic cursing and frog transformations . . . There were different levels to magic, too. His broken bones and poisoned flesh, his eyes and tongue — he'd cured those, but they weren't really cured. In part he was *keeping* them cured, just as he was *keeping* his clothes in existence . . . and halfway up his new ladder, he realized that he had relaxed his control over those wish-garments, and they weren't there anymore. He made a mental note to dress himself again when he got to the top, then ignored the problem. The ladder, likewise, was going to flicker out of existence as soon as he took his mind off it, although the bronze would last longer than the wood, as some compensation for being harder to create in the first place. The wall that was blocking the djinns . . . and the shaft would shrink back to its original size, so he'd better keep *that* firmly in mind while Inos's Aunt Kade was inside it!

Moreover, once he'd reached the level of the main cellars he was working with masonry instead of solid rock, and he had to be careful to thin the stones without shifting them or collapsing a wall. And his far-sight was telling him that the exit was going to put him in a crowded courtyard, so he was working on the shaft and the ladder at the same time as he began to wonder about making himself invisible. He was also rippling the ambience horribly. Probably he could develop a smoother touch with practice, but every time he added one more rung to the ladder, he seemed to shake the palace like a tambourine. Amazing that no one else noticed! . . . everyone ought to be falling down and shouting earthquake. Lucky the whole palace had a shield around it, although it wasn't a very good one, and it bulged oddly in places, but it would probably be enough to mask his activities from any sorcerer outside. Gods! They'd feel him in Krasnegar otherwise. Lith'rian had made a few ripples, but Rap was creating tidal waves. Rookie!

Twinges of pain told him not to forget his own body. Now there was another sort of sorcery: healing. If he took his mind off himself now, then he'd snap back to almost the same near corpse he'd been before. He was keeping himself whole with magic, but he was also encouraging his natural healing. Maybe that natural healing was a sorcery the Gods did, but he could certainly feel the mending going on at a deeper, slower level, another sort of occult. Even as an adept he'd been able to speed up his natural healing. He thought that now he'd be able to do it for other people, as well. Like Inos. Burns? Yes, he thought he could.

Of course a full sorcerer would be able to do an instant, total cure with the creation magic, but a mere mage would just have to be patient and keep his occult bandages in place until his healing was complete. He'd also have to be careful where he slept for a few nights; someplace where a whiff of gangrene wouldn't bother anyone. He could put a sleep spell on himself, couldn't he? . . .

Removing his beard and the bloodstains — that had been yet another sort of magic, a *go-away* magic. That was permanent, he thought. No time to work it out . . .

The original opening had been a very small grille, high in the wall of the building. Rap opened a new one at ground level, with an inattention anticharisma around it, and he scrambled out onto the courtyard flagstones, hot already from the early-morning sun. He kept his eyes closed against the glare while he gazed around at the blue sky and the kites floating up there. Flowers and fountains and fine horses, and the occult wall around the palace blocking any farther view. The djinns were going frantic down in the cellars and the dungeon . . . far too many of them in the dungeon; they were passing out from lack of air.

A troop of mounted guards went right by him without a glance at the new opening in the wall, or the naked . . . *Whoops!*

Now he was pushing his ability to dangerous limits, juggling too many hatchets, keeping himself healthy and clothed, and the shaft open and the ladder in existence, and everyone else distracted, and an eye on the princess and Jalon . . . Jalon? . . . making their way up to the surface. And he mustn't forget about his mind, either. Too much calm and he'd fade out and drop some of the hatchets. Too little and he'd have to deal with the crazy boy in there who'd been bent to breaking point by fear and agony and just wanted to scream and scream . . . that was another healing that was going to take patience. Nights were going to be tricky, certainly.

Then he took the princess's hand and helped her out; she was blinded by the sunlight. And then Jalon, and it was good to see the little jotunn, and give him a hug and thump on the back. He'd shaved and cleaned up since Rap had last seen him as their boat sailed into the bay; but he still smelled strongly of salt water. And Jalon seemed absurdly glad to be able to hug Rap, trying to keep his eyes closed against the light and weep with them at the same time, mumbling nonsense.

Rap let go of the shaft and it began to shrink at once. The guards weren't through the bricked-up doorway yet, and when they arrived, both ladder and shift would have vanished. Let the red horrors chew on that problem!

Inos's Aunt Kade was staring at the squad of brown-clad family men approaching. They went striding blindly by her. She glanced down at her filthy, gory robe, then at Rap. Then Jalon. She pushed back her wild-flying white hair, and her fingers discovered the bloodstains even there . . .

"Can you escort us safely back to my quarters, Master Rap?"

"Certainly, ma'am."

"And then I do hope you both will join me for breakfast. We have much to discuss."

4

At the top of the long staircase, two very bored guards slouched outside the door to Kadolan's suite. They were not the gymnasts she had seen in the night, but they looked no older, nor any more impressed by their responsibilities. She could, of course, complain to Prince Kar about the quality of the protectors he had assigned to her — despite her fatigue, the absurdity of that whimsy made her chuckle. When Rap touched the door and the lock clicked, one of the youths looked around, vaguely puzzled, but he obviously did not register that three people were going in.

In her chamber, Kadolan changed back into her night attire and passed her soiled garments out to Rap, who promised that they would be seen no more. Then she wiped some stains from her hands and face and rang for her attendants. Astonishingly, the sun was not yet far above the horizon.

The housekeeper. Mistress Zuthrobe, had not impressed Kadolan even before the night's revelation of what her young wards were getting up to with the guards. Now Zuthrobe soared into panic when told that the sultan and sultana were expected for breakfast. She flew off without inquiring how Kadolan had received such a message unbeknownst to her staff. Intrigue was certainly catching, Kade decided, and it was endemic in Arakkaran.

55

This had been the hardest night of her life, but excitement was still buoying her up, and a warm tub refreshed her. Then she hurried out to her balcony to find a sumptuous meal already being demolished by a starving faun and . . . *bother!* . . . the imp guttersnipe, Thinal.

Rap jumped up when she approached, but the little thief just leered, displaying a mouthful of irregular and dirty teeth. He was wearing nothing but a ragged pair of shorts. He needed a shave, a haircut, and a very thorough washing.

Seeing that conversation would have to wait — and feeling pleasantly hungry after her night's exertions — Kadolan helped herself to some generous portions and joined in the feasting. No one spoke at all while the eating continued.

Able at last to study him properly, she was surprised at how large and — er — husky, Master Rap was. He was the only faun she had ever met, but she had always understood that fauns were one of the smaller races. Even allowing for the fact that he was sitting next to the puny Thinal, Rap seemed big, larger than most male imps, approaching jotunn or djinn size. Of course he was part jotunn — as was Inos, of course.

Off in the distance, troops of guards were hurrying to and fro, and she could guess that she had thrown the palace authorities into unprecedented turmoil. The thought was not unpleasant.

As her appetite waned she began to wish that Doctor Sagorn was present, to provide some cultured discourse, or even Andor, were he sober. Almost any of the five would be better than Thinal, who tended to stare at her with an appraising, avaricious gaze even as he chewed. He made her feel like a pet rabbit in the presence of something feral, and hungry. His eyes were red-rimmed and he yawned a lot, often when he had his mouth full.

His manners were atrocious, by any standards. Master Rap, on the other hand, was handling his skimpy cutlery — and when necessary his food — very well, much as she did herself. He might require less coaching than she had been anticipating, in order to turn him into a respectable consort for Inos. She wondered if he would consent to having his hair curled; obviously it would never lie flat.

Inos and Azak must have sailed by now, but a mage ought to be able to arrange good-quality transportation, and perhaps even speed its passage. Most ships stopped in at all the major ports along the coast. So she would pursue, with Master Rap's assistance, and at Brogogo, therefore, or Torkag, they would intercept the sultan. Then Rap could cure Inos's injuries and use some occult persuasion on Azak to get the marriage annulled. It was still, of course, a marriage in name only.

Once Inos and the faun had been reunited under Kadolan's tutelage, they could all start giving some thought to the problem of Krasnegar. And if that was insoluble, then a comfortable estate within some pleasantly civilized corner of the Impire ought to be within reach of a mage. Just like one of the poet's romances — the lovers would find a happy ending!

Feeling extremely pleased with herself — and properly grateful to the Gods, of course — Kade selected another pomegranate. These tropical delicacies certainly helped to compensate for the absence of some of her more familiar favorites.

The two youths ate much faster than she did, but all three seemed to reach their capacity at about the same time. Thinal belched and pushed his chair back. He set to work paring his toenails with a fruit knife. Kadolan dabbed her lips with a linen napkin. Rap poured her another cup of coffee, and one for himself.

Then he glanced at the door and frowned. "You have a visitor, ma'am. I think I can keep us unobserved."

That seemed likely, after their unremarked return across the palace complex. Before Kadolan could ask what sort of visitor, Mistress Zuthrobe came hurrying in, veiled and wide-eyed with fright.

"His Highness Prince Kar, ma'am!"

Again Kadolan opened her mouth but was prevented from speaking. Without waiting for her invitation, Kar strode out onto the balcony, shadowed by two of the fearsome family men. He came right to her chair and stared down at her with a sinister little smile, as if he were a teacher and she an errant pupil.

She had met the baby-faced chief of security a couple of times at the wedding rehearsals, but even those brief, formal encounters had explained why Inosolan found him so intimidating. The presence of two obvious interlopers at Kadolan's table was no help in this instance, even if Kar did not seem to notice them.

He turned to regard the Zuthrobe woman, who was fidgeting in the background with the apparent intent of chaperoning the unorthodox interview. He did not need to speak — his expression alone was enough to send her fleeing back indoors. Then he resumed his baleful inspection of Kadolan.

"You are expecting company, I understand?"

She plied him with her most innocent smile, "Well, Inosolan called on me last night. I am aware that she has departed."

"And?" A smile so thin on Kar implied a scowl.

From the corner of her eye, Kadolan could tell that the invisible Thinal was making obscene gestures at Kar, causing Rap to grin faintly.

"And I understand that the departure is to be kept secret as long as possible. I thought I could start a rumor that they had eaten breakfast here, muddy the waters a little."

His eyes were chips of pink granite. "His Majesty is touring the northlands this morning."

"Oh!" Kadolan said. "Well, that's nice. Then I have provided a secondary alibi?"

"You have weakened a cover story that cost enormous preparation. You did not eat all that by yourself."

Beginning to feel flustered, she waved a hand at the empty air beyond the balcony. "Of course not, your Highness."

Now his smile would have frozen the marrow of her bones had she not had a mage within reach. "I feel that these quarters are inadequate, ma'am. We may be able to find you something more appropriate and more easily guarded."

"These are quite satisfactory. I find the antiques fascinating. Something is wrong?"

"Intruders are prowling the palace. Guards have been murdered — and the faun has escaped!"

"I am delighted to hear it," she said calmly. "If you think I am hiding him, then I grant you leave to search my quarters."

"My men already did." Kar spun on his heel and strode out, his spurs jingling. His flunkies followed.

Thinal grinned and cocked a final snoot at his back. Rap frowned.

"Well!" Kadolan said, annoyed to find that her heart was beating faster than was seemly. "I thank you, Master Rap. Your powers are a welcome reinforcement in Arakkaran!"

The youth smiled faintly, but he was still keeping his true feelings masked.

"Perhaps," she suggested, "we should now compare notes and make some plans?"

He nodded. "First I must escort Thinal down to the gates and see him safely on his way. It would not be fair to keep Gathmor in suspense any longer."

"Gathmor?"

"Another friend. A good friend. A sailor. You saw him once."

"I did?" The conversation was already slipping away from the path she had planned.

"In the magic casement. He was the third man present when Sagorn and I met the dragon."

Gods! "The prophecy was fulfilled?"

"The first one . . . " The faun frowned suddenly. Looking very uneasy, he added, "And now I suspect that makes the other two inevitable."

A duel with the infamous Kalkor? Torture in the goblin lodge? Horror-struck, she said, "Surely not! Why?"

"Because obviously the casement was working correctly. Why did I not see that earlier?" He shook his head, puzzled. "Some things are very clear to me now, things I never knew before."

"The words bring wisdom?" She took a shaky sip of coffee. "Then perhaps you can explain something that is puzzling me, Master Rap. My word of power never seemed to make much different to me, nor to my sister-in-law, when she was alive. I assumed that it had very little strength, as it were . . . that it had been diluted in the remote past by too many sharings, or that it was wearing out. Yet it has produced extraordinary abilities in you. Surely you were not capable of all this yesterday?"

Again he shook his head, his gray eyes unreadable. After a moment he said, "I do know more about that! It . . . it isn't easy to explain."

"Oh, we have lots of time."

"We don't, not at the moment. But it isn't that. I mean, I feel a strong urge not to talk about such things. The words are secretive by nature!" He glanced at Thinal's ratty eyes. "This must be why nosy mundanes like Sagorn have so much trouble finding out!"

The thief nodded and smirked.

"I'll try, though." Rap took a deep breath. "There seem to be three things involved, ma'am. First, of course, is the mere number of words. One makes a genius, two an adept. Then mage and sorcerer. All are different. Rarely a genius will have occult power, as I did, but not often — and so on. The number of words is important in itself. Everyone knows that."

"Like the number of wheels on a coach."

"Yes! A wheelbarrow, or a chaise, or . . . " He smiled his diffident little smile. "I don't know anything with *three* wheels! Or a wagon — all different. But the number of words matters most. My farsight, for instance, is much stronger than it was, but mainly I have skills now that I never had before. Mage skills. And then the words themselves can be weakened by sharing. We knew that."

"I'm not as good as I was," Thinal muttered, looking resentful.

"You're still the best!" Rap said quickly. He wiped his forehead, as if feeling a strain. "That sort of comparison is all right when you compare one person's power before he tells a word, or after he gets more of the same word . . . but it doesn't mean much when you compare one person with another. What's more important then is . . . the third thing . . . I never realized . . . "
He paused.

"What third thing?" Thinal demanded.

"It's a sort of native talent." Rap stared unseeing for a moment, a young man wrestling with great problems. "When I was only an adept I could feel the ripples. Lith'rian didn't like that!"

"Ripples?" Kadolan said, confused. Did he mean *Warlock* Lith'rian?

"It's like a vibration. The world shimmers. I thought I was going to shake my own teeth out making that ladder. I expect I'll develop a gentler touch, when I've had some practice. Hope so! I can't tell within the palace, but I think I could sense sorcery a great way off now."

"Sheik Elkarath is a mage, and he said he couldn't. Not at all, he said."

Rap nodded, then slumped back in his chair, breathing hard. "Then I'm better than him. It may be our words, but more likely, it's this third thing — us, ourselves. I'm just more . . . responsive. That's the way I see it."

Some people had innate musical ability and could learn to sing, or play any instrument they chose. Others, like Kadolan herself, had a stone ear for music. So this nondescript stableboy had another sort of inborn ability, a gift for magic, something she did not. She felt mildly resentful about that. It explained Inos, though. Perhaps Inos had no gift at all, or very little, so her word of power was of no use to her. That seemed most unfair! And there were the tales of the legendary great warlocks of the past, the Thraine — who had left no notable successor, so far as she could recall.

She wondered why the servants were not coming to clear the table, and realized that the faun might be keeping them away.

Then he roused himself and glanced inquiringly at the imp, as if ready to leave.

"What about Inos?" Kadolan said quickly.

Rap leaned back and studied her unwinkingly. "What about her?"

"Her accident. The burns?"

He nodded glumly. "I was responsible for that, I suppose, in that I killed the sorceress. If I can find Inos, I shall try to repair the damage. The curse on the sultan must be a sorcery, though, and I can't do anything about that."

"And her marriage?"

"What about her marriage?" the faun asked coldly.

Suddenly concerned, Kadolan said, "It was all a terrible mistake!"

His face was so infuriatingly wooden!

Rap said, "I asked her if she had married of her own free will. She said she had. She was not lying, ma'am! I can detect lies; I could even then. It was her choice."

"But . . . But . . . But she thought you were dead! She had seen your ghost, she thought!"

He shivered, very slightly. "And I saw her . . . But she knew I was alive when I asked the question." A trace of pain showed, and vanished again. "Has Inos ever said she loved me?"

Probably her face was telling him *no* before she could open her mouth. "Well, she spoke often of your childhood. She was very upset by your death."

"And she was very angry at me for interrupting her wedding."

This was awful! "Of course Inos was upset! It was a disaster! She had not had time to think, to remember the God's words, to work out the implications."

He did not comment, just looked at her.

60

"Free will is a nebulous term, Master Rap! Under the circumstances, she had no real choice but to marry the sultan. It is often easier to lie to oneself than to admit unpleasant truths."

"She did not lie to me, ma'am. I am certain of that."

Horrors! This was not at all what Kadolan had expected!

"And she stayed silent when the sultan ordered me thrown in jail."

"That was for your good!"

Thinal guffawed.

"I mean," Kadolan said stiffly, "he is insanely jealous! Anything she said would have only made him angrier."

Rap shrugged, slightly.

God of Love!

"And you? How do you feel about her?"

"With respect, your Highness, that is not relevant."

Kade wrung her hands, searching for an argument, an excuse, an explanation. "I beg you. Master Rap! I *beg* you to rescue my niece from an inappropriate and unwanted marriage!"

"She is a married woman!" Rap exclaimed, shocked. "Your Highness, you cannot mean that!"

"You must see — "

"No I don't! I won't even consider it!" He set his jaw.

"You are being very difficult!"

"You are making improper suggestions."

"But —"

"I won't listen!"

"Stubbornness is not an attractive trait."

"So Inos always told me."

Thinal snickered. Doubtless he also was recalling what Sagorn had said about this mulish faun. Kadolan stopped drumming fingers on the table and composed herself. "I think you must ask her again . . . er . . . sir. About free will."

Again he shrugged slightly, and again moved as if to rise.

"Now," she said hastily, "Inosolan and the sultan have not long sailed. If we hurry down to the harbor — the three of us and your other friend, if you wish — then surely we can find a ship heading west? If money is a problem, I have some brooches and things I can sell. Then we can overtake them at the next port, or even chase them all the way to Qoble, if necessary."

Rap shook his head.

No? "Then what do you plan to do?"

The big gray eyes studied her. "I plan to remain in this palace for some time. A week, at least, perhaps longer. With your permission, these quarters would be good, or I can find others. I need to complete my healing. I must also learn to control my powers — here, where I am shielded. Otherwise I shall just give myself away to some warlock or sorcerer and be enslaved. Also, my friends need time to rest, all six of them."

Reluctantly she concluded that it was not an unreasonable request. She nodded. "You are most welcome here, and they also, if you can hide them."

Thinal snorted. "I wouldn't rest here. Pickings're too good. Got my eye on a well-stocked little whorehouse down by the docks."

Kadolan regarded him with distaste, but the technique that worked so well on underlings at Kinvale and Krasnegar seemed to be ineffective on him. She turned her attention back to the mage. "And when you are ready, you will take me with you when you go after Inos?" She heard an unpleasant whine in her voice, but now she was wondering if he might just desert her, and the prospect was terrifying. The rest of her life in Arakkaran?

"I will not abandon you, ma'am. Not after what you did for me."

How deeply was he prying into her thoughts? "I am very grateful for that promise, Master Rap."

His eyes seemed to go out of focus, staring at the space above her left shoulder. "But . . . I do not go after Inos."

"What? But —"

"Qoble is in South's sector."

"You fear Warlock Lith'rian?"

"Or he fears me."

She did not ask what that cryptic remark meant. Thinal seemed as puzzled as she.

"I sail," he said softly, as if not speaking to anyone. "I sail . . . but north. Yes, a big port on a big river."

Ghostly fingernails scratched at her skin. The mage was using some sort of occult power she had not met before. Foresight? The imp seemed to have the same odd foreboding she did, for he drew back his lips in a snarl. But Ollion was another possible way to the capital.

"And then?" she whispered.

Beads of sweat showed on the faun's forehead. "Then," he whispered, "then . . . Hub, I think. It must be Hub. The palaces?"

All the world's problems came to Hub eventually. She herself had often said that the Krasnegar question would be settled there. Perhaps it had been settled already — or perhaps that was yet to come. She began to feel a surge of hope. Hub!

"And there, Master Rap? What happens in Hub?"

For a moment there was no answer. The gray eyes widened . . .

Then Rap screamed and covered his face with his hands.

62

Best-laid scheme

> But, Mousie, thou art no thy lane,[1]
> In proving foresight may be vain:
> The best-laid schemes o'mice an' men,
>   Gang aft a-gley,[2]
> An' lae'e us naught but grief and pain,
>   For promised joy.
>   BURNS, *To a Mouse*

---

[1] *no thy lane:* = *not alone*
[2] *a-gley:* = *awry* (*Ed.*)

4

Several ways

1

A s always, Inos took longer than anyone else aboard to find her sea legs, but by the time Star of Delight had called in at Brogogo and then rounded the Corner of Zark into the Summer Seas, she was well enough to sit up and start taking stock of her companions.

Kar, of course, had stayed behind to hold off the jackals. Who came next on Azak's loyalty list?

Zana's presence was less surprising than it first seemed. A sultan could hardly take his wife traveling without some female companionship, and if there was any woman in the world whom Azak trusted, it was the older half sister who had reared him. He had spoken of her briefly once or twice in the desert, and those had been the only glimpses he had ever revealed to Inos of his youth or childhood. He would probably have been willing to die for the old woman, and most certainly willing to kill for her. From Inos's own point of view, although Zana was not Kade, she was as acceptable a lady's companion as anyone who could have been found in the court, even granting that

Zana's own loyalty would put Azak's well-being ahead of anyone else's by several leagues.

Apart from Azak himself, there were nineteen men in the party. Only one of them she recognized as a prince, and that was the massive and aging Gutturaz. He, too, seemed a surprising choice, but any brother of Azak's who managed to reach middle age must have demonstrated both a gift for survival and a rare lack of ambition.

The other eighteen were youngish family men, a bloodcurdling collection behind their red whiskers. But facial hair was not worn in the Impire; without comment, Azak shaved off his beard at Torkag, and every one of his followers was clean shaven before *Star of Delight* sailed on the next tide. Somehow their ruddy faces looked even more deadly than before.

And there was Azak himself, who shared her kennel-size cabin. Of course they had shared a tent for months in the desert, but Kade had always been there, also. Then, too, he had been occupied much of the time in being first lionslayer, usually coming to bed after Inos had been magicked asleep by the mage and often departing before she awoke in the morning. And they had never been both there in daylight.

Two days out of Torkag, *Star of Delight* was becalmed. The sun blazed overhead, the sails hung still as icicles, and there was nothing to do but fall down and melt. With men all over the deck, Inos retired to her cabin. So did Azak.

They each had a narrow bunk, on opposite walls, but hardly a cubit apart. She lay under a sheet. He had stripped down to a cloth she would have described as being on the narrow side of skimpy. Perhaps he was letting her satisfy her maidenly curiosity about the male physique. Perhaps he was bragging, although Azak never really bragged about anything — he merely stated the obvious. Or perhaps he was trying to make the best of an impossible situation, staying as close as possible to normal married behavior.

He was too long for the bunk and almost too wide for it, a shiny copper giant, everything a girl could dream of. Poor Azak! The scorpion had been scotched but the sting remained in the wound. And the hideous burns on her face still hurt. They were oozing now — she might never smile again. Azak's lifelong infallibility seemed to falter when Inos was around.

He felt her scrutiny and turned his head lazily. "My love?"

"Azak?"

"Hot, isn't it?" He went back to staring at the ceiling.

She had never heard him utter fatuous chit-chat before.

After a moment she whispered, "I will say it when I can. It will mean more if you know it is honestly meant."

He studied the overhead. "Were it not for the curse, I would have you babbling it by now — and meaning it."

"I am sure you would. I wish you could." Did she? Did she really? *My love. My darling. Beloved. Lover.*

Why not? Many a woman in Pandemia had learned how to love the husband fate had dealt her. Why should she be different? Very few would have such a husband to love.

Trust in love!

Footsteps sounded over her head. The ship barely rocked, and the usual creaking, squeaking noises were depressingly absent. Even the gulls were silent.

She thought of Rap, pacing a cell back in Arakkaran. Honest, well-meaning, blundering Rap. Azak might be persuaded to write . . . No, give him a little longer to heal his pride. He was not truly vindictive, Azak. He might be deadly, but he usually had a logical purpose in what he did — apart from his insane jealousy, of course. After the disaster of the wedding-night kiss, he had blamed himself for not thinking of the danger; a lesser man would have blamed her, or the Gods, or even Rap . . .

It was too hot to talk. It hurt too much to be silent. "Azak?"

"Mmm?"

"How do we travel? I mean, in the Impire? Am I to be Hathark again? And what name and station will you —"

"I shall be Kar!" He chuckled at her surprise. "It is as good a name as any. My own might be recognized, as I am so memorable. We shall be sons of the Sultan of Shuggaran. The treacherous dog is something of an Imperial supporter, which may help."

"But . . . what about your appeal to the Four?"

Azak frowned at the planks above him. "There will be no appeal to the wardens. We travel merely as young princes seeking knowledge. It is not a Zarkian custom, but the imps will see nothing odd about rich young men jaunting around the world."

Inos raised herself on one elbow to study him better. "If you wanted a harem girl, you should have brought a harem girl! I happen to have a brain, and now you have roused my curiosity."

He rolled his head again and flickered one of his rare smiles. "I haven't beaten that out of you yet, have I? All right, my queen, just remember that none of the others know. Except Zana, of course. As far as my brother and the rabble are concerned at the moment, we are spying, and I brought you along to divert suspicion. You understand?"

The smile had gone, and the red eyes were menacing.

"Of course," she said. He had been gelded, and no shame could ever be worse for him. His court might have guessed, but the matter would never be discussed.

Azak nodded and sighed. "I must find a sorcerer, and no sorcerer except a warden ever dares reveal his existence. So I must seek out one of the Four, a warlock. The witch of the north is not . . . No, a warlock."

Why not Bright Water? Probably he could not bear the thought of begging for help from a woman. It would not help that the woman in question was supposedly three hundred years old.

"Then who?" Inos asked. "Not Olybino, obviously." East was the occult backer of the imperor's legions.

"Nor Lith'rian, obviously."

"Why not Lith' . . . Oh, you mean because he sent Rap?" Despite the heat, she shivered then at Azak's glare.

"Exactly. That leaves Zinixo — obviously. He is only a youngster, they say. He should be sympathetic."

Poor Azak! There were no words to say. She wished she could grip one of those big hands and squeeze it. She lay back to avoid his gaze and considered. How maddening not to know more about these mysterious wardens!

"And isn't he supposed to be Olybino's enemy?"

"So the gossip says. When the legions make war, historically the other wardens tend to oppose East. East supports the army, and the imperor does, also, of course. That's two out of the five, so the other three are inclined to balk. It isn't much to go on, but it is all we have."

Inos wiped her streaming brow and adjusted the sticky sheet. They would all be cooked before they ever reached land again, and that would solve all their problems.

"Azak," she said cautiously, "why are you so reluctant to make a formal appeal to the Four? It would give you some sort of legal status on the journey — the Impire ought to grant you safe passage."

"No! With war coming, I dare not risk falling into East's clutches. And what sort of argument do I have now, with Rasha dead? She can't meddle in politics now." His voice had gone very harsh and forbidding.

She persisted, gently. "A monarch needs heirs —"

"No!"

Pride? An appeal to the Four would be a much more public affair than a private audience with one of them.

She let the silence hold for a moment, then said, "How about me? I have been abducted from my kingdom by sorcery. I still have cause to appeal. And you escort me . . . "

He swung himself up, dropping his long legs to the floor, and humped over in a crouch as he reached for his clothes. He was inflamed with sudden anger. "I said 'No!'"

She turned her face away, guessing the rest.

The Krasnegar matter was supposedly all settled now, or so they had been told. Azak would not risk unsettling it again. Finding a ruler for Arakkaran was easy — much too easy — whereas she might yet seem like a uniquely acceptable answer for Krasnegar.

If the Four did give Inos back her kingdom, then they would expect her to rule it. Once Azak had promised to go and live there at her side. Obviously that promise was no longer relevant.

There would be no appeal to the Four if he could help it.

2

A year ago he'd been content to be Thorie. Now he wanted to be called by his full name, Emthoro, and Shandie didn't like that, because it had been Dad's name. So they settled on Thorog, which was the name of the hero of a book Cousin-Thorog had been reading until Aunt Orosea had found it and taken it away. The Book-Thorog was always visiting ladies' chambers, and Cousin-Thorog told Shandie about some of the things he had done to, for, and with the ladies and — even more unlikely — some of the things the ladies had done to him.

It all sounded rather sick-making and boring, but Shandie didn't say so. He knew what grown-ups did on a bed, and most of it seemed to be just the same thing every night, and pretty stupid. None of the things Book-Thorog had done.

Cousin-Thorog was thirteen, and hence thought he knew a great deal more than Shandie did. He probably didn't know quite as much as he was hinting, though, because Shandie was sure no girl in the Impire would ever want to kiss anyone with that many pimples or such funny-shaped eyes, even if Thorog was tall, like his father, the Duke of Leesoft. And Shandie, while he had yet to understand the merits of kissing and that sort of stuff, had seen a lot of that sort of stuff going on sometimes when he was supposed to be asleep.

Rather to his astonishment, Shandie had discovered himself alone with his cousin — no grown-ups around at all! He tried to remember the last time this had happened. He had wondered, with a shiver of panic, if he even knew how to speak to anyone not-grown-up anymore, but apparently Thorog hadn't noticed anything wrong with his talk. Of course, Thorog was doing most of the talking.

They were in Thorog's room, and Thorog was just finishing dressing himself. He didn't have a valet of his own yet . . . Shandie did! The wedding called for formal dress, of course, but not *court* formal, so that was all right. Formal was only a hundred years out of date, instead of thousands. No togas.

Thorog wanted to get back to Leesoft quickly, although he had just arrived in Hub. This was hunting season, he said.

"You'll stay for my birthday, day after tomorrow?" Shandie said hopefully.

"No. I mean, I'm here to represent the family at the wedding today. Dad said I can come home anytime I like as soon as it's over, and I don't want to miss his big stag hunt."

"It's raining!" Shandie glanced at the streaming panes and thought wistfully of going on a stag hunt, or even being able to sit on a horse again. As long as he behaved himself at the wedding, he thought he would get a birthday party, though. Ythbane and Moms ought to be in a good mood, after all. He wondered if he'd know any of the boys who'd be invited.

"Won't be raining at home! Rains more in Hub than at Leesoft."

"How d'you know?"

"Dad says so."

Shandie retreated from that battle and tried again. "What else d'you hunt?" he asked wistfully. And after the list ran out, "You ride every day?"

Thorog was taken by surprise, busily hauling on a stocking. His legs were much longer than Shandie's, but not much thicker, and Shandie was rather ashamed of his arrow-thin calves. But at least Thorog wasn't getting dressed up in a toga. Even to look at a toga made Shandie shake now.

"Don't you?" Thorog demanded.

The thought of sitting a horse was very unpleasant so soon after yesterday's formal court function. "I never . . . almost never ride."

"Why not?" Thorog looked thoroughly disbelieving. "You're not *scared* of horses, are you?"

"Course not!"

The nasty glint did not leave Thorog's eye. "Sure?"

"Sure!"

"Then why not?"

Shandie shrugged. "Just don't have time. Too many f-f-f-formal functions." He plunged ahead loudly. "Now that Grandfather's birthday's finally over, there won't be so many f-formal things I have to go to."

"What do you do at them?" Thorog demanded, standing up and squeezing his feet into his silver-buckled shoes without unbuckling them.

"Just stand beside the throne." *And I always fidget, no matter how much I try not to. But this wedding isn't that sort of function, so I won't get beaten. I hope.*

"Shandie," Thorog whispered with a quick glance around the obviously empty room, "does Grandfather ever say anything now?"

Shandie shook his head. "Not in weeks. Why?"

"Mum asked me to ask you. Don't tell."

"Course not." Shandie shook his head again.

"When are they going to proclaim a regency?"

"About a month, I think. They want to get the wedding over first. Why are we whispering? The whole court knows all this."

Thorog said, "Oh!" and looked disappointed.

Suddenly there was a gap in the conversation. Now might be a good time to try to get an answer to a question that was really bothering Shandie. He had been dying to find someone he could ask. His books were vague on the matter, and Court Teacher was evasive. He took a deep breath and decided to risk it.

"Thorog . . . what d'you know about *puberty?*"

"Puberty's what I'm in the middle of," Thorog said, drawing himself up straight and looking challengingly at the mirror.

Shandie sniggered. "You mean like messing up a cravat?"

"No, I mean like growing hairs on my lip — and other places," he added mysteriously.

"What hairs on your lip?"

"Well, once it starts it comes very quickly, Dad says. And it's started!" Thorog looked even more mysterious.

"Where?"

"Down here."

Now came the problem that had been really torturing Shandie. "Thorog, *what color is it?*"

Thorog stuttered and said brown, what color did he expect it would be?

"It isn't . . . blue, is it?"

A very strange expression came over his cousin's face. He clumped over to where Shandie was sitting on the edge of the bed. "Why, Shandie?"

Surprised, and a little nervous, Shandie said, "Well, it can be blue, can't it? Hair *down there?*"

"Who has blue hair there? I won't say you told me, honest. Except to Mum, and she won't tell anyone."

"How should I know?" Shandie said quickly, alarmed now.

Thorog dropped his voice. "The only people with blue hair are merfolk. Their hair is blue, all of it. Very pale blue. Even eyebrows, I suppose. They're very unhairy people, legs and arms, but I expect their grown-ups have hair *down there* like any others. If a man had some merman blood in him, he might have blue hair, and then he'd have to dye his hair so people wouldn't know. But I don't suppose he'd bother dying the bit *down there*. All right?"

Shandie nodded gratefully. That explained things, although it was odd that Thorog was so knowledgeable about merfolk. "And what's wrong with having merfolk blood? I mean, is it worse than troll blood, or elf blood?"

"Nothing wrong with a little *elf* blood," Thorog said snappily. "Dad says jotunn wouldn't be too bad, either. But merfolk . . . you know why Grandfather doesn't rule the Kerith islands, young fellow?"

"Because they don't fight fair," Shandie said. "Mermen won't stand and fight. They pick us off with cowardly attacks in the dark, one at a time. It's happened . . . "

"Fight fair?" Thorog went back to his mirror. Amazingly, he seemed to be satisfied with his cravat, for he set to work on his hair. "If someone invaded your country, would you care about fighting fair?"

Shandie had never considered the question.

"And why do the centurions let the men run around to be killed one at a time in the dark? They don't do it fighting dwarves in Dwanish, or elves in Ilrane. Why fighting mermen? Never asked your books that question?"

"No," Shandie said in a small voice.

"Well, it's the merwomen who do the damage. They sing, or dance, or just show themselves. And the army falls apart. You know how dogs flock to a bitch?"

"No."

"Bees to a queen, then?"

"No."

Thorog rolled his eyes. "You spend far too much time reading and hanging around court functions, my lad! You should get out of doors more. But that's why you'll never be Imperor of the Keriths, Shandie. *Sex!*" he whispered dramatically. "Men go crazy!"

"Oh!" Shandie said.

"And that's why merfolk aren't welcome, not anywhere. They bring quarrels. Why don't jotnar ever trade in mermaid slaves?"

Shandie considered that, then said, "Why not?"

"Because they can't bear to part with them!" Thorog crowed in triumph. "Now, who do you know with blue hair *down there?*"

"Oh, no one! Say, you don't mind if I slip up to my room for a moment?"

He didn't sleep with Moms anymore. He had a new room now, all to himself, and his medicine was there. He was beginning to feel scratchy-twitchy, and the only cure he knew for scratchy-twitchy was a mouthful of his medicine. He headed for the door.

"Why," Thorog said, staring, "do you walk that way?"

"'cause I peed my pants on your bed," Shandie said, and was gone before his cousin had finished making sure he hadn't.

3

Seven hundred leagues to the west of Hub, in a cold and clammy dawn, Ambassador Krushjor shivered under a fur robe on the deck of an Imperial war galley. Fog hung over the sea like a white mystery, and the sea roiled slowly and painfully below it, dark and menacing. In a pouch at his belt lay very imposing documents, rolls of vellum decorated with heavy wax seals — an edict granting safe conduct to the imperor's trusted and dearly beloved cousin and a missive welcoming the thane of Gark to the City of the Gods. Aged clerks, well inured to hypocrisy, had muttered oaths as they penned the words.

If a jotunn felt chilled, imps froze. Rowers, archers, legionaries, officers . . . their teeth chattered like castanets all around him, and their swarthy hides were a livid blue in the dubious light. Moisture glistened on their armor as it glistened on plank and rigging and sword.

The possibility of treachery had been evident to both sides right from the start. Thane Kalkor had listed many possible days and sites at which he might appear to learn how the imperor had answered his arrogant request. This was one of the places and one of the days, but not the first, nor the wheels of the secretariat had turned with glacial slowness, and even the ambassador's decision to bring the reply himself had not saved it from being delayed by bad weather.

Krushjor glanced at the sky, contemplated time and tide, and decided to hang around for another half hour in the hope that some of the imps might contract pneumonia. He, after all, knew for certain what they could only suspect — that the documents in his pouch were worthless forgeries. The safe conduct had been carefully phrased so that it became effective only when it was delivered, and there was not one chance in a million that his dear nephew Kalkor would blunder into a trap as obvious as this one.

A long way to the south, in a fog even thicker, a bonfire crackled and steamed on a reach of rocky coast. A bowshot seaward, a rugged sea stack provided a notable landmark, although it was presently invisible. Shiny, lethargic swells drifted in to the shore, summoning just enough energy as they died to break the surface and slap small ripples of froth on the shingle. Seabirds like toy boats bobbed at the limit of vision. The rocks and grasses were as wet as the sea, the air heavy with scents of weed and the restless ocean.

Shivering, stamping his boots, and tending the fire, an aging jotunn named Virgorek cursed his vigil and the Gods who had brought him to such a pass. He was Nordland born, blue-eyed and blond like all jotnar, but burdened with a most atypical fondness for security. Long ago, at fourteen, he had killed a man who had raped his sister. And killed his sister, also, of course, for submitting. The incident might have boosted his career considerably had the man's family not possessed more fighting men than his own. Discovering that his life was worth less than a cormorant's egg, Virgorek had fled from his homeland and sought his fortune in the Impire; and in time he had found himself living in the capital, serving on the staff of the permanent Nordland embassy there.

The pay was excellent, for few of his countrymen could tolerate indoor work, and they pined without the smell of salt water in their nostrils. He had estimated that a couple of years of such drudgery would earn him enough to return to the sea and buy his own boat so that he could end his days in respectable fishing, brawling, and smuggling. He had overlooked the sheer impossibility of anyone but an imp managing to hang onto money in an impish city.

After five years of this degradingly honest labor, he was wiser, but also older and poorer and no more content. Indeed, when he contemplated his debts and domestic problems back in Hub, he could think of no sane reason why he should return there.

Meanwhile he must spend two hours at dawn here, on every one of eleven specified days, in the slight hope that Kalkor would choose this one time and place out of a handful of others. Virgorek had no way of knowing whether the documents he bore were the real ones or merely more of the forgeries. This was the seventh time he had gone through the same useless ritual, and the only good thing about this one was the fog. This was authentic orca weather.

The dory had crept almost within hailing distance before he saw it. His first sensation was annoyance that some stupid local fisherman had blundered into the rendezvous and would have to be killed in case he gossiped. Then he noticed the solitary rower's gold hair. And finally he registered that the man's back and arms were bare. In that weather, such deliberate discomfort ruled out any normal fisherman. Virgorek's heartbeat speeded up considerably, and he began rehearsing the passwords.

Just before he beached, the rower expertly turned the dory and backed water for a few strokes. Then he rested on his oars.

"What do you catch, stranger?" Virgorek called.

The response took long enough that he had almost given up hope, but the newcomer was merely studying him and the enveloping fog.

"Bigger than you expect" came the expected reply at last.

Virgorek held up his pouch.

"Bring it!" the visitor commanded.

Reluctantly the ambassador's emissary stepped forward into the icy clutches of Westerwater. He waded out through the puny waves. Before he reached the boat, his teeth were starting to chatter, and the freezing water was almost up to his groin.

"All blood is red," he said, thinking that his own might be turning blue by now.

"And beautiful," the rower said. He was wearing nothing but a pair of leather breeches, and his lips were white with cold. Even the damp could not darken his heavy pale hair. His eyes were an intense blue, glittering arrogance.

His face was callous — and also clean shaven, which was strange indeed if he was a raider, a sailor on an orca ship. Even more strange, he bore no tattoos. He still looked mean enough to eat trees.

But the passwords had been correct. With relief that his vigil was over and he need never return to this godsforsaken headland, Virgorek fumbled at his pouch.

"Get in," the stranger said, waving a thumb at the bows.

The ambassador's emissary hesitated, and the raider's fingers strayed to the hilt of the dagger in his belt. Virgorek scrambled aboard and huddled himself into a shivering knot. The boatman pulled a few strokes, sending the little craft leaping seaward. Then he hauled the oars inboard and scrambled back off his thwart. "You row. Warm you."

Virgorek unwound and edged over to sit amidships; then he was toe to toe with the raider. Maybe Hub was not the worst place in the world to live. Maybe a diplomatic career not the worst fate a man could suffer.

"Give me the pouch," the stranger said.

"It is for the thane's eyes only."

The steady sapphire gaze was a nightmare of unspoken threat. "I will give it to him."

He must be one of Kalkor's men, and one of the most trusted. By definition, then, he was a killer with no scruples at all.

Virgorek passed over the pouch and took the oars. He had not rowed in years, but a jotunn learned boats before he learned fighting, and fighting before speech. He put his back into it, to show this uppity youngster, and in a few moments he began to feel his blood run warm again.

The raider's change to inactivity must be chilling him, but he showed no signs of it. He leaned back, a statue of hard muscle and icy stare, and for several minutes said nothing. Then he bent and found a third oar, which he pushed out aft and tucked under his arm to steer. He seemed to have no compass, and the world ended less than a cable length away in all directions. He did not look worried. He did not look as if he ever worried.

Virgorek pulled and pulled and soon began to feel hot. He had been letting himself get soft — palms, and arms . . . He did not slack the pace he had set.

"How far?" he panted.

"Far enough."

With his free hand, the stranger opened the pouch. He took out each roll in turn, staring hard at the seals and inscriptions as if he could read them. Almost certainly he would be faking . . . he wasn't even moving his lips! Very few jotnar ever learned to read, because their eyes were not good at close work.

But then he returned the safe conduct to the bag and tossed the imperor's letter overboard unopened. Virgorek considered a protest and then thought better.

Then the third scroll, the letter from the ambassador, followed the second. That was too much.

"Hey!" Virgorek said, lifting his oars from the water. The vellum would float, and the ink might not wash out if it were recovered quickly.

"Hey what?" the stranger said, unwinking.

"That's important!"

"No it isn't. It would merely warn Kalkor that the Impire plans to set a trap for him. He knows that."

Suddenly the raider smiled.

Virgorek dipped his oars again quickly. He didn't like that smile. A few years among imps made a man feel tough, but now he wondered if he was any more important than those discarded scrolls. That sort of thinking untoughened a man awfully fast.

"Why is he doing this?"

"Doing what?" The blue eyes widened; the smile widened.

"Going to Hub! Putting himself in the Impire's clutches! They'll never let him escape!"

Still smiling . . . "Who knows? I've never met anyone brave enough to question him."

Oars creaked. Water hissed by the planks. The pace was telling on Virgorek now, and he regretted his initial enthusiasm.

The raider leaned slightly on his steering oar and the dory veered, and yet nothing showed in the ubiquitous white fog.

"Why don't you ask him?" he said. "When we get to the ship?"

Virgorek wondered if he had ever known real fear in his life before. "No! I don't think I will."

"Then you may even see land again," Thane Kalkor said pleasantly, "but only if you row much faster than this."

4

Autumn rains always brought on Ekka's rheumatics, and this year they were especially painful. Ominously bad. Reluctantly she had taken to her bed, and she lay there now, buttressed by warm bricks wrapped in flannel, sprawled back on a heap of pillows, and wishing she had not demanded to see her face in a mirror that morning. A gray complexion definitely did not go with her amber teeth.

And just as a final, unbearable irritation, here was her idiot son, fatter and more incompetent than ever, shifting from shoe to shining shoe at the foot of her bed and tugging his pendulous lip. An impeccably dressed nincompoop! The thought of Angilki ever trying to manage Kinvale without her was enough to make a God blaspheme.

"It's from the imperor!" he wailed again.

"I can see that, dolt!" Even her old eyes knew that imposing seal, and she could make out enough of the crabbed scribe's hand.

"He wants me to come to Hub!"

"So?"

"So what?"

"So, what are you waiting for? Or are you planning to refuse?"

Angilki's already sallow face turned even paler. Perhaps he had hoped she would write a note to excuse him? He had never been more than two day's ride from home in his life.

"But why? Why me?"

Because the imperor had recently granted his gracious leave for this lumpkin to style himself King of Krasnegar, that was why, and now the bureaucrats had found some law or reason — the two were rarely compatible — requiring the pawn to move to the center of the board. The purpose might be as trivial as a public homage or as terminal as attainder for high treason. The only certainty was that Angilki was now involved in Imperial politics and must do as he was told.

She could not face the thought of trying to explain all *that* to *him*. The less he knew the happier he would be.

When she did not speak, he added, "And the foundations for the new west portico . . . "

"God of Worms!" she muttered. "Give me strength! Go and pack your bags and saddle a horse. And you'd better take a lunch."

"One lunch? It'll take me weeks and weeks!"

Ekka shut her eyes and waited impatiently for the sound of the door closing.

5

Far to the east of Zark, below the hazy white of a maritime sky, *Unvanquished* dipped her bowsprit in salute to an advancing green mountain. The wind was boisterous, just right for sailing.

The crew were cheerful, not realizing how far from land they really were, and Rap was moderately content — no sorcerer was likely to detect his cautious experiments this far out in the Spring Sea, or wish to investigate if he did. He was learning. He could even adjust the weather now, within limits, and without rippling the ambience very much. Since his injuries had

76

completed their healing, he had almost caught up on his sleep. He still had nightmares, though, and probably always would.

If Jalon and Gathmor had been his only companions, he would have taken the warlock's boat for this trip north, but he could never ask the princess to ride in that. It might be booby-trapped, anyway, so that the warlock could follow its progress, or even call it to him. Lith'rian was sneaky, perhaps the least trustworthy of all the Four. Olybino was said to be stupid and the other two were just plain crazy. The elf was a trickster, and treacherous.

A gust of spray blew over the bows and did not touch Rap. He took hold of the rail as *Unvanquished* tipped her bow skyward. His jotunn blood thrilled to the creak of rope and spar, to the green gleam of light through the glassy edge of the wave ahead, and the swoop of the albatross astern, wheeling its wings against the sky. Fish swirled, myriads of them down in the main, and sometimes he sensed great somber shapes that might be whales, deeper in the cold dark. Most happily would he sail on forever. Landfall was going to bring back his troubles, and danger — and responsibility.

Captain Migritt dozed in his cabin, the cook cooked in the galley. Within a labyrinth of tackle stowed in the glory hole, Pooh was stalking a rat. The gnarled little gnome was about the most entertaining person aboard — Rap had already spent hours with him, hearing his yarns, chuckling at his ribaldry. No one ever talked to gnomes, and yet they were friendly, easygoing folk once you got past their odd customs and their stench, and once they got over their surprise and suspicion. He liked Pooh.

And there were voices, all over the ship . . . He could muffle them and ignore them, if they did not talk about him. But some of those voices did talk about him, often, and then the conversations were as hard to ignore as if they were right at his back.

Now, down in the princess's cabin, all three of them were on about him again.

Gathmor, gruffly: "Yes, he's changed. Do you think any man could suffer as he did and not change?"

Sagorn, supercilious: "It was not that. When he first recovered he was not like this. It was whatever he saw in his vision that did this to him."

Princess Kadolan, concerned: "Then we must try to find out what he saw and see if we can help."

Then both men together, saying that they had tried.

Gods! — how they had tried, Gathmor and all of the five by turns! Cursed mundane busybodies.

He had never asked to be a mage. Had the princess given him a choice, and had he been in fit state to think, he'd have refused the third word of power in the dungeon. He had really wanted to die then. He had never wanted occult power at all, except that he'd thought he could help Inos. So he'd trapped Sagorn with a dragon and become an adept. That was not a memory he cherished. Serve him right — see what it had brought him! Inos had a kingdom now. She had a royal and handsome husband, at least in name. Maybe she would be content with that? No, not Inos. She was too much a real woman not to want to have a real marriage, with children and . . . and a real husband. Gods! Why did a man have to fall in love? He drummed his fists on the rail. Why must a churl fall in love with a queen, and then not have the wit to know it and tell her so at once, so she could laugh and thank him politely and lay the whole matter to rest right away?

Then he'd have stayed in Krasnegar and been a wagon driver.

Then she'd have married Andor.

What business of his if she had?

What could he do now? Cure her burns, yes. Easy. That would be no harder than smuggling her aunt out of Arakkaran, which he had accomplished with no trouble at all. He couldn't remove her husband's curse, nor win back her kingdom — a mere mage could not take on the Four, no one could. Anyway, he wasn't going to be around much longer and she must have resigned herself to losing Krasnegar when she married that big barbarian . . . chain a man down and mash his bones? Inos had not known about that, her aunt said, and her aunt never seemed to tell a lie. She bypassed the truth when it was bothersome, but he had not seen her lie.

And here she came now, swaddled in wool and leather, a rolypoly figure staggering along the deck to speak to him. Her white hair was blowing like a flag and her cheeks were rosy as sunsets already. So now it must be her turn to try and comfort the moping faun.

He steadied her a little — not so much that she would notice — but he did not turn. When she arrived at his side and grabbed at the rail, he glanced around as if he had not been watching.

"Ma'am!"

"Master Rap!" She was beaming. She obviously enjoyed sailing. "This is wonderful weather! Is this your doing?"

"A little of it. Not much."

A gust of cold spray came over the side and he deflected it from both of them. She noticed and laughed shakily.

"Oh! Oh, that's splendid! You are a very helpful traveling companion!"

"I won't be much use ashore, I'm afraid. I shan't dare exert power there. Especially when we get near to Hub."

"Of course, I quite understand. I am so excited! All my life I have wanted to visit Hub. I never thought a mage would turn up to escort me — it's quite like a poet's romance!"

She smiled at him with faded blue eyes, the worry and inquiry quite obvious behind the feigned cheerfulness,

He would not think about Hub. Silence fell.

"I had a long chat with Captain Migritt at dinner last night," the princess said. "About Shimlundok. That's the eastern province of the Impire. Even after we reach Ollion, you know we still have to cross the whole width of Shimlundok Province, more than a thousand leagues!"

Rap had eaten dinner with Pooh, down in the cable locker, but he had heard most of the conversation anyway. "What'd he tell you, ma'am?"

"Well, he suggested that we start by sailing up the Winnipango. It's navigable for a very long way now, he says, since the new locks were put in. Well, they're not really new, because they were built by the Impress Abnila . . . "

The captain had also admitted that it was a very roundabout way to travel, slow at the best of times, and impassable when the military had need of it and cleared civilian traffic out of the way. "But then Doctor Sagorn pointed out that the Winnipango is a very winding . . . "

Small wonder the sorcerous rarely made friends with mundanes.

It was a shame that Lith'rian's boat had been left behind in Arakkaran — to sail up a long, long river in that might be fun. Of course the shifting winds would snarl all the other travelers, and the magic might attract the notice of the warlock of the east. Even a much lesser sorcerer would be dangerous to a mere mage. The boat was gone anyway. Rap discarded a vain dream.

The princess finished repeating what she had learned about the Winnipango. "So Doctor Sagorn suggests that we should purchase a traveling coach and proceed overland. He thought you would probably be able . . . consent to drive it for us."

"It would be a real pleasure, ma'am. I'd like that."

"Oh, that's good! Do you suppose Master Gathmor will wish to remain in our — your — company?"

Nothing was going to detach Gathmor from Rap now, although his craving for revenge on Kalkor was sucking him into waters deadlier than he could imagine.

"He might just agree to dye his hair and face," Rap said, "and if Darad could hold him still for long enough, I could remove his mustache."

"Oh!" Then she realized that he had actually made a joke, and laughed a little too hard.

"He can be our footman, then." She smiled, hesitated. "Master Rap, would you forgive me a personal question?"

"Of course, ma'am."

"Those marks — the tattoos around your eyes. I understand that those were put there without your consent . . . "

He removed the tattoos and she blinked, and then laughed again, nervously.

"If I may say so, you are much better-looking without them."

He would never be better-looking than almost anyone else except a troll, so why did it matter? She was trying to imagine him sitting beside Inos on a throne for two, and that wasn't going to happen.

"I can't make them go away, really away," he explained. "They'll reappear as soon as I forget about them, or go to sleep. And a sorcerer might notice the magic — in a way I'm more conspicuous without them than I am with them. Conspicuous to people who matter."

She nodded and apologized, but he left the tattoos invisible for now.

"I used to wonder," she said hastily, "why Sultana Rasha did not just make herself young and beautiful and leave it at that."

He hated talking about sorcery now. "I'm sure she could have. I wondered the same about Bright Water. I'm sure she could make herself younger with a sorcery, and it probably wouldn't be very noticeable to another sorcerer, not as detectable as magic. But suppose sometimes she wants to look herself again, or chooses to look like someone else entirely? Then she'd have to cast another sorcery on top of the first. Pretty soon they'd pile up like overcoats."

"What would happen then?" the princess asked, looking worried.

"I have no idea, ma'am, but you couldn't keep changing a gown into a coat and then . . . a nightshirt, maybe . . . and so on, and not have the cloth fall apart on you eventually, could you? So I think that sorcerers probably just use magic on themselves, not sorcery — temporary, not much more than illusion. Like what I just did to my face."

She chuckled, thinking he was in a better humor. "When will we round the corner into the Morning Sea?"

"A couple of days, I expect."

"And how long after that to Ollion?"

"A week at least. Longer with stops on the way."

She paused, then said, "Is that an estimate, or can you see?"

"It's an estimate, ma'am. Foresight is tricky."

"Yes?"

He didn't want to be interrogated like a child, but he must not forget that he owed her his life, even if he didn't really want it much now. She had certainly risked her own for him.

"Premonition and foresight aren't quite the same," he explained, floundering at finding terms for the ineffable concepts of magic. "I got a little premonition with my second word, although that's unusual, and I seem to have some foresight now. I used premonition when I said I wouldn't follow Inos west to Qoble. What would have happened, I don't know, but it would have been very bad. It'll never happen now, so I'll never know. Foresight . . . Even sorcerers have trouble with that, and it's especially hard to foresee yourself, because you start to get nervous, and make plans . . . I wish I could say this better."

"Oh, do take your time, this is fascinating!"

The ship rolled forward over a crest, showing waves marching on over the endless ocean to meet the boundless sky. Why could he not dwell out here forever on the clear clean sea? Who needed land?

"A witch, a sorcerer, and at least one warlock all tried to foresee me and failed," Rap said suddenly. He hadn't meant to. He decided it wasn't her he didn't want to tell, but nosy old Sagorn. To ask her not to repeat his words would not be fair, though. "You remember what the magic casement showed when I went near it? A white glare?" He noticed that his voice was rising and his fists had clenched on the rail. He tried a small calming magic on himself.

"Of course."

"It hurts!" Rap said. Ishist had told him that. "I foresaw me arriving in Ollion, I think, and we will travel in a coach, a big green one. And then I think I caught a glimpse of Hub — I don't remember exactly. And then . . . " He shivered despite himself. "White! Like the sun . . . please, I don't want to talk about it."

He was shaking, and his fists had clenched again. She covered one with a wet, chilled hand. "Of course! I'm sorry I pried . . . I won't tell the others what you said."

She was absurdly concerned and apologetic. Evil take it, but he didn't want to be mothered, either!

"That's all right, ma'am. I should have explained sooner. Something awful happens in Hub . . . I'm afraid you'll have to manage without a seer. A foreseer, at least. Anytime I try to look forward now, even a couple of hours, all I can see is — that."

And his premonition was growing worse every day.

"Then you must stay away from Hub, Master Rap!"

Her sympathy was quite genuine. He forced himself to fake a smile. "I don't think I can escape. It's destiny. I think I'm as helpless as . . . as a pebble in a chicken's crop."

And everyone knew where they went. Meanwhile, in the glory hole, the rat made a dash for escape. Rap reached down and turned it, and Pooh grabbed as it went by. Rap laughed aloud, and the princess gave him a strange look.

6

Dearest Aunt, Greetings!

Please excuse the lack of a date and address, which would be proper. I have quite lost track of the days, but I can give you a rough idea of my location. I am writing this on board a nasty little ship — from which I hope to escape very shortly! — close to Elmas, which is in Ilrane! We have crossed the bar and are riding the tide up a very still river. (You may not think so from my handwriting! This was the best pen I could find. I had to ask a sailor for one, and he must have thought I said marlinespike.) The Big Man is writing to his brother, and so I shall ask to have this note enclosed. It may be the last chance I get to write to you for some time, and of course I must be circumspect with names, etc.

Now, my news! I am well, and quite a confident sailor now. We made very poor time at first. The notorious Kerith Passage was a lamb, a sleepy kitten, a featherbed, crystal calms alternated with drowsy zephyrs . . . thick cream, one long lullaby! You get the gist. And HOT! The Big Man was ready to snap the mainmast with his TEETH! Our ship was a week late and almost out of fresh water when we got to Ullacarn. None of us went ashore there. Our merchant friend is probably still lurking around, even if his superior is not — yellow hat. You know who I mean. But even he might still be around sometimes, because his friends are thicker than ever. The Big Man will be telling his brother all about that, though. We silly women mustn't worry about men's affairs, must we?

Then we set sail for Angot. The usual route follows the coast, and I was quite looking forward to seeing Thume again — from a safe distance! It was not to be.

Despite its name — which the captain assured me is historical, not geographical — the Sea of Sorrows is renowned for the gentlest sailing anywhere in the Summer Seas. Don't believe anything a sailor tells you, Aunt.

If that was CALM, I cannot imagine what STORMY looks like!

In my honor, I suppose, it mounted one of the worst typhoons the old-timers can remember. My literary skills are quite inadequate to describe it, but it did do wonders for my abilities at praying. Star of Delight was more fortunate than many fine vessels, I fear.

But the Gods were merciful and the return of fair weather found us with half our rigging and a bad list, somewhere southwest of Qoble. Except that we had bypassed three planned stops, we were slightly ahead of our original schedule when we limped into the world-famous harbor at Gaaze, which I had never heard of. It's on the other side of Qoble from Angot.

So I was back in the Impire proper! How long it seems since you and I crossed the pass at Pondague with Andor and that horrible proconsul! Yet it isn't much more than half a year.

Gaaze (which has, as you know, a world-famous harbor) looks to be quite a pleasant city, but I barely set foot there. The Big Man and a couple of his friends went ashore first and came back very soon with fists clenched and brows knotted! Djinns are no longer welcome in Qoble, they were told. In fact, a general roundup of djinns was expected at any moment!

So, even if the passes were still open, we could not get into the Impire through Qoble.

Fortunately, the Big Man was able to buy early passage to Ilrane, and here we are, two days later, safe and sound in elf land. None too soon, either! This is a dirty old tub, which stinks of bilge like sewage, and whose principal cargo seems to be fleas. Believe it or not, Aunt, its official name is Lady of Many Virtues and Much Beauty. *Even the captain has better names for it.*

So now we hope to find horses and head north. That is, if we can get permission! Elves, I am told, are very suspicious of strangers. I shall not be sorry to see the last of the sea, but this may be my last chance to send a letter — I'm afraid the Imperial post will not be calling in Zark from now on. What fools men are!

I do hope you are well. My Dear Kade. I miss you and long to see you again. I expect you are keeping busy, knitting overcoats for camels or something.

And what about Rap? I have tried to speak to the Big Man about him, but he refuses to talk on that subject at all. I shall make one more effort before he sends off his letter to his brother, and hope I can persuade him to relent. Rap is no threat to anyone, and he was only trying to help. I am sure that if he were to be banished from the kingdom, nothing would ever drag him back. If I do manage to arrange this, will you try to see that Rap has some money when he leaves, and give him my best wishes? I should love to have heard all his adventures. He was duped by a warlock, I fear, and what happened really wasn't his fault. I am sure he meant well — please tell him so, if you can. And if I can't win a release for him, do see if you can do anything to ease his captivity. But I'm sure you'll have done your best already.

From all the stamping on the roof, I assume that this floating pesthole is about to dock, so I'll close this letter now . . .

The harbor at Elmas was a river mouth, flanked by steep wooded hills that were reflected on the mirror surface. Half a dozen ships lay at anchor. Small boats flitted around them, most being rowed in the total calm. A few were being poled near the shore, and there oxen plodded along a towpath, hauling barges. Inos, standing on deck beside Zana, decided that she was not impressed with Ilrane so far. There was nothing to see, because the valley curved abruptly both upstream and seaward. She felt deliberately shut out, and said so.

"Secretive people," Zana agreed, and nodded approvingly.

Soon, however, the little tenders began to flock around *Lady of Virtues,* and elves came swarming over the side. Azak's entourage of djinn fighting men made up most of the passenger list; most of the crew were jotnar. By comparison with those, the elves looked puny. They also all seemed extremely young, an invasion of children. But their mirth and the lilt of their voices illuminated the air like birdsong, and their skimpy garments fluttered and flamed like butterfly wings. Most of the men wore only a loincloth, the women very little more, and all were barefoot. Every few minutes one would jump over the side to cool off and come swarming back up the ladder or anchor chain, laughing and sparkling. With golden skins and haloes of golden curls and their outsized eyes flashing in every shade like diamonds, they were children of light and sky, who barely belonged to the earth at all.

Inos was entranced. The Uphadly girls she had met at Kinvale had been part elvish, but they had seemed no more than imps with permanent jaundice. These merry golden children were magically different from imps, and a most welcome change from the sullen djinns and rancorous jotnar who had been her only companions for so long. She decided she might enjoy her visit to Ilrane, and she wondered about clothing. At the moment she was enveloped in a chaddar, swathed and veiled so that only her eyes showed. It was a comfortable enough garb for the dry glare of the desert; in this salty, muggy maritime air, she felt half boiled.

"Zana?"

"My lady?"

"If I were to strip down to about what those girls there are wearing and then jump overboard — what would Azak say?"

Zana's ruby eyes widened amid a million tiny wrinkles. "I doubt if he would ever allow you back on the ship."

Inos sighed — true! And there was the matter of her mutilated face. She would have to become reconciled to wearing a veil, or else learn not to mind people staring at her.

The deck bustled with elves and jotnar, plus the djinn passengers who persisted in getting in the way. Azak had just finished a long conversation with an elf, who had accepted a coin and gone ashore by the most direct route, his arms flashing like bird's wings as he swam. He was moving very fast, almost leaving a wake, so he at least must be as young as he had seemed. Azak was watching, leaning on the rail by himself. Now was the time!

Inos strode over and waved her letter under his nose, "Dear?"

It did not feel so strange now. She would work her way up to more passionate terms later, and maybe the use of the words would begin to feel natural. Sincerity by self-hypnosis . . .

"My love?" He smiled approvingly — he knew what she was doing and seemed to appreciate the effort.

"I should like this to go to Kade, please? With your letter to Kar?"

"Of course." Azak took the letter in his big swordsman's hand. "You have sealed it? I must read it."

And now . . .

Or had he really just said what she thought she'd heard?

Yes, he had. "You do not trust me, husband?"

He smiled down at her blandly. "It will take me time to learn to trust you, my darling. Men of my country do not give trust easily."

When you tell me you love me, I will tell you I trust you.

Inos took a couple of deep breaths and then said in the sweetest tones of which she was capable, "Then read it by all means."

Azak broke the seal. He turned around to lean his back against the rail and proceeded to read the letter. Suddenly he looked up, his face dark as an arctic storm. "You spoke with a sailor?"

"Zana was there!" Inos said hastily.

"Ah! Your pardon!" He went back to reading, while Inos wondered how much it would take to bribe Zana — even if she had any money, which she hadn't.

Azak finished, nodded, folded it, and slipped it inside his robe. "It will be sent. You were discreet. You do realize that the chances of it reaching Arakkaran safely are slim?"

"We can but try."

He nodded. "And don't bother pleading for your boy lover. The matter is closed."

Another, even deeper breath. She laid her hands on the rail, stared at the green hillside, and forced her voice to stay soft and level. "You are being very unfair, husband. He was never my lover. I have had no lovers in the past and I have sworn to be true to you in the future. I resent your choice of words."

"We shall not discuss it further."

Inos turned on her heel and walked away before she said anything that would make matters even worse.

She sulked for quite a while in her reeking cabin. Why would Azak not listen to reason? Why could he not see that royalty should always reward loyalty? . . . that Rap had been a puppet . . . that locking him up was grossly unfair . . . that he could easily be dumped on the first handy ship and dispatched out of her life forever?

Insanely jealous! It was the only explanation. Where she was concerned, obviously, Azak was not his normal rational self. She must learn to watch her step very carefully.

Meanwhile she could listen to the racket while elvish stevedores unloaded whatever cargo the ship had brought, and loaded food and water and whatever goods Ilrane exported. Pulleys squealed over elvish laughter. The whole affair seemed very inefficient, out here in the river — why not use quays like any normal port? Were the elves truly so terrified of spies, or did they just enjoy making things difficult?

Eventually she heard Azak's voice raised and decided to go back on deck. She found Zana watching the argument. Indeed half the crew, all the passengers, and most of the elves were watching the argument. Only the elves seemed to be finding it funny, for Azak was trying to browbeat a girl about half his size and much younger than he, and he was making no progress at all.

"Who is *that?*" Inos demanded.

The girl was strikingly beautiful, even for an elf. She was shining wet, as if she had swum out from the shore, and yet her blaze of golden curls flared out around her head in a glory. She wore nothing but a very scanty pair of blue shorts, like a boy, but she was emphatically not a boy. She stood aggressively with hands on shapely hips, and her bare breasts, small but firm, were graced with aureoles and nipples of fiery copper red that held every male eye on the ship. Even from a distance, the flashing brightness of her big jewel eyes was obvious, and she was smiling up at Azak's fury with defiant amusement. In his present emotional state, the sultan was hopelessly incapable of dealing with *that.*

"Some local official," Zana muttered, glowering over her yashmak. "She forbids us to disembark."

The ship was bound back to Qoble, Inos knew. She did not want to spend another minute on the horrible thing, and she certainly did not want to return to Qoble and an Imperial jail.

"What story is he telling?"

"Too many stories," Zana said angrily. "First he said he was just a tourist. Then, when she refused him admittance, he said he wanted to consult a sorcerer. So she accuses him of lying. He is not doing this very well, my lady!" From Zana, that was a surprising concession.

But the discussion seemed to be over. The elf girl shrugged — with remarkable results — and started to turn away. Azak almost grabbed her shoulder, and restrained himself at the last moment. His clean-shaven face was brilliant red with frustration.

He shouted, "Wait!"

Inos hauled off her headcloth and veil, swiftly unpinned her hair, and strode forward.

The elf turned back and stared at her, her mother-of-pearl eyes flickering gold and rose and then pale blue.

"Go away!" Azak roared.

Inos ignored him. "I am Inosolan, Queen of Krasnegar."

The copper-red lips pouted in surprise. The multihued eyes were noting the green of Inos's eyes, the golden hair, the scars. "I am Amiel'stor, Surrogate Syndic of Elmas, and Deputy Selectman of the Stor Gens."

Whatever . . .

"I have been deprived of my realm by sorcery. I wish to appeal to the Four, in Hub."

Amiel'stor glanced at Azak, and then back to Inos. "You are with him?"

"He is my husband. Forgive his prevarication. He merely wished to keep my troubles secret."

Azak growled and was ignored.

"Another story?" the girl asked skeptically.

"I will swear by any God you wish," Inos said.

The elf was disconcerted — she could not keep her eyes off those burns. "Your face?" she whispered.

"Sorcery. A curse."

Amiel' looked back at Azak. "You agree with this now?"

Cheeks burning like flame, Azak nodded.

"That is different!" She hesitated, frowning at Inos's scars. "Beauty always . . . The ship will not sail until the morning tide. Tonight the two of you shall dine with me. I will refer the matter to higher authority — my son is Port Warden for Elmas."

Her son? She looked about fifteen.

"You are most kind," Inos said sweetly. She began to loop her hair up again, preparing to cover it.

Amiel' nodded, then turned and vaulted nimbly up on the rail. She raised her arms, leaped out in a dive as graceful as a seabird. She was gone, and there had been no sound of a splash.

Inos looked up to meet Azak's fury. "I think I saved the day?"

"You are a meddlesome slut!"

"But it paid off." She would not let him cow her.

His fists were balls of murderous bone and the curse he bore made them especially dangerous to a woman. He was shaking with the effort of self-restraint.

"Don't be childish, dear," Inos said, barely keeping the tremor out of her voice. "It takes a woman to deal with a woman. It worked!"

"But only because it was a woman! Cover your face! Zana tells me she never heard you ask a sailor for a pen! If you ever again dare to speak to a man when I am not present, I will have you flogged!"

Inos had jotunn blood in her, and she could only stand so much. Remembering the onlookers, she managed to keep her words low, for him alone. "You arrogant bastard! Had I not intervened, we would be on our way back to Qoble right now! A marriage is a partnership, and the sooner you learn it the better, Azak ak'Azakar!"

"Not where I come from!"

"But where you are now. And since I have just done you a considerable favor, there is something you owe me . . . "

"If you are referring to that lover of yours . . . "

"He is no lover —" Their voices were rising.

"He is dead!"

"What?" She reeled back. Looking at Azak's face, she did not doubt. "Dead!"

"You promised no bloodshed!"

He stepped forward to loom over her, his mouth working with rage, bloodred eyes almost starting out of his head. "There are ways to kill a man without shedding blood! The family men understood me, even if you did not. Do you want me to list all the things they did to him? They —"

"No!" She put her hands over her ears.

"As you will. He took a surprisingly long time to die, but he is most certainly dead now."

Sudden wrenching nausea wiped away her anger. She should have guessed why Azak would not talk about Rap.

He nodded in gruesome satisfaction at her dismay. "And be warned, sultana! For you to as much as smile at any man is to sign his death warrant! Do you understand now?"

7

Shandie giggled softly. When he moved his head — *like this* — the whole room moved — *like that!* Funny! He did it again. And even in between times it was going up and down and sometimes round and round, and everything was all very nicely woozy,

He was lying on his bed, legs dangling over the edge, nothing on but his tunic. Silly tunic. Mookie had been trying to put Shandie's toga on him, and Shandie had kept dropping it, or falling over, and now the toga was a rumpled mess and Mookie had given up. Much better. Poor Mookie.

Woozy woozy woozy!

Mookie had been weeping. Valets were *not supposed to* weep! Mookie had gone away, and now here he came back again, with Moms. Oh, dear! Moms would not think it funny, maybe.

Moms was shaking him . . . the room going wild, all ways at once! Very funny — now he was trying to explain about the room, but his tongue was tying itself around his teeth, tangling itself up like his toga, and he had started to giggle again and couldn't stop. Maybe the wardens would think it was funny. He would tell them. Going to see the wardens, going to see the wardens . . .

Mustn't move when the wardens come.

And here was Ythbane, nasty butt-beating Ythbane. Beat all you want today, Ythbane. Can't feel a thing.

"What's the matter with him?" asked Ythbane.

Moms: "He's been at his medicine again."

"Gods! Can't you keep him away from it for a single morning?"

"He's sneaky! He hides it and then says it's run out, asks for more . . . "

"Well, he's got to be there! Try some black coffee or something. Brainless brat!"

"You! Leave us!" That was Moms speaking-to-the-servants voice. Oh, dear, was Mookie in trouble? Poor Mookie.

"Now you listen to me, Yth!"

Yth? Surely Moms never spoke to Ythbane like that? In her speaking-to-the-servants voice?

" . . . is all your doing! Gods forgive me, why did I listen to you? That foul stuff was your idea — what is it anyway, laudanum? — and you've turned my son into a —"

"Of course it isn't laudanum! Laudanum? Don't be crazy, woman! It's a gentle elvish nostrum. And you know how much our future is going to depend on . . . a suitable attitude?"

Words words words . . .

"But you're making him into a —"

"Never mind now. Gods, the investiture'll be starting in —"

"Even if it isn't laudanum — I don't care what it is — we've got to stop him taking it —"

No, not the medicine! *Not take away the medicine!* Then the scratchy-twitchy feeling would come, and he'd feel sick, and his head would throb . . .

Hear himself making a funny noises, trying to sit up. Trying to talk. Can't talk to say not to take away the medicine, please not take away the medicine . . .

"Looks like he's coming round a bit. Get him dressed up, and we'll put him on a chair over at the side and maybe nobody will notice."

"But it's not just today! He's like this half the time now, whether there's a ceremony on or not, and —"

"Maya! Beloved!"

"Er . . . yes?"

Oh, good. Ythbane using his sweetie-pie voice. Calm Moms down. Wonder if they'll do it on this bed? Awful small for three.

"I've been neglecting you, my darling. But you do understand how busy I've been, don't you? And from now on I'm regent, and things will be a lot easier — and a lot better between us two. You'll be wife of the regent, and first lady again, and you and I can have a lot more time to ourselves again. In fact, I'll promise you — right after the state dinner, you and I will slip away . . . "

Sweetie-pie sweetie-pie sweetie-pie . . .

89

Going to see the wardens . . .

Maybe formal ceremonies weren't *quite* so terrible, Shandie thought, if you could sit down for them. And Moms had said he could move if he wanted to, as long as he didn't fidget too much. She was sitting beside him, on a gold bench thing, and she would nudge him if he fidgeted too much. He was still woozy, but a very nice woozy.

He kept wanting to yawn. Mustn't yawn. He was hardly trembling at all today. Must be the medicine, or else the sitting down.

Nobody was paying much attention to him, over here near the east door. Today was a north day. He could see all of the Rotunda instead of just half of it. Important day! All of the Senate seemed to be here, filling up the whole north half. Some of them were right behind him, even — noisy old men, coughing and wheezing all the time over his head. The south half was all junior nobles and important people and a few assemblymen. For weeks and weeks the court had talked of nothing except who'd got tickets and who hadn't.

Important day. Going to see the wardens! Getting quieter. There was a very loud senator just behind Shandie. He kept saying things in a voice like a hoarse trumpet, and whoever was with him was trying to hush him.

" . . . real Evilish disgrace, that's what it is! Everyone knows he's a mongrel. Merman blood in . . . Mm? Well, it's common knowledge. Mongrel sitting on Emine's throne? Mm! Can't think what Emshandar was thinking of when he made him a consul. Told him so myself. Well, hinted anyway. What? Speak up, man!"

Shandie squirmed just a little and tried to swallow a yawn.

It was a nuisance being down on floor level, instead of one step up. But he could see the back of the Gold Throne and the Opal Throne beyond that, in the middle, and all of the others when people didn't get in front of them. Lots of people were fussing around, getting ready. Grandfather hadn't been brought in yet.

All the seats were full, 'cause this was a very-special-important formal ceremony. Today the wardens would come! He shivered a little, and glanced at the White Throne on his right and the Blue Throne on the far side, but they were still empty. He was almost in back of the Gold Throne, near the aisle. People were still coming in and squeezing into their seats. Ever so many people, though; he'd never seen the Rotunda so packed.

And lots of people coming and going on the floor, ministers and secretaries. There was Marshal Ithy with his gold uniform and the red crest on his helmet. Lots and lots of lords.

This would be a bad seat if the sun came out. The Rotunda got very hot in summer, but today was rainy. Trouble was, all these people were making it stuffy. Mustn't yawn!

90

"Think the wardens'll go for it?" The old senator was still mumbling. "Wouldn't be surprised if they didn't show up. That'd show him! Show us, too! Sneaky business. Never saw so much grease. Mm? What?" There was a mumbling sound, and then he spoke more quietly. "Resolution, indeed! Should have been a formal Bill, three readings and recorded vote." Mumble, mumble. "Yes, but it's from two dynasties back. Emshandar always talked of updating it; never got around to it. Anyway, it says next of kin, not some upstart halfbreed flunky!" There were more hushing sounds.

The floor was clearing, notables hurrying out so they could make a formal reappearance. Shandie's attention wandered to the big table before the Opal Throne. Those things lying on it must be Emine's sword and buckler! He'd never seen those, and he couldn't see very well now, and he tried to make himself a little taller, and Moms flashed a frown at him and he subsided quickly. See them later . . .

"Sneaking it through in the middle of the order paper?" the old man said, snorting. "All over before half the Senate knew what was going on! Oh, I think the wardens may argue. They'll want Orosea, you wait."

A fanfare drowned him out, and the crowd stilled. Then everyone stood up, so Shandie did, 'cept in his case it was more standing *down* and he could see even less. The Council was coming in through the south door, dividing at the Blue Throne to pass around either wall, passing on the outside of the thrones; he'd never seen this properly, 'cause he was usually part of it. The hall was very still, except for a shuffle of footsteps. Half the parade went right by in front of him, but he didn't look up to see their faces. He knew when the marshal came along, though, in his shiny uniform and a smell of new leather. He liked Marshal Ithy. He told Shandie war stories.

" . . . good man," rumbled the old senator. "Very sound. The Zark thing . . . time we showed those pinkos!" He chortled. "Besides, they're due to be milked again, mm? Get those taxes down . . . "

Hushing noises . . .

The parade joined again at the north end, and advanced to the center and the Opal Throne. And here came Ythbane, striding by in his purple-hemmed toga. The old senator growled, then winced as if someone had trod on his toe or jabbed him in the ribs.

They'd changed precedence! Usually Moms would be last in the left-hand line, just behind Ythbane, and Shandie last in this line after Consul Uquillpee, going along the east side on a north day, looping back to meet in the center. And here was Grandfather, in a carrying chair. Asleep. He slept all the time now. Oh, dear. He did look old today, and ill.

Someone sniffed loudly in the senatorial benches above Shandie's head. "Evil-begotten shame . . . ten years younger than I am, you know . . .

fought beside him at Agomone. Good man. Great man." *Sniff!* "Evil-take-it shame to see him go like that . . . "

And Grandfather was not going to be put on his throne! The chair was placed by the dais, but then the bearers departed. Shandie was surprised, and the old senator mumbled angrily. So did some others. Now everyone was sitting down again. Shandie scrambled up on the bench beside Moms, who looked down at him and nodded absently. Then she turned her attention back to the action, the men and a few women standing before the throne, three or four of the very old ones on chairs.

The Rotunda was ever so quiet. Even the noisy senator had gone quiet. The dean of the Senate was being led forward. Marshal Ithy said he was older'n anyone 'cept Bright Water. He did something and was led back to his seat.

A herald began to read out the joint resolution, all *whereases* and *be it therefores*.

Shandie felt a yawn coming on, and stopped it, and realized it was quite a while since he'd needed to yawn. He wished the bench had softer cushions. Leather was hard and he wasn't used to sitting still, only standing still. He hoped the ceremonies wouldn't go on too long, because he might need some of his medicine soon.

Thump! Ythbane had just put the Imperial seal on something. Must be the resolution. Had he said his usual things about Grandfather accepting it? Shandie had not been paying attention.

Now what? Ythbane *undressing?*

"God of Whores!" the noisy old senator behind rumbled. "We going to have a whole coronation ceremony now?"

Ythbane had taken off his consul's toga. Shandie glanced up at Moms, but she didn't seem upset that he was standing there in just his tunic like a servant. Now Consul Uquillpee was helping him put on a purple toga. Like Grandfather's! That didn't feel right, somehow.

The deaf old senator didn't think so, either. He was getting even louder, going on about Imperial Honors. But Moms was smiling, so it must be all right.

Ah! Here came the big moment. Shandie felt a tremor of excitement cut through his wooziness. One day he was going to do this! One day he would call on the wardens to acknowledge him as rightful imperor. One day he would put his arm in the straps on Emine's buckler like that, and take up that sword, and then walk all around the throne like that, holding them up for the audience to see. They weren't very impressive. The buckler was all dented, and the sword was bronze, too. Why wouldn't a great imperor like Emine have had a good steel sword? Shandie felt cheated, somehow.

92

Now Ythbane had completed his circle and was facing the Opal Throne. Suddenly Moms grabbed Shandie's hand and squeezed it very tight, and he looked up at her in surprise. She was chewing her lip, watching Ythbane intently.

The old senator tried a whisper, and in the cavernous silence it came out loud as a bugle: "One gets you five they won't show."

No one else said a word. Ythbane went up one step.

"Won't honor a mongrel," the senator growled.

The second step. Ythbane was in front of the Opal Throne.

He turned to face across at the White.

Why was he waiting like this? Was he scared, a little, maybe?

Ythbane struck the sword against the buckler and produced a dull Clank! Shandie felt a surge of disappointment. He'd expected a bright, ringing Clang! that would echo away for a long, long time. No wonder the sword and buckler were both so battered-looking, if every imperor in three thousand years had bashed them together like that.

Then came a long hissing sound from all around the rotunda as the audience drew in its breath. A lady was sitting on the White Throne.

Well! She wasn't so old! Moms looked older'n that. She wasn't green, either. About the same middle-brown shade as Shandie himself; maybe a little yellower. Floor-mat color, coconut. Her hair was black, and coiled up on top of her head. She wasn't beautiful, certainly, but not 'specially ugly. There was something odd about her chiton, though. It sort of glowed a bit, and the folds were kind of misty, as if the cloth were flowing fog. It made Shandie woozier, so he looked away.

Ythbane saluted with the sword. If Bright Water did anything, Shandie missed it, because when his eyes went back to the White Throne, it was empty again.

A rumble of disgust came from the old senator. From several old senators, from the sound of it.

Ythbane had turned to the east now, and Shandie instinctively froze. He could only see the back of the Gold Throne, anyway.

Again the Clank! of sword on buckler, and Warlock Olybino answered the summons immediately. Shandie saw the gold-crested helmet over the back of the Gold Throne.

Moms sighed and relaxed. Two was enough, he remembered. Ythbane had been confirmed as Imperial regent by the Four. Well, that wasn't much of a ceremony!

The senator grunted angrily. "Disgusting! A mongrel! Can't think what the wardens are thinking of!"

But that wasn't right! Shandie knew. Court Teacher had told him — all the wardens came for was to show that the candidate hadn't gotten there by sorcery and wasn't a sorcerer. As long as he'd succeeded by mundane means, they didn't care if he'd used an army, or poison, or anything. He had Emine's buckler and sword, and he wasn't a sorcerer, that was all. Very rarely in all history had the Four refused to recognize a new imperor or a regent.

Ythbane saluted. The warlock rose and responded, and was gone again. Shandie rubbed his eyes. It was hard to believe that you'd seen something — someone — when they weren't there any more and you hadn't seen them going away.

Now Ythbane strode round to the back of the Opal Throne. South was an elf. Shandie had not seen any elves around court for so long that he could hardly remember, except for a few dancers and singers, and they'd all been very young. No grown-up elves, except maybe Lord Phiel'nilth, the Poet Laureate, and he didn't seem very old, either.

The other two wardens would certainly come now and make it unanimous — that's what he'd been told. It wouldn't matter if they didn't. Ythbane was regent now, and poor Grandfather was going to die soon, and Shandie mustn't think about that, or he might start crying and future imperors mustn't, not ever, 'specially in public. He would really get beaten for that, and he'd deserve it, too.

There was a man sitting on the Blue Throne. A boy? He didn't look very much older than Thorog, and no taller. Could that be Lith'rian himself, or had he sent a grandson or someone in his place? Maybe elves looked like that no matter how old they were? He was wearing a toga, and an odd blue one, like folds of captured sky. His golden skin and golden curls were sunshine in that sky, and his smile was brilliant. His face was very bright and his eyes were . . . odd. Elvish? Thorog's eyes were sort of slanted like that, big and queer. Shandie'd never thought of that before.

With gold skin and hair like that, an elf really ought to be warlock of the east, so he could have a throne to match. That was a funny idea! And a red-skinned djinn to be West, and a jotunn North, 'cause jotnar were so pale. How about South? No blue skin, but blue hair — a merman? That would be much tidier, and he'd arrange it when he got to be Emshandar V.

Ythbane had saluted. The boy rose in a graceful shimmer and bowed very low to him. Shandie's Deportment Teacher would have loved to have seen that! That was how a toga should be worn, too. The audience murmured appreciation — and then surprise, as the warlock sank down on his throne again, leaning back and crossing his ankles as if preparing to stay a while. His smile seemed even more rakish than before.

The regent hesitated. The elf waved a hand in a *carry-on* gesture and then crossed his arms also. He was smiling, perfectly at ease. Why not? Whoever would beat a warlock if he misbehaved? And the great Warlock Lith'rian looked as devilishly mischievous as any cheeky upstart page at the moment.

Ythbane was so obviously at a loss that Shandie wanted to giggle. Then the regent moved around to face west. *Clank!*

Silence.

And more silence . . .

"So he's only got three!" the old senator muttered.

Still nothing had happened, Ythbane facing the Red Throne, and the Red Throne remaining stubbornly empty. Warlock Lith'rian put a hand in front of his mouth to smother a graceful yawn.

"Elves and dwarves!" the senator muttered. "It's not the merman, it's the elf, mm?"

Ythbane gave up. With a guarded scowl at South's obvious enjoyment, he stamped around to the front of the Opal Throne and sat down. Shandie was watching Lith'rian, and he vanished at the exact same instant. The audience rose to its feet and cheered the new regent.

After the cheering came the speeches, and they went on a long time, and Shandie wished it would all stop so he could go and take a mouthful of medicine, because he was starting to feel scratchy-twitchy.

8

At the top of the slope the foremost riders were reining in. Here the trail emerged from trees, onto a grassy ridge. Gratefully Inos reined also, and slowed her sleek bay mare to a walk and then a halt. Its breath blew white in the high air, and she felt the wind chilling her heated skin. She looked out over yet another garden landscape: fields and farms and lakes, glowing in evening sun. All of Ilrane seemed to be one great picturebook.

She had ridden with an Imperial army across taiga and tundra in winter. She had crossed the Central Desert on a camel in summer and the Progistes Range on a barrel-ribbed mule. Yet she had never known a ride like this one. Four days of almost uninterrupted canter . . . horse after horse, in relays . . . . meals snatched in the saddle, and brief, brief nights when she had lain like a stone in straw or under a blanket in some cedar-scented attic . . . Every bone ached, and she was raw from hips to ankles. Elves did nothing by halves.

The only good thing about her numbing daze of exhaustion was that it blanked out any chance to brood on her terrible error.

Then she saw what had caused the halt. Very far off, beyond the hills, a pinecone shape stood faint against the sky. One side gleamed brilliant, sparkling, the other was blue with the haziness of great distance. It was the closest she had yet seen a sky tree. Even fainter, beyond it, shone peaks that must be the start of the Nefer Range.

"Valdoscan," said a voice.

95

It was Lia', the leader of this strange expedition. In her trim silvery leather riding clothes she seemed no older than Inos herself, and yet two nights back she had mentioned her grandchildren. Only her obvious fatigue hinted now at her true age. Then Inos remembered her full name — Lia'scan.

"Your home?"

The girl — woman — smiled wistfully and cupped a hand to the brim of her cap to see better. "Indeed! I was not born there and have visited it but rarely . . . but every elf belongs to a sky tree, as a bee belongs to a hive."

"Some day I should love to see a sky tree."

"Few indeed are the nonelves who have ever visited one. But if that is your wish, Inosolan, then it may be so."

Startled, Inos paused to think. She looked over the rest of the company. In Elmas the elves had agreed to help after all — help her. And they had not merely granted the visitors right of passage, they had escorted them posthaste, although they had rejected Azak's private army, limiting him to three men. He had chosen Char, Varrun, and Jarkim, sending Zana and the rest off with Gutturaz to find their way back unscathed to Zark and the coming years of glory — or so it was to be hoped.

Inos and the four djinns rode unarmed, while their elvish escort bristled with shiny swords. They might be slight, but they all moved like hummingbirds. Half of them were women. They rode like swallows on the wind. Azak was still more sulky than grateful.

"My lady," Inos said, "I don't think I understand. We are on our way to the Impire, are we not?"

Lia' glanced around. Azak was edging his horse toward them. She kicked in her heels. "Let us walk awhile, Inos. Our mounts will grow chilled if we keep them standing."

Inos put the mare into motion and rode at her side, still puzzled.

"You are indeed on your way to the Impire," Lia' said. "By noon tomorrow you will cross the border. We can take you by unguarded ways, and we can furnish you with documents that should carry you safely after that — no one but a border official knows what a real passport looks like. Your weapons will be returned to you, although you will be wise to keep them hidden. All will be done as was promised."

"So?" Inos said. The rest of the company was following, but a trio of elves had moved in behind her to cut out the djinns. This little chat had been carefully planned.

The elf looked at her with challenge. "Is this what you truly want, child? There is an alternative."

"Which is?"

"No elf can resist beauty, in any form. It was the damage to your face that won Amiel's support, and, through her, the favor of . . . other people. Important people."

"I think you are no nonentity yourself, ma'am."

Lia' smiled. "Never mind what I am. Elves revel in fancy titles and laugh at them also. What matters is that the warlock of the south is an elf. He is greatly honored by his people. We fear him, of course, but we also admire him and what he has done."

The trail wound back into trees again, and both women twisted to take a final look at the iridescent glory that was Valdoscan. Then it had vanished.

"Lith'rian spends much time at his own enclave, Valdorian. It is on the far side of Ilrane, but still closer than Hub. If you wish, then that could be your destination."

"He would heal me?"

"I am certain he would." The opal eyes flickered viridian and cobalt.

"And my husband's curse?"

The childlike face grew bleak. "It was decided that this offer would be made only to you."

"I see." Temptation! Was this some sort of a test?

"Azak is not the sort of person who readily gains sympathy from an elf," Lia' remarked snidely.

"He is a remarkable man," Inos insisted, "and a fitting ruler for a harsh land."

"And a fitting husband for a well-born lady?"

"You presume far, ma'am."

Lia' laughed halfheartedly. "Forgive me, that was vulgar! But you puzzle us, Inosolan. Why did you ever marry that boor? You did not yield to manly caresses, for his lips would burn you. I do not think you are a witless child to be bewitched by muscles and ruthlessness. So why? Not merely to share a throne, for a sultana is no more than a housekeeper." Receiving no response, she pressed harder relentlessly. "They say that the God of Love plays dice with our hearts. Do you love Azak ak'Azakar, Inosolan?"

No.

Inos did not speak.

She was thinking of Rap.

Why had she not seen earlier what the God's words had meant?

Too late, too late!

"He is a barbarian, Inos."

He tortured my lover to death, the man who loved me, who crossed the world to help me.

She gulped at the thought. "If I accept your offer and seek out Lith'rian, then what happens to Azak?"

"We shall give him the choice — he may return whence he came, or proceed to the Impire. But I suspect he would be betrayed to the Imperial military."

Inos glared at her companion. "You are ruthless yourself, my lady."

Lia' nodded sadly. "Elves often are. It surprises people, sometimes. Even ourselves. But we agreed to help you only. And now I want your answer."

"One more question. Would Lith'rian restore me to my kingdom?"

"I have no idea whatsoever." Elves cared nothing for politics outside their own convoluted affairs.

Inos looked back. Azak was glaring at her. The positions of the horses suggested that he had been trying to edge forward and the three elves were deliberately blocking him.

He killed the man who loved me.

Kade was hostage for her return to Arakkaran.

She thought of a lifetime with Azak. She tried to think of what a life with Rap would have been like; her throat tightened and her eyelids burned. *Too late, fool, too late!*

She had a word of power. How much did that interest the warlock?

She had made solemn promises to the Gods that she would be a wife to Azak.

She had promised her father . . . but the Impire had dealt her kingdom away like an unwanted kitten.

And she hoped that she had standards of her own. What would her father have said?

Or Rap, for that matter?

"I am Azak's wife," she said. "I will not betray him."

Lia' shook her head sadly. "Spoken like a fool — or an elf. Or a queen, I suppose. It is what I expected. May the Gods bless you for it."

9

"You seem worried, Uncle!"

"Worried? No, not at all! Me worried? Absurd! Why should I be worried?" Ambassador Krushjor tossed his silver mane in the wind and folded his arms and leaned against the rail as if he had never known worry in his life. A jotunn on the helmsman's deck of a longship was in his natural element and should be as carefree as a dwarf in a diamond mine or a gnome in the town dump.

Of course his nephew, Thane Kalkor, was utterly insane, but that was quite normal for a jotunn raider. All the truly successful thanes had been mad as rutting sea lions — sanity would distract a man when he should be concentrating on his killing and raping. Mindless cruelty and destruction were by definition done for their own sake, without logic or reason. Meanwhile fifty or so brawny jotnar were rowing *Blood Wave* up the languid waters of the Ambly, and Krushjor had come to make a courtesy call, which meant he must spend a few hours at least in the madman's company. Both were large men, and the sailor holding the steering oar was even larger, and the platform was very small. Krushjor felt strongly disinclined to jostle his maniacal nephew.

And his maniacal nephew kept smiling at him with his inhumanly bright blue eyes, as if he could read every thought in Krushjor's head. Every time he moved — to wave his contempt at the crowds on the bank, or study the position of the naval escorts — he seemed to settle back a fraction closer to his uncle. He must be doing it deliberately. What happened when the imaginary chip fell from his shoulder?

The sun shone. The silver ring wound and twisted. Two imperial war galleys kept pace ahead, four more astern. As the procession turned each bend, staying as close as possible to the inside curve where the current was least, great crowds of imps swarmed on the shore, running like ants, waving, jumping up and down and cheering. They were not cheering this impertinent intruding jotunn pirate, only the accompanying honor guard of the Imperial navy — which was polished and scrubbed and armed to the armpits, and also completely outclassed.

Kalkor was playing with them. Time and again he would snap an order to the coxswain to up the stroke. Then *Blood Wave* would leap forward as if to over-take. The vanguard would move frantically to cut her off, and usually become hopelessly entangled in doing so. Then Kalkor would rein in his crew and let the Imperial navy straighten itself out again. His men were barely sweating — they could have rowed figure-eights around the escorts for him had he wanted. The day before, the choleric Imperial admiral had tried putting four ships in the van and two astern. Kalkor's feints had put half the flotilla aground within an hour.

Not in centuries had a raider progressed so far up the Ambly, perhaps never, even in the troubled times of the VIIth Dynasty, or the XIIIth.

The shores were lined with civilian traffic — barges and cargo boats, galleys and gondolas, all shooed aside to let the fleet pass by. Their crews watched the procession in sullen silence. Behind them the orchards and hop-fields were golden; rows of peasants bent with their sickles, reaping corn, not looking up at all.

Krushjor had pulled an oar in a longship in his youth, as had most Nordlanders. He'd been good enough to become a thane, leading a few raiding expeditions of his own then, taking out boatloads of his more promising youngsters to season them in the ancestral traditions of rape and pillage, for

99

all jotnar learned in their cradles that if they ever grew soft, the Impire would be all over them like fleas.

Officially, he was still Thane of Gurtwist, his realm kept safe under the aegis of the Moot while he served abroad. Thanedom came partly from birth and partly from prowess. To become a thane required three things, the wags said — bloodlines, bloodthirst, and bloody luck. He'd done all right, but he'd never intended to make a lifelong career out of rape and pillage. Indeed, he'd been returning from his farewell tour when he'd gone after a tempting merchant ship and in the skirmish had received a very ill-placed sword cut. He'd made his way home to Gurtwist before it began festering, but for a month or two thereafter the Cods had seemed very anxious to weigh his soul.

In the end his recovery had been complete except for one small detail, a lingering defect that would not interfere with pillaging but disqualified him totally for the other half of the profession. Had that disability become generally known, he would have been a ruined man, and likely a dead one soon. As a ruling thane, he would not have been able to hide his shortcoming for long, but a need for a new Nordland ambassador to the Impire had come along at the opportune moment. Krushjor had engineered his own nomination, accepted with a proper show of reluctance, and sailed away to live with the enemy. He was safer there, for no one in Hub took notice of his private life, nor cared anyway.

So to travel on a longship again brought back happy memories of his violent, lusty youth. Compared to Kalkor, though, he had never been more than an amateur. Times were relatively peaceful now, and raiding wasn't what it once had been — men might be allowed to flee if they left their valuables behind, and women were often spared if they submitted pleasingly. Kalkor was a throwback to the Great Days, to legendary raiders like Stoneheart, or Axeater, or Thousand-Virgins.

He was mad beyond question, if sanity was to be judged by the behavior of other men. But mad in exactly what way? Why had he plunged himself and his crew into this impossible trap? When the first letter had arrived, Krushjor had been certain that it was some sort of a joke, or an elaborate subterfuge. He had been aghast when his nephew had actually accepted the safe conduct and put himself into the enemy's power. The old man dearly wanted to know why and also to know what might be expected of him personally — but anytime he drew near to the topic, his nephew would smile, and the madness would sparkle up in his blue-blue eyes, daring Krushjor to ask that one impertinent query. And Kalkor himself was certainly the only man aboard who knew the answer. A thane's crew never questioned.

Why, for another matter, did he have a goblin on board? A goblin was hardly less likely than a silo, or a tannery. But the goblin was there, rowing with the rest, his black hair and khaki skin making him conspicuous among so many blonds. He seemed tiny in that company, and yet he was handling his oar with apparent ease.

"It's so tempting!" Kalkor sighed. He was staring at a wide water meadow, completely covered with gawking imps.

Krushjor could see more temptation in the city that lay behind the mass of spectators. It was unwalled, of course, here in the heart of the Impire, and its old stones and planks were sun-worn, mellowed by centuries of peace.

"They've left the town unguarded, you mean?"

His nephew raised pale eyebrows in mockery. "Have you forgotten, Uncle? Imp towns are always unguarded! Guarding requires courage, remember? No, I was just wondering what would happen if we made a feint at that crowd — drew our swords and faked a landing. How many would be crushed in the panic, do you suppose? Care to lay a wager?"

His eyes danced with merriment, but there was a crazy longing there, too. Perhaps a week or two without the smell of blood was beginning to sap his self-control.

"The imps would put so many fine-feathered shafts in us that we'd look like a poultry market. And they'd claim you'd broken the truce."

The madman's eyes gleamed even brighter. "But Nordland would never believe them. Would they risk a war?"

"Yes," Krushjor grunted, trying to seem impassive.

Kalkor sighed and leaned back again, surreptitiously nudging him a fraction closer to the edge of the deck space. "And I should be deprived of my great ambition."

"Which is?" The question slipped out before the older man could stop it.

"Why, to see the City of Gods, Uncle!" Kalkor smiled at him mockingly. "Don't the imps have a saying — 'See Hub and Die!'?"

If that was what he wanted, he was going to be satisfied. What else did he plan to do beforehand? And whom did he want to take with him?

10

Iron hooves thudded, iron-rimmed wheels thundered.

Less than a year ago, the sunniest summit of all Rap's dreams had been to become a wagon driver, but the limit of his ambition had been a rickety dray loaded with peat and salted beef. He could not have imagined a vehicle one-quarter so grand as this opulent coach, with its cunning suspension wrought of dwarvish steel, with its gilt trim and glass windows and all those shiny carriage lamps. He certainly would never have imagined its team of six giant bays pounding along the imperor's highway at a pace that snatched the

101

breath from a man's lips. To be the coachman on such a wonder would have seemed a dream of ecstasy to that lonely rustic lad of Krasnegar.

Well, now he was a mage and there was nothing to it. It was not unpleasant, though. It did keep a man from brooding, maybe.

Usually Gathmor sat up on the box beside him, but this was the last leg of the day's progress, so he was clinging on at the back as if he were the genuine footman his fancy livery denoted. Gathmor still dreamed vain dreams of revenge on Kalkor. He had agreed to stain his face and hair, and he was short for a jotunn. He had even removed his beloved floorbrush mustache, to seem more impish. Rap could have dissuaded him from coming, at least for a few hours — for long enough to have left him behind at Ollion, by the sea where he belonged, but Rap had been reluctant to use mastery on a friend, and he hated himself for his stupid scruples. He did not know what awaited Gathmor in Hub, for his foresight would not work on anyone other than himself, but at least nothing could be more improbable than finding Kalkor there.

Rap was driving now with his eyes shut, because evening was coming and the ruddy western sun hung unpleasantly close to dead ahead. The wide pavement stretched toward it as straight as an arrow, flanked by neat hedges to restrain the cattle. Good dairy country, this. Earlier he had seen forest and near desert and desolate swamp; he had caught faint glimpses of the snowy Qobles, far to the south. Now the hills were green — impossibly green for so late in the year. The trees were mostly bare, and the harvest gathered, yet the herds could still graze their fill, and to a Krasnegarian that seemed very odd.

Everywhere he saw prosperity: white farms and great mansions, villages and big cities. The Impire rolled past as if it would never end, rich and safe and powerful.

And yet . . . out of sight of casual travelers on the Great East Way, behind the nearest hills, the wealth grew more patchy. There were hovels there, whose inhabitants wore rags. And when the highway rolled through the hearts of great cities, then behind the great-fronted buildings — in the back streets and alleys — a seer could find slums and misery without much searching. The Impire was more than he had ever dreamed, and considerably less than it thought it was.

The world had certainly grown in the last year.

How would humble little Krasnegar seem to him now?

On the sumptuous padded benches inside the coach, Princess Kadolan and Doctor Sagorn chatted pleasantly together, saying nothing of any importance, so far as an eavesdropping mage had noticed. When she arrived at her destination, her companion would be Andor, though. Sir Andor would have been mentioned in the letter the courier had borne on ahead in the morning, so it would be Andor again tonight.

It didn't always work, of course. A few times they had lodged at post inns, especially when they had first left Ollion, but the princess had spent a lifetime entertaining guests at Kinvale. She was acquainted with hundreds of the Imperial nobility, and as she drew closer and closer to Hub, so more and more of them lived within reach of the Great East Way, or their relatives did. They welcomed her like long-lost kin, they feasted her and tried to make her linger. Failing in that, they wrote introductions to others ahead, their own friends and relations. They sent couriers to warn of her coming. Kade was proceeding in royal style from mansion to mansion. The straw pallets and pottery bowls of the inns had given way to silken sheets and golden plate.

Her coachman and footman boarded with the servants, of course, and that suited both of them. As far as Gathmor was concerned, that also suited Princess Kadolan, but she kept trying to persuade Rap to play a grander role. A postmaster expected to provide postboys along with his horses, she said. She would gladly hire such men to drive her equipage. Then Rap could be her secretary, perhaps, or a Sysanassoan prince on vacation, if he wanted. She appreciated now that he was capable of faking anything, of fooling anyone, and yet she still cherished dreams of taking him in hand and polishing him up to be a fitting consort for Inos. Rap had politely declined. When she had grown more pressing, he had gone stubborn on her again. His premonition would not let him be happy, but he was less miserable when he was being as near to his real self as possible.

A courier of the Imperial mail went galloping by and vanished into the sunset. Rap pulled out to overtake two lumbering wagons. Traffic was always heavy on the Great Way. That morning a whole legion had trudged by, five thousand solid young men bound eastward to the wars, singing a rousing marching song with their heads held high and their eyes glazed.

Rap had wondered how many of them would ever return, and if they were wondering the same.

He had wondered how it felt to be a sword in the imperor's army. Did it make a man feel important? Or very unimportant? Strong or vulnerable? Proud? Ashamed? Scared? He recalled what the outlaws in Dragon Reach had told him about freedom.

One thing driving did do was give a man time to straighten up his thoughts and lay them out in rows.

The Imperial posts were set about eight leagues apart, usually in little villages or in market towns. At those he would turn in one team and hire another. The ostlers would try to browbeat him, of course, always. Anxious to hire out postilions to ride those horses, they would insist that even a faun couldn't handle six from the box. They would refuse to believe him when he said that a shoe was ill-fitting or a fetlock sore before he had even lifted the animal's foot. And so Rap would apply a hint of mastery, and get whatever he wanted, and despise himself for doing it.

But he was circumspect, for there was magic everywhere. Ancient ruins and tiny cottages still held faint vestiges of occult shielding. Here and there he saw things or people blurred by a curious shimmer that suggested they were not what they seemed. In the towns he often sensed the ripples of the occult at work; at night in the great houses he would feel Sagorn prowling the library or Andor recruiting a winsome servant maid to cheer his bed. He knew when Thinal took up a collection for a good cause.

Before the expedition had even departed from Arakkaran, the princess had produced some brooches and strings of fine pearls, requesting that Sir Andor sell them to finance the journey. Perhaps she had a rough idea of what first-class passage cost on a fine ship, but she obviously did not grasp the expense involved in bowling along the Great Way in style at twenty-five leagues a day.

And yet perhaps she suspected, for she always became uneasy and fretful when Andor wandered off to visit the markets in the cities. Pawnshops were his objective, of course, although they were never mentioned. The ongoing finances were being unwittingly contributed by the princess's hosts, her friends, and Thinal was her agent. Rap wondered if Inos would have found it funny, as Gathmor did. He didn't.

But if the princess did guess that she was thieving, she was willing to do even that for Inos.

And here, at last, was the turnoff. He did not doubt, for a mage needed few directions. He slowed the coach to a stop before the awe-inspiring gateway. A man came running from the gatehouse, tugging his forelock for the gentry. He swung the flaps, and Rap sent the team cantering up a long driveway, graveled and wide. Rich parkland stretched out on either hand, and turrets showed over the trees ahead.

Now Andor had replaced Sagorn, and the princess was peering into a hand mirror. They'd done twenty-two leagues today, less than usual. Tomorrow they would try to do better. And tomorrow, as every day, Rap's premonition would lie even more heavily on him. It scratched at him constantly, telling him to turn back, turn back!

Eventually the journey would end. Of course he might go mad first, but otherwise the spires of Hub and the waters of Cenmere must inevitably crawl up out of the smoky distance. Then he would discover what awful destiny awaited him there behind the fearful, agonizing white glare of his foresight. The magic casement had given him three prophecies, and two were left to come — and yet, somehow, he thought that the white glare took precedence over those. He dared not pry at the future now, to find out.

In Hub, perhaps, would be Inos. The princess was confident of that, or tried to be so. Rap hoped so. He would like to see Inos again, to cure her scars and to assure her that he bore no ill will. What would she care, though, for a stableboy's forgiveness? Who was he to forgive?

There was nothing to forgive.

He spoke a thought to the horses, and the great coach rolled gently to a halt before wide steps and a massive archway surrounded by centuries of ivy.

Even before Gathmor had dropped to the ground, a great door flew open. As happened on so many evenings, a middle-aged lady in a fine gown came racing down the stairs with her arms held wide, shouting "Kade! Aunt Kade!"

11

The nearside front wheel caught in a pothole; the carriage lurched and a spring broke with an audible crack. Horses shrilled in fright, and the rig bounced to a shuddering, canted halt.

For a few moments Odlepare sat and listened to the roar of rain on the roof. Beyond the windows, all was black — or as near to it as no matter.

He could hardly believe that there would be only one pothole on a major highway within a hundred leagues of Hub, but even if there was, the king's coach would have found it as surely as swallows return in the spring.

"What's happened?" Angilki demanded, the sulky, pouting expression of his doughy face just visible in the last, faint gleam of evening.

"A broken spring, I fear, your Majesty."

"That's very inconvenient, Odlepare." At least he could remember his secretary's name now. He had tended to forget it during the first few weeks.

"Yes it is, Sire. We shall not make Hub tonight."

His Serene Majesty, King Angilki the First of Krasnegar, Duke of Kinvale, et cetera, had noticed a milestone that morning and had been convinced by it that he was within one day's drive of the capital. Thereafter nothing would satisfy him but to prove it. Who was Odlepare to point out that Hub must be considerably larger than Kinford, or even Shaldokan? Reaching the extreme outskirts at this hour would not solve anything.

"Extremely inconvenient! You are not suggesting that I spend the night in this diabolical contrivance, are you?"

"I am sure there will be an inn somewhere nearby, Sire."

With the fat man's luck, though, it would be considerably less comfortable than the coach would be. But of course the fool had insisted on pushing on after sunset. He could always be trusted to push his luck, King Angilki, and he invariably had the worst luck imaginable. Angilki the Unruly. King Angilki the Last. The rain had not stopped since they left Kinvale, and yet every night

105

someone had remarked with regret on the glorious weather that had just ended. Angilki brought winter with him. Very likely the sun broke out as soon as he departed.

Someone was going to have to go out in that downpour . . .

It had been the fat capon's fearsome mother who had conscripted Odlepare for this Evil-begotten journey, summoning him to her sickbed.

"Without proper guidance," she had said, "my son is more likely to arrive in Krasnegar than at Hub. I have decided you are the only one of his regular confidants who can tell east from north."

Odlepare had resigned on the spot.

She had bought him back with a promise of a bonus equal to ten years' wages. He had counted every minute of those ten years going by. Accidents and temper tantrums, absentmindedness and endlessly repeated dissertations on the next round of renovations planned for Kinvale . . . He had aged twenty years in the last six weeks. Had it only been six weeks?

God of Greed, forgive me!

A rap on the door. Odlepare pulled down a window and recoiled as icy rain slashed in at him. "Yes?"

The postilion, sodden: "We have a broken spring, Master Odlepare,"

"His Majesty surmised as much. Have you by chance observed any inns or hostels recently? Even a private establishment of quality?"

Any of the minor gentry would be honored to provide hospitality for a benighted king — at least until they discovered just how benighted a king could be, The postilion could not possibly be wetter had he spent ten years underwater, so Odlepare need not offer to go exploring himself.

"There is an inn just across the road, master."

Odlepare shuddered. This was going to be even worse than he had expected.

"It's called the Soldier's Head," the postilion added hopefully.

"And I expect it will smell like it. You had better send someone across to count the bedbugs."

His humor brought him a black glare, warning him that he had spent the day inside the coach, while the postilion and coachman and footmen had not.

"There is an inn across the road, your Majesty," Odlepare reported.

"Excellent. Where is the umbrella?"

"I recommend a cloak also, your Majesty . . . "It would take more than an umbrella to keep a shape like his dry in weather like this.

Using all of the interior of the coach. King Angilki the Unwieldy struggled into his voluminous sable overcoat. Odlepare found the umbrella, the door was opened, and the two footmen helped their master to clamber down, while Odlepare attempted to hold the umbrella overhead. It leaped in his hand and then turned itself inside out. By that time he was already soaked and it was too late to hunt up his own cloak. He climbed down, unaided.

Wrapped and billowing, Angilki was leaning against the storm. He very rarely addressed any of his retainers except Odlepare, and he could have identified none of the others by name, but even in near darkness the iron brace on his right leg made a postilion recognizable. The king was waving a finger under his nose and, while most of his angry bellowing was muffled by the high collar pulled over his face, enough was audible to convey his meaning.

"Evil-accursed carelessness!" he bleated. "Serious error . . . grave inconvenience . . . dismissed without notice . . . no references . . . your job to look for hazards . . . "

Despite the cold and his already drenched condition, Odlepare was fascinated. He had never seen the fat fool so aroused before, and there seemed to be an excellent chance that the dismissed postilion would retaliate with a right hook to the jaw, or some equally appropriate demonstration of lese majesty. But no, alas! Modern youth was sadly lacking in the nobler virtues — the man merely cowered back in dismay, accepting the destruction of his livelihood without a murmur. How disappointing!

Angilki ended his tirade. With a final bellow that was probably "Odlepare!" he spun on his heel, stormed around the back of the immobilized coach and straight into the pothole, falling prostrate and hurling a deluge of icy, muddy water over his secretary.

12

"You do yourself proud, uncle!" said the newcomer, glancing around the hall. Having just come in from a very dark and moderately stormy night, he was screwing up his eyes against the lamplight.

Krushjor flinched. He could, of course, reply that this was a very modest mansion by Hubban standards, but the raider would probably not believe him. "It is our national embassy — would you want the Impire to believe that Nordlanders are barbarians?"

"Yes," Kalkor said, without hesitation. "This sort of decadence disgusts me." He scowled at the marble pillars, the soft rugs, the chintz-covered chairs.

"It is customary," Krushjor insisted uneasily.

"It is revolting."

The thane was still wearing only his leather breeches and boots. Dagger and broadsword hung at his belt. He was soaking wet from the rain and ought to be chilled to the marrow, although he did not seem so. With a practiced eye for value, he chose the richest rug and wiped his muddy boots on it.

107

The embassy staff had been lined up to receive the noble visitor. Most of them were jotnar, and even they looked apprehensive. The imps among them were obviously terrified as the killer strolled down the line, deadly blue eyes inspecting them.

Krushjor was wishing he had not dressed himself up in local finery to greet his nephew. Probably Kalkor believed that fine clothes were decadent also. He would never comprehend that in Hub a handshake was worth a hundred fists. "Would you care for a hot bath?"

"No."

"Then may I present our embassy staff?"

"No. At least, not most of them. I want a meal, with red meat and strong wine. I want a room with a straw pallet. And . . . " The raider looked over the staff once more. "Are any of these women your daughters, Uncle?"

"No." Krushjor felt himself tense, and hoped his dangerous nephew would not notice.

He did, but he misunderstood. The sapphire eyes twinkled with sudden amusement. "You are wiser than you look. Very well — I shall have that one and that one."

"But . . . "

"Yes?"

Krushjor gulped. "I am sure they will feel honored."

"I don't care what they feel," Kalkor said. "Send in the meal as soon as it is ready. Them and the wine now."

13

The innkeeper had insisted that the room would sleep seven. So Azak had paid for seven, but five tatty pallets pretty much covered the whole floor. A single lantern dangled from the sagging ceiling, smoking and guttering, stinking even worse than the heaps of sodden, horse-saturated garments by the door. There was no other furniture. Inos had folded her bedding into a thick bundle and was sitting on it, pouting at the ratholes in the wainscoting opposite, while Azak was leaning back against the wall, legs straight. The other three all sprawled full length, still gnawing desultorily at the last of the rolls and smoked meat. No one could find energy enough for talk. Rain beat steadily against the casement, and a draft whined somewhere. Downstairs the tavern patrons were into rousing chorus already. They would sing half the night away, but they would not disturb Inos's sleep.

The ride through Ilrane had been hard, a physical torment of uninterrupted riding. In the Impire danger had added a new element to the strain, while Azak had set the same brutal pace, racing from post to post as if he were an imperial courier, bribing the postmasters to give him the best horses, paying penalty for what he had done to the last lot. Day after day of unending pounding, and now also rain and gales and winter cold. The effort needed to keep a horse cantering through sleet and near darkness was enough to kill a woman all by itself.

Ranchland and farmland, city and town — the Impire had flowed by in wet and gloom without Inos appreciating any of it. This style of traveling was not a beneficial exercise that one grew accustomed to. It was an ordeal to bleed one's strength, to crumble mind and body to ruin.

Every night she was convinced that she could take no more of it. Every morning she somehow found the strength to clamber on a horse again and ride one more league.

Then another.

And another . . .

Azak knew what he was doing, though. Talk of war was everywhere: tales of djinn atrocities and provocations, imps in Zark being molested, maidens abducted and hidden away in vile seraglios, needing rescue. Much the same stories had been used a hundred times before, about djinns or dwarves or elves as politics required. There were other slanders that could be dragged out when needed to justify war on other races, fauns and trolls and merfolk and anthropophagi, who could be depicted as subhuman. The legions would march in the spring, but the taxes were needed now, so the people must be prepared.

In Zark Azak was conspicuously huge, in the Impire a giant. He could have dyed his face and hair, but not his eyes. The civilian population was hostile — several times he and his company had been booed in cities, and once almost stoned, while the military reacted to djinns like dogs to cats. On the highway they would give chase, and half the postmasters refused to do business with the enemy until they had obtained permission from a centurion, or at least an optio.

Six or seven times a day Inos had found herself ringed by armed men with twitchy sword arms and hate in their eyes, but so far the elves' document had been respected. She had no idea what was in that imposing forgery, for Azak kept it to himself, but it cowed the average centurion like a blaze of dragons. Yet one or two had clearly remained suspicious, and that reluctance to believe was becoming more and more evident as the travelers neared Hub. Here in the center, even a common sword-banger would likely be better educated and more sophisticated than his provincial equivalent. Sooner or later some smart young legionary was going to take the strangers in for questioning, and then the wasps would be in the jam.

The post inns offered a wide range of board, from sumptuous to squalid, and Azak invariable accepted the cheapest. He had plenty of gold, he just wanted to avoid notice. His strategy was likely sound, for djinns in the dining rooms or public baths would have attracted attention and hostility. Each evening he hired a common sleeping room, bought food, and kept his company out of sight as much as possible. Wise, perhaps — but the wretched living conditions were doing nothing to improve Inos's state of mind.

"Two days to Hub," Azak said suddenly, and she jumped, realizing that she had been almost asleep.

The other three men exchanged glances. Then Char sat up stiffly. "Majesty . . . " He stopped at the look he received. "I beg pardon — Master Kar."

"Better! And you are about to be presumptuous. Well, go ahead and get it over with!"

Char flinched and looked at the other two as if to see if they were still with him. "We were wondering . . . why do we stay on the Highway? Surely we would be less conspicuous if we —"

"— traveled overland," Azak said. "By the lanes and byways?"

"Yes . . . Kar."

"Because strangers off the beaten track are rare and therefore conspicuous. We should seem furtive, hence suspicious. Because only the Great Ways have horse-posts, so we should have to buy livestock of our own, and half a day of this would kill them. Because time is short and we must travel by the fastest route. Do you question any of those points?"

Char shook his head vehemently.

Azak stretched, as if it hurt to stretch. "You don't have the brains you were born with. Now take away those scraps so the vermin don't fight over them all night." He turned to Inos. "Beloved, do you wish to go outside?"

"No."

Azak's red eyes swung back to his men. All three scrambled to their feet and headed for the door, Char carrying the remains of the meal. The door thumped shut behind them. Azak twisted himself around, turning his back on his wife. Even he moved like an old man.

Wearily, aching everywhere, Inos spread out her bedding and then dug in her saddlebag for her jar of elvish unguent. Trying very hard not to wince aloud, she hauled off her clothes and began salving her abrasions, gently massaging the bruised muscles at the same time. Many of her blisters had bled, and even the clean bits were black and blue. She did this every night, and Azak always turned his back. That might be a politeness — for her sake — but more likely he was avoiding the torture of viewing beauty he could not possess. If so, he had not guessed how little allure he was missing at the moment.

She had never wanted anything in her life so much as she now wanted a bath and change of clothes. She wondered if there were a God of Suppleness, Who might listen to a repentant cripple. She really ought to go the bathhouse, but Azak would insist on escorting her there, and a djinn hanging around those quarters might well provoke a lynching. She promised herself that she would do it tomorrow.

"Azak?" she remarked as she smeared.

"My love?"

"Where will we go in Hub? You can hardly expect to walk up to the Red Palace and have the warlock ask you in for a cup of tea. These things take time."

"Some inconspicuous hostelry."

"I have friends and relatives in Hub. Senator Epoxague is a distant —"

"No."

"Kade always spoke very highly of his daughter, and —"

"No!"

Useless to argue with the ox. Her head was stuffed with rocks; she could hardly keep both eyes pointing in the same direction. Maybe in the morning she'd try to talk some sense into him. She squirmed to an even more painful position to get at some of the difficult places.

"Inos, I want your parole," Azak said.

He had turned around and was watching her, but she was too weary to feel embarrassed. Besides, he was her husband and entitled to look. And her battered brain seemed strangely unable to digest what he had said. "Parole? What do you mean, parole?"

His face was in shadow, but she recognized the expression. Here we go on the *insanely jealous* ride again . . .

"I mean that you will make no approach to these friends and relations, nor —"

"Gods give me strength!" Inos muttered. She capped the salve jar and pushed it into her saddlebag. "You think I'm planning to desert you, is that it?"

"You are my wife!" he shouted.

Yes, that must be what he was thinking. And she recalled the elves' offer, Lith'rian's offer. After a few days' consideration, she had somehow seen as obvious what had not been obvious at the time — that the offer must have come from Lith'rian. Who would dare commit a warlock to anything without his knowledge, or venture to speak in his name? Who knew what a warlock looked like? Inos might even have met him. He might have been one of the riders, possibly even Lia'scan herself.

What a fool she had been not to accept! By now she would be a pretty girl again, instead of a freak; dancing at balls in Hub, perhaps, while Azak would be rotting in an Imperial jail. That would be a kinder fate than Rap had met in a Zarkian jail.

She pulled on her filthy nightgown, thinking that her whole life seemed to be a steadily growing mountain of errors, a human trash pile.

"Your parole!" Azak demanded angrily.

"Parole?" Inos repeated. She had not told him about the message from Lith'rian. She wasn't going to. She grunted with effort as she reached for the blanket. "I'm your wife. I swore oaths to you and to the Gods. Why should I desert you now?"

His eyes shone like rubies — not like sane, ordinary-sort-of eyes. "You are in the Impire and have the advantage of me . . . "

Inos eased herself down on her back, and then had to rise on one elbow again to pull the saddlebag over. She heaved it behind her head as a pillow, and even that was an effort. "You already have my most solemn vows, husband. What more can I say? I am a woman of my word." She sank back with a sigh and pulled the scratchy cover up to her chin. "You can let the three deadly virtues back in now, if you want. I'm respectable."

He came scrambling closer and knelt beside her, glaring down menacingly. Mad as a bull camel at mating time? No — it was just that Azak was accustomed to holding all the cards, and here he was out of his element and unsure of himself.

"You're tired," she said. "Don't get carried away."

"You will swear your parole! Swear that you will not —"

Inos failed to suppress a yawn. "Azak! If I wanted to escape from you, and turn you in to the Impire as a spy, and return to my friends . . . do you really think it would be difficult?"

He bared his teeth in fury. He actually had a hand on his dagger, too. It would be funny if she wasn't so beat.

"Swear, or I shall tie you to the saddle, and tether . . . "

"Oh, don't be so silly! You're my husband and I'm stuck with you. If I wanted my freedom, *darling*, all I need do is scream. In the postyard. In the streets. Even right now." She yawned again, enormously. "Help me, sirs, these wicked djinns have taken me prisoner and are dragging me off to their den of lust. I haven't done that, have I? I don't mean to. Now can I go to sleep, please?"

It was likely only a moment, but when Azak spoke again his voice jarred loudly, as if she had already slid over the lip of sleep.

"You are right," he said, "and I am wrong. I apologize."

Amazing — historical! "Mm? Well, don't be surprised if it happens again some time." Sleep . . .

112

"This senator? Would he truly be willing to help, or would he turn us over to the imperor's torturers?"

"Don't know if he has any torturers," Inos mumbled. "Not officially. Of course Epoxague will help. I'm a relative, sort of."

"I am not!"

"Yes, you are. They'll be thrilled to discover they have a sultan in the family. The nobility always stand by one another. Unless they actually catch you plotting treason, yes, they'll help."

"Then tomorrow you will send a letter and set up a rendezvous."

"Yes, dear. Tomorrow. Now may I sleep?"

Several ways:
>   As many several ways meet in one town;
>   As many fresh streams meet in one salt sea;
>   As many lines close in the dial's centre;
>   So many a thousand actions, once afoot,
>   End in one purpose . . .
>   Shakespeare, *Henry V*

5

Trysting day

1

At a hostelry on the outskirts of Hub, Andor had just sold the great coach. It had served its purpose well, but it showed the wear and tear of that service — two of the fancy lamps had fallen off, and a steadily growing crack in one of the springs had been worrying Rap for the past few days. He had mentioned it to Andor, so he could draw it to the buyer's attention, but Andor hadn't.

Now Andor had rented a town carriage, a smaller but even more opulent contraption, suitable for a lady of rank. "Really ought to have the Krasnegarian arms emblazoned on the doors," he remarked cheerfully. His broad hat and stylish cloak glistened brightly, although the rest of the busy yard seemed drear under a steady drizzle and a lowering dank sky.

It was still barely noon. Gathmor was up on the carriage roof, fastening wet rope over the luggage with expert sailor knots. Rap was making friends with the two grays he had selected. Foggy and Smoky, he had named them, and they were content with that.

1 14

Princess Kadolan was fretting under an umbrella. She looked bedraggled, her hair lank in the wet air. "I am still not sure that I agree with Sagorn's plan," she said.

Andor smiled and opened his mouth, but she stepped quickly over to Rap. "We should have consulted with you," she said. "Doctor Sagorn and I had a long talk again, this morning — about our best course of action."

They had been arguing the point for days, and Rap had rarely bothered to listen. He was in Hub, and premonition was making his skin crawl. It lay on his heart like lead. "Ma'am?"

"I have many friends here, although most of them I have not seen in years. Senator Epoxague, for example, is a third cousin of mine and a person of some standing in the court! But Doctor Sagorn feels that we should go to his house, and . . . ah . . . lay low for a few days." She paused, and added wistfully, "I dislike being furtive, I suppose."

Rap could see that she was just impatient to find Inos. He pondered for a moment. He dared not call on his foresight for aid — that terrible white agony would be upon him instantly. Instead, he weighed premonitions, and neither course felt any less ominous than the other. He discovered that he was curious to see Sagorn's dwelling. Andor's, also, of course. How did the five manage to keep their great secret when they stayed a long time in one place, where they might become known?

But his occult talents were of little help, and that meant he must use his native wits. He did not think they were likely to be of great assistance.

"I am inclined to trust the old man's judgment, ma'am," he said uncomfortably. "After all, you can reveal your presence at any time, but you can't vanish again once you have done so."

Failing to find an ally, the princess bit her lip. "I suppose that's true." She nodded a gracious surrender to Andor and headed for the carriage step, where Gathmor was waiting to hand her in. She paused and looked him over with approval. "You are a very skilled footman, Captain! I hardly ever notice you now, and that is the mark of quality service."

Gathmor stood stiffly at attention, a seemingly model retainer in shiny livery. "Sailors can turn their hand to anything, ma'am," he said, "even if they *hate* it!"

Princess Kadolan recoiled, then disappeared into her new carriage without another word.

"Well, that's settled, I suppose," Andor said, a gleam of amusement on his too-handsome face. His raiment would have cost a factor's clerk in Krasnegar about three lifetimes' wages.

Rap gave Foggy a final pat while he looked the rig over once more with farsight.

Andor paused at the carriage step. "The driving will be tricky, my man. I'd best give you directions."

Rap's nerves were too taut for jesting. "Just say right or left when you want me to turn. You needn't shout, either."

Andor flinched. "You can hear what we say inside?"

"When I want to. Right or left out the gate?" Rap hauled himself up on the perch without waiting for the answer.

"Left!" Andor whispered crossly, and went to join the princess.

Hub was huge. Andor had told him so, long ago, but Rap had never envisioned so many leagues of busy streets and ostentatious architecture, and it all grew grander and grander and busier and busier as he drove steadily into the heart of the capital. Row after row of tenements for the poor gave way gradually to respectable homes, and then to the great houses of the nobles beside parks, to monuments and grandiose public buildings and temples . . . above all, temples. Dozens of temples.

Even in the gloomy drizzle, Hub was overpowering. He could not imagine how glorious it would be in sunshine.

Inside the carriage, Kade was as excited as a child, and Andor smugly acted as tour guide: pointing out, naming, explaining. "The temples are why this is called the City of the Gods, ma'am. Every single God has a temple of Their own. 'Tis said the Imperial secretariat just keeps building them, so that whenever a new God is added to the list, there is a temple ready waiting to be dedicated."

"Fancy! Well, I must visit some. And since it must have been the God of Love who appeared to Inos, I should perhaps start with Theirs."

"Er . . . I advise against it! A lot of dubious characters hang out around that one."

Rap had little time to eavesdrop on the passengers or admire the city or brood about his future. Despite himself, he was being forced to exercise some of his powers, and he had no idea how mundane drivers could survive unscathed in such tumultuous traffic. Carriages wheeled everywhere, all driven by maniacs, while the rest of the population seemed to be holding footraces and watersports on the same streets in fruitless efforts to stay dry. He thought he would much rather drive over the causeway to Krasnegar at high tide in a gale. He survived only because he had absolute control over his horses, and over all the other horses, as well — his passing provoked much well-phrased cursing.

It was a danger, of course. Some sorcerer might detect him, some warden's votary out hunting for recruits, but he thought that very unlikely. He had learned how to use his talents now without shaking the ambience much, and he had just become aware of another safeguard, here in Hub — there was a background shimmer of sorcery and magic going on all the time. To track down a whisper of animal mastery amid all that occult hubbub would be almost impossible.

He caught a fleeting view of the golden turrets of East's palace, and a much briefer glimpse of the Opal Palace beyond, and then Andor's instructions led him south, away from the center.

Dark was falling by the time he heard the welcome news that the hostelry ahead was his destination. He pulled into the yard and stopped, and for a moment just sat limply in the sudden peace, wiping his eyes and feeling as if he'd been wrestling white bears underwater. Whatever dread fate his foresight had seen in Hub . . . could it be any worse than the traffic?

A groom was holding cheekstraps, Andor counting out gold, Gathmor yelling instructions at the boys swarming over the baggage, and a quartet of trolls was shambling forward.

Rap jumped down and went to thank Smoky and Foggy. Normally he would have insisted on rubbing them down himself, but a quick scan of the stables showed him they would be well boarded — and Andor was sending him glances.

"We've only a bowshot to go," he was saying. "We don't need porters, do we?" The travelers had amassed an amazing amount of baggage, and that morning he had insisted that it all be crammed into just two trunks.

So Rap exchanged shrugs with Gathmor and said he thought they could manage. Then he beat the sailor to the larger box and hoisted it onto his shoulder with no help from the scowling trolls.

Wielding the princess's umbrella for her with his usual aplomb, Andor led the way out of the yard, across the street, into a lane too narrow for a carriage, down a short flight of stairs, turned left at an intersection, and into a shadowy court.

Then up some stairs. Across another courtyard . . .

The steady downpour was showing no signs of waning, and a spiteful wind hustled it along these constricted passageways. The trunk on Rap's shoulder grew heavier by the minute. Water was running into his sleeve and down his collar. Ankle-deep floods swirled garbage along gutters and paving alike, and periodically managed to soak his feet.

The next alley was a gap so narrow that pedestrians must walk in single file, and the two human camels had to watch their elbows and knuckles. Nothing was straight for more than a few paces, no angles were right; the buildings were a labyrinth, their height squeezing the darkening sky to narrow slits. More steps . . .

"Some bowshot!" Gathmor grumbled, puffing.

117

"Arrows fly straight." Rap just wished that the old lady would walk faster.

"Good spot for an ambush."

"Don't see anything lurking." Rap had not been neglecting his farsight, but so far it was confirming what his eyes said — that this was an area of blighted trades and decaying residences, but relatively harmless. The buildings were obviously very old, but that must be normal in Hub.

Gathmor paused to shift his load to his other shoulder. "Easy for you!" he grumbled.

"Yep!" Rap said. "Want me to take both?" But he was using honest muscle, not power, and he was both surprised and pleased to have outlasted the sailor. He shifted his load over, also, though, and they carried on — across a rubbly empty lot, through the gloom of a covered wynd, stopping at last before an inconspicuous door set almost flush with the wall. It was cobbled together from rough planks; it had no distinguishing marks at all.

"And here we are!" Andor said cheerfully. "Not exactly a fashionable address, but certainly not a slum, either. Discreet —"

"Open that door, or I drop this on your toes!" Gathmor snarled.

"Ah! Well, if you insist. Magic time!"

Andor placed his lips close to a knothole in the door and whispered something to it. Rap felt a shimmer as it swung open.

"Goodness!" the princess said.

"Magic door! You can buy anything in Hub if you have the money."

That was sorcery, not magic, but a large number of such occult gadgets in operation would explain the steady vibration Rap sensed in the ambience. With sighs of relief, he and Gathmor entered and thumped their loads to the floor in unison. The dingy little room was bare except for a shabby rug and a row of pegs holding a few assorted hats, cloaks, and a couple of lanterns. The only lighting came from a small transom, grimy and barred, plus a few chinks in the door; the staircase ahead was inky dark. Andor closed the door carefully, then fumbled with flint and steel.

"This is an odd place," he said. "What my associates and I like most about it is that it has entrances on three different streets. Thinal and I have been known to come in a skylight, also."

Rap's farsight was already exploring an astonishingly complex series of rooms and hallways and staircases, a human-scale ants' nest carved out of a dozen adjoining homes by the simple process of stealing away a room here and a room there. Only by tracing out the pathways through the maze could he determine which chambers belonged to this residence and which did not. Even the neighbors might not realize that this labyrinth existed in their midst.

He easily detected the hand of Sagorn — room after room filled with books, rolled charts, hermetic apparatus, and piles of bizarre paraphernalia —

118

but he also noted several walk-in closets completely stuffed with gentleman's clothing, and an attic workshop littered with artists' equipment and parts of musical instruments. Thinal seemed to be represented only by a small secret cupboard under a stair tread, half full of gems and gold trinkets — nothing but the best, of course. Of Darad there was no sign at all, but Darad would have no reason or desire ever to come to Hub.

The lantern flickered into life, casting a golden glow on weary faces.

"The place needs a good cleaning," Andor admitted. "We hire a servant every ten years or so, for a few months. We're overdue. It may not be the style to which you are accustomed, ma'am, but it does provide a very suitable lair for a group of men bearing an ancient curse."

"You did not design it yourselves?" Rap asked.

Andor had turned toward the stair. He turned back, as if reading something in Rap's tone. "No. It's very old. We were lucky enough to hear of it when it came on the market, and Sagorn purchased the freehold. Why?"

"About two-thirds of it is shielded. I suppose the rest of it was added in later, but the original was the work of a sorcerer."

For once Andor was at a loss. Then he laughed uneasily. "Our lucky word at work?"

"Certainly," Rap said. "You probably owe your lives to it, because all of you jostle the ambience at times. It's always seemed like a miracle that you have escaped detection for so long . . . so, here's the miracle."

"Gods! We do? Then you will show me which parts are safe before you leave?"

"Gladly."

Andor shrugged, visibly unnerved by the news. Then he again headed for the stair, holding the lamp high and offering his arm to the princess. In silent consent, Rap and Gathmor moved to opposite ends of the same trunk and hefted it between them, leaving the other for a second trip.

Settling in was a brief process. Andor assigned bedchambers to everyone; the other men delivered baggage and then brought buckets of water from the pump in the cellar, which was itself ankle-deep in runoff that day. Cleaned up and refreshed, the visitors gathered in the main drawing room and discovered that their host was no longer Andor.

Long and gaunt in a silvery robe, Sagorn was leaning against the mantel and surveying the room with the supercilious sneer that meant he was displeased. He was wearing a black skullcap, an affectation Rap had not seen on him before.

The chamber was large but sadly in need of cleaning: the fireplace full of ancient ashes, tables thick with dust, shelves festooned with cobwebs. Rap did not know how much detail the others could make out in the gloom filtering through the grubby windows, but the smell of dirt was unmistakable and the princess's expression unusually bleak. Sagorn himself was making no move to light the candles.

He nodded to Gathmor as he entered, the last to do so. "Take a seat, Captain."

"Think I'll stand." The sailor folded his arms and scowled. The princess had perched on a straight-back chair. Rap had let himself sink into a cushioned divan, to see if it was as soft as it looked. It was, but smelled unpleasantly of mildew.

"I assume that Andor called you so we could have a strategy meeting?" the princess said.

Sagorn chuckled cynically. "Only partly. Our fastidious friend was shamed by the quarters he had to offer you. He decided that as it had been my idea to bring you here, I ought to take the blame." He raised a hand to forestall her denial. "And he was right! I apologize wholeheartedly, ma'am. I had failed to notice in the last few years how neglected the place has become. I tend to become lost in my studies, you see . . . The house is a disgrace."

"Well, we shan't hurt for a day or two," the princess said cheerfully. "What do you propose we do now?"

"Food, I suppose," Sagorn said. "And information. How real is this war? Has Inosolan arrived in Hub, and have her djinn companions? They may have been forced to turn back, you know. What of Krasnegar? What rumors of the Four? And we might try to ascertain which of your friends and relations are in town, ma'am. The same for my political cronies. When we have answers to those questions, we shall have more questions to answer!"

"And how can I help?"

"I'm not sure! There are taverns not far away where Thinal can often pick up gossip. Andor can visit some of his acquaintances." His raptor eyes swung around to look at Rap. "Our mage should be able to gather news by occult means."

"Only by eavesdropping," Rap said. "But that's safe enough."

"And mastery. If Andor can worm out secrets, I'm sure you can."

"I suppose so," Rap said unhappily.

"You might interview a legionary or two. And the captain . . . " Sagorn eyed Gathmor doubtfully.

Gathmor sneered. "The captain stays home and makes things shipshape. Filthy, lubberly crew you are!"

"Then I shall be cook and homemaker," the princess said.

"Ma'am —"

"No, truly!" She beamed up at him, amused. "I love cooking, and I very rarely get the chance. But I can't produce a meal from an empty larder."

All eyes went to the darkening windows. The markets would be closing, or closed.

"This place is shielded." Rap had just discovered he was ravenous. "How about chicken dumplings?" He was remembering a very special treat his mother had made for him maybe twice or three times in his childhood, the best thing he had ever tasted. With his occultly flawless memory he could recall that taste exactly, and his mouth was suddenly watering like the weather. It was the nicest sensation he'd known in days. Maybe, just once in a while, it was good to have powers beyond the mundane.

"Of course!" the princess exclaimed. "You can make food appear by magic, like Sheik Elkarath did!"

"Oh, yes. I'm not sure what happens afterward, though. We may all wake up very hungry in the night."

"Well?" Sagorn snapped. "Why stop with such plain fare? I am sure her Highness would prefer, say, fricassee of pigeon breast in truffle and caper sauce."

"Anything at all," Rap said. "If you let me know what you want it to look like, I'll produce it. But it's going to taste like chicken dumplings."

2

Along every great highway of the Impire, the horse posts were numbered. In her letter to Senator Epoxague, therefore, Inos had suggested that Post Number One on the Great South Way would be a suitable place to meet. She knew the road would go that far, but she had no idea where it went within the city. What she had not anticipated was just how large a staging post could be.

The letter had been borne on ahead by the next passing courier, and a message to a senator was sure to receive dispatch treatment. Azak had set a gentler pace thereafter — to be less conspicuous, perhaps, or to let the letter arrive and produce results. That night the innkeeper had called in soldiers to inspect his suspicious guests, but the elvish passport had worked again. Inos kept expecting it to fail.

And at noon the next day, it did.

South Post Number One was huge, enormous. Not only the Great South Way began here, but the Pithmot Way also, and a spur of the Great East Way. Here the stagecoaches and the Imperial mail began and ended their runs. Here private travelers arriving could turn in their posters, then hire cabs for transport within the city; the outgoing could rent mounts or whole equipages of horses and coaches and servants. Halls and yards and paddocks and stables sprawled like a small township, bustling with couriers and messenger boys and porters and ostlers and cutpurses. There were a thousand horses there, and

121

almost as many people, all seemingly milling around in the rain, all shouting. Wheels rumbled and splashed. The air was thick with the smell of wet horses. There were also soldiers.

Inos had not foreseen the difficulty of meeting someone she did not know, and who did not know her, because she had expected a far smaller place, and never such a turmoil. For two days she had been dreaming of a friendly family senator appearing to provide hospitality and protection, and perhaps a little sane, cultured relaxation after half a year of mad adventure. He might very well have answered her plea and come to the rendezvous, or sent someone in his place, but how could they locate each other? She had not dared mention that she was traveling with four djinns.

They had turned in their horses and recovered their original deposit. They had left that office, and now they were outside in the rain and Azak was leaving the next move to her, scowling ferociously but saying nothing as the minutes crawled by and she stared this way and that way and wondered where on earth to go first. Horses and travelers milled past, and then — from all sides like wolves emerging from a forest — legionaries closed in with drawn swords.

Followed by her four djinn companions, she was escorted indoors and then up a somber staircase to a room that already contained a tribune, a centurion, and one unremarkable civilian. About a dozen legionaries filed in with the captives, and spread around, still holding naked blades. There was one table and no chairs. The door was then closed, and bolted.

Fear throbbed at her temples; the forgery had been exposed, the senator had betrayed her. The deliberate overcrowding of the room was designed to add to the stress; she felt she could hardly twitch without contacting an armored torso. They were all around, eyes too close. She could smell the leather and the polish and the men's breath.

The tribune leaned back against the table and read over the passport. Then he regarded his five captives with satisfaction. "This is very good work," he said. "A very good fake."

"No, it isn't," Azak replied.

The tribune smiled and handed it to the civilian, who was young, balding and bookish — an inoffensive little man, obviously dangerous, else he would not be there. He carried the document over to the window and peered at it, holding it almost at the end of his long nose. "Yes, very fine," he concluded. "Elvish, almost certainly." He continued to study the penmanship.

The tribune turned his patient smile on Azak. He was a short man, and middle aged; surprisingly old for a soldier. His face and arms were swarthy, weatherbeaten, but he could afford an expensive uniform, the bronze inlaid with gold. His dark eyes glinted brighter than his helmet. "Now the truth?"

"You have the truth," Azak replied evenly.

"The persons named in that forgery have never heard of you."

"Of course not. I'm coming, not going." Azak had not blinked, but Inos felt her heart sink another notch. Obviously every spy and every doubting official along the Great South Way had sent in a report. A tidal wave of reports must have hit Hub, all at about the same time. The authorities had merely let the suspect strangers complete their Journey, right to the gates of the capital. Now they would be examined to find out what they were; taken apart in the process if necessary.

The tribune looked Inos up and down. "Uncover your face!"

For ladies to wear riding veils was not unusual, but normally they removed them indoors. Inos took off her hat and pulled the veil free of her collar. She was so filthy she could barely live with herself. *I am the long-lost Queen of Krasnegar, in the far northwest of Pandemia, and my large, equally evil-smelling companion is my husband, sultan of a powerful state in Zark, in the extreme southeast. We are here to meet with a prominent member of the senatorial order. What else would you like to hear?*

The tribune nodded, as if he had just confirmed what had been reported. "Not djinn, not pure anything. Part elf and part what?"

"No elf. Imp and jotunn."

"Who branded you, and why?"

"That is my business."

He shrugged, as if the point were of no import. "You are consorting with djinn spies, traveling under forged papers. Worse may befall you than that."

"It is not yet noon," Azak remarked calmly.

"What of it?" asked the tribune.

"We are to be met here by an important person at noon. I suggest you restrain your curiosity until then, Tribune."

The tribune folded his arms. "Do I really look so gullible? You can gain nothing by insulting me."

"If you truly believed that our credentials were false, you would have dragged us away in chains long since. My authority is unusual, I admit, but that is not your concern. Just wait until noon. I cannot guarantee that your questions will be answered, but you will be stopped from asking any more of us." Azak folded his arms also.

He was filthy and travel-worn, and a red-hairy thigh was visible through a tear in his breeches, but the Sultan of Arakkaran knew all there was to know about intrigue. He was probably right — the tribune was still not quite certain. Djinns were fair game at the moment, or very soon would be, but the

123

war was not yet official. There could be diplomatic moves underway still, and the man was smart enough to know that.

It felt like already past noon to Inos, although the weeping gray sky made the point debatable. It felt like past time for the senator to show up if he was coming. He might be out of town, and her letter still on its way to wherever he was. He might have thrown it in the fire as a fake. He might have turned it over to the secret police, and this tribune might be just playing with her by not mentioning it.

Had she not persuaded Azak to let her send that letter, then their case would be hopeless. If someone did not answer the letter very soon, then their case was hopeless anyway.

"Any doubts. Scrivener?" the tribune asked.

"Oh, none at all," said the young man. He tossed the roll of vellum on the table.

"Right." The tribune spoke to the centurion. "Search them."

The centurion sheathed his sword and signed to two men to do likewise. They advanced on Azak, who glared but offered no resistance while the men poked and peered. They clinked his bags of gold on the table, they relieved him of two daggers and a couple of thin knives Inos had not known about.

Then Char, Varrun, and Jarkim were given the same treatment.

The tribune eyed Inos thoughtfully. "Are you carrying any weapons or documents?"

"None."

"You swear this by the God of Truth?"

"I do."

"Very well. Now, we'll start with that one." He nodded at Char.

The two legionaries grabbed Char's hands, spun him around, and slammed his face into the wall. Then they held him there. Azak took a step forward and was stopped by a hedge of swords. The centurion threw a heavy punch at Char's kidneys and kicked his ankle. Inos shut her eyes.

Char took two more blows in silence, then he began to cry out. Azak growled wordlessly.

"Ready to talk?" asked the tribune.

"You will regret this!"

"Carry on. Centurion. Don't be so squeamish."

"Look!" the ineffectual little civilian said.

Inos looked. The man was still standing by the window, and must have been staring out of it for the same reason she had been keeping her eyes closed.

"A carriage with armorial bearings has just driven in, Tribune. And its outriders are Praetorian Hussars."

"God of Torment!" the tribune said.

It still wasn't quite settled. The hussar who exchanged salutes with the tribune was several ranks lower, but he was young and glamorous and supremely satisfied with himself and the status that came with his plumed helmet. He was very tall and almost chinless, but any man who could win his way into the Praetorians had great influence to start with, and just being a Praetorian gave him much more — he was almost certainly a future lictor, at least. There was very little fight left in the tribune.

But the passenger in the coach was no senator, merely a portly, well-dressed lady who looked astonishingly like a younger version of Aunt Kade. Swathed in warm, soft furs, she directed a cold, hard stare at the rain-soaked waif standing in the mud beside the carriage, surrounded by troops.

"You know this woman, ma'am?" the tribune asked glumly.

"No."

He brightened. "No?"

"She wrote to my father, claiming to be related to us, but neither of us has ever met her. Moreover, the person she claims to be has been reported on unimpeachable authority to be dead."

The tribune beamed.

The chinless young hussar frowned silently. He had obviously decided that he approved of Inos, despite her disgustingly bedraggled condition. "Can you prove who you are, miss?"

Azak burned in silence in the background.

"I am Inosolan of Krasnegar, and this must be Lady Eigaze."

In the coach, the dumpy lady lowered her eyebrows skeptically. "My name is hardly a secret."

"Kade has told me much about you."

"For example?"

"You spent a summer at Kinvale, and won the heart of a young hussar by the name of . . . Ionfer, I think."

"My husband is Praetor Ionfeu. You will have to do better than that."

"Well, she also mentioned a certain spinet recital where the spinet would not stay in tune, possibly because of a hedgehog crawling around its insides. And a covered soup tureen, which, when the footman lifted the lid in front of Ekka —"

"Inosolan!" the woman shrilled. "Whatever happened to your face, child!" She came stumbling down the steps in the rain and threw her arms around Inos.

"May the Gods be with you next time, Tribune," the brash young hussar remarked in a pleased voice.

3

Kade habitually made pretense of being scatterbrained. Her former protégé, Lady Eigaze, carried imitation to the point of parody; she maundered and sniggered and prattled. But she was a senator's daughter and had a will of her own when she chose to show it. One glimpse of the battered and bleeding Char was enough to slide the velvet hand into the iron glove. Her flabby form seemed to stiffen into muscle, and she glanced up meaningfully at her bold escort.

"Tiffy, darling?" she murmured dangerously. "Do something?"

He beamed at the tribune. "Sir," he said . . .

Then the full weight of the Imperial establishment came crashing down on that unfortunate officer. He found himself requisitioning a coach and rushing off *in person* with his victim to the finest military hospital in Hub, with Varrun along as a witness, and under strict orders to report *in person* to the Lady Eigaze before the sun set, lest his career be permanently blighted.

The lady was tough. When Inos presented a gigantic barbarian as her husband, Sultan Azak of Arakkaran, Eigaze smiled without a blink and offered her fingers to be kissed. Azak excused himself on the grounds that he was too travel-soiled to touch her.

And when Inos protested that she also was unfit even to enter the senator's grand coach with its fine poplin upholstery, Eigaze again snapped her fingers to bring forth a miracle. The Number One Post Inn produced hot tubs and soft towels and clean raiment. Inos felt her head swim at the sudden release of tension. The ensuing meal was the finest she had eaten in weeks, and yet all she could register was the unending stream of babbling nonsense proceeding from her distant cousin, and the expression of astonishment and reluctant respect on Azak's shiny-clean, fresh-shaven features.

But when those formalities where over, when Inos and Azak had been installed on the green poplin upholstery and space found on the back for Jarkim between the footmen — then Lady Eigaze settled down to some ladylike chatter that concealed more serious purpose. The Praetorian Hussars cleared a path through the traffic, the carriage rumbled smoothly along, and Inos made a desperate effort to pull her soaring wits back to earth. She was euphoric with a newfound sense of freedom and escape; Azak must be feeling even more trapped than before. She could tell that he was reviving all his dark suspicions of her motives. Now, even more, it was Inos who held the cards, and he did not trust her not to betray him.

"It is, obviously, a very long and unlikely story, my lady —"

"Eigaze, dear."

"Eigaze. It might be easier if you just told me how much you know first, and then I can add the rest."

"Inos, dear, now I think I know almost nothing. The first thing we heard was that there was trouble in northwest Julgistro last spring, with goblins raiding. Father came back from the Senate one night absolutely *livid!* And then we heard that your father had died. That much is true?"

"Yes," Inos agreed, that much was true.

Eigaze muttered condolences. "And that you and Kade had gone off back to Krasnegar with a military escort. Then the escort was ambushed on its return, and there were terrible stories of atrocities. The Senate . . . You can imagine! *Goblins!* Worse than gnomes, even! The Impire has never, ever, had trouble with goblins before. Of course Father and I were concerned, and we wrote to Ekka. And then came word that you and your aunt were dead!"

"Who," Inos asked intently, "said so?"

"The imperor, dear. It was in his report to the Senate. Of course he'd told Father earlier, being a relative of sorts — usual courtesy. He told him he got it from Warlock Olybino."

"Aha!" Inos said, and exchanged glances with Azak. Suddenly things began to seem much clearer. Olybino had failed to purchase Inos from Rasha — or steal her, perhaps, if he had tried that also. So he had just made the problem disappear by reporting that she had died. Who would question the word of a warlock? So then, when Inos had turned up in Ullacarn, she could no longer be of any use to him, and he had just sent her back to Rasha. Aha indeed!

"And what did the imperor decide to do about Krasnegar?" Inos asked, before her hostess could fire another round of questions. The carriage was racing along a wide avenue lined with glorious buildings, and Inos knew vaguely that she wanted to gape at them like a tourist, but she also knew that this was not the time to indulge in sightseeing.

Eigaze frowned. "I think that was after his Majesty's health began to fail. Consul Ythbane . . . he's regent now, of course . . . he proposed that since the direct line had died out — for Kadolan would have been next in line to you, of course — Angilki had the best claim. But Krasnegar didn't seem worth a war with Nordland, and the Zark campaign was already scheduled, and the dwarves were starting to get difficult, not to mention goblins. By that time we had received a reply from Ekka, and Father was able to report that the duke would have no interest in becoming a real ruler. So the compromise was that Angilki would have the nominal title, and rule though a viceroy chosen by the thanes. The Nordland ambassador agreed, and a memorandum was initialed."

Lady Eigaze's wits were no dimmer than Kade's, obviously.

"Very convenient!" Inos muttered. "Except for the citizens of Krasnegar."

"They're not the imperor's responsibility, dear, unless you wish to declare that you hold the kingdom in fief from him?"

"Certainly not!" Inos said hurriedly. "Well, obviously the warlock was lying."

Lady Eigaze seemed to pale slightly, and coughed. "Even warlocks may make mistakes, dear, sometimes, I suppose. And Kade, you say, is safe and sound, back in . . . er . . . "

"Arakkaran," said Azak.

"Thank you." She eyed this inexplicable savage with obvious bewilderment and then chose a safer subject. "This is all quite extraordinary! Angilki knew nothing of this at all!"

Inos felt a quiver of premonition. "Angilki?"

"Oh . . . of course you won't know! He's here in Hub, dear! He showed up two nights ago in a terrible state."

"Angilki? The duke is here?"

"Why, yes, dear. The regent summoned him when — but you can't know that, either, I suppose." Lady Eigaze was starting to look worried. She reached in a locker and produced a box of chocolates. "He has a broken ankle. Angilki, I mean. He had a dreadful journey, poor man. And he's not a duke, now, he's King of . . . Oh, dear!"

"What else don't I know?" Inos demanded.

"Have a chocolate? No? Your Majesty?"

Azak declined. "Please just call me Azak," he added, "as we are all family now."

"Gods bless my soul!" Eigaze muttered, and ate three chocolates in quick succession without taking her eyes off him. Djinn relatives would not be welcome news in Hub at the moment.

"Why did the regent summon Angilki?" Inos asked determinedly.

"Because of Kalkor, dear. He's a Nordland thane —"

"I know of Kalkor. He is another distant relation, extremely distant." Inos remembered the vision in the magic casement and grimaced. "In fact, I saw him once. The more distant the better with that one! What of Kalkor?"

"He is — Oh, Holy Balance!" Eigaze took another chocolate, and her eyes grew very wide. "Darling, I may have made a serious error!"

"What error?" Only years of dealing with Kade kept Inos from grabbing the woman by her fat throat and shaking her.

"Well, your letter arrived this morning, after Father had left for the palace. I didn't really believe that it was genuine, of course, so I didn't send word to him. I nearly didn't come at all. I had to cancel a dress fitting. Oh, dear!"

Azak was scowling. Inos could feel her heart pounding.

"What about Kalkor, Eigaze?"

Two more chocolates . . . "He is in Hub also! That's what today's court is all about! He requested a safe conduct, and of course the regent granted it, because he'll never manage to escape again afterward, and he arrived a couple of days ago, and that's what today's business is — Krasnegar! When Angilki arrived at our house, Father sent word to the palace right away, and they came and dragged the poor man out of bed in the middle of the night and hustled him off . . . "

"Krasnegar? Today?" Inos cried, feeling Azak's eyes burning into her. "Should we go and —"

"Oh, it's too late now, dear! They'll have started, and even I couldn't get you in, or even get word to Father now."

"But what does Kalkor want? Recognition of his claim?"

"Sure you don't want a chocolate? Nobody knows! The belief is that he's totally insane and wants to fight Angilki for the throne."

"*Fight Angilki!*" Inos remembered the deadly, muscled warrior she had seen in the casement and the overweight, ineffectual duke. She started to laugh. The idea of those two locked in battle was absurd.

"That's the only theory anyone's come up with, darling!" Eigaze wailed softly and popped the final chocolate in her mouth. "The jotnar have some ancient savage ceremony to solve such disputes among themselves. They call it a Reckoning, Father says."

"A fight with axes!" Inos sobered suddenly.

The casement had prophesied a duel with axes.

But obviously, somewhere, the course of events had gone awry. Now it was not she whom Kalkor was challenging, but Angilki.

And Rap, who had been destined to be her champion, was dead.

Azak was smiling.

4

Moms had cut down Shandie's medicine. She'd also found the spare bottle he'd hidden under the dresser. He was starting to feel scratchy-twitchy already, and the ceremony had barely started. Perspiration was running down his face, and it was awesomely hard not to shiver. He tried to concentrate on what was going on, to take his mind off his medicine.

The King of Krasnegar had a cast on his foot, and he was fat. Managing a toga and a crutch at the same time must be pukey difficult, but he looked as if he'd have enough trouble managing either one by itself. Shandie didn't think much of the King of Krasnegar.

Shandie didn't approve of imps being kings, anyway. Imps owed their loyalty to the imperor. Maybe dwarves or anthropophagi or people like that could have kings — he hadn't decided — but not imps. Still, this king was really only a duke, and he'd just done homage for Kinvale to the regent, so that there

wouldn't be any misunderstandings, and he'd looked very funny when two heralds had to help him kneel down with his cast and his toga and his crutch.

He'd had to read his speech, tool Disgusting! And he'd mumbled it so
badly that no one had heard him.

If that was the King of Krasnegar, then Krasnegar had very low standards.
The fat man didn't know a thing about court behavior. He'd been given
Consul Humaise as a sort of keeper, to stay close and whisper instructions.

Oh, why didn't they get on with it?

With a funny little thrill of fright, Shandie thought about pretending to faint.
Then he'd get carried out! Ythbane would beat him raw, of course, but then
Moms would let him have lots of medicine. Be worth it, maybe, for the medicine.

Pay attention.

The jotunn was . . . Well, he sure had muscles. And he wasn't as fishy-
white as most of them — browner. His hair looked very pale, even for one of
them. Moms said they were murdering brutes, and this Kalkor looked mean
enough to kill anything with his bare hands, but he did have muscles, and he was
bare from the waist up so he could show them off. He wasn't hairy and tattooed
like the ambassador and his followers. Disgraceful to come to court dressed like
that! He didn't look very humble, either. Of course jotnar didn't, usually.

Unexpectedly catching those blue, blue eyes on him, Shandie looked
away quickly and stared at the White Throne. This was a north day, of course.

Pay attention!

"The ambassador never had authority to waive my claim to Krasnegar,
Highness." Kalkor had a very creepy sort of smile — a nasty sort of smile.

"But a Reckoning? That seems a very barbaric custom to us. Thane."
Ythbane was using his lead-him-into-a-trap voice.

At Kalkor's side, the duke-king nodded vigorously. Even standing still
before the throne, he was having trouble balancing on his crutch and keeping
his toga from unraveling.

The raider was as relaxed as a cat on a cushion. "Written agreements seem
very decadent to us, your Highness. Two men who need to write down what
they have agreed to obviously do not trust each other."

"Then why not settle your differences with King Angilki here in amicable
conversation and discussion, and bind your agreement with a handshake?"

Kalkor did not even glance at the fat man beside him. "If I shake his hand,
he'll have two casts to worry about."

In the background. Ambassador Krushjor guffawed, and his men followed
his lead.

Behind Shandie's shoulder, Ythbane sighed. "Well, the Impire is not
directly involved, as we have said." He was speaking loudly, so the senators
would listen. "King Angilki is our loyal subject only as the imperor's cousin of

Kinvale. He does no homage to us for Krasnegar. I repeat — we are merely offering our good offices, as friendly neighbors to both sides."

The jotunn laughed so harshly that Shandie jumped. "Of course, of course! And in a minute or two you're going to have some perfectly marvelous idea to suggest, aren't you? I can hardly wait."

The Senate rumbled with disapproval.

There was a pause, then, until Consul Humaise leaned forward and whispered something in King Angilki's ear.

"Er, what?" King Angilki said. "Oh, yes! Look, Kalkor —"

The jotunn whirled on him. *"Thane, to you!"*

The fat man almost fell over. "Er, Thane. Yes. Thane!"

There was another pause. He seemed to have forgotten what he was going to say, or even that he had been going to say anything.

Kalkor smiled his creepy smile at Ythbane again. "Strange friends you have, your Highness."

Ythbane chuckled, very softly, and Shandie felt his insides quiver. He usually heard that noise when he was on the writing table.

"We are confused. You cannot seriously propose a duel between yourself and the king, when he has a broken ankle?"

Kalkor folded his arms, and for the first time dropped his smile and scowled. "I can't seriously propose a duel between me and that *slug* at any time. This isn't what I expected! But it seems to be what I'm stuck with. No, we allow the respondent to name a champion."

"Your Majesty?" Ythbane said.

Angilki looked blank for a moment, and then said, "Oh? Me? Er, yes?" His face was very red and shiny, and there was a vein pulsing in his forehead. He wiped his face with his toga.

Ythbane spoke slowly, as if prompting a child. "Thane Kalkor is willing to allow you to name a champion to fight in your stead. The outcome will settle the fate of the kingdom. That is right, is it not, Thane? The loser loses on behalf of himself and his heirs forever?"

Kalkor's amusement returned. "Of course. You mean he actually produces heirs?"

"But if King Angilki nominates a champion, then we assume that you have the right to name one also?"

The jotunn shrugged. "I never have and never will."

"Well, then." Ythbane had switched to his close-the-trap voice. "We are sure neither side wants a war, and a personal duel is much less bloody. We suggest that you accept, King Angilki."

"Oh. Right! Yes, I accept!" The fat man nodded vigorously, which was fun to watch.

"A Reckoning?" asked the thane.

"A duel in Nordland fashion," the regent agreed.

Thane Kalkor flipped his head in a curious gesture. For a moment Shandie did not believe what he was seeing, and probably no one else did, either, but there was spittle on Angilki's cheek.

"By the God of Truth," the thane proclaimed, "I say you are a liar, by the God of Courage a dastard, by the God of Honor a thief. May the God of Pain feed your eyes to the ravens, the God of Death give your entrails to swine, and the God of Life nourish grass with your blood. The God of Manhood shall support me, the God of Justice spurn you, and the God of Memory will lose your name."

In the ensuing silence, the duke raised the hem of his toga and wiped his face. He seemed almost stunned.

Ythbane laughed, then. "How picaresque! Your victim may now name his champion?"

"I advise it."

Everyone looked to Angilki. "Ah. Yes? Well. My champion? Let's see, it's a short name . . . " The king's face seemed to redden even more. Maybe he was feeling scratchy-twitchy, too? Shandie could feel the shaking coming on, and his mouth was so dry he could hardly bear it.

Consul Humaise whispered something in Angilki's ear again.

"Ah! Yes. I call on, er, Mord of Grool . . . to be my champion!" The king dragged an arm across his forehead and leaned harder on his crutch.

The audience rumbled with astonishment and excitement.

Kalkor shook his head in disgust. "I can guess, with a name like that." He pouted sourly at the regent. "Do we get to see the champion now, your Highness, or will you unveil him in the morning?"

"In the morning? Is that not rather soon? The arrangements —"

Kalkor folded his arms again. "There is no room for discussion. You agreed to a Reckoning, and so we are bound by the rules of a Reckoning. Disputes are usually taken to the Moot on Nintor, but I can't imagine your fat friend going there, and he has accepted the challenge. Failing that, by the rules of Reckonings, the battle must be held at noon on the day after the challenge, and on the closest suitable piece of ground . . . Do I hear his champion arriving?"

A thunderstorm of laughter roared from the senator's benches, and even from the commoners'. Shandie risked a sideways glance at Ythbane, who had his head turned away, and then farther yet, past him, until he could see the west door and what was causing the laughing. A troll was coming in, wearing armor. Its heavy, shambling tread seemed to shake the rotunda. Shandie had never been really close to a troll before, and this one seemed much bigger than most. Even two steps up, he wasn't level with its muzzle. It was even taller than Thane Kalkor, although jotnar were supposed to be the tallest race of all. Its low-slung arms were as long as a horse's legs. It had a helmet like a coal shuttle.

He, not *It!*

The troll stopped beside Angilki and boomed out over his head, "You called me, Majesty?" He knew his lines better than the king did. The whole Rotunda rocked with mirth and sheer delight — senators, nobility, commonality — and the noise seemed to swirl around and around like a wave in a teacup. Heralds thumped their staffs for quiet. It eluded them for longer than Shandie could ever remember. He wished he could laugh, too. He was shivering.

Kalkor had been waiting in tolerant amusement, like a grown-up humoring children. He obviously did not think that the laughter was directed at him. "Mord of Grool, I presume?" he said, as the tumult finally died away. "If you come in second will your orphans and widow be able to collect?" He was smiling a really happy smile now.

"The king's champion is acceptable, then?" Ythbane said, and again the hall bubbled with laughter.

"Oh, yes. A close relative is the normal choice, and I can see the resemblance."

"You still do not wish to name a champion of your own?" The regent's question raised more titters.

"No. I expected something like him. Of course he must dress properly."

"Perhaps Ambassador Krushjor can loan us an expert to see that all the proprieties are observed?"

"I am sure he can."

Shandie's hands were quivering like a bird in a net, and his head was thumping. If the ceremony didn't end very soon, he would pretend to faint and take the beating. He was twitching so badly now that Ythbane must have noticed, so it would be pants down again tonight anyway. He might as well fake a faint and save himself any more of this. Very, very soon!

Kalkor had turned to face Angilki, who quailed. "We meet tomorrow, then!"

Angilki shuddered and licked his lips. "Yes."

"And you are aware of the Ultimate Rule, aren't you?" Kalkor asked, and a strange silence settled over the Rotunda as subtly as an overnight snowfall.

"Wha . . . What rule?"

The jotnar turned his blue smile on the regent again. "A Reckoning is a mortal challenge. Either challenger or respondent must die, regardless of who does the fighting. Champions may alter the odds, but not the stakes."

133

Angilki uttered a strange bleating sound.

Ythbane's voice came out hard. "You mean that if you can beat the troll, then you get to kill the king, also?"

Kalkor snapped his fingers.

Ambassador Krushjor flushed scarlet, but he strode forward. "That is indeed the Ultimate Rule, your Highness. Obviously, it is the only fair way to stage a mortal challenge when substitutes are allowed."

"A duel between willing warriors is one thing," Ythbane said, "but a cold-blooded —"

"You both agreed to the rules!" Kalkor roared.

Even his great bellow was almost lost in the surging anger of the audience. King Angilki made the strange noise again, but probably no one farther away than Shandie heard it. The heralds were thumping their staffs again. Shandie's head was thumping, too. Crimson-faced, King Angilki had come to the edge of the steps and was shouting at Ythbane. No one was looking at Shandie, so he risked wiping the perspiration streaming down his face. What in the names of the Gods would Ythbane do to him if he *threw up* beside the Opal Throne?

But then Angilki stumbled backward and crashed to the floor, and lay still.

Silence, stunned silence.

Oh, good! Maybe now they would stop all this silly ceremony and Shandie could go and beg Moms to give him some of his medicine.

5

"And that about sums up my day," Senator Epoxague said. "No . . . One other thing. The duke seems to have suffered a serious seizure. The doctors are concerned."

"Oh, dear!" Eigaze wrung her fat hands.

"I am sorry to hear it," Inos said. "Rough seas are not his waters. He asks only to fish his own little pond and be at peace with the world."

"I believe that!" The senator was well preserved for his age, dapper and quiet, and unusual only in that he wore a small mustache, a rarity among imps. He was a small man, yet he radiated power in an astonishing way. There were always six or eight people in attendance on him, but they kept their distance as if he were surrounded by an invisible fence. He had shown no visible surprise at finding his drawing room occupied by a supposedly dead relative and a djinn sultan. He had merely settled into his favorite chair and listened attentively to a brief summary of their problems, without comment. Then he had reported on the events at court.

"And now," Inos said, "I expect you would like to hear my story in more detail?"

He shook his head. "First a quick supper. After that we shall be joined by some other people." He smiled. "And then you may talk till dawn, I warn you!"

Inos returned his smile gladly. The knots in her nerves were starting to unravel. This magnificent house had a strong flavor of Kinvale about it, which might be Eigaze's influence, or just the style of the Imperial nobility, but was soothing in either case. Eigaze had furnished a respectable wardrobe for her shipwrecked relative at incredibly short notice and, best of all, had borrowed a skilled cosmetician from a neighboring duchess. The burns still showed, of course, but now everyone could reasonably pretend that they didn't.

Azak, at her side, was rigid, and so far he had been silent. Now he said, "So this Kalkor dies tomorrow at the hands of the troll?"

Epoxague flashed him an appraising glance and rubbed his mustache with one finger. "That, of course, is the plan. Gladiatorial combat was outlawed by the present imperor's father when I was a boy — I can only just remember seeing one — but it is common knowledge that such things continue in private. This troll who goes by the name of Mord of Grool is the accepted current champion. His handlers were very pleased to accept a match with only one man, even a notorious fighter like Kalkor. Mord will take on four imps or two jotnar, sometimes."

Inos broke the silence. "Then why is there any doubt?"

Epoxague sighed. "There were rumors . . . Gods know who starts them! But the talk was that Duke Angilki's seizure was more than mundane."

Inos shivered. "The wardens?"

The senator shrugged. "Perhaps. To use sorcery within Emine's Rotunda, so close to the throne . . . that would be either an act of the Four, or of a total madman."

"Kalkor? You are saying that Kalkor is a sorcerer?"

"I am saying nothing. It is only rumor. But Angilki was probably about to withdraw from the contest, and Kalkor seems to want the battle. That man is either quite mad to come to Hub, or else he has a means of escape that the regent has not counted on." Epoxague smiled grimly as he rose from his chair. "Or both?"

The lamps burned late that night in the Epoxague mansion. Inos had not been introduced to all the people present. Some were undoubtedly relatives, others must be political cronies and advisors. At least one was a marquis, but nobility was of much less weight in Hub than in the rest of the Impire. What counted in the capital was influence, and a senator had plenty of that. Epoxague held several hereditary titles, but he did not bother to use them, and he dominated all the others present. They sat in rows and listened in silence. A few were women, and Eigaze was there, near her father.

Surprisingly, so also was the chinless young tentpole they all addressed as Tiffy, who had turned out to be Eigaze's eldest son. Out of uniform he seemed even younger and cheekier, and at dinner he had attempted to flirt with Inos in flagrant defiance of Azak's murderous glares — conscious of her ravaged face, she had been grateful for his efforts. Like the rest of the company, he now listened in deferential silence.

The senator sat in front, occasionally sipping at well-watered wine. Inos and Azak had been placed on a sofa facing this formidable audience, and Inos talked.

She told the whole story, in as much detail as she could recall. She even told things that Azak had never heard — about the magic casement, and Rap, and the prophecies. She told of the curse, which he had forbidden her to mention. She did not mention her own word of power, which she was beginning to think was a myth. On only one point did she fudge the truth, and then she thought she saw the senator raise his eyebrows a fraction, as if he could hear the difference, like one off-key string in an orchestra. Rap, she said, had died of his wounds. To brand Azak as a murderer would be betrayal, and she had sworn to be faithful to him.

Azak was still and silent as a marble statue. He was seeing the enemy in its lair, some of the most powerful people in the Impire, and she knew it must be a climactic experience for him. Whether he was impressed or disgusted she could not tell, but Azak understood the ways of power, and he must be noting and learning. A wise man knows his enemy.

The room was large and opulent. Crystal mirrors and fine porcelain gleamed amid fine furniture, and yet there was a patina of age on everything; the rugs were starting to show wear and the ceiling friezes were yellowed above the sconces. This was not the sparkling-new decor of Kinvale nor yet the sunlit splendor of Arakkaran; this was old wealth, sure of itself, long established and deeply rooted in the governance of the greatest state in Pandemia.

Finally she came to the end, her throat sore with talking. She took a long drink. The candles had burned low. Her scabbed face throbbed, and she feared that the paint had started to flake off it, in which case she must look like a gargoyle. Perhaps in time she would learn to live with disfigurement.

It would not be easy, though.

"I think I have only one question," the senator said. "When exactly did your father die? On what day did this sorceress abduct you?"

"I'm not sure," Inos said. "We had been traveling the taiga for weeks, and I'd lost track of time. Azak? When did I arrive in Arakkaran?"

"The day after the Festival of Truth. I believe you honor the same day, your Eminence."

136

Epoxague nodded. "Any other queries?" he asked. Although he did not turn, the question was obviously addressed to the audience at his back.

Silence.

At last Tiffy spoke up. He was by far the youngest, and his intervention was therefore so unlikely that he must have been rehearsed beforehand. "How closely is her Majesty related to us, Grandfather?"

Tension reared — silent and invisible, and yet so palpable that Inos thought the candles flickered.

Epoxague stroked his mustache. And then he said, "Not close as his Grace of Kinvale — but close enough."

It was acceptance. Despite the danger she brought, the quiet little man was saying he would not throw her out in the street, and he had made the decision on behalf of the whole clan. That showed real power, she thought. A faint shimmer ran through the audience, a shifting of feet, a drawing of breath, as the minds worked over the problem.

And the senator now looked to Azak. "My house is honored to have such a guest, your Majesty."

Azak released a very long sigh and seemed to sink lower in the sofa. "The honor is entirely mine, your Eminence."

Inos glanced sideways at him. He was a very astonished djinn.

"Your position is difficult," Epoxague said. "Both your positions! The King and Queen of Arakkaran and Krasnegar? I have heard of far-flung realms, but never one so far-flung as that."

The audience smiled uneasily. He had identified the ultimate impossibility: Azak and Inos could not rule both kingdoms. One or the other must be dispossessed.

"Boji," the senator said, without turning, "how long since the Right of Appeal was invoked?"

"Last dynasty," a grizzled, heavyset man grunted. "Hundred years or more."

"Tomorrow," the senator told Azak, "I must present you to the regent. Until that is done, you are in some danger — and my own position is ambivalent."

Azak nodded. "I appreciate that."

"And the best excuse for your presence in Hub is an Appeal to the Four."

The sultan squirmed — Inos had never seen him so discomfited. "I had hoped that a private approach to one of the wardens —"

Epoxague shook his head. Choosing his words carefully, he said, "Which one? Obviously Olybino is unthinkable. He is not only the power behind the legions, he is already involved in this affair somehow. Bright Water is . . . unpredictable; and she also must be involved, for East certainly tried to protect the troops on that disastrous retreat from Krasnegar, and he was blocked.

137

Only the witch of the north could have done that, up there. What she wants, I do not know. Maybe she worries only about Krasnegar, and not Arakkaran. Lith'rian, also, has been meddling in your realm, and I cannot guess what his interest is, except that warlocks sometimes play games with us mundane mortals. And elves do not think like other people," he added sourly.

Inos was enthralled. Here, at last, was a man who knew something about the shadowy wardens and their secret ways. Some of what he was saying she had heard before, but for months she had wanted to hear it from someone who could speak with authority.

"West?" Azak muttered when the senator did not continue.

The caution became more marked. "Ah! We know very little about Warlock Zinixo. He is no older than Tiffy here, and new to his office. So far he has been very inconspicuous. When he succeeded, he refused the traditional address of welcome from the Senate. He did not appear at the regent's confirmation."

After a pause for thought, Epoxague added, "All dwarves tend to be distrustful; he seems to have that caginess to an unusual degree. There is no doubt that South hates him. Elves cannot abide dwarves, and vice versa. When Zinixo struck down Ag-an, then Lith'rian and Olybino together tried to blast him on the spot."

Someone coughed warningly.

The little man did not turn. "I have that on the highest authority," he said calmly.

That was news to some of his audience, at least. Bland faces registered surprise. Lips pursed and glances flickered. The little man ignored them.

"So West has good reasons to fear the others. Bright Water may be his ally — at times, but who would rely on such an ally?

"Besides," he concluded, "you have a very beautiful young wife, your Majesty. I recommend that you do not ask favors of Warlock Zinixo."

Azak flushed and scowled at Inos.

Epoxague glanced over his shoulder, as if to include the other listeners. "Can anyone fault my logic? I can't see a private appeal working at all. Anyone disagree?"

No one disagreed.

Azak scowled. "Why should an appeal to the Four be any better, then? My case is hopeless!"

Was he only concerned by the thought of his curse being discussed in public, or did he fear that the wardens might give Krasnegar precedence over Arakkaran and order him off there to be husband to the queen? Inos could not ignore a tiny shoot of hope sprouting in her heart. She was stuck with Azak until death, and she would make the best of him; but Azak in Krasnegar would be a sight easier to live with than Azak in Arakkaran.

"Shaky, but not quite hopeless, perhaps," Epoxague said. "Put them all together, as the Council of Four, and they may remember their responsibilities. They have a duty to suppress political use of sorcery. They will wish to uphold the Protocol, for it also guards them from one another. So they may well agree to cure your curse, heal your wife, and spirit you back to your realm. It would be an easy demonstration of their powers. Ashlo, what do you think?"

"It is possible, your Eminence," said the one who Inos thought was a marquis. "The best bet under the circumstances, I should say. Collectively they often cancel out one another's petty schemes."

The heavy man addressed as Boji cleared his throat. "The regent will have a vote if they split."

Epoxague and some of the others chuckled, sharing some political thought they preferred to leave unspoken. The senator turned his bright eyes on Inos.

"You also must be presented, and as soon as possible. You realize that you are in extreme danger, even here, now?"

"Er . . . no!" Inos said, shocked. She had been feeling more relaxed than she had in months, euphoric almost.

Epoxague smiled grimly. "A warlock reported you were dead. If you appear in public, he will be shown up as either a liar or a fool."

She nodded dumbly, deeply shaken. She should have seen that!

"So we must make you appear in public, and as soon as possible! Can you think of any way in which Kalkor can have learned of the vision you saw in the casement?"

"No, your Eminence."

"Mmm. But I think he must have." The little man rubbed his chin. "Something he said today . . . He did not expect that duel to be fought against a troll, nor against Angilki. Perhaps Bright Water told him. He is one of hers, you know — a jotunn raider. She has always had a goblin fascination with death and suffering. You are certain that the Rap man is dead?" His eyes were sharp as rapiers.

Inos looked to Azak. Let him answer this one!

"I saw him the night we left, Eminence. Gangrene had set in. It was incredible that he was still alive at all. I am sure he could not have survived another day."

At least he had not been hypocritical enough to express regret, but the senator was studying him closely.

He must be able to guess how Azak had felt toward the man who had disrupted his wedding.

And now he was frowning. "Well, you must be presented at court, Inos. Tomorrow."

The Boji man coughed. "I hope you'll warn him — send a note to let the regent know what you're going to spring on him."

"I daren't!" Obviously worried now, Epoxague uncrossed his legs and crossed them the other way. "If East finds out that Inosolan is in Hub, then she will *not* be in Hub, and Gods know where she may be, alive or dead. Ashlo, you'll see Ythbane before any of us. Could you drop him a warning that I'm going to dump a load of garden grower on him, but without being specific? At least he'll know to have a smile handy."

The marquis muttered his compliance, not looking very happy at the prospect. Again Inos felt impressed by the senator's power.

He sighed. "Olybino's not the only one who's going to be embarrassed. Ythbane will have to withdraw recognition of our unfortunate cousin as King of Krasnegar. Of course Kalkor will then withdraw his challenge to Angilki and that is good, with this scent of sorcery in the air . . . except that Kalkor . . . "

His frown twinkled into a smile. "How fast can you run, Inos? I wonder what it costs to hire Mord? Cousin Azak, in the interests of economy, would you consider taking on the thane as your wife's champion?"

He wielded humor with a sharp edge. It isolated Azak as the stranger, the barbarian warrior in a room full of urbane politicos — and it raised again the ultimate impossibility of uniting two kingdoms at the opposite ends of the world; it asked Azak to decide between them.

The barbarian was subtle enough to see all that. He clenched his jaw, and the room waited.

Inos knew what was coming. It was inevitable — and it was also horribly logical and reasonable. Who could choose the barren arctic rock over the jewel on the Spring Sea?

"I think my wife must relinquish her claim."

Everyone looked to Inos. Abdication? That would solve the regent's problem and might therefore save Epoxague himself considerable trouble. Abdication was implicit in her marriage to Azak. She had promised her father — but then she had promised Azak later, and the God of Wedlock, also. And she did not know if her kingdom would accept her, or if Nordland ever would, or even how much kingdom the imps had left for her.

And yet that tiny sprout of hope had not withered yet. This was certainly her last chance to see Krasnegar again, and she was not going to throw it away until she must.

"I should prefer to wait until my husband has made his appeal to the Four," she said.

140

Epoxague nodded and seemed to relax slightly. "A good response! So Kalkor must delay his challenge until the Four have heard the case. I must say I dislike the thought of our cousin of Kinvale being axed to death on his sickbed, and I am sure the thane is capable of that." He nodded in satisfaction. "Yes, we can block this outrageous contest tomorrow. The regent will like that. That is the nugget in the rockpile!"

The little man rose and turned to face the company. "I shall present Inos at the Campus Abnila tomorrow — it must be done in public. Do any of you have any questions or comments or advice?" He studied the silent faces. "Speak up! I know this affair could harm us." Still there was no response. He was pleased. "No? Well, then I suggest an early night. Mord of Grool fighting Kalkor the raider? That news must have gone through the city like a tornado, and the streets will be chaos in the morning."

Everyone rose then. The company broke up into groups. The doors were opened, people began drifting away.

Some came forward to greet Inos and shake Azak's hand. He was obviously astonished at this generous friendship being extended to him through his wife. Inos could see the doubts and suspicions struggling below the surface — in their own fashion, djinns were every bit as untrusting as dwarves — but he was being as gracious as he knew how to be in mixed company. The men's reaction to him was so guarded that she mostly could not read it.

The few women present were all eyeing the sultan in a way she ought to be finding very pleasing.

Not a man in the room looked more handsome in doublet and hose. He towered over them all, even young Tiffy, who had departed and now returned, glumly waving a note.

"I am ordered to the Campus by dawn, Grandfather. You'll have to trust yourselves to Drummer, I'm afraid. Are your affairs in order, your will up to date?"

"Think you'll recognize a dawn when you see one?" the senator countered. Then his smile faded. "Don't take this lightly, lad. Half the city is going to turn out to see the pirate fight the troll. There are going to be crowds like you've never known. And if Inos's arrival stops the battle — as it should — then there may very well be a riot!"

Trysting day:
> By the nine gods he swore it,
>   And named a trysting-day,
>   And bade his messengers ride forth,
>   East and west and south and north,
>   To summon his array.
>   Macaulay, *Horatius at the Bridge*

141

6

Pilgrim soul

1

At the same time as he had outlawed gladiatorial contests, Emthar II had also dismantled the arenas. The greatest of them all, Agraine's Amphitheater, he had renamed the Campus Abnila, in honor of his mother. All the stonework had been torn down and removed, and a great oval of grass installed over sand where multitudes had bled and died for centuries to amuse the populace.

Being situated midway between the Opal and Gold palaces, the Campus Abnila was convenient for martial displays and sports events, but neither of them compared in popularity with its former glories. A grassy bank enclosed it for the convenience of spectators, but there were no facilities for handling crowds.

The regent had chosen the Campus as the site of the Reckoning, and it was a very logical choice, but the day happened to coincide with the festival of the God of Commerce, a holiday for most of the populace. The news of the planned spectacle had rippled out across the city the previous evening. By daybreak, vast mobs were surging through the streets, bound for the Campus Abnila.

The weather was cool, the skies drab and threatening. Recalling her prophecy in the magic casement, Inos had been confident of rain, but so far the showers had held off. She sat in the great carriage beside Eigaze. Azak occupied two-thirds of the opposing seat; the senator had the rest. Their escort comprised a mere four of the Praetorian Hussars, and they could do little to speed the coach's passage through the teeming throngs.

Downgraded from absolute monarch to guest and tourist, Azak was tense and surly. Eigaze prattled, but her nervousness showed. Inos felt gloomy, unable to keep memories of Rap out of her mind. Things had gone awry, and the fault was hers, for not heeding the divine warning she had been given. Today's Reckoning had been preordained, either here or on remote Nintor, but Kalkor should have been matched against an occultly endowed Rap, not some brutal professional killer. Mord of Grool, indeed! The very name degraded the battle to a sordid public spectacle.

And it should have been her regality at stake, not the fatuous Angilki puppet show.

Somewhere garments had been found to fit Azak; perhaps they had been specially made in the night. Inos also had been gifted with suitable clothes. She did not know whose they were — obviously not Eigaze's — but for the first time since her marriage she was traveling unveiled. Her hostess and her maids had done the best they could to mask the burns with cosmetics, but the swellings and suppuration could not be hidden. The paint was probably wearing off already. Inos was going to meet the regent and his court looking like a monster.

Epoxague was calm, but uncommunicative. He was a man of power, a confident of imperor and regent, yet he was obviously risking Imperial anger for Inos's sake. Without his support, she would now be in some ghastly jail. She ought to feel grateful, and happy. Why could she not quash her regrets? Why, too, this strange foreboding? Suppose the horrid Kalkor actually won! Suppose the match was called off and the crowd rioted, as the senator had predicted! The day held potential for infinite disaster.

She was about to be presented at court. Even Kade had never achieved that great honor. For Kade's sake, also, Inos mourned — poor Kade! Stranded in far-off Arakkaran, again denied her lifelong ambition to visit Hub . . . had she been present, she would have been gawking at all the great buildings and chattering like an excited starling.

Even Eigaze had fallen silent.

"Eminence," Inos said suddenly, "tell me about the regent?"

Epoxague raised his eyebrows. "Ythbane? He has only held the position for four or five weeks . . . "

He thought for a moment, and then spoke with even greater care than he had used when talking of the wardens the previous evening.

143

"These are troubled times for the Impire, Inos. It would be treason to say so, of course, but there is a school of thought that says we may soon see the end of a dynasty. Agraine's line has given us many great imperors, and perhaps the greatest impress of them all, Abnila. Emshandar was — is — a great man, but his reign has been cursed with much bad fortune. His wife and his son both died young, and now he has been taken with a great sickness."

He sighed, and shook his head. "His grandson seems to be a weakling. His daughter, Orosea, is a kindly person, but it is hard to see her rivaling her great-grandmother."

"The regent?" Inos asked again.

Epoxague smiled faintly at being thus cornered.

"You will probably find him charming. He is charming! His origins are obscure, and he keeps them that way, but it is a common belief that he has merfolk blood in him. That is rare. Some merfolk boat was storm-wracked on a coast somewhere — it happens often, and the results are always bloody. If a merboy is washed ashore, then the local women pursue him and the men knife him in consequence. The opposite is true of a mermaid, of course. Rarely one of the resulting children will survive and be reared. When it reaches adulthood, the same results inevitably follow . . ."

He caught her eye and saw that she was not to be distracted. "Ythbane, then. In his case, apparently, there was a second generation. The story is that his father died at fifteen at the hands of a lynch mob, having already impregnated some man's wife. That is only rumor, of course. Quarter merfolk are very rare! Or perhaps his remarkable success with women created the legend."

Eigaze tutted. "Father, I really don't think you should repeat such scandal."

"Perhaps not. But if it is true, then Ythbane inherited only part of the merfolk curse — he can charm women, but men do not react badly to him. And he is undoubtedly gifted. Emshandar always preferred commoners as his confidential aides, because the great families are constantly feuding and that muddles aristocrats' loyalties. He noted Ythbane's talents early and used them well. The Senate was horrified when he made the man a consul — Emshandar always enjoyed shaking us up. When the fever took Emthoro, though, Ythbane went after his widow."

"Father!"

"It's quite true, dear. Orosea was happily married, Uomaya was mother of the heir. Ythbane knew what he was doing. He is shrewd. He is a skilled politician. Who better to be regent and guardian of the prince than his mother's husband? Of course the imperor wasn't expected to last quite so long . . . " The senator veered smoothly to another topic. "And today's events . . . he may be planning to reinstate gladiatorial contests. That would be a very

144

shrewd move!" He glanced up at Azak beside him. "You know how unpopular regents always are?"

"We never have any," the sultan said, "but I suppose they lack the divine authority of the blood?"

"Right. Also, governments must often do unpopular things, and a newcomer will always blame the previous administration. So Ythbane is in a difficult position. He must rule for Emshandar until he dies — it can't be long — and then, if he has not already become too hated, he can hope to become regent for the prince, until he comes to his majority. By historical precedent, the young imperor will then repudiate his former guardian and turn on him. The history books are full of such cases."

He chuckled. "So do not be too hard on the man! A regency is a thankless and dangerous job."

"What I don't like," Eigaze said suddenly, "is how he keeps dragging the old man out to every function and putting him on display like a stuffed corpse!"

Her father blinked at her in astonishment. "Now who is indulging in dangerous talk?"

"Well, it's true! And that poor little prince!"

"Careful! A prince must learn early. He will succeed in . . . what . . . eight years only? And the presence of the imperor lends authority. Don't repeat those remarks to others, Eigaze!"

His daughter flushed and turned to the window. Inos caught Azak's eye, but it was unreadable. Obviously Epoxague was a Ythbane supporter, the sort of canny politico who would always be found on the winning side.

And it was none of Inos's business. If the appeal to Four could be arranged, she might find herself back in Arakkaran within days, properly married to the sultan and legally ex-Queen of Krasnegar.

And Rap would still be dead. Neither wardens nor gods could undo that.

She, also, turned to look out the window.

2

Never before had Inos seen a truly large crowd, and she found it scary. Half a league from the Campus, the coach was blocked completely. The senator and his guests were forced to proceed on foot, with their Praetorian Hussars striving to open a path for them. The crowd's temper was brutal, because most of those who had come were not going to see the spectacle. Crested helmets of legionaries showed all around, yet even they could not shift the struggling, rumbling sea of people, for it was solid as pack ice, with nowhere to go. Inos was well aware that any minute one of her guardian horses might trample someone and thereby spark a riot. The short walk took well over an hour.

But the Imperial army was still the most efficient organization in Pandemia, and the imperor's compound had been demarcated and fortified as if to withstand a full-blown siege. The entire Praetorian Guard seemed to be present, bright and deadly, an unbroken cordon of steel and bronze and muscle.

Their leader was a weatherbeaten tribune, who saluted Epoxague smartly and only then registered Azak beside him. The expression that at once overran his face impressed Inos as the most memorable event of the day so far.

Greatly relieved to be out of the crush, the newcomers climbed the grassy slope, to find more guards at the top, and many civilians, but nobody very happy. A canopy of purple leather flapped mournfully over a portable throne and a dozen or so chairs. Despite a damp smell on the wind, no rain had fallen yet.

Before them lay the field, larger than Inos had anticipated. Except for two small tents at east and west, the grassy oval was bare, outlined by a solid ring of soldiers with arms locked, struggling to hold back the throng that covered the bank. Plumed hussars rode slowly around within the cordon, directing the effort.

Latecomers would be fighting to climb up on the outside, those on the flat crest were pushing inward to the edge to get a decent view, while the early birds on the inner slope were being relentlessly forced down against the human fence. Inos was very glad she was not out there among the squirming, heaving, cursing citizens of Hub.

Even the lowering sky seemed to threaten disaster. Already there were rumors of citizens being crushed. Expected festival was turning into probable calamity.

More dignitaries and important guests continued to arrive, standing then in despondent talk, grumbling about the unruliness of the common herd. Many of them seemed disheveled, their opulent cloaks fussed and rumpled.

Inos stood as close to Azak as she ever dared get, ignoring the curious stares being directed at the two of them, wondering how the paint on her face was holding up. Eigaze was pale and oddly taciturn, Epoxague was smiling and nodding to acquaintances — yet discouraging conversation and the obvious curiosity about his astonishing djinn companion. Pages circulated with refreshments.

An hour or so dragged by and noon was nigh when a fanfare announced the arrival of the regent. Inos forgot her troubles and watched in growing excitement. The limp figure in the carrying chair was obviously the old imperor himself, a wasted hank of cloth and bone, and now Inos understood

Eigaze's disgust. That pitiful relic should be dying in peace somewhere, in a comfortable bed. She wondered if he was being deliberately abused to hasten his end, but just to pose the question would be sedition.

And then came the royal family, led by Regent Ythbane himself. He was short and lean and pale-skinned. His cloak was of purple velvet, trimmed with ermine, spangled with imposing orders and bright sashes. There were enough miscellaneous jewels in his osprey-plumed hat to qualify it as a crown. He moved with a studied grace, nodding and smiling to the courtiers' bows. Even at a distance, Inos felt his charm and his authority. When he reached the inner slope of the bank and was visible to the crowd, he stopped and stood at attention for the imperial anthem. The ensuing cheer sounded thin from so large a congregation.

Princess Uomaya was a disappointment, running to plumpness, almost blowzy. She also was decked out in purple, but it did not flatter her complexion and she was not wearing the garments as well as their cut deserved. Ten years ago she might have been a wondrous beauty, or even five years ago; but she had let her face sag into a permanent expression of defeat and resentment.

The small boy with them was whey-faced and puny, his legs thin as broomsticks within his hose. He was strangely subdued and much less interested in events than seemed right for a child of his years. Now Inos saw why Eigaze had called him a "poor little prince." Uomaya had a chair beside the throne, the boy stood on the regent's other side, staring out blankly at the empty field.

Obviously the marquis had passed the message, for Ythbane was barely seated before his eyes searched out the senator. They narrowed ominously at the sight of the djinn.

A curly-haired page came running to Epoxague, who nodded to Azak and began working his way through the throng. Inos followed with her heart starting to pump. Every girl in Pandemia dreamed of being presented at the imperor's court one day. She had been no exception, but she had always visualized the kindly old imperor in a great shiny ballroom, not this muddy grass and a substitute who seemed to be half regarded as a usurper, seated on a rather ugly thing of gilded wood under a low-slung leather canopy.

The closer courtiers reluctantly made way for the arrivals. Ythbane's face was dark with suspicion. "Senator! We were advised that you had something important to tell us?" The accompanying expression was warning that it had better be good.

"Your Imperial Highnesses!" Epoxague bowed to the regent and then to his wife. The onlookers watched him with calculating eyes. "First, I have the honor to present a distant relative, who arrived at my house unexpectedly last night — his Majesty Azak ak'Azakar ak'Zorazak, Sultan of Arakkaran."

Azak removed his hat in impish style, but then he doubled over in one of his djinn gymnast's bows.

The regent flushed angrily. "An emissary, your Eminence? This is neither the time nor the place!"

Epoxague, Inos noted with surprise, was nervous. "No, your Highness! His Majesty visits the City of the Gods merely to invoke the Right of Appeal to the Four."

Ythbane was clearly surprised, and yet perhaps relieved that his war was not imperiled. He glanced at some of the onlookers — advisors, likely — and then made a fast decision. "That right is enshrined in our oldest traditions, your Majesty." He relaxed his frown. Epoxague had dropped a hint earlier that a mere regent might enjoy boosting his personal prestige by showing how he could invoke the great occult council. Perhaps that calculation was going on now in Ythbane's obviously quick wits. "We shall enjoy hearing of your petition very shortly. If it meets the requirements of the Protocol, then we shall fulfill our ancient responsibilities and facilitate your suit."

And then he noticed Inos. No djinn, she! His eyes narrowed again.

"'First', you said, Senator?"

"Second, your Majesty . . . " Epoxague drew a deep breath and glanced around as if to make sure than Inos was still there and had not been magically transported to some far corner of the world. "Your noble predecessor was badly misinformed. This lady is the wife of Sultan Azak, Sultana Inosolan of Arakkaran … "

Ythbane began to shape a formal smile, and stopped abruptly.

" . . . and also a distant relative of mine . . . and also the rightful Queen Inosolan of Krasnegar."

"You are joking!" the regent said flatly.

"I fear not, your Majesty. She is, as you can see, very much alive. Reports of her death appear to have been ill-founded."

The regent, his wife, the courtiers within earshot . . . stunned silence . . . shocked glances . . .

Ythbane was the first to recover. "Can you prove your claim, ma'am?"

Inos rose from her curtsy and faced him squarely. "I will make it before the wardens, should your Highness so desire. Or before any other sorcerer who can detect falsehood."

Ythbane's lips moved in silence. Then he turned his head and bellowed, "Ambassador Krushjor!"

An elderly, massive jotunn shouldered his way through the crowd. He wore a metal helmet and a long fur cape, clasped at the throat and gaping to display the silver-furred chest below it . . . Nordlanders spurned shirts. His blue eyes were blazing with fury.

148

"Your Highness?"

"Thane Kalkor must be advised that there is a third claimant to the throne of Krasnegar."

The jotunn put his fists on his hips and the cloak gaped wider to reveal a jewel-encrusted belt buckle and crude leather breeches. "The Reckoning must proceed. Once a challenge has been uttered, there is no way to withdraw it."

Ythbane's pale cheeks flushed again. "But Duke Angilki may very well wish to recant his claim."

"He made it falsely. He must suffer the consequences."

Epoxague said, "But . . . " and then fell silent.

The regent turned to look at the vast crowd ringing the field. It was growing impatient, its voice a menacing undertone of anger, like some restless sea monster wakening in the deeps.

And at that moment a man in a red cloak emerged from one of the tents and raised a trumpet to his mouth.

"Stop him!" the regent shouted.

"I can't and you can't!" the ambassador said. "With *all* due respect, your Highness, here you are merely another spectator at a sacred ceremony."

The brazen notes of the challenge came drifting over the campus, and the crowd noise died. The mounted patrol cantered to the far end of the field, then lined up to watch the action.

Ythbane shot a glare of fury at Inos, and she stepped back hurriedly. The senator took her elbow and led her aside. He looked shaken. "Didn't work!" he whispered.

"I am sorry," she whispered. "Your kindness has brought you trouble." ·

He shook his head angrily and muttered, "Never mind now."

The Reckoning was going ahead. Was that good news or bad news for Krasnegar?

Everyone was watching the field. Another man emerged from the other tent to repeat the process. Red cloak flapping in the wind, he blew an answering refrain. Then they both stepped back inside.

"Is this what you saw in the casement?" Azak whispered, somewhere above and behind Inos.

"Roughly." Why was there no rain, though? The sky was dull enough, but in the prophecy there had been rain falling.

The two contestants emerged simultaneously, each wearing only a fur wrapped around his loins. Kalkor was too far off for Inos to recognize, but his silver-gold hair and pale bronze skin were unmistakably jotunnish. The other was grotesquely bulky, with skin of a muddy mushroom shade, and he seemed to have a woolly beard, although she could not be certain at that distance. It

149

was only when she compared him to the spectators on the banks nearby that she saw he was a giant, as meaty as an ox and perhaps even taller than Azak.

Behind the two contenders, the attendants reappeared, each bearing an ax. A painfully angular lump grew in Inos's throat as she watched the ritual of transfer. She had foreseen Kalkor's part of this ceremony in the magic casement's vision.

Now there was no Rap there, being her champion.

And no rain falling. The casement had been a flawed prophet.

Kalkor swung his weapon up on his shoulder — as predicted — and went marching smartly across the grass. The troll shuffled forward to meet him, idly waving his own ax as if it were a fly whisk. The crowd murmured appreciatively.

Then the troll stopped and raised a tree-trunk arm over his head, spinning the huge weapon around like a baton to show how easy it was. The crowd rumbled and roared in delight. Mord of Grool, the favorite, was about to wreak justice on the murdering raider.

Kalkor had also stopped and was watching.

When the troll ended his display, Kalkor lowered his ax to touch its blade to the grass and then hurled it heavenward. It went spinning up, and up . . . higher even than the onlookers on the bank . . . it seemed to hang in the air . . . and then it began to fall, faster and faster. Kalkor reached out and caught it effortlessly, without needing to move his feet. The spectators groaned a low, grievous cry.

Could mundane human muscles have performed that miracle unaided? Inos knew just how heavy those axes were, because the casement had shown Kalkor straining to hold his out at arm's length. Yet now he was suddenly able to perform circus stunts with it?

"Sorcery!" muttered the senator's voice somewhere near Inos.

Nobody argued.

The two combatants began to advance again through the silence, more slowly this time, holding their weapons ready. They came to a halt just out of each other's reach, and perhaps they spoke then, taunting each other.

The troll moved first, with unexpected agility. Wielding his ax like a saber to take advantage of his superhuman reach and power, he made a horizontal lunge at his opponent's neck. Kalkor did not attempt to parry, nor was he foolish enough to attempt the same stroke — lacking Mord's great bulk, he would have overbalanced at once. Instead, he skipped nimbly back, holding his ax in both hands athwart his chest. The troll followed, jabbing repeatedly with the great blade. Kalkor withdrew, staying out of reach. The crowd started to jeer.

This might go on indefinitely, Inos thought. Trolls were reputed to be tireless; they had been known to work until they dropped dead.

Kalkor did not wait for that to happen, and he struck so fast that Inos had to take a moment to work out what she had just witnessed, because she had not registered the movements. The thane must have ducked and sliced upward at the troll's wrist and slipped away again before the ax could fall on him. She was not alone in her surprise — for an instant neither the onlookers nor Mord himself seemed to realize what had happened. Relieved of its burden, Mord's arm had jerked upward of its own volition. The colossus just stood there, arm raised high, staring at his life's blood hosing from the stump. Belatedly Inos closed her eyes and put her hands over her ears to shut out the animal howling rising from the spectators.

When she looked again, Kalkor was standing on the corpse, holding the great head in the air, rotating slowly so that all might see its face.

Azak whispered in her ear, "I always did want to visit the City of the Gods. We barbarians have so much to learn about *civilization.*"

3

"Give me Angilki!"

Kalkor had arrived at the base of the bank, as near to the throne as possible. He still held the great ax, and he wore the troll's lifeblood as if it were an honor. Hair, face, torso — all were joltingly red on so drab a day. The centurion had already told his men to draw, and a cordon of swords stood between the blood-soaked thane and the slope. He looked madly angry, ready to scythe through them with his ax.

Leaning forward on the throne, the regent seemed scarcely less enraged. His scheme to rid the world of the raider had been a disastrous flop. "He is not here. He is in the infirmary."

"Get him!" the thane screamed. "He should have been here! He must be fetched. He must be brought out to me so I can have my satisfaction!" He was rocking from foot to foot in his fury, barely in control of himself. "I demand his head!"

The legionaries were about as taut as longbows fully drawn. Inos had watched jotnar brawl on the streets of Krasnegar and she knew their frenzies, but she had never seen a true bloodlust before, a mad-dog ravening.

Rain was starting at last, in scattered, splashy drops. The crowd seemed to be easing back, although there were no gaps visible in it yet. The hussars were riding the lines again.

"You have won your contest," Ythbane shouted. "You are not about to murder a sick man in cold blood."

"You agreed to a Reckoning! Angilki must die!"

"Not if I can help it! There is another claimant to the throne of Krasnegar."

151

That news worked a strange magic on the thane. His gibbering wrath vanished like a snuffed candle-flame. He stilled, and his eyes traveled over the group near the throne until they settled, eerily blue even at that distance, on Inos.

"Aha!" Now Kalkor yelled in glee, and tossed the ax over his shoulder like a pinch of salt — it traveled a good ten paces. Legionaries reeled aside as he stepped forward. He ran nimbly up the bank and angled over to Inos, coming to a halt so close to her that their toes were almost touching. She could not retreat, because Azak and Eigaze and the senator were all behind her, together with several other people. Else she might have fled, screaming. She tried not to cringe before the bloody killer.

He was very big. Not quite as big as Azak, but certainly big enough to intimidate. She had to bend her head back to see his beaming smile, and the stench of blood on him made her nauseous. Fists on hips, the infamous murderer and rapist surveyed her gloatingly.

"So you have arrived, Inosolan! What a hideous mess you have made of your face. That excludes one option, anyway. And where is that raccoon-eyed faun of yours?" He glanced around, and his height let him scan the whole court party.

The courtiers were at a loss. Ythbane was seething at being thus ignored. The rain grew steadily more persistent.

Inos's whirling wits grasped onto one solid thought — Epoxague's guess had been correct. Kalkor knew of the prophecy. He even knew of Rap's tattoos, and he had picked out Inos so easily that he must have been given a detailed description of her.

He had also passed through the line of guards with no apparent effort.

"Dead! Rap's dead," Inos said, tugging her cloak around her and fighting a need to shiver. Everyone but Azak was quietly backing away from the murderous madman.

The sapphire eyes came back to hers in a flash. "Oh, that was very careless of you. You have spoiled my fun." He flashed a smile, white teeth in gory mask. "Quite sure?"

"Yes."

He accepted that without hesitation. His mood became petulant. Rain was thinning the blood on him, running in red trickles down his chest and face. "Very annoying. And who will be your champion now? Anyone worthwhile?"

"Come here, Nordlander!" Ythbane roared from the throne.

Kalkor ignored him, his glittering gaze rising to rest on Azak, who was marginally taller, but perhaps only because he was wearing boots.

"This?" The jotunn laughed scornfully. "A camel-loving djinn?"

"My wife withdraws her claim," Azak said with astonishing calm. "Keep your rotten little kingdom."

Ythbane jumped off the throne and came striding over. Praetorians rushed to follow. His wife moaned and put a hand to her mouth, staring after him. The little prince just gaped as if he were halfwitted.

Inos said, "Azak —"

"Be silent, wife! You need not challenge, Thane. She acknowledges you as King of Krasnegar."

"No, Azak!" Inos shouted. "I said I withdraw my claim only if —"

Azak roared, "*Silence!*" at Inos, just as the regent arrived beside her and Kalkor spat in her face. She cannoned back into Epoxague, shocked speechless.

"Stop!" the regent snapped. "There will be no more of this!"

Kalkor turned the ice-blue glare on him. "Hold your tongue, imp! I am a Nordland thane — violate your own safe conduct and I promise you the coasts of the Impure will burn for a generation." His bare shoulder was higher than the regent's fine plumed hat.

Shakily Inos wiped her cheek with a linen kerchief. Before either Ythbane or Azak could speak again, Lady Eigaze uttered a loud shriek from the background.

Kalkor's scowl had just come back to Inos . . . suddenly it became a broad smile.

Inos looked past him to where three people were arriving at the bottom of the slope beyond the line of legionaries: a hussar leading his horse and escorting a well-dressed elderly lady, and a . . .

It was not the hussar she saw. Nor the lady. Only the youth at the back.

Only he registered, a nondescript young man in the simple brown garb of an artisan. Bigger than an imp, smaller than a jotunn. Tangled hair already dripping wet. Stupid, stupid tattoos around his eyes.

Inos screamed, "*Rap! It's Rap! He's alive! Rap's alive!*" She jostled through between the regent and the thane and flew down the bank with her cloak streaming high behind her and her arms spread out in welcome and her feet barely touching the ground.

4

It had been late the previous evening when Rap had dropped in at the hostelry to check on Foggy and Smoky. He had spent the day in gathering news, which meant snooping, which meant applying occult charm to make people talk of what they didn't necessarily want to discuss. What they did want to discuss — particularly some of the women — had often shocked him considerably.

The task had left him feeling cheap and soiled, and the only relevant thing he had learned was that Kalkor was in Hub. Impossible, but confirmed by many.

153

He had found the ponies well content, being tended by a young faun stableboy, who had mostly wanted to know how Rap had managed to grow so big. When that had been explained, he had passed on a dramatic new story about a battle scheduled for the following day.

By the time Rap returned to the house, Andor had just arrived with much the same information, and everyone was talking at once, on a variety of topics.

Gathmor, of course, was gloating. Kalkor was in town, and Gathmor had a wife and children to avenge.

The princess was puzzled and fretting, because there was no word of Inosolan. If the Impire had recognized Angilki as King of Krasnegar, then where was Inos?

Andor was adamant — tomorrow's spectacle was no place for him, nor his friends, either. "The crowds will be immense!" he insisted. "People will get trampled and crushed. I am not going, and neither are any of you! It is madness."

Rap was feeling the cold fingers of premonition on his skin. He knew that he at least was going to be there. "What do you want, ma'am?" he asked the princess. There was no doubt what she wanted.

But what she said was, "Advise me, please, Master Rap?"

Foresight he dared not use. He had been two days in Hub now, and the fearful white horror must be very near now. But he thought about going and then about not going, and he compared his premonitions. He sensed danger, yes, and dark menace, but behind all that there was something new — a pure, high note of joy like the song of a flute. It could only be Inos, seeing Inos, and it squeezed his heart and hurt his eyelids.

"I think we should go, ma'am," he said.

"We shall go, then," she agreed happily.

And Gathmor? No need to ask him.

"Not me!" Andor said.

"Darad. I think."

"And I will not call Darad! Not in Hub."

"Darad!" Rap insisted, and despised the mean satisfaction he gained from seeing Andor flinch.

So it was decided.

Gathmor was content with his footman's livery, but finding clothes that would fit Darad was a problem, and Rap himself wanted some inconspicuous, noncommittal garments. Clothes produced by magic might attract occult attention. He took a lesson in sewing from the princess, and sat up most of the night, tailoring as if he had apprenticed to the trade for years.

By morning Gathmor was in a rapturous state of mind that Rap distrusted. He tried halfheartedly to dissuade the sailor from coming, but without using power on him the effort was wasted. What bothered Rap most was the dagger concealed in Gathmor's doublet, although an opportunity to strike at Kalkor seemed highly improbable and Rap could always magic the weapon away if it seemed likely to be used. Kalkor had occult powers of his own, and no mere mundane sailor was going to end his career.

And Darad was no more trustworthy, for he also had a score to settle with the savage thane.

They left at dawn, yet despite Rap's peerless control the carriage became stalled in traffic and crowds a long way from the Campus Abnila. Reluctantly leaving the horses in the care of a couple of shifty-eyed youths, he set out on foot with his friends.

Darad's great bulk was a help, but more valuable still was the constant tremor of magic that seemed to infest the capital like a winter dog. It was even more in evidence than usual, so obviously Rap was not the only wielder of power striving to reach the arena. There might be occult cutpurses around also, working the crowd as Thinal would. Seers would be trying to lay bets.

Rap used as little mastery as possible, but he gradually cleared a way for himself and the others. Large men moved aside without quite knowing why they did so, and step by step the princess and her escorts fought their way up the outside of the bank, and across the top, and then down the interior slope, until they had a prime location directly behind the arm-linked cordon of soldiers, close to one of the two little tents. The troll was in there, Rap knew.

And that was as far as they could go. Now all that remained was to wait until the regent's party arrived and the duel began.

The royal enclosure was empty at first and then gradually filled. Suddenly Rap's heart began to beat much faster . . .

"Surely I am not mistaken," Princess Kadolan said. "Is that not the sultan? And Inos!"

Over the past few weeks, Rap had been gently curing her shortsightedness, but so subtly that she had not been aware of his meddling. Her back pains had gone, too, and she had not missed those, either.

"Can't be certain," Gathmor grunted. Jotunn eyesight was legendary, a handy trait for sailors, but Rap's farsight was now well beyond the limits of mundane perception.

"Yes, it is," he muttered. Tragedy! He could cure those awful scars, but to do so at such a distance would be difficult, and dangerous for him. He would do it, of course, but later, when he could get closer. He would do it for her sake — he didn't care what she looked like, only what she was.

Her misfortunes had not broken her spirit; her star burned brighter than ever. Inos! Oh, Inos!

More than anything he wished he had been able to tell her, just once, how he loved her; how he always had. He couldn't tell her now.

155

Inos, married.

Standing close to her big, handsome djinn.

Being presented to the regent.

Rap did not eavesdrop on what was said, although he could have done so. He just watched glumly.

Then the antique trumpets brayed, and battle was joined. It was disgusting. Kalkor used magic. Rap felt the ambience shake as the ax whirled skyward and again during the thane's murderous attack. He had known Kalkor was a seer, and had suspected even back on *Blood Wave* that the raider had more than one word of power. Obviously he knew at least three, to be able to control his weapon in the air like that and so easily penetrate the gladiator's guard . . .

Why not? Words of power were a form of wealth. They could be looted like anything else. The troll had never had a hope.

Kalkor disabled him and then chopped him down like a tree and jeered at him as he bled to death. Then butchered him. Finally he went stalking toward the imperial enclosure, still bearing his ax. So this was the ritual savagery that he had once described to Rap as a sacred ritual?

Gathmor and Darad had begun to twitch with bloodlust of their own, and Rap regretfully laid a trance on both of them, so that they just stood and smiled vaguely at nothing. That was safer for them, he told himself angrily. By the time it wore off, the thane would be long gone elsewhere.

The weary fence of legionaries still struggled against the press of the crowd, because they had orders to do that. The fancy young men on horses were moving around again.

"Ah!" the princess said. "That tall one on the gray, Master Rap! You see? He visited Kinvale last Winterfest — he knows me! Can you make him come this way?"

"Yes, ma'am," Rap said.

It was time.

*   *   *

Pilgrim soul:
> How many loved your moments of glad grace,
> And loved your beauty with love false or true,
> But one man loved the pilgrim soul in you,
> And loved the sorrows of your changing face.
>   Yeats, *When You Are Old*

7

Whispered word

1

The legionaries had already opened a gap; Inos ran through it. She went by the hussar and his horse, she ignored the astonished Kade, leaving her with hands raised and smile wasted . . .

She would probably have thrown her arms around Rap and very likely have kissed him, except that she seemed to stumble into an unseen feather bolster that brought her to an unexpected, gasping halt. His eyes were big and gray and unreadable.

"Rap!"

"Hello, Inos."

"Oh, Rap, Rap! I'm so glad to see you!"

"Me, too. To see you."

"You're well?"

"Yes. You?"

"Fine."

Why were they whispering?

157

"Rap, I thought you were dead again . . . Oh, Gods!" She laughed. "I mean, again I thought you were dead."

Alive! Rap was alive!

He was not smiling, not even that bashful little grin she remembered so well. He had not bowed to her, as he had at their other dramatic meetings. He was just regarding her with a wistful sad stare, as if trying to fix her in his memory.

"No. Not dead. Not yet, anyway. How was your journey?"

"Fine — no it wasn't. Horrible! Yours?"

"Not bad."

They were standing in the rain, staring, mouthing nonsense like morons. Or she was, anyway, and why was he so solemn?

"How did you come?" she asked. "I mean, did you come by sorcery, or really travel, like ordinary folk?"

Argh! She should not have said that.

"I traveled. With your aunt. And Sagorn. And Gathmor, but you don't know him."

No need to ask *why* he had come. The God had told her that. "Not the goblin? Sagorn and the others, of course. You all survived the imps, then . . . Oh, Rap! I do so want to hear it all."

"Inos, I think we're keeping some important people waiting."

She backed away a step. He looked like Rap and sounded like Rap, and yet somehow he didn't, either. "You are Rap? Really Rap? Not a wraith, or some horrid magic trick? Azak said you were dead. He said awful, terrible things and I believed him and oh, I'm so glad you're all right and how did you escape from the jail?"

"That's a long story."

His face hardened. There was a strange, unfamiliar strength there, and no sparkle in the big gray eyes. He had changed. But so had she — they weren't children anymore.

"You are Rap, though?"

"I'm Rap. And Azak . . . Well, never mind Azak."

"Rap, what's wrong? There's something wrong, isn't there?" She could not see what could possibly be wrong now. Rap was alive, and she wasn't ever going to believe him dead again unless she saw his head on a pike, and — "Oh, Gods! Of course! Kalkor's here, Rap!"

He nodded. "I know that."

"The casement . . . Did you meet a dragon, Rap?"

"Yes, I did. Here's your aunt, Inos."

Belatedly Inos spun around to Kade and embraced her. If she couldn't hug Rap, then Kade was next best thing, maybe.

But Rap had been right. Monarchs did not enjoy being kept waiting, and they could send armed men. Ythbane did so, and in a minute Inos found herself being firmly escorted back up the bank, and then standing between Azak and Kade under the awning, although the shower had almost ended. Kalkor was in the group, also, snow-white teeth shining within a pink-streaked face, studying her with a contented smile that struck her as completely insane.

And Rap. They weren't all lined up before the throne like errant children, but she felt as if they should be. Epoxague was in the group and even Eigaze, although she was hardly involved, and even the unfortunate hussar who had agreed to bring Kade over. He looked more frightened than any of them.

Then Kade was formally presented by Eigaze, which explained why she was included. The court party was now clearly divided into those involved in the Krasnegar affair and the great majority who weren't, and most of those outsiders were perforce standing outside the awning, openly scowling at this new symbol of status.

The little prince was staring at his own shoe buckles, shivering and ignoring events all together.

Ythbane nodded in approval of Kade. "Yes, the reports all mentioned that Inosolan was accompanied by her aunt. Obviously you have had some strange adventures, ma'am."

Kade simpered, which completely concealed whatever she might be thinking. "But none more exciting than this moment, your Highness!"

Formalities disposed of, she was waved back. The white-faced hussar was explained and excused, and he departed with very long strides. The regent fixed a bleak eye on Epoxague.

"Well, your Eminence? Have you any further surprises left to brighten our day?"

"No, your Highness," Epoxague said. "I am being surprised myself now."

"You may be more surprised yet," Ythbane retorted sourly. "This is hardly the place . . . " For a moment his attention went to the great crowd around the campus. It was obviously thinning out now. Some ominous clusters of activity hinted at casualties being attended, but there had been no disaster. Yet the roads would not become passable again for a while yet. He shrugged.

"But we might as well get started. And who is this young man? A goblin supporter, obviously. A faun?" He glance around. "Jotnar and a djinn. A troll! We have a motley assortment of participants!"

Kade spoke up quickly. "His name is Rap, your Highness, a retainer of my late brother's. He has been accompanying me on my travels."

Oh, very neatly done! The regent nodded and lost interest in Rap. How fortunate that Inos had not embraced him!

But why had Inos not embraced him? She had spread her arms and then been somehow distracted, or stopped. Had Rap done that? That called for sorcery, surely. And he had not said how he had escaped from Azak's jail, although obviously Azak's horrible story had been a basket of lies. This strange melancholy . . . was Rap oppressed by the thought of the duel with Kalkor? She knew she must not keep staring at him, but her eyes wouldn't listen to her. Rap himself seemed to be studying the old imperor, who slept on in his carrying chair, a shriveled relic swathed in a tasseled wool rug, oblivious now to all events in the great realm he had ruled for so long.

"Sultana Inosolan!" Ythbane fixed her with a glittery gaze, and she jumped. She was suddenly aware that the regent's reported influence on women was no myth. Small, and not especially handsome, he was yet dominating the assembled court much more than a mere throne ought to account for, or all his jewels and finery. Despite that absurd wooden chair and the ugly canopy above his head, he was projecting power and dignity. No one else was talking. Only Kalkor seemed unimpressed, silently observing proceedings with a silent sneer on his demonic and grotesquely bloody features.

"Sultana Inosolan," the regent repeated thoughtfully. "We can agree on that title, surely?"

Inos hesitated. Azak shot her one of his lion glares, but she resisted it. Rap was alive, after all, and now she knew that Azak had always been a delusion. Perhaps she had not been very fair to Azak, but then he had not been fair to her at all. Her consent to the marriage had been extracted by open threat.

Always she had assumed that Rap was dead, so she had never even considered him — not since her father died, anyway . . .

No, that was not true. She had *never* thought of Rap as a lover. She had never allowed herself to think of him that way, for he had been only a stableboy and all her upbringing had insisted that she would have to marry a noble. That had been her great error. Only after he had turned up alive in Arakkaran had she realized how she felt about him, and then it had seemed too late. But it wasn't too late! Rap was alive, and her marriage to Azak had never been consummated. It wasn't a valid marriage yet.

To bring that up now would really put the wolves in the fold.

A lifetime with Azak? No — a lifetime with Rap!

Evil take her upbringing!

Her mind was wandering like a songbird escaped from a cage.

"Your Highness?" she said, trying to school her face into Kade's most witless expression, feeling even more witless under it.

Ythbane's eyes narrowed. "You can hardly expect to be both Queen of Krasnegar and Sultana of Arakkaran. Which is it to be?"

"Er . . . " Inos looked up again at Azak's murderous stare. Then she turned to look at Rap, and for a moment saw . . . Then it was gone. His face became completely unreadable. What had she seen? Pain? Longing? He had crossed the world to be at her side, and now come halfway back again. Surely she need not doubt what Rap wanted?

She was descended from a long line of kings. She raised her throbbing chin defiantly. "Your Highness, my husband wishes to appeal to the Council of Four. Until they have heard his petition and rendered judgment, then I cannot decide where my best interests lie."

"Ha!" Kalkor crowed. "She does not recognize me as King of Krasnegar!"

"You be silent!" Ythbane shouted. He glanced around. "Where is he? Ambassador Krushjor! Come and remove this naked savage. Wash him and clothe him decently, or throw him back in his cage if you prefer, but get him out of my —"

"Watch your tongue, upstart!" Kalkor snarled. "Does this female recognize me as King of Krasnegar? For if not, then I challenge her to a Reckoning."

"You'll do no such thing!" Ythbane shouted. "We have had quite enough of that murderous nonsense."

Azak's harsh djinn voice boomed out. "Your Imperial Highness, the jotunn assaulted my wife in your presence. Can you not apply suitable discipline?"

The court drew breath at the effrontery. Ythbane's pallid face flushed bright. "Unfortunately, not easily. He has diplomatic immunity. We could have him shipped across the border in fetters, and that is beginning to seem like a very good idea."

"There is a prophecy," Kalkor said.

Ythbane looked startled. "What prophecy? Prophesied by whom?"

"Ask the woman."

Everyone looked back at Inos.

"My ancestor, the Sorcerer Inisso," she said, "— he left a magic casement in his tower in Krasnegar. It prophesied for me. It prophesied that Thane Kalkor would fight a duel, a Reckoning."

"He just did," the regent snapped. The Kalkor affair was entangling his court like a net, and his anger was both obvious and understandable.

It was also starting to make Inos jumpy, or perhaps it was all the eyes on her doing that, although that was even sillier. "Not against a t-troll. And for me. In the p-p-prophecy, his opponent —"

"Magic casements do not prophesy," Rap said.

Now all eyes went to him.

"And what do you know about magic casements, young man?" the regent growled.

"I have some power," Rap admitted.

The watchers quivered. Suddenly, although no one visibly moved, there was a gap around him. Even Inos felt a shiver of alarm — Rap had met a dragon, and dragons belonged to the warlock of the south. It had been Lith'rian who had sent him to Arakkaran. Who or what was this strangely somber Rap?

He was Rap, wasn't he? Really Rap?

Kalkor broke the silence with a chuckle that raised the little hairs on the back of her neck. "He is the one I fight."

"We want no more Reckonings," the regent said, but he sounded less confident than before.

For a moment there seemed to be an impasse, as if no one knew what should happen next. The crowds were leaving, streaming over the bank and out of sight; the legionaries were falling out and slumping on the sodden grass to rub their shoulders and mutter curses. The rain was starting again.

And Inos was thinking furiously. The casement had shown Rap fighting Kalkor, and then it had shown him dying in the goblin's lodge. If he did fight Kalkor, then he survived, surely? Of course she didn't want Rap to die at all, but if both prophecies were inevitable, then she couldn't do anything to stop them. And if they weren't inevitable, then she wanted to let this one happen and stop the second. That was logical, wasn't it?

If he didn't fight Kalkor, then she was going to have to yield her kingdom to the thane. She could not bear the thought of the decent, humble folk of Krasnegar being handed over to that monster.

And as if he could read her thoughts —

"Do you recognize me as King of Krasnegar?" Kalkor asked, blue eyes mocking.

"No!" Inos said.

"Then, by the God of Truth, I —"

"Stop!" the regent shouted. "We have had one murder committed here today, and we want . . . want to make it perfectly clear that . . . " He paused. Then his voice dropped. "That, if there is indeed a prophecy, then we are going to have another."

Senior courtiers hid astonishment behind well-trained nods. Ythbane drew himself up on his throne, scowling. The lesser onlookers glanced at one another in worried surmise. A whirl of wind napped cloaks and buffeted the awning. The shower drummed harder on it.

"But who will be the lady's champion?" Kalkor asked with a cynical smile. "Sultan Azak?"

Azak's face flamed dark mahogany. "Not me!"

"He spat on your wife," the regent said.

The sultan glared murder at him, but he folded his arms and kept himself under control. "Not me. I care nothing for Krasnegar."

So where now was the overbearing bully-boy of Arakkaran? Where was his prickly djinn honor? Inos felt her lip curl in contempt, and did not care who might notice.

Yet she did not understand what was happening. Only Kalkor seemed to know that.

"You will hire no more trolls," the regent said. "Not after what happened to Mord. If we allow this affair to proceed, then who will be your champion, lady?"

"Rap?" she whispered.

Rap said, "No."

Ythbane glanced from Kalkor to Rap and back again, as if he had had a sudden understanding. "Is sorcery permitted in Reckonings?"

"Certainly not," Kalkor said.

"Then, Sultana, we think you had best yield to Thane Kalkor before it is too late."

The bystanders had caught the hint. Kalkor had felled the Impire's best gladiator like a blind farmhand, and this strange young faun had admitted to being a sorcerer.

If not the faun, then who else could accept the match?

Kade's gentle voice intervened. "Master Rap —"

Rap said, "No."

Inos clenched her fists. She knew Rap's stubborn look, and there it was. "Not for me, Rap. Think of the people of Krasnegar!"

He shot her a glance of pure agony, then set his big jaw again. He said, "No," again.

The wind thumped the awning, and the patter of raindrops speeded up. A few groups of citizens still lingered, chattering or watching the royals in their compound, but the great crowds had gone from the grassy bank, leaving it tattered and muddy. The legionaries were forming up in their cohorts.

"This is so disappointing!" Kalkor said, with a sneer. "Master Rap, what of your destiny?"

Rap said, "No."

"Well, perhaps I can reassure you. Krushjor!"

The jotnar were huddled at the rear of the enclosure, well back from the awning, being spurned by the gentry. Now the old ambassador stepped forward a pace and called, "Thane?"

"Send over our most recent recruit."

"Now what?" demanded the regent suspiciously.

Bloodsoaked and half naked, Kalkor bowed low, more in mockery than respect. "One of the persons included in your Imperial safe conduct, Highness. An old friend of Master Rap's."

The jotnar had opened their ranks to release a short, broad youth. He wore impish garments, but he was certainly no imp.

Inos glanced back at Rap. If Kalkor had hoped to elicit some emotion from him, he had failed. Rap watched without expression as the newcomer walked forward. But even back in Krasnegar Rap had possessed farsight. He must have known who had been hidden in there.

Khaki skin, lank black hair . . . straggly bristles around an oversized mouth spread now in a gruesome smile . . . teeth like white daggers. He was about the shortest person present, except for the prince, but very thick and burly. This was the same young goblin Inos had seen with Rap before, the one Rap had said wanted to kill him. The one who did kill him in the casement's vision. She had forgotten his name.

Courtiers cleared out of his way with glances of distaste.

"Hello, Flat Nose." Angular eyes gleamed.

"Hello, Little Chicken," Rap said evenly. "I sort of expected you would turn up soon."

The big grin grew wider yet. "The witch gave me a promise!"

"You would be a strong swimmer, I expect; once you learned."

The goblin nodded cheerfully.

"Would someone care to explain?" Ythbane said in a dangerously low voice. "Witch?"

Rap shrugged. "It is another prophecy, your Highness. The anthropophagi tried to eat him, but I expect he was too tough for them."

The goblin chortled and the regent flushed furiously.

"We have taken all the insolence we will tolerate. This court will adjourn to the palace, and we will have some real answers if it takes hot irons to get them."

"But we have a challenge to consider," Kalkor's mild protest stilled the fidgeting courtiers. "We were trying to stiffen the faun's backbone. You did meet the dragon, I suppose?" he asked of Rap.

"Yes."

"I thought you would. And yet you distrust the casement? Such a shocking lack of faith! Or are you trying to break the chain before our green friend gets his hands on you?"

Rap said, "No."

"What then of your great love for Inosolan? — the love you confessed to me so touchingly when we had that delightful chat on my ship?"

Rap said, "No," a little louder than before.

Oh, Rap, Rap!

"And where is the courage you displayed so convincingly last summer? Where is the hero who tried to sink me and my crew?"

The onlookers drew breath in surprise.

Rap said, "No."

"Afraid, Master Rap?"

Rap looked down at the turf and said, "Yes!"

"Truly, I am chagrined!" Kalkor's sapphire eyes danced with mockery. He turned and stared thoughtfully at the arena, almost empty of civilians now. The legionaries were forming up, preparing to leave also.

Again Inos noted the little prince beside the throne. He was very pale, and shaking as if he had a fever. The mute stare he was directing at his mother seemed to hold some sort of appeal, but she was hunched in her chair, sulking and paying no attention to anyone. Had she no concern for her son's health? And why would a boy of his age not be more interested in this talk of fighting and sorcery? Was he halfwitted? Had Epoxague been hinting at that this morning?

Kalkor sighed, regarding Rap again with his habitual contempt. "I suppose I shall just have to bear my sorrows and accept the responsibility of kingship so harshly thrust upon my reluctant shoulders. Here, then, my friend — a remembrance! A parting gift."

With a flick of his hand, he tossed something across the group to Rap, as if playing catch.

Apparently without thinking, Rap reached out and caught it . . . whatever it was . . .

Something red.

Something about the size of a closed fist . . .

Rap yelped and leaped back, dropping the strange object as if it had burned him. He vanished, completely. Courtiers cried out and recoiled in alarm from the empty spot where the faun had stood.

The gift, whatever it was, had vanished also, but the grass there was spotted with blood.

Ythbane leaped to his feet. "What was that?" he barked. "What's happening?"

Kalkor moved his rain-streaked shoulders in an exaggerated shrug. "I really have no idea, your Highness. Apparently Master Rap has been called away by urgent business. A friend unexpectedly taken sick, most like." He chuckled gutturally.

The regent was clearly at a loss, and the onlookers flinched as realization came to them also — there had been two evident sorceries. The faun had vanished, but the jotunn had thrown something that he had not been holding only moments before, and he certainly had no pockets in that tatter of fur he wore.

Then Rap was back. The courtiers surged away again, isolating the two antagonists. Rap's face had turned sallow and his eyes bulged. He stared at the thane and made choking noises.

Kalkor sighed. "Not literally a heart of gold, of course, but I'm sure he had many admirable qualities."

"Monster!" Rap cried, his voice breaking. "Demon of Evil!"

"Flattery will avail you naught. Spare me your unseemly protestations of gratitude."

"Heartless monster!"

"Heartless?" Kalkor repeated, looking hurt. "Oh, no! Not me! Him, yes, but what would you expect of a mere sailor? You didn't try to put it back, did you?"

Rap turned on Inos, and she cringed before the unexplained horror she saw in him.

"All right!" he shouted. "I'll do it! Take his challenge and I'll kill the swine for you!"

He spun on his heel and ran.

"You!" Ythbane yelled, starting. "Come back here! Guards — catch that man!"

Praetorians jerked into motion. Courtiers scattered.

Chasing him would do no good, Inos knew. Not if Rap was now a sorcerer. "Inos!"

She glanced down at Kade, who was staring at her with obvious joy. "Your cheeks, dear!"

Inos raised fingers to the cosmetic flaking from her face, and there was no soreness there at all.

2

The afternoon seemed to go on forever.

When Ythbane selected his victims, Inos was first on the list. She was shipped off to the palace in a very bouncy coach, accompanied by three steely-eyed legionaries who refused to talk, or explain, or answer questions of any kind.

The Opal Palace was world famous, but she was taken in through a back door and hence saw nothing to impress her. Then she was left in a room of blank walls and hard benches where her jailors were now women, built like basalt basilisks, and no more interested in conversation.

Of course emperors and their replacements were dangerous persons to offend, and Inos knew she was in considerable danger. She discovered that it did not seem to matter very much. If they boiled her toes, they could not

166

spoil this day for her. Rap was alive and well! Nothing else mattered. Let Azak worry about his curse, and Arakkaran, and the stupid war. He could go home alone and chase goats all day for the rest of his life — and breed sons all night, for that matter — and Inos would not care if he didn't even say good-bye.

Kade had escaped, too, and that was wonderful, but the big thing was that Rap lived, and he loved her. He had cured her burns. He would be her champion at the Reckoning. Rap was a sorcerer! Indeed Rap seemed to be able to work miracles, and she would never doubt him again, nor doubt the power of love.

She had likely been sequestered to give her time to worry herself into a panic. In fact, she had indulged in an hour or so of dreamy contemplation when she was taken off to be questioned by the regent himself. He was obviously in a foul temper. With half a dozen secretaries taking notes, she talked and talked and talked. She had no secrets to conceal, nothing to keep back. Ythbane himself paced the floor like a caged animal, and did not suggest that she might wish to sit. He was a shrewd interrogator; he had a very powerful personality. She did not think she could have held back anything had she wanted to.

But she had nothing to hide. Did she love this Rap boy? Yes. Had it been he who healed her scars? Who else? Did she want to go back to Arakkaran? Never. Did she want, hope, expect to become Queen of Krasnegar? If it would benefit the people, yes; otherwise no. Where was Rap now? She had no idea. Would he turn up to fight Kalkor at noon the next day? Certainly! He had said he would, and he had always been reliable.

At last Ythbane sent her away, demanding that Kade be brought in next. Inos was returned to her cell, but three of the men she had thought to be secretaries came with her, and they began the questioning all over again. Hunting for inconsistencies, they took her through her story three times more — twice forward and once back — until her head ached and she could barely croak.

The early dark of winter had already fallen when she was rescued by a messenger from the regent. At last she was allowed to wash her face and freshen up. She thought she might have won a battle, somehow, or that Ythbane had lost one.

She was escorted to a delightful pink-and-gold drawing room, where Kade and Eigaze sat by a cheerfully crackling fire, cheerfully sipping scalding green tea from exquisite porcelain cups and nibbling tiny sandwiches. Inos collapsed into a very soft chair and stared at them in disbelief.

"A slice of lemon, dear?" said Kade. "Do have something to eat. Try the cucumber ones. Do you suppose the cucumber is *occult* at this time of year?"

"Imported from Pithmot, I expect," Eigaze said, "but I still think the fresh, local ones have more flavor."

Rap! Come and rescue me from these maniacs! "No cucumber for me," Inos said. "It makes my nose shiny."

Eigaze switched targets in midreach and went for the watercress instead.

"Well, do eat something, dear," Kade said. "We may have a long night ahead of us."

Inos gulped the hot tea gratefully. "Tell me!"

Kade beamed. "The wardens! His Highness has decided to invoke the Four, and we are to visit Emine's Rotunda and attend! Isn't it exciting?"

"And so rare!" Eigaze exclaimed. "Outsiders are very rarely admitted when the Four are called. You are greatly honored."

"We are to be fitted for our gowns very shortly!"

Honored? Exciting? Inos drained her cup. *Rap! Quickly!*

3

Kade was squeezing Inos's hand very tightly. But then Inos was squeezing her, also, as they walked together through the gloom.

Emine's Rotunda might not be as large overall as the Great Hall in Arakkaran, but it was certainly large enough to humble anyone, and no internal pillars marred its wide expanse. Whether the fabled Emine had ever set eyes on it was unknown — it was old beyond record. Tradition said that sorcery had built it; only sorcery could have preserved it since the shadowy dawn times of the Impire. It smelled old. It was filled with curious little echoes and dark whisperings. Somewhere overhead was the famous dome, with its soaring stone ribs and crystal windows, but on a rainy night like this there was nothing to be seen up there but impenetrable blackness.

In the center stood a forest of giant candelabra, each one twice the height of a man, branched like a golden tree with blossoms of fire and fruits of crystal. Inos wondered how many servants had taken how long to light so many hundred candles. Yet each gold tree stood on its own plot of brightness, with shadow seeping in between them — the Rotunda was just too big to illuminate properly. Beyond the enchanted glade the darkness lurked unharmed. The banked seating around the walls was barely visible, still and empty, and the roof remained a mystery. Whatever drama was to be played, this was quite the creepiest setting Inos had ever seen; Rasha's dome in Arakkaran had been a country kitchen by comparison.

When she arrived with Kade, half a dozen men were already present, wearing military uniforms or crisp white togas. Others came drifting in behind her, and a couple wearing red togas were necessarily senators. Another sported a purple border and would be one of the consuls. They stood in groups, muttering together in low voices — she had already noticed that all the imps in Hub, even the oldest, held themselves in stiff-backed soldier style. She did not recognize any of them, but she caught some glancing in her direction.

She would have felt slighted had they not. She and Kade had been hastily fitted out with white chitons. They felt like costumes for a masquerade ball — probably because, like togas, they were garments normally seen only on statues or in historical lithographs. The folds clung to her body, and her arms were bare. Chitons were not unlike nightgowns, and whereas Kade's was woolen, warm, and matronly, hers was sheer enough to be unpleasant on this damp, cool evening. Men had just better look!

Two women entered wearing red chitons. They were both elderly, of course. More men in uniform: proconsuls, and a tribune.

She noticed a newcomer staring at her, a man in an especially impressive uniform. His breastplate was inlaid with gold, and the horsehair crest on his helmet was scarlet. She thought back to a lecture that Proconsul Ygginggi had given her once at Kinvale, and decided that this must be the marshal of the armies. She could not recall his name, but it was short . . . Ishy, maybe? . . . something like that. He looked tough, but not unpleasant. She turned her gaze elsewhere so he could admire her profile also.

She found herself staring at the Opal Throne.

Of course all this playacting and the whole great building — everything was designed to draw attention to one spot, the center. Unconsciously she had been fighting back, perversely refusing to look where she was supposed to look. Like a rabbit ignoring a snake, in the hope that it would just go away.

The heart of power. It was a wide and ugly thing in itself, squatting on a two-step circular dais and lit by two candelabra of its own. This was the imperor's chair, the seat of power, the hub of Hub, the navel of the world. She assumed that by day it flamed brightly. Under the candles it was mostly black, glowing here and there with baleful embers, crawling hints of blood and gold, grass and sky; restless stains of ancient evils. She thought of a dreaming dragon asleep on a hoard of candlelight.

From that potent center radiated four points of color, inset in the gray granite of the floor. The four-point star, symbol of the realm. Each triangle stretched out into the encircling darkness — yellow, white, red, and blue. Where each would narrow to nothing stood another throne on a single-step dais. Those must be the thrones of the wardens, and each had a single candelabrum right behind it, shedding its own isolated puddle of light.

The Opal Throne was facing toward one that Inos recognized, in a stunning flash of memory. It glittered gold below the many fires of its candelabrum. She knew who would sit there.

Despite her cynical desire to scorn such theatricals, she was impressed. A large part of the history that packed so many books in her father's library had been brewed right here, in this great antique chamber, on these five thrones. Oceans of blood had flowed from this spring. The chill and damp were raising chickenflesh on her arms, but the awesome scent of raw power was certainly helping.

Suddenly Azak came striding in, taller than anyone, and accompanied by the tiny form of Senator Epoxague. They were an ill-assorted couple, both clad in togas, one white, one red. Surely Azak had never worn such an absurd garment before, or ever dreamed of doing so, and yet she could not help but note how good he looked in it. His bare right forearm was ropy with muscle, and his hair was burnished copper and gold in the candlelight. At his side, the old senator seemed frail and scrawny, almost pitiful. Poor man! He had risked his career for her, and might be going to pay a heavy price for that kindness.

Azak had seen her, and came to her, looking her over carefully — especially her chin and her newly healed cheeks.

"You are well, my love?"

"I am, sir."

He frowned at that, and then looked to Kade. "And you, ma'am?"

Kade bobbed a small curtsy. "Very well, your Majesty."

"I have not yet heard how you departed from Arakkaran, nor how you brought Master Rap with you."

Kade flaunted her daftest simper. "The regent himself asked me the same question. I explained that I had obligations to others that prevented me from answering that."

Trust Kade to defy even Ythbane!

And Azak, also! The giant flushed angrily, but he did not pursue the matter. Here he was a guest, not a despot.

"We are very grateful to your Eminence," Inos told the senator.

He smiled wryly. "Imps regard family ties as important, Inos."

"I shall never forget," she said.

He sighed. "It was unfortunate that we did not manage to stop the duel. I fear much trouble will flow from that."

Just then Kalkor himself came stalking in, accompanied by Ambassador Krushjor. Their jotunnish garb of leather breeches and boots was a defiance of the cold; their pale hair shone gold under iron helmets. They glanced around contemptuously and then chose a location where they would see all five thrones, as everyone else had done.

At their heels, as if in attendance on them, came the young goblin, and now he also was wearing jotunn garb, his skin shining much more obviously green under the candles. No one would ever suggest putting a goblin in a

170

toga, and he was not a diplomat who could sport his own ethnic costume. Goblins' ethnic costume was likely even less respectable than jotnar's.

In a moment Little Chicken noticed Inos, and his angular eyes widened slightly. Then he grinned toothily at her. She very much wanted to have a chat with that young man, to learn why he now consorted with jotnar, and how he and Rap had escaped from Inisso's chamber. But to go near Kalkor would be to beg for trouble. It would also provoke Azak into a foaming fit.

From time to time Inos recited to herself a little speech she had composed, explaining how her marriage was not valid and she now wished to have it annulled. The logic had seemed quite convincing at first. It felt frailer near Azak, somehow.

A quartet of bearers brought in the old imperor, laying his chair beside the central dais. Oh, that poor old man! Why could they not let him die in peace? The bearers departed.

That would seem to be everyone, Inos thought.

She was right — in the distance a door thudded closed, and a moment later Ythbane strode in from the darkness, heading for the Opal Throne. He wore a purple toga, but there was a small bronze shield on his arm, and he carried a short sword in his right hand. Behind him came hurried the spindly little prince, looking both cute and pathetic in his toga. He stared straight ahead, ignoring everyone. His mother was not present.

The regent mounted the two steps to his throne and turned to look over the company. The prince went up one step and then around to the right of the throne. He turned also, and then seemed to freeze, like a statue.

The kid ought to be in bed, Inos thought angrily. Didn't the Impire know how to look after its future rulers?

"Sultan Azak!" Ythbane proclaimed. "Are you prepared to present your petition to the four wardens, occult preservers of justice within all Pandemia?"

"I am." Azak's voice was deeper, and harsher.

"Then we invoke the Council of Four on your behalf, as is our ancient right and obligation." Ythbane raised his sword, and all eyes turned expectantly toward the gold throne.

Clank!

Well! Inos doubted that even a warlock could hear that silly little noise all the way from the Gold Palace.

For a moment nothing happened. No one seemed to breath. The Gold Throne remained empty below its shimmering candelabrum.

Then the flames in that golden tree shrank and died, and went out. The throne faded away into the darkness, still empty.

The spectators looked back to Ythbane. His mouth hung open, and even the prince below him was showing a similar astonishment.

171

Obviously the regent was at a loss. His eyes sought out a couple of the senators, as if seeking guidance. If the Right of Appeal had not been exercised for a hundred years, no one would be an authority on procedures. Had someone forgotten something?

Setting his jaw, Ythbane strode around to his left, so that he faced the Blue Throne, the seat of Warlock Lith'rian. He raised the sword again. Before he could use it, the same invisible fingers snuffed those candles also, and the Blue Throne vanished away into the night.

The wardens were rejecting his call.

Inos peered around: Azak, darkly furious . . . the regent even more so . . . the dumbfounded audience . . . Kalkor showing all his teeth and enjoying the drama . . . the little prince wide-eyed . . . Or was the kid trying to stifle a smirk?

Before the regent could move, the candles over the White Throne of the north throne glimmered and died also.

"Too bad!" a heavy, sepulchral voice said.

The Red Throne of the west remained lit, an ugly monstrosity of granite carved in bas-relief. There was a boy sitting on it.

The regent went around to the back of the Opal Throne and bowed. "Your Omnipotence does me honor."

"I don't mean to."

Not a boy — a young man. One day at Kinvale, Andor had taken Inos to visit the duke's slate quarry. The dwarves she had seen there had all been very short, with massive shoulders and heads, and complexions like gray sandstone. Despite his youth, Zinixo's hair was iron gray. He must be shorter even than the goblin, Little Chicken, for his feet looked as if they did not quite reach down to the floor. Although his thick forearms rested on the sides of the throne, the position was awkward for him, hunching his shoulders up near his ears. His toga was the mysterious dark red of iron cooling on a smith's anvil. He seemed to be wearing no tunic below it, for his right arm and shoulder were bare; so were his overlarge feet.

He bared a mouthful of teeth like white pebbles. "You're too early, Regent. Too impatient! Try us —" The grating voice stopped, and he cocked his big head, as if listening to something. His eyes were restless, furtive. Inos remembered what Epoxague had said about dwarves being cagey and distrustful. They were also reputed to be mean-spirited and avaricious.

Either the little prince could no longer bear not being able to see the warlock, or else he decided that he should not have his back to him. Whatever his reason, he spun around to face the other way and then went very still again.

Zinixo apparently decided that there was nothing amiss and resumed his smirk. "Try us again tomorrow, mongrel."

A sorcerer insulting a mundane that way was rather like a boy torturing an insect. Maybe Olybino was not so bad as Inos had thought.

Ythbane flinched at the gibe, but his voice stayed level. "You will hear the sultan's petition then?"

The dwarf laughed with a sound like millstones. "No! He won't trouble us. But there will be other problems. In fact, you weren't even going to ask the right question tonight."

Ythbane had his back to the watchers, but that taunt made him stiffen visibly. "What should we have been going to ask, your Omnipotence?"

The warlock glanced over the company and then pointed a finger in a gesture that would have poked a hole in an oak door. "Ask him!"

The candles above him flickered out simultaneously and both he and the throne vanished. The throne was still there, though, in the shadows. The dwarf was not.

Everyone was looking where he had pointed. But which one had he meant? One of the two jotnar, or the goblin?

4

Inos awoke as the door opened. She was magically, instantly awake, with her eyes wide to the darkness, knowing that she had been asleep for some hours. A faint gleam from the window showed the dim shape of the intruder. The door closed without a click, but she had already recognized the familiar woolly-blanket feeling of a calming spell on her mind.

"Inos?" the expected whisper said.

"Hello, Rap."

She thought of Azak, waking to find Rap in their bedroom . . .

"The sultan won't waken," Rap said, dropping the whisper but keeping his voice soft. "You won't scream or anything if I —"

"No. There's a housecoat somewhere, if you can find it."

He must have removed the spell at once, because her heart started to pound with excitement. She felt him toss the gown on the bed for her. She sat up, realizing that sorcerers could see in the dark; in fact, they could probably see through dwarvish chain mail, so the coat would make no real difference to him. The ritual would make her feel better, though, and it dispelled any last, lingering doubt that this was the genuine Rap.

She climbed out of bed and wrapped herself, shivering slightly with excitement. A faint glow sprang up in a lantern on the mantel. Rap was by the

173

window with his back to her. He turned around, and they gazed at each other across the width of the room.

The bedchamber was grand enough by most folk's standards, but it was definitely not what a palace should offer a visiting king. The furniture was an odd assortment, the wall frescoes were peeling and faded, and an old-fashioned fustiness suggested everything had been inadvertently left behind by the previous dynasty. Such pettiness might be intended to show Ythbane's anger at the humiliation Azak had brought him, or perhaps it represented some household flunky's contempt for djinns. Who cared?

The bed had been big enough, and that had been all that mattered. On the far side of a protective bolster, Sultan Azak slept soundly.

She raised a hand to her face. "Thank you for this, Rap."

He shrugged. "It was easy. Bones take time, but skin is easy."

"Thank you anyway."

He was still wearing very plain workman's clothes, and they were wet. His hair was soaked, although even that wouldn't make it lie down completely. Rap had always had very stubborn hair. He spoke first, smiling sadly at her.

"Magic can make you as you were, but even sorcery could never make you any more beautiful."

Well! That was new! And he wasn't even blushing as he said it.

"Thank you for that, also, kind sir. You are a sight for sore eyes yourself." She sat on the edge of the bed, glancing across at Azak. He had one brawny arm outside the covers, and his hair was a red puddle on the pillow. No, he was not going to waken.

Rap was staring at Azak also, squinting in an odd way. "I can't do anything about his curse, I'm afraid. I can sort of see it, though."

Inos was in no immediate hurry to have Azak relieved of his curse, but to say so at the moment would not be in the best of taste. "See it? What does a curse look like?"

Rap scratched his head. "Hard to describe. Like there's a glass cloth on him, a fuzziness. It kind of shimmers . . . I can't put it into words. I wouldn't know what it did if your aunt hadn't told me, but I'd know he had a sorcery on him."

"Rap, sit down! I want to hear all about your adventures, and how you escaped from the tower, and how you met the dragon, and —"

"Your aunt can tell you all that. We may not have time for it right now. It wasn't easy — finding you." He glanced around; she suppressed the unnerving thought that he was looking *through* the walls and ceiling instead of at them. "There's a big dark blank over the palace. A silence. What I mean is, no one else's using magic in it. I don't want to give myself away to the wardens."

"Wardens? Rap, Ythbane tried to summon them tonight, and they wouldn't come. Only the dwarf."

Rap's eyes widened. He walked over to a chair and sat down. "Tell me, please!"

So she told him what had happened. He listened solemnly, his face giving away nothing at all. His woodenness was beginning to unnerve her. Rap had always been so transparent!

"Zinixo's a little horror," he muttered, when she had done. "He's terrified of the others ganging up against him. He expects everyone else to be as mean as he is."

"You know him?" And he knew Lith'rian, of course. Truly, Rap was full of surprises now. Had she ever been asked to judge her childhood friends for the one Least Likely to Consort with Warlocks, Rap would have won hands down.

"I haven't met Olybino," he said, "but I did meet the other three. You met Olybino, your aunt says."

"He wasn't very chummy, either."

Rap pulled a face. "It's what sorcery does to people. Sagorn knew. It makes them unhuman, somehow, in the end."

She grinned. "But you're still all right? So far?"

He shrugged. "I hope so."

She still couldn't tell what he was thinking. Was that the start of it? Rap had always been as readable as a signpost, but he certainly wasn't readable now. She sensed a worry in him, though.

"All right, I'll ask Kade when I get the chance. Oh, Rap! I am so madly happy you're alive! I thought the imps had killed you, and when I saw you in the desert I thought you were a wraith! I thought your ghost had come back to haunt me! You have to explain that to me, too. And then you turned up alive again, and I was so happy — then Azak told me you'd died in jail after we left. He told me a terrible story about you being beaten to death . . . I'm afraid I believed him, Rap. I'm sorry. I thought it would be in character for him to have let that happen to you, so I thought he was telling the truth. But you're all right! That's wonderful, Rap! Do just tell me how you escaped and rescued Kade?"

"Ask her."

"Just quickly? The highlights?"

"Ask your aunt."

"Rap!" she said crossly.

He got up off the chair and began to pace to and fro across the room, not speaking,

Obviously he had come here for some reason — breaking into the Opal Palace in the middle of the night must be a dangerous thing for him to do, no matter how great his powers were. There was one obvious reason for gentlemen to sneak into ladies' chambers like this. She did not think Rap would attempt anything so crude as that.

So why was her heart galloping? Because she was hoping he would? She knew what would happen if he did try to carry her off to his personal den of iniquity — and it would not involve Sultana Inosolan screaming and spoiling the fun. She would leave Azak a heart-warming note.

"Rap, if you fight Kalkor tomorrow —"

"Today. It's not far off dawn."

"Today, then. Is it certain? I mean, can you be sure that he won't kill you? Even with the third prophecy, can you be sure of winning?"

He was over by the window, and behind her. "No."

Eek! So that was it.

"Then don't! I won't risk losing you again, not just for Krasnegar. I mean, even if you do win, there's no guarantee that I'll ever be queen. *We must break the chain somewhere!* We mustn't let the goblins get you, the third prophecy. What did you mean when you said that magic casements don't prophesy?"

"It'd take too long to explain."

"Well, never mind. Just give me a minute to get some clothes on, and we can go."

"What?" He was back by the dresser, where she could see him, and he was staring at her with a very shocked expression.

She smiled. "I love you. Rap! Did you doubt it?"

Now his face was as readable as it had ever been — he colored all the way to his ears. "Inos, no!"

"Of course I do! I admit I didn't realize back in Krasnegar, but I should have! You might have dropped a hint or two, you know. Boys are supposed to make the first move."

He frowned at her in dismay and shook his head.

"Of course I love you!" she said crossly. "It's what the God tried to tell me, and I was too stupid to —"

"Inos! You're a married woman! A sultana! No, listen to me . . . " He sat down on the chair again and looked pigheaded. "You know how Andor used mastery on you? Well, when I got my second word of power, I found myself using mastery on him! I could make Andor believe anything I wanted! I couldn't help it. And now —"

Twaddle! "Let's not talk about Andor. Horrible man!" She smiled at him, this grown-up, solid, solemn Rap. Very much what she would have expected —

176

reliable, competent . . . when he knew what he was doing, that is; probably still inclined to blunder without proper guidance. Still, he'd managed to get here. Maybe Sagorn had helped. But honest, trustworthy, faithful. Just what a woman needs.

"I admit that I still didn't realize, even when you turned up in Krasnegar the night that Father died. Oh, I should have! You'd run all the way to Pondague and then back again, just for me, and I still didn't see. But I was very shaken that night, and still under Andor's spell a bit, and I wasn't thinking straight. But —"

"You married Azak. I asked you if —"

"Rap!" she shouted, forgetting that her husband was sleeping on the bed behind her. "You'd just turned my wedding into a circus and killed all those guards and —"

"Inos!" he said softly, and her tongue seemed to freeze. "My ambition was always to be your sergeant-at-arms, when you became queen. You knew that! Now I know I'd never make a soldier, and I'm very happy that you've found such a fine royal husband. I know I'm just a nothing! We're not children anymore." He looked very earnest, but Rap had always sounded pompous when he tried to tell lies. Not enough practice, likely.

She laughed and jumped up. "Turn your back, Nothing, and I'll get dressed, and we'll run —"

"No. Sit down! Now listen. I'm trying to tell you something! I'm a mage. I can make you do anything I want. Anything at all. And, yes, I do feel very strongly about you."

"Oo, that's it? Feel strongly? You run through the taiga, you cross the whole world to come to me, you fight dragons . . . You're quite sure you feel strongly? So . . . "

"And it leaks!" he shouted.

Azak stirred briefly. Then he rolled over and went still again.

"Leaks?" she echoed stupidly.

Rap nodded, looking miserable. "I can't help a little mastery leaking out. That's what you're feeling. Every time I look at you . . . I'm sorry, Inos. That's all it is. When I'm not around anymore, then you'll recover. But I'm afraid I'm making you feel that way. That's all it is, really."

More twaddle! "Oh, no it's not!"

"Oh, yes it is!"

They scowled at each other.

She snorted. "Indeed! And who are you to say whether I'm in love with you or not?"

"I'm a mage. Yes, I know you're telling the truth. I can see that."

"Kind of you to mention it."

"But that's not the point! You're saying what you really believe, but you're believing that because I . . . Because I want you. Yes, I do want you, and I'm making you feel that way."

"Oh, is that so? Well, let's just prove a point! Come here."

She started to unwrap her housecoat and Rap said, "*Inos!*" Kade herself could not have sounded more scandalized.

She fastened the housecoat again miserably. "Rap, I really do love you! I married Azak because I didn't have any choice. Rasha was going to do terrible things to —"

"Inos, please?"

She fell silent.

"I didn't come for that. I would never! And I didn't come to take you away. I just came to ask a favor."

She stared at him, the way he slumped in the chair, the dejected way he held his head. This was not like him. He was readable now, and he was in real trouble.

"Rap? What favor?" *Anything!*

He sighed. "Kalkor's a sorcerer."

"Oh, no!"

"I think he is. I'm not sure. He's at least a mage, but I think he's a full, four-word sorcerer. That's why he can risk coming to Hub — the Impire can't kill him. When he wants to go, he'll just vanish." He studied her bleakly for a moment. "And if the Impire can't kill him, then I certainly can't! I can feel magic being used, Inos, and he used big power on the troll. Maybe he's just a clumsy mage, but I think he's a full sorcerer."

"That's what Zinixo meant!"

"Must be — he was pointing at Kalkor. See, the regent was going to forbid another Reckoning, and Kalkor changed his mind for him. I felt that one, too. And to use power on the imperor — or his regent, I suppose — is a direct breach of the Protocol."

"And the day before, he struck down Angilki right in the Rotunda . . ."

But Rap did not know that story, so she had to explain that part also, while he stared at her solemnly with his big gray eyes. Stupid tattoos! Why didn't he magic them away? Oh, Rap, Rap! Who cared about tattoos? Wonderful to have him back . . .

"So why don't the wardens punish him?" she demanded at the end.

"I don't know. Maybe they want me safely dead first? No, that's stupid — I'm worse than the dwarf. Seeing enemies everywhere."

"So Kalkor's a sorcerer. And you're not?"

He shook his head. "I'm only a mage. Three words."

She felt a shiver of panic. If Kalkor killed Rap, then she was going to go back to Arakkaran, married to Azak, and Rap would be really dead at last. She'd thought those nightmares were all over.

And then she understood, and relief washed over her like light through a shutter thrown back. She would make him ask, though! For even doubting. "Tell me!"

"Would you . . . would you mind . . . sharing your word of power? I know it's an Evilish big thing to ask of anyone, but . . . " Then he must have sensed her amusement, because he stopped, and almost seemed to smile.

"I'm sorry to have to ask you, but I'm afraid. I mean, I'm afraid that without that, I won't be able to kill the bastard." His face went wooden again.

"Why did you change your mind, Rap?" she asked softly. "What was it Kalkor threw at you that made you change your mind?"

Wooden, very wooden . . . "I don't want to talk about it." He shivered.

"Where did you go when you left us?" Nosy!

For a moment she thought he wouldn't answer. Then he said, "To a funeral, and I won't talk about that, either."

"Well, it doesn't matter. Kalkor's a monster. If you can kill him, then you'll be doing us all a favor, and of course I'll share my word with you." And a lot more than that.

His relief was so obvious that she almost felt hurt. "You will?"

"Did you doubt?" She smiled pityingly at him, and she thought she saw him mask a blush.

"Thanks, Inos, It may not matter for very long."

What did that mean? Well, she didn't care, and there were worse problems to talk about.

"It will weaken your power, of course," he added reluctantly.

"Oh, no it won't! I just hope it'll do you more good than it has done me. Ever since Father told it to me, I've been waiting to see what difference it would make, and it hasn't made any. Not at all! I've never developed any special talent, nothing. Elkarath said I was using power once, when we were in Thume, but I wasn't conscious of doing anything. It must be a very weak word. Rap. Half of nothing is still nothing."

He shook his head. "That may not be right. Sagorn thinks that the words have different properties and suit different people. Or don't. Meaning yours may just not be right for you. That could be, but I think it's something else. I think some people have a real talent for magic, and the words help those people. Others haven't got the knack, somehow. If a boy's naturally clumsy, then he'll never make a swordsman, no matter what training he may get. I was like that. Some sorcerers are naturally much stronger than others. I don't think Rasha was very powerful at all."

"She zapped me all the way across Pandemia."

Rap snorted. "That wouldn't be hard, with the magic casement open. It would have acted like a . . . hard to explain. Anyway, even if your word hasn't done anything for you, I think I have a very good knack."

"Yes, I think you do. You're making me feel giddy. I could absolutely swear that I'm insanely in love with you."

He did blush at that. "Please, Inos! Be serious! If you will share your word with me, I will try to kill Kalkor."

She laughed. Glad of the excuse, she walked over to him, where he sat uncomfortably on the chair, and she laid a hand on his shoulder. It felt surprisingly solid. She bent to his ear, remembering how she'd watched him tell a word to Rasha.

"This is how it's done?" she whispered.

He squirmed a little. "Yes."

She kissed his cheek. "Like this?"

"Inos! Please!" He wasn't moving a muscle.

She chuckled. She could smell the damp of his hair, and he needed a shave. "What's it worth?"

"My life," he said hoarsely.

That sobered her. "Sorry, Rap!" She whispered the gibberish her father had told her on his deathbed.

Then she straightened. "Well?"

He looked up at her. "That's it?"

"That's it. So much fuss for such a lot of nonsense!"

He swallowed and licked his lips. "You're sure?"

Doubt . . .

"Yes. That's what Father told me."

Rap said nothing. He looked down at his fists, clenched tight on his knees. "Rap? What's wrong?"

"Inos . . . That wasn't a word of power."

"It's what Father said!" But was she sure? Had she perhaps got the *angoo* bit mixed up with the *engip* bit?

He shook his head and rose suddenly.

He was much bigger than she remembered. Solemn gray eyes.

"It's not a word of power, Inos. Hearing one of those . . . You know, it's like having your head explode."

"But . . . "

"Do you remember when he told you? Did you feel anything?"

"No," she said. "Just surprise. I thought he was raving again."

180

"Then it isn't your fault."

"Rap! What do you mean?"

His face was very close, and it was wooden as a three-masted schooner. She could read nothing in it.

"I mean that sometimes words must get lost. Maybe your father was too far gone. Maybe it was his father. The chain got broken somewhere. Someone forgot, or didn't hear right."

"No! No! No!"

"'Fraid so. You'd have felt the power when he told you, and you didn't. That's why you've never developed a talent, Inos. You don't know a word of power!"

It made awful sense. Horror fell on her, chilling her. "But Kalkor?"

Rap shrugged, not looking at her. "Maybe he's only a mage, like me. Just have to hope so." He didn't sound very confident.

"Then you'll be all right?"

"Then it'll just be a question of which of us is stronger — and I'm pretty strong, I think. If we cancel out completely, then it goes back to muscle, and he's . . . But that's not likely. Lith'rian was very shocked when he discovered I could feel magic being used, and I was only an adept then. I think he was worrying about what I might become if I ever learned more words."

"And if Kalkor knows four?" She waited. "Rap? Can a mage fight a sorcerer?"

"Can a mouse fight a cat?"

"Rap!"

"Different animal, it'd be no contest. Duke Angilki's still unconscious?"

"That's what they said tonight — still in a coma."

Rap nodded bitterly. "No help from his word, then. Go back to bed, Inos, and I'll put you to sleep."

He stepped away as she tried to put her arms around him.

"Rap! Stop being idiotic! Forget Kalkor! He's not worth your life. Forget Azak! And forget Krasnegar! Let's go now! You and me. Pick anywhere you like and I'll go with you."

"No. I'm going to go and look for another word." He had his stubborn look on.

"You don't need to kill him for me. Rap, because —"

"I'm not doing it for you. Nor for Krasnegar. I'm doing it because I want to. Now go to bed."

"Idiot! Almost dawn? Sagorn's been hunting for words for a hundred years, and you expect to find one before noon today?"

Suddenly his eyes were very big. She could see nothing but his eyes.

"Go back to bed, Inos."

She went, and slept, and Rap departed.

Whispered word:
>   It is the hour when from the boughs
>   The nightingale's high note is heard;
>   It is the hour when lovers' vows
>   Seem sweet in every whispered word.
>   Byron, *Parisina*

8

Fortune's fool

1

He ran north, knowing that what he sought would be somewhere to the north, near the White Palace. Near the lake.

He ran through the rain, wishing he still had the legs he'd had in the taiga. First sailoring and now weeks of driving had spoiled him for running, and he was trying to hold back on magic.

Running into rain; running into dawn, too. His time was draining away. He had not slept that night, and would not. There would be a long sleep ahead, if this last chance failed.

This was his third day in Hub, and the inexplicable white horror must be very imminent now. It would come today, he thought. *God of Justice, let me kill Kalkor first!* He still had no more clue as to what it was, for he feared it too much to use his foresight at all. It might be just death. That was the logical explanation — that the Gods blocked a man from seeing beyond his own death. Yet two wardens had failed to read his future and Ishist had said it hurt to try. If this other fate saved him from dying in the goblins' lodge, then it might be a good thing, although he doubted that even the goblins could inflict more agony than he had sensed in the white glare.

Meanwhile there was nothing to do but run as fast as he could.

He did not always manage to stay mundane, even after he'd left the palace. Legionary patrols challenged him periodically, a lone man running the streets at night. In the narrower ways, ill-defined shadows moved as if to close in on him, action before query. Each time he just drew an inattention spell over himself and ran on unhindered.

He tried not to think about Inos.

Poor Inos! How his lustful thoughts had confused her! Being a mage was a hateful thing. But if the wardens took the curse off her husband, she would soon be safely back in Arakkaran, embarking on the life she had freely chosen before Rap had blundered in. In time she would forget him.

He thought instead of Kalkor. He unbottled the rage that had foamed inside him for hours, letting hatred fuel his running. The pains came, in his legs first and then a burning in his chest, but he thought of Kalkor and his anger gave him the strength to run on.

The faun in him went away. The jotunn ruled alone, riding his soul, ranting and rousing. As fatigue and exhaustion built, so did the bloodlust. He had never lost his temper since his childhood except once — almost — in Durthing. That burst of fury had frightened him, but it had still not taught him what a jotunn rage could be. Now he felt it in its full adult form for the first time. It was wonderful, irresistible, intoxicating. He might regret this after, for as long as he might live, but now that did not matter. Nothing mattered.

Blood and destruction and satisfaction . . . only those.

By the time he drew near to the northernmost of the five hills and the shielded mystery of the White Palace, milky dawn was seeping into the watery sky. Traffic was picking up in the city, populating the rain-swept streets with carters and early-rising apprentices. Any he spoke to answered his questions willingly and swiftly, and eventually he found one who could direct him to the place he sought.

It was a big ramshackle building in its own well-wooded grounds, a relic of prosperity within an area that was sliding into slumhood. Men and even families came and went, but the owner of this property was immortal.

If Rap had guessed wrongly, and his quarry slept on the longship moored in the lake, then he was a dead faun.

He went over the wall of the Nordland Embassy faster even than any cat could have managed, into a once-fine estate that had been allowed to sink into forest, unattended. There were no dogs — true jotnar detested them — and dogs would have been no problem anyway. The problem was Kalkor.

Breaking into the Opal Palace had been less risky than this, because there was a sorcerer in here somewhere, and merely touching his mind with farsight might awaken him.

Dragging his aching feet through the sodden shrubbery of abandoned garden. Rap began to probe the big house ahead. Already a yellow streak marred the eastern skyline, below the rain clouds. Even a thane was not likely to oversleep on a day he must fight a mortal duel.

Farsight drew a blank in the great bedchambers, but a Nordlander might spurn those as decadence. Rap switched his attention to the back, the former servant quarters, and there he soon found Thane Kalkor already awake, and busy with a recreation from which he would not be easily distracted. He might well go back to sleep afterward.

So Rap could concentrate on his main quarry. More swiftly now he continued scanning, room by room. There were surprisingly few people in the great sprawling mansion. The crew of *Blood Wave* would mostly be sleeping aboard, of course, not trusting the imps.

He finished the rooms. Nothing. He tried the cellars. Blank. Then the attics. Likewise.

Despair!

Failed! By the time he could reach the lake, the sailors would be awake. Fool! Fool! He had guessed wrong.

He stood in the cold rain and earthy-scented shrubbery and faced the unpleasant truth that Kalkor was going to chop him to pieces. His only recourse now was to try to sneak into the house and try to kill the thane while he was distracted. Sneak up on a sorcerer, mm?

And then he registered a collection of decaying wooden sheds and outhouses around the back of the house. There! In the woodshed. Of course.

It could not have been easier. He trotted around and found the door ajar. He sent a wakening nudge ahead of him, to where his quarry lay on a moldering old rug on the bare dirt, with a rag tied around him as a token garment. He would have chosen this place of his own free will, loving the temperature and the smell of wood.

As Rap entered he sat up and stretched. Even a full-grown timberwolf might have envied his yawn.

"Hello, Little Chicken."

The goblin squinted at the shadow in the doorway. "Flat Nose?"

"Yes." Rap sank down gratefully, cross-legged on the dirt, still panting. Weary, weary! He ached all over, but especially his legs. Amid the high-heaped firewood there was barely enough space for him; he was knee to knee with the goblin. But it was good to get out of the rain at last, and good to sit.

"You come to visit an old friend?" Little Chicken's angular eyes glinted with satisfaction. He scratched himself busily. "Or you want something, maybe?"

Rap's fury had refined itself now to pure purpose, his mind was icy clear. "Yes. Need something. You know, in an odd way I'm glad they didn't get their goblin stew."

"I think I know why you're glad. Flat Nose!" The goblin chuckled, gloating a little. "Thane told me you'd come."

Oh, he had, had he? Rap checked quickly, and Kalkor was still at it, heedless of his intended victim trespassing.

"We'll get to that. I'm really curious — how did you escape?"

Little Chicken pointed to a scar on his thigh. "Put an arrow in me, took me prisoner. They'd eaten their fill that night. No room for goblin."

"So they kept you to fatten you up?"

Once Rap had been afraid of Little Chicken and his monstrous ambitions, but that was over now. The goblin could save Rap's life or condemn him to death this day, but that was the limit of his power at the moment. True, the wardens had foreseen a great future for him, and Rap had assumed that it involved ruling Krasnegar. A mage's insight, plus the smattering of news and rumor he had collected in Hub had shown him how wrong he had been. Now Bright Water's interest and help were understandable. What lay in store for Little Chicken was something quite unrelated to Krasnegar, but it did involve Rap and the third prophecy.

"They tie you up or cage you?" Neither would detain a man with the goblin's occult strength.

The big tusks flashed again. "Caged me. I let a day or two go by and then left. Lots of jungle on the wet side of the island . . . Took a woman along to do the cooking." The ugly khaki-hued face was just as easy to read as anyone else's.

"What was her name?"

"Couldn't work my tongue hard enough," Little Chicken said offhandedly. "I just called her 'Woman' and she did what she was told."

"How did she feel about this?"

The goblin shrugged. "Seemed happy. After the first couple of days, said she wouldn't run away, so I could leave her untied at nights." He leered. "Good man for her! Strong!"

All the time Rap had been a sailor, living in Durthing, the goblin must have been hiding out in the Nogid jungle, letting his wound heal, tended by the girl he had stolen. There were a lot of things he wasn't saying, though.

"And then you sailed away and left her?" No, that wasn't right . . .

"Paddled a tree trunk across to next island. Woman said we could get to another imp fort after six, seven islands."

So Little Chicken had gone hunting his destiny and she had chosen to go with him. He wasn't lying about her feelings; the anthropophagous woman had genuinely fallen in love with her goblin kidnapper. Likely he had treated her as well as he had been able, for women were useful. Was it possible that Little Chicken had ever done anything so ungoblinish as to fall in love? On the verge of taunting him with that, Rap suddenly drew back.

"Bad current," the goblin said. "Big storm came."

"I'm sorry to hear that." A mage could sense the real sorrow under the pose of indifference. How strange! HOW sad!

The rest of the tale came easily. Heading westward again in *Blood Wave*, Kalkor had encountered a log floating in Dyre Channel with a near-dead goblin on it, but that was exactly the sort of freakish coincidence that words of power could produce, and of course the goblin knew a word, also. Kalkor must have seen his own destiny then, for he had known of the three visions in the casement. That must have been when he had conceived his mad expedition to Hub.

"So he forced your word of power out of you, and that made him a sorcerer?" Rap asked.

Little Chicken flushed olive at the insult. "You know goblins better than that! He was a sorcerer already. Didn't need it!"

That was good news, maybe. Little Chicken's word had come straight from a fairy. No one else shared it — yet. A strong word.

Rain drummed on the roof of the shed and dribbled through leaks. Again Rap scanned the house. Kalkor had finished what he was doing and seemed to be asleep again. The woman lay at his side, sobbing in silence. Elsewhere men were starting to stir, though. Even jotnar might feel the chill of this clammy morning and decide to light fires. He must be quick.

Little Chicken stretched again. "Why'd you agree anyway? I saw. Didn't use magic on you?"

"No. Not directly." Of course Kalkor could have changed Rap's mind as he had changed the regent's, but that would not have been playing the game the way he wanted it played.

"How then?" the goblin asked. "You're stubborn as a mother bear, Flat Nose. I know."

Despite his fury and grim purpose, Rap chuckled. "Well, thank you, Little Chicken!" Those awful weeks in the forest had faded in his memory until he could look back on them with something like nostalgia. Oh, the innocence of youth! He had not been a mage in those days. "Remember Gathmor?"

The goblin nodded, visible now as a gray shape in the dawn. "He was on the longship with you, then? Thought it sounded like him."

"He was a good man. Little Chicken. He came to Hub with me."

187

The angular eyes widened in understanding. "Yes, good man . . . What did Kalkor throw you yesterday?"

Rap shuddered. "His heart. It was still beating."

The goblin thought about that, then shook his head. "Bad way to kill a man. No honor." He had strange ideas about good ways to die, but it was a tribute.

"I must kill Kalkor!" Rap said. His fury flickered into flame, making his hands shake.

Little Chicken shrugged. "He said you'd come here, wanting my word."

"Will you share it with me?"

"No." The big fangs showed again. "Nice being strong."

"You'll still be plenty strong if you share it."

The goblin shook his head. "How many you got already?"

"I'm not saying."

"And I'm not telling." He brayed an unexpectedly strident laugh. "You can't magic a word from me, Flat Nose. What else you going to try?"

Rasha had inflicted pain on Rap and then threatened to use it on Inos, but neither of those techniques would work on the goblin. If his anthropophagous lover had lived . . . but Rap could not injure an innocent woman, no matter what his hatred.

That left persuasion, or threat. "If Kalkor kills me, then you don't. You can't take me back to Raven Totem if he's held up my head at the Reckoning."

Again the goblin chuckled. "That's what he said you'd say. But if I do tell you, then you're a sorcerer. So he said. Can't torture a sorcerer."

If Kalkor knew that Rap was already a mage, then he was taking an astonishing risk in leaving the goblin's word lying around unattended, as it were. Either he was insanely confident of his own sorcerous prowess, or he knew something Rap had not thought of.

The wardens, maybe? Nordland raiders were Bright Water's prerogative; the witch of the north might intervene to defend Kalkor against sorcery.

Or perhaps he had forsaken this entire meeting and knew for certain that the goblin was not going to share his word of power. Rap dared not use farsight.

He checked again and the thane had not stirred from his pallet. Possibly Kalkor was just relying on a word's reluctance to be told — Little Chicken had never been cooperative, and now he was enjoying being obstinate and forcing Rap to beg. Quite likely Kalkor also was sleepily enjoying the fruitless struggle as he rested alongside his most recent victim.

Rap's jotunnish blood was racing. The trembling in his hands had spread all the way to his shoulders. His anger needed a victim, and if he couldn't make the young goblin cooperate, he would certainly kill him. Perhaps that was the outcome Kalkor had foreseen? That would amuse him.

"If I promise?"

"Promise?" the goblin scoffed. "Promise to let me slay you? A sorcerer? Won't work, Flat Nose. Just have to trust the Gods."

"I want to kill him," Rap said, beginning to feel desperate, "for Gathmor. And this is my only chance. Tell me your word of power, and I swear that I'll fulfill your prophecy. I'll come back to Raven Totem with you and let you kill me."

The goblin fell silent, but Rap could see the start of indecision in his ugly face.

"What about the woman? You fixed her burns."

"She has another chief. I told you she was a chief's daughter and must marry a chief."

"Won't take her?" Little Chicken looked disbelieving.

"No, I won't take her. She chose that one."

"Not doing this for her?"

"I told you — I'm doing it for Gathmor. Kalkor's death won't help Inos."

The goblin shook his head. "Don't care. Won't tell you my word, Flat Nose. Tell me yours and I'll kill thane for you. Then take you back to Raven Totem."

Rap was struggling to keep his teeth from chattering with fury. The despicable green runt had no idea how close he was to death. "Tell me or die! I swear I will kill you, Trash! Gods spurn my soul, but I'm going to kill you."

The angular eyes flashed. "Not trash now!"

But his looks didn't support his words. Rap quickly reached for memories. He had never untangled the intricacies of the goblins' custom, but he could do that now.

"I say you're still my trash, goblin!"

"Not trash! Saved you from the imps in Milflor!" Again untruth registered to a mage's insight: taut neck, sweat-filmed skin, speeding heart. Little Chicken was lying.

"No, you didn't! They didn't intend to kill me, and I'd have gotten away without your help! And I called you back when you attacked the soldiers. You disobeyed my order, so what you did didn't count!"

Little Chicken was tense with rage, but he wasn't denying the accusations. Rap chuckled as he saw his guesses scoring.

"So you're still my trash! But Kalkor's going to kill me today unless you share your word with me. You can save my life this time! Then you won't be trash any more; really not."

The goblin pouted, considering. He looked up slyly. "Then I get to kill you — very, very slow?"

"I'll endure as long as I can. Longer than anyone ever has."

It was a gruesome promise, but a meaningless one. The white-fire destiny was going to destroy Rap first, probably before the day was out. He wasn't going to survive long enough to see Raven Totem again.

"You swear, Flat Nose?"

"I swear it by any God you want."

"I think you're a man of your word, Flat Nose." The goblin grinned and licked his lips. "Much honor! I'll do it! I'll tell you my word."

2

Rain drummed mercilessly on the sodden tent, seeping through seams to drip onto Rap's head, puddling around his feet. He could hear the spectators slithering on the slick mud of the bank outside, but the crowd was much smaller today and would see little of the contest through the driving mist that obscured the field — much of which was already a silvery marsh. Thunder rumbled overhead in clouds thick as mud. The magic casement had predicted the conditions exactly.

The magic casement had arranged the whole thing.

That was what magic casements did! Much more than just prophesying, they warped the flow of events to serve their owners' interests. Just who the Krasnegarian casement regarded as its owner was yet an unsolved mystery, but apparently not Kalkor, for it had already destroyed him as surely as it had destroyed Inos's great-grandfather. Rap had told Kalkor of the duel and Kalkor had contrived to make it happen for his own amusement, but he would never have thought of it without the casement's prompting.

The casement had trapped him. He would never reign in Krasnegar now, because he had used power on the regent to force the second Reckoning. That was a violation of the Protocol and must bring retribution from the wardens. No matter what the outcome of the duel, Kalkor would die.

Some things were very obvious to a sorcerer!

Rap had seen the bitter truth just after his visit to Little Chicken, but it made no difference to him, for his jotunn bloodlust was still an agony in him. He would avenge Gathmor's death at any cost at all. It was not a task he could leave to the wardens' justice — he himself must make Kalkor pay, or die trying. He could barely remember his father, but his father had been a jotunn, descended from generations of killers, and that jotunn blood pumped now in Rap. He was not doing this for Inos. Officially he was her champion, as the casement had suggested, but in his own mind he was fighting to avenge a friend, most callously murdered to gratify the raider's whim.

190

Blood!

He slumped on a low stool and wished his bones were not so heavy, his muscles so throbbingly painful. He was keeping himself mundane, and suffering for it, out of some strange perverse desire for misery. He had not slept at all in the night, and little the night before.

A smelly length of bearskin lay heaped on the wet grass beside him. Opposite, on another stool, sat an ancient jotunn whose name had not been offered. In his overlong red robe, he held a great battle-ax across his lap and was busily running a whetstone along its edge, although it was already sharp enough to split gossamer. A horned helmet and a battered bugle lay at his feet.

"You must get ready!" he growled, frowning shaggy white brows. He disapproved of Rap. Mongrels should not be allowed to participate in sacred jotunn ceremonies, and this one did not look much like a fighter anyway.

"There's time yet," Rap snapped.

What he really should be doing was practicing sorcery. Hearing his fourth word had been a cataclysmic experience, greater than any of the others had produced. His mind still jangled from it. Perhaps the goblin's word had been especially strong, or perhaps this was just what being a sorcerer was. He felt as if he had been given an extra set of senses.

Now he knew the ambience itself, like a whole additional occult world superimposed on the mundane. He could see it without seeing it — or smell it, taste it, feel it, hear it, and none of those words fit exactly what he knew. It was another plane, to which he could move without leaving where he was. Hub was a great city to his eyes, but in that other set of dimensions it was a universe of shadows inhabited by glowing beacons of sorcery.

Beacons, or standing rolls of thunder, or monstrous shapes, as he chose. Between them were the little whirls and flashes of minor magics: a woman using glamour to ensnare a lover, an occultly gifted cook producing a masterpiece of pastry for a lord's table, a merchant sweetly swindling an unsuspecting opponent. He could see them as they were, if he wished, or he could view their extensions in the ambience, their projections of power. Purple and shrill, pungent or angular and angry — words and concepts had become totally inadequate to convey even the thoughts, and to describe them to a mundane would be impossible if he tried until the sun went out. Small wonder that sorcerers were not like other people.

Did all sorcerers perceive these things so clearly, or was such insight a function of strength? And how strong was he? He felt giddy with power, omnipotent. Was that a dangerous self-delusion? Could he truly be as mighty as he sensed?

On the far side of the field, Kalkor stood in the other tent, too excited to sit. He was steadying his ax upright with one hand and sharpening it with a

191

stone held in the other, and he had already stripped down to the fur wrap, ready for blood. Then he felt Rap's attention and looked up, blue eyes shining with mad joy.

Rap glanced into the ambience and there he saw Kalkor as a transparent, naked image of himself. In that dimensionless space he might have been standing an arm's length away, or far off in Nordland. But there was more than just a wraith there; Rap also sensed red, twisted hatred like a coiling fire. Death and rape and atrocity sparkled in it and there was nothing human.

"*You die soon, halfman!*" Kalkor said, and his flames flailed hotter, gloating.

"Why?" Rap asked. He kept his arms on his knees and sent out his message without speech. The old man beside him did not look up. "*What do you hope to gain by this madness?*"

Kalkor laughed, and his laughter was blood spilled steaming on snow and women writhing in savage thrusts of pain. "*If you do not know, you are unworthy to know.*"

"*You seek to win a kingdom with sorcery. The wardens will not allow it. Already you have transgressed against the Protocol!*"

"*The wardens?*" The jotunn sneered. "*I do not fear the Four! Olybino has three wars on his hands already and dares not rouse the jotnar, also. Bright Water applauds me. She sought me out on my ship one night, clothed only in occult beauty, seeking my strength and relishing my overpowering will.*"

Rap could not tell if this was truth or madness.

The twisted web of fire became a thing of claws and scales and poison fangs, clamoring in discordant dirge. "*So I have two on my side, and the regent also will shun further war! I will carry the vote, and the wardens will not intervene!*" Physically Kalkor stood in his tent on the far side of the campus, a long bowshot away, but with that contemptuous outburst he seemed to snap his fingers right under Rap's nose.

Rap wrestled down his own dread fury, resisting the urge to hurl a bolt of power at the monster. The worst thing was, what the thane said might even be true. If the magic casement had foreseen that Kalkor's succession would best serve the future of Inisso's house, then Rap was the one who had been tricked! The other claimants, Inos and Angilki, had been sidetracked and Rap was doomed to die here.

Oh, poor Krasnegar!

Horrified, he peered deeper into the nightmare pit of Kalkor's mind. He found no fear. He could hardly even find much interest in the outcome of the Reckoning, for the raider had long since lost any sense of human life being valuable, even his own. His insanity in forcing the match made a sort of weird sense, therefore. To a man who sought his thrills from danger, every new escape became a challenge to risk more the next time. Death and rape and loot must pall at last, and yet there was nothing else to gain if that was what a man lived for. So he had sought out occult power also, and that had made the problem worse. If he survived today's spectacle then he must just seek a grander way to die, for now only death itself remained as the ultimate, inescapable, goal. And perhaps fame, as the thane who had sailed his ship to Hub and gambled a kingdom on a Reckoning in the capital of the Impire.

Appropriately, thunder clamored in the murky sky, and thousands of hands went over ears in the crowd. The downpour seemed to gather strength.

"*And what after me?*" Rap asked. "*Do you slaughter the regent? Or that husk of an imperor? The boy, perhaps? What is the last verse of the war song?*"

An explosion of unholy mirth turned the monster into a glittering, jagged monolith on a baleful starlit moor. "*You will never know! But I shall have immortality!*"

The duel would begin soon. The Imperial party was arriving. Azak was there, his skin glowing red with Rasha's curse. Incompetent slut she had been! That spell was a shoddy piece of work. Inos, also, looking distraught and yet desirable enough to drive a man madder than Kalkor. Poor Inos, knowing not a single word of power!

"*You can't win, you know,*" said the thane's mocking whisper in the steely calm of the ambience. "*I am a raider! I bow to no man. I recognize no law but death.*"

"Nor I!" Rap said angrily.

And the thane struck.

In the mundane world, nothing happened at all. The two old jotnar supporters sat by their principals, quite unaware of the occult confrontation in progress, but in the ambience Kalkor's misty image slashed Rap across the face with a cat-o'nine-tails like the one he had brandished before him on *Blood Wave*.

It was not intended as a mortal blow, nor even to disable; the result should have been merely a vicious jolt of pain. The whip did not exist, nor did the wooden staff with which Rap deflected the sorcery, for those were only mental pictures of the invisible, images of the unimaginable . . . yet Rap barely restrained a counterstroke with his imaginary club that would have crushed the ogre's skull.

Kalkor looked mildly surprised, and also amused. "*Not bad!*" he murmured.

"*Let's try that again,*" Rap said, reaching out in the spectral plane as if to offer a sailor's crushing handshake or a bout of arm wrestling.

Kalkor struck back at once, a monstrous sword thrust at his opponent's arm.

Rap preferred the handclasp. It didn't matter how he thought of it, or how Kalkor did, either. What mattered was pure occult power.

Now they matched strengths, and in Rap's vision the opposing fingers were soft as a child's. He squeezed, meeting so little resistance that he hardly noticed it; rejoicing as he sensed that he was inflicting hurt, as he saw the jotunn's eyes brim with swift-rising panic. Satisfied, he withdrew quickly before he maimed the man. With his ax, Kalkor could doubtless cut Rap to ribbons, but in sorcery he was a pushover.

The thane recoiled with a cry, so that his aged companion looked up in surprise. The ambience filled with bubbling slime and a fetor of decay. Gifted with strength and wits, with courage and beauty and high birth, Kalkor had abused them all until, after a lifetime of conquest, he had come to believe that no man could ever best him at anything.

And now he knew better.

Low, dismal dissonance, a frothing pit exuding noisome stenches of terror . . .

Rap peered in disgust at the filth. He saw fear at last, but not enough fear to please him. "*No, Thane! I will destroy you as you destroyed Gathmor. But first I will make your bowels run, like a craven's. You will flee from me, and I will chase you all around the field. Finally, you will grovel on your knees before the crowd. You will beg the regent to have mercy and stop the match, and he will refuse. The imps will have great sport today, and for years the poets will sing comic songs about the Nordland raider who came to Hub to strut, and ended running from a faun.*"

Kalkor bared his teeth, and visibly braced himself. "*No one will believe! They will know that you are using sorcery!*"

"*Maybe! But they will have a good laugh first.*"

The raider was no coward. He had worn out his fear of death long ago, and now he seemed to master his fear of mockery. "*And so you will avenge your sailor friend?*" he demanded.

"*Yes!*" Rap shivered with anticipation. "*Oh, yes!*"

"*Will you indeed?*" The thane shook his head with a disbelieving smile. "*Gathmor . . . if that was his name . . . how would he feel about that?*"

Rap's joy faltered. Gathmor had hated sorcery and despised it.

"*And yourself?*" Kalkor persisted, blue eyes shining inhumanly bright. "*There is very little satisfaction in slaying a man with sorcery — believe me, I know! Will it feel better than just leaving me to die of old age? I should enjoy that less, you know!*"

"*I will have justice!*" Rap yelled.

"*Not with sorcery, you won't, little faun! I grant you are a stronger sorcerer than I, but I am a Nordland thane, and to use your powers against me will be an infraction of that Protocol you quote so glibly. The witch of the north must avenge me. We both die, then? Is that Justice? Why not just strike us both dead now?*"

Kalkor chuckled as he measured Rap's dismay. Visions of fire and bleeding flesh . . .

"*Well, Master Rap? What is it to be? Do we both die by foul sorcery, or do we strive as men together, you seeking vengeance and I immortal fame? Shall we not agree to leave one of us alive afterward? There is a kingdom at stake also, remember! Battle of sorcerers, Master Rap? Or man to man?"*

Gathmor!

Rap was doomed either way . . . but he thought of Gathmor, and his jotunn self raged against faunish common sense telling him he was about to do something crazy. However frail his chances against the monster thane in mundane battle, there lay his only chance of real satisfaction.

Kalkor saw his hesitation and sneered, again the arrogant, confident master of *Blood Wave*. *"Coward!"*

Even a half jotunn could not take that.

"Man to man, then, you bastard!" Rap leaped to his feet and ripped off his doublet.

He had spoken aloud — his red-robed companion looked up in surprise. At the far side of the field, Kalkor's equally ancient second lurched to his feet and reeled out through the tent flap into the rain, grabbing up his bugle and helmet in passing.

He staggered, then, bewildered by his own unexpected move, for it had been Rap's doing.

An explosion of thunder made him jump and look up nervously, as if expecting Gods to appear in wrath. When nothing more happened, he raised the mouthpiece to his lips rather shakily and began the ceremony.

Fanfare of challenge.

"Ah!" Rap's supporter laid down the ax, took up his own trumpet and headgear, and tottered outside to sound the response.

Rap girt himself in the fur and followed.

Rain wrapped him in a clammy shroud, but the cold could not quench the fire of his rage. He fidgeted angrily from foot to foot while ancient ritual was mumbled at him in some long-forgotten dialect.

Kill Kalkor!

Kalkor's tent was barely visible as a blur of blue on the far side of the arena, but the jotnar performing the ceremony there were invisible to mundane sight.

Kill Kalkor!

Rap's heart was racing, throbbing, every beat saying "Kill him." *Killhimkillhimkillhim* . . . Every muscle twitched with eagerness. He wanted to shout at the old priest or whatever he was to hurry up; but at last the gaffer ended his mumbling and raised the ax — holding it vertical, straining. Rap knew from the casement's vision that Kalkor would be accepting his ax one-handed, in formal ritual. He had no such pretensions. Snatching the weapon with both hands, he . . . he very nearly dropped it. It was appallingly heavy,

195

a flared blade as wide as his chest and a polished metal shaft longer than his leg and too thick to close his fingers around. He had no idea how to fight with such an idiocy.

Kalkor did.

Heaving the monstrous thing onto his shoulder. Rap began to trudge forward over the wet grass. Rain blew in his eyes and dribbled icily over his bare skin. His legs ached, he was groggy from lack of sleep, but he had agreed not to use sorcery in this Reckoning. He would fight Kalkor on his own terms, man to man with axes.

Thunder roared directly overhead, stunningly loud, its echoes rolling away into the distance and merging with the underground rumble of the vast audience. Among the thousands of spectators who had come to watch this duel, very few would see the outcome in such a downpour.

Directly ahead, Kalkor appeared dimly ahead from the mist, as nearly nude as he was, bearing an identical ax. One of them was going to die very shortly, and very bloodily. This was what the magic casement had foretold.

But it had not said which one.

No farsight . . . no sorcery . . . Wholly mundane, Rap advanced, more cautiously now. Kalkor moved his ax from his shoulder, gripping it with both hands like a quarterstaff, holding it almost upright. He was the expert — Rap copied the move. They came to a halt about three paces apart, standing in a puddle.

The crowd had fallen silent. Rain hissed on the grass.

Kalkor was smiling, white teeth in a bronzed demon face. He wore an icy calm, but the crazed jotunn bloodlust showed in that smile. One of the great killers. Sooner slay a man than bed a woman . . .

Gathmor!

"Ready to die, halfman?"

Rap made no answer, watching the bright sapphire eyes, keeping a wary guard also on the ambience, alert for sorcery. Thunder rumbled far away.

Kalkor advanced a step.

Rap did the same.

The thane raised a quizzical, mocking eyebrow. "It will be quick," he promised, trying an experimental wave of his ax, a high sweeping motion, not close enough to connect.

Rap ignored the move. Watching. Waiting. It had better be quick, for the jotunn had twice the muscle he did and could outlast him. His arms and wrists ached already . . . one battered finger could be fatal in this game.

Kalkor frowned and came a half step closer. They were within range now. "Go ahead! You first. You need the practice!"

196

Rap had given his word. He wasn't using sorcery, not farsight, not even insight . . . but he felt a sudden hunch that Kalkor was not quite as confident as he should be, or was trying to seem. Could there be something bothering him?

"How long have you known your words of power, Thane?" His dry mouth made the query a whisper.

Kalkor just smiled . . . slowly raising his ax and sliding his right hand lower, nearer the end of the long shaft. Muscles were tensing in his right leg.

Rain dribbled unattended into Rap's eyes. "How long?" he persisted. "How long since you fought anyone without sorcery to help you, Kalkor?"

The thane struck, ax still almost vertical, foot following for balance, a chop more than an arc, aimed at Rap's chest . . . that was how it was done? . . . Rap countered shaft to shaft, arms straight to withstand the jotunn's bearlike strength. The impact rang over the arena, but it also jarred every bone Rap possessed and sent him dancing wildly backward, while a leering Kalkor followed with another stroke.

This time Rap sidestepped and parried with his blade along the massive handle, a long screeching slice trying for Kalkor's fingers. The thane deflected it in time, but now he was the one to leap off balance.

Wild joy surged up in Rap. Kalkor was stronger; but he was faster. And he still suspected that the man had forgotten how to fight without the aid of sorcery. That had been a clumsy retreat.

The axes were too heavy to swing like sticks. The men could move themselves faster than they could turn their weapons. That was worth knowing.

Now Rap was pursuing, lowering his ax under his opponent's guard. Kalkor had the advantage of height, but his legs were as vulnerable as the rest of him. Unexpectedly, the thane countered by swinging even lower, aiming at Rap's shins in the sort of clumsy wide stroke that Rap had already ruled out.

He was certainly supposed to jump over this one, and Kalkor would have twisted the handle to raise the blade and catch his feet, but fortunately the night's running had left Rap so stiff that he rejected the move on instinct, leaping back and ducking his ax to catch Kalkor's, hoping to hook the blades and jerk the slippery handle from the thane's grasp. *Clang!* He had underestimated the inertia . . . Kalkor thrust, and almost sliced through Rap's leg, but not quite, and he was within the thane's guard then, so he rammed a knee at his groin.

Nice try . . . Kalkor twisted and they rebounded apart, neither injured. Wary and panting, the two circled . . .

Flicker!

"Stop that!" Rap gasped. He wasn't certain, but it had probably been foresight — this close even a sight in use would be detectable to a sorcerer. "Once

197

more and I blast you! I swear!" He remembered Andor remarking that foresight made a deadly fighter.

Kalkor bared his teeth and said nothing. His eyes were wilder than before
even. Not quite the pushover he had expected? Keeping sorcery suppressed
when you had cheated with it for years must be a very big distraction.

Rap would tire first, though. His shoulders were coming apart already. His
fingers were freezing and cramped, slipping on the smooth metal.

Clang! Clang! Mostly they just avoided each other's cumbersome strokes,
but some connected. *Clang!* Rap was doing most of the retreating, but they
were dancing around each other so much that they had drawn no nearer the
crowd. Rap's speed would fail before Kalkor's strength did. The thane's face
was a rictus . . . could he look as bad? . . . His heart was going to burst.
Killhimkillhimkillhim . . .

And then Kalkor tried a straight rapier thrust as if wielding a pike and Rap
fended with a downward counter as Sergeant Thosolin had taught him. It was
an error — the thane dodged and Rap could not stop his stroke before he had
buried his blade in the turf. He hurled himself flat beside it as a murderous
return slice hissed above him. But while he was there, Kalkor's foot slipped on
the slick grass; he staggered and stepped too close, so Rap swung a fist and
caught the back of the jotunn's knee.

Kalkor went down also.

Then Rap could leap up with a yell of triumph and jerk his ax free.

For a brief instant that seemed to last an hour, the men's eyes met — Rap
swinging the great ax high overhead with what he suddenly knew to be the
last of his mundane strength . . . Kalkor on his knees and facing death, his
face a mask of horror and shock as he tried to twist out of the way. Then Rap
had both feet planted and his ax descending.

Glory! Gathmor! With a wordless scream he brought the dread blade down,
giving it every scrap of muscle he had left, but Kalkor reached into the clouds
and hauled down the lightning.

3

"*Cheat! Yellow cheating coward!*" Rap could barely hear his own howls through
the ringing in his ears. He danced on the puddles in his fury.

That had been very close, though. He had healed his hands, but his ax was
still glowing red; charred grass steamed and hissed around it. Half the spectators were still trying to find out what had happened, and most of the rest were
on their knees in the mud, madly praying. The bone-chilling downpour
roared unceasing.

"*Rotten cheating sneak! Man to man?*"

But Kalkor could not answer. Kalkor was dead, cooked. He stank of roast pork. What had happened, anyway? It had all been so sudden! Rap reached back with hindsight — and that was a trick he hadn't known he had — and saw himself ablaze in violet fire . . . No wonder the crowd was wailing! He had felt the ripple of sorcery coming and thrown a shield around himself. Then he had blazed like a God within the lightning, but he did not understand why then it had left him and melted his ax and struck the thane who had summoned it — *that cowardly turd, who had used sorcery after swearing not to* . . .

Very close! In hindsight, it looked as if Kalkor would have escaped by a hairsbreadth and Rap's ax would have buried itself in the ground and left him to Kalkor's nonexistent mercy . . .

So who had killed Kalkor? — Rap, or the Gods, or Kalkor himself? Rap didn't know. What mattered was that Kalkor had died thinking the faun had beaten him.

Well, good!

Gathmor would have approved.

Gathmor was avenged.

Hollow victory, which didn't bring Gathmor back.

Kalkor had been the one to use sorcery, not Rap. Would the wardens accept that, though? It might not have seemed like that.

The two old jotnar in their red robes and horned helmets were creeping forward, drenched and timorous, coming to inspect the outcome. Rap turned on his heel and walked away.

Now what? Of course he might just try to disappear from Hub, but he didn't think he could evade the wardens if they really wanted to catch him. The mysterious destiny of the white flame was waiting for him, wasn't it? He still felt a premonition. He tried a tiny sliver of foresight and recoiled at once. Yes, it was still there, implacable and very imminent. Shudder!

He thought about running away, and his premonition hardly eased at all, so flight would merely delay it a little. It seemed to be inevitable. Besides, he had a belated wedding present to give Inos. He headed for the royal enclosure.

The two old jotnar shouted after him, wanting him to do ritual butchery on the corpse, and he ignored them.

He certainly wasn't going to turn up in front of Inos with just a furry skin around him and even furrier faun legs showing below it. He detested his legs. As a child he had hated his squashy nose and his impossible hair, which the others had all laughed at. He had grown used to those eventually, but then his legs had sprouted like hayfields and given him something much worse to dislike. He wished that when the Gods had stirred up his mixed heritage. They had given him jotunn legs.

Still, sorcerers could solve such problems. He did not even need to retrieve the garments he had left in the tent, nor hunt out a private place to change. As he walked through the rain he clothed himself in a whole new outfit. He made good practical garments, of comfortable soft leather, like the work clothes Factor Foronod wore in the field. He made them in a plain, serviceable brown. They were sorcerous, not magical, and therefore permanent. The difference was quite obvious to him now.

Splashing along in his new boots, then, he brooded. Kalkor's death had solved nothing. It had not brought Gathmor back, and it left Krasnegar without a monarch. It had certainly not soothed Rap's jotunn temper. Left to itself, that terrible anger might last for days. If anything, it was worse than before, because now there was no relief in sight, no one to strike at. He could feel it rampaging inside him, seeking a victim to destroy. It might not matter very much, because he was going to die very soon.

Why? He didn't want to die in burning agony! He didn't want to die at all, and knowing it was coming made it even worse.

The cordon of legionaries opened a gap for him grudgingly. Today's canopy was much larger than the previous day's, and most of the royal party had managed to huddle in below it, leaving their guards out in the rain with the servants. Were they frightened of catching colds?

Rap stalked up the bank to the smarmy little regent on his stupid wooden throne. He used the smallest bow he thought would not be an open insult.

That had been noticed — he detected the hidden smiles and frowns from the various political factions represented. The Imperial court would always be a creel of lobsters, all slithering and biting to get on top. He despised them, these wealthy parasites in their embroidered cloaks and fancy gowns, in their elaborate ruffles and padded tights. He had not thought much of them yesterday, and today he could read them like posters with his sorcerer's insight. The contempt was mutual; he could see their curled lips and cocked eyebrows as they scorned the yokel sorcerer, their little shared glances of nervous mirth.

In the open at the very back of the crowd Little Chicken was smirking as he thought of all the barbarous things he was going to do to Rap. Dream away, little green monster! Poor wee goblin, doomed to be cheated of his victim! When Rap had left him in the shed, he had been busy crushing firewood with his bare hands to see how much strength he had given away. Well, he would get it all back soon.

Near him the burly old Nordland ambassador was trying to seem impassive, but his satisfaction was perfectly clear to a sorcerer. Obviously he hadn't enjoyed having Kalkor sniffing around his private peeing tree. No mourning there, Kalkor. No mourning anywhere.

200

The big chunky djinn stood swathed in his despicable curse, and rigid with fear and guilt. He was hiding them well beneath an arrogant sneer, but not well enough. He had tried to kill Rap most foully, and now his victim was a sorcerer. Bladder feeling a little tight, Sultan? Bowels a little shaky? The giant was not unlike the dwarf, Zinixo. Why must such distrustful men always assume that others were as vindictive as themselves? Did he think Rap would now make Inos a widow? Yes, he did, because that's what he would do in Rap's place. Murdering savage! How could Inos have ever . . . but that was her business.

"A most fortuitous bolt of lightning, Master Rap," the regent said. "I understand from the ambassador that you are now entitled to style yourself 'Thane Slayer!'"

Oh, he was a nasty one! He made Rap's skin creep. He had no magic, though. Seen through the ambience, he looked just the same as he did in the mundane world, except that farsight penetrated such trivia as clothes, and hence showed that despite his impish features he was part merman, with his hair and eyebrows dyed black to disguise the fact. His twisted ambition was a deformity of the soul.

"Call me whatever you wish, Highness." Reluctantly Rap turned face and mind to Inos, and met a smile like a summer dawn. Her cypress velvet cloak was spangled with a million fine diamonds of moisture. He toyed briefly with the thought of making them real diamonds. Well, at least Little Chicken wasn't the only one pleased to see him survive the Reckoning. But why must she show it so blatantly? Even the mundanes were reading the look on her face.

Inos, no! Stop that!

Her aunt stood nearby, beaming proudly at her sorcerous protégé as if he were all her own invention. Well, he didn't mind her.

"I think we shall now adjourn this court to the Rotunda," the regent announced. The thought was making him uneasy, most likely because he had been sadly humiliated there last night, but he was hiding his feelings behind his usual pomp. "We shall require the wardens to certify that the thane died by an act of the Gods and not by sorcery."

And he had the impudence to smirk at Rap as he said it!

"It was sorcery!" Rap said grimly.

The merman mongrel paled, and the courtiers around him all recoiled a step. His frowzy, sourpuss wife uttered a wail. Even the little boy lurched back.

Rap took a harder look at the little boy.

What in the name of all the Gods was wrong with *him*?

None of Rap's business! He had never really wanted to be a sorcerer. Or had he? He had stolen a word from Sagorn and then groveled to get another

201

from Little Chicken. He had schemed as hard as he could to become a sorcerer — whom was he trying to fool?

The old man in the background, wrapped in his rug like a parcel and
wedged into a chair — he must be the old imperor. Rap had heard good things
of him, poor man. His light burned very low now; and yet there was still light
there. Yesterday, as a mage. Rap had been sorely puzzled by the old man's afflic-
tion. Today, his stronger sorcerer wisdom found the trouble at once. He shuddered as he sensed the pulsing black spider-thing inside the old man's skull. That
did not belong there! Could he remove it without destroying the surrounding
brain? Very likely he could, but that was not his business, either. He couldn't go
around curing all the ills in the world. Imperors were off limits anyway.

The lumbering machinery of Imperial politics was still grinding along the
muddy track of mundane thought. "Then you may have violated the Protocol,
Sorcerer," the regent was saying. "The thane was an ambassador at large from
Nordland, and Nordland may take the view that . . . " He droned on, talking policy and right of succession and other drivel.

The sycophantic courtiers standing around him all nodded in sad agreement, sneering at the poor rustic who knew no better, taking comfort from
thoughts of the guardian wardens.

Was that what the white agony meant? — that Rap was to be judged by
the Four and put to death by them? No, Lith'rian and Bright Water would
surely have recognized their own hands in that mysteriously cryptic future.
That couldn't be it.

So why did the Evil-take-them wardens have to meddle at all? Why must
they come after him, when they had left Kalkor alone for so long? Where was
the justice in ignoring the atrocities of an odious cur like Kalkor and then
punishing the one who had ended his career? Rap's temper was bubbling
higher, pressing hard against the limits of his control.

Again he looked at the little boy, who was staring at him with hollow eyes
and chalky face, shivering in his thin hose and doublet. The kid's little backside was a monstrosity of welts and bruises, and there was something like a
cowl over his personality, a web, a mist . . .

Horrible!

"So we shall require you to attend," the regent concluded imperiously.
"Also our council, and Sultan Azak, and —"

"That won't be necessary!" Rap snarled. He isolated Azak's form in the
ambience, a dully mundane giant wearing only the sheen of sorcery on his
skin. Rap took hold of it and ripped — it came away like a film of soap bubble and he discarded it.

He flipped back to mundane senses. "I have cured the sultan's problem
for him, your Highness. If you will just grant him safe conduct back to his

home, then he and his wife can depart." He smiled at Inos. "A wedding present for you!"

Inos gasped and looked up at Azak. Azak stared at Rap and then looked down at Inos. Princess Kadolan uttered a shriek of alarm and put both hands to her mouth in obvious consternation.

Error?

Azak held out a clenched hand to his wife. Inos shot Rap a look of horror and then gingerly touched a delicate finger to the massive red fist. Of course nothing happened — did they think Rap could wield lightning against Kalkor and then not know when he had canceled out a clumsy spell like that curse?

Azak took Inos in his arms and tried to kiss her.

Her instant repugnance sent a burst of fury through Rap, and he hurled them apart, so that they both went reeling back.

Inos! Why was she looking at him like that?

Oh, Gods! He wasn't leaking anything now, not a whisper.

She really did love him? She didn't want big Barbarian Muscles after all?

Inos, oh, Inos! A mongrel wagon driver? *You're crazy, Inos!*

Then why had she . . .

He thought of madcap Inos putting her horse over ditches, of Inos scrambling up cliffs after birds' eggs and getting herself so horribly trapped that he and Krath had almost had to stand on their heads to haul her up to safety, of Inos charging recklessly into brawls on the waterfront to break them up and nearly being broken up herself in the process . . . Inos the headstrong . . . Inos who never stopped to think . . . Inos the impetuous . . .

He pushed the memories away. She had married that man of her own free will. It was too late!

And her feelings now were quite obvious to everyone. The djinn was black with fury, breathing hard, fists clenched.

"Oh, you cured his problem, did you. Sorcerer?" the regent said. "It seems to us as if your assistance was not entirely welcome."

The odious courtiers burst into raucous laughter at such wit.

Rap grappled with a rage that threatened to choke him.

And lost.

Fury!

His anger headed for the lecherous Azak and then swung away, for Inos's sake. It hovered briefly over the crazily impulsive Inos herself and retreated even more quickly. It peered longingly at the looming vulture nests of the wardens' palaces in the distance and shrank back in baffled impotence.

And so it returned to the easiest victim, the smirking little regent on his wooden throne.

Teach *him* to make jokes about Inos!

Rap reached out with sorcery and cured the imperor.

4

For a few moments nobody noticed. The old man opened his eyes and blinked at the shadowed crowd under the canopy, at the noisy torrents of water gushing off it near him and the gloomy rain beyond. Rap sent a surge of strength into the emaciated body — the mind was already burning up bright and clear.

The regent had risen, so the honored few with chairs were rising also. Flunkies were dashing off into the downpour to summon coaches; soldiers were running to alert the hussars.

Ythbane glanced around the crowd, selecting the favored ones who would be allowed to attend the meeting with the Four.

Then a lady squealed. Courtiers looked where she was looking and backed away in haste, pushing those at the edges out from cover. An aisle opened between the old man and the regent.

Ythbane made a fast recovery. "Your Imperial Majesty! You feel better today? You delight us! Medics!"

"Consul?" The voice was strong. "Would you explain what we are doing here? Is this some sort of nature festival?"

The regent — or possibly ex-regent — staggered. Then he turned to stare at Rap, and all the other eyes came around to Rap, also.

Rap allowed himself a satisfied smirk, and let it grow wider as he saw the horror and confusion spreading over those well-fed, pampered faces. This felt better than anything that had happened since he healed Inos's burns.

It felt much better than killing Kalkor.

"And who is that young man?" The imperor was alert enough to see that he must be important.

Ythbane was beyond speech, and some anonymous courtier answered for him. "He is a sorcerer, your Majesty."

"Ah." He seemed to understand instantly. "What day is this?"

Someone told him, but Rap's attention was distracted by Inos's aunt, who came pushing through the crowd to him, shoving roughly, making up in determination what she lacked in size. Her kindly face was ashen with worry.

"Master Rap! Is this your doing?"

"It is, ma'am!" He wanted to laugh aloud at the consternation he had created. Pompous parasites! The look on the regent's face   . . .

The princess wailed. "But isn't that a violation of the Protocol, using magic on the imperor?"

"And if it is?" Rap demanded, his anger flaring again.

She cringed back, a frightened little old lady.

"Rap!" Inos had arrived also, looking even more worried than her aunt. "You didn't!"

"I certainly did!" He lowered his voice. "And I don't care! They're going to burn me for killing Kalkor, so now they can burn me in a good cause. You don't prefer that horrid little merman regent do you?" He had gotten loud again. Oh, well . . .

"Rap! You idiot!"

"Who are you calling an idiot?"

Inos stamped her foot, but wet turf was not satisfying for foot stamping. "You, of course, you idiot! Blundering nitwit! Numbskull! Clown!"

"Oh? And who are you to criticize? Who went and jumped into marriage with a man who gives her gooseflesh when he —"

Rap bit his tongue. The big djinn was following his wife through the crowd, dodging his fancy hat around the water-loaded bulges of the awning. He had heard and he was not very pleased. Other people were listening, also, and they looked both scared and amused at the same time.

They could surely see the anger in Inos's scorching glare, well matching her angry words. What they would not see was the underlying fear, which was much stronger, although it was not fear for herself. At the moment she was only concerned about Rap. She was far more worried about him violating the stupid Protocol than she was about the way he'd cured her husband's curse and made her marriage possible — and yet she really didn't want to be married to the djinn at all, since even the thought of kissing him nauseated her. So at the same time as she was shouting names at Rap, her face was sending him different messages altogether. It was very confusing, even for a sorcerer. It could be mind-smashing wonderful if there was any future to it.

But it didn't go anywhere. He was doomed, and she would just have to adjust to married life. Her husband could touch her now and obviously intended to do so immediately —

As Azak put a hand on her shoulder, Inos flinched but did not look around. The signal her eyes were sending to Rap became a plea for help and rescue, even while she continued to shout insults at him.

"You always were a blundering chucklehead! Gullible, Rap! That's what you are! You never would think out what other people really wanted. You always accepted anything anyone said and took it at face value . . . No one else could ever possibly believe for one minute that the wardens would ever punish anyone for killing that Kalkor horror! In fact, that's obviously what Warlock Zinixo meant last night and the reason why they wouldn't listen to the regent then, because they *wanted* you to go ahead and kill Kalkor. But you couldn't see that! Oh, no! You had to go and slap them in the face by med dling with the imperor and *no one's* allowed —"

"You don't know what you're talking about! Wardens *eat* sorcerers!" She hadn't been to Faerie and she didn't understand the politics.

"Eat them?" Inos said blankly, stopping her tirade to breath a little.

"They give their words to a votary and then kill them. Do you think they're going to pin a medal on me?"

She pulled free from Azak's grip and lurched at Rap in fury, trying to pound at him with her fists. "Then what are you waiting around here for? Go away, you idiot! Run! Run!"

He took hold of her wrists and she was helpless. No sorcery required He lowered his hands so she was pulled against his chest. "It won't do," he said softly.

She looked up at him in dismay. "Not do why? What?"

He shook his head: too long to explain. Her face was very close to his Red lips. Green eyes, full of fear and longing. Scent of roses.

And then he became aware that people were staring at him expectantly The imperor in his chair was peering along an avenue of people. He wanted Rap.

Rap released Inos reluctantly. He'd been really enjoying that last bit. He walked over to the old man.

Emshandar had been tall for an imp. His bones were still large, but now his flesh was so wasted that the dusky, spotted skin hung limp. His neck looked like a fishnet hung on a hook to dry, and his face had fallen in around his teeth. Streaks of white hair hung limply from his scalp. The nose was a knife blade, yet there was fire in the eyes still, and Rap had not put all of that there. Even huddled under a wool rug the old man bore an aura of authority.

Behind the beaming faces surrounding him, most of the courtiers were in a state of panic. All their fine calculations had been spilled in the mud by the unexpected sorcery. Who was in charge now? How long would this remission last? How long till the old man died anyway? His daughter-in-law, who was now the regent's wife, was standing very close, trying not to be visibly ill, trying to keep her usual pout turned up in a smile.

It was very satisfying — and yet very unsatisfying, too, because when Rap had been a mundane he had hated the way the sorcerous seemed to play games with ordinary folk. Now he was starting to do it himself. He'd been a sorcerer only a few hours.

He sank to his knees on the grass by the imperor's toes. "Your Majesty?"

"It seems that we have been ill for several months, and today you healed us with sorcery. Is that correct?"

"It is, Sire."

The dark old eyes were filmy, but as shrewd as any. They appraised Rap carefully and then flickered vaguely over the watchers and listeners. He wanted to know why, and he wasn't going to ask; not here, not now.

He brought his attention back to Rap. "We shall reconvene this meeting in warmer and drier climes. We can command the rest —" Yet the old fox knew that his authority was now far from settled. "— but you can only request!" He glanced up. "Marshal Ithy?"

"Sire?"

"How many legions will you need to bring in this man?"

The soldier was a hard man, and a worried one, but he had a sense of humor. "More than your Majesty can readily muster, I fear."

"We fear the same. Sir Sorcerer, will you graciously agree to ride with us in our own coach?"

He wanted a private chat, of course, but his eyes were also saying that there were mundane means to undo what Rap's sorcery had wrought. He was vulnerable. He wanted protection! That seemed very amusing, when Rap considered it.

"I shall be greatly honored, Sire. I am at your Majesty's service."

"Are you, indeed?" The imperor was relieved. "Very well! Consul?"

With murder in his heart and a smile on his face, Ythbane said, "Me, Sire?"

"You. Sorcerer Rap will accompany us in the great coach. We require everyone else here to attend us in the Emerald Hall an hour before sunset. Yourself we may summon sooner."

Ythbane bowed, but Rap could not understand how he expected his face to deceive anyone at all.

As Rap rose to his feet, he saw one person who was in no doubt how he felt about the imperor's recovery. Squeezed between his mother and the side of the old man's chair, the little prince was gazing at his grandfather with a joy so great that he had even forgotten his own pain. The pinched features were still mantled to Rap's occult senses by that mysterious, unholy cowl, but there could be no mistaking the boy's relief and happiness. He sensed Rap's gaze, looked up at him in alarm — and ventured a wistful little smile of thanks.

And Rap's temper flashed up again. Someone must pay for what had been done to that child!

5

The great coach was great indeed, emblazoned in bright enamels and gold fittings. It had big windows of clear crystal draped with muslin; the door carried the Imperial arms picked out in gems; the interior was upholstered in purple silk.

Four stalwart Praetorian Guards supported a canopy over the imperor's chair as he was borne to this stupendous vehicle, and others lifted him in. Rap did not know which impressed him more, the coach itself or its eight white geldings with their jewel-encrusted harnesses and shiny plumes. If he was going to his funeral, as his aching premonition suggested, then he was certainly going in style.

Everyone stood back to let him enter also, and Ythbane was not the only onlooker whose inner thoughts were plotting that funeral. Rap moved toward the door, then swiftly detoured in two long strides to snatch up the little prince.

The boy gave a squeak of alarm. His mother and the regent began to react, and were momentarily frozen by sorcery. Rap swung the lad up high, stepped up on the footboard, and stood him inside.

"I think this one also, Sire!" He followed the boy in.

The Imperial eyebrows swooped down, and a haze of color suffused the parchment face. "You presume far, Sorcerer!"

"Suffer me this, Sire. I have reasons! Sit, lad."

With a worried look at his grandfather, the boy eased himself onto the seat opposite. The old man frowned as he registered the awkward movements. Then he shouted for the door to be closed, ignoring the angry faces peering in.

Rap settled at the prince's side and gave him a friendly grin that had a trace of occult reassurance included. "I ought to know your name, your Highness, but I don't."

"Shandie," the lad whispered. "I mean, Emshandar like Grandfather."

"A great name, then!"

"They call me Shandie, mostly."

"I'm Rap, but you can call me Rap."

The lad sniggered and wiped rain from his face. He began to relax, beaming excitedly at the imperor.

Harness jingled, the coach rocked smoothly off along the road. Ythbane was glaring after it, and other faces besides his had lost their fake cheerfulness also. Rap brought his attention back to his illustrious companions and the opulence of his surroundings — ivory door handles, gold lamps. Humble old Krasnegar seemed very far away now.

The old man adjusted the lap robe that had been tucked around him, clearly planning his first question. Rap spoke first.

"Shandie, I'm going to heal those bruises for you, but first I want you to let your grandfather see them."

The lad blushed scarlet, then just as quickly paled. "You mustn't use magic on me . . . er, Rap. I'm family!"

"Well, I've already bent the Protocol pretty badly, and I don't suppose one boy's battered butt will make a great deal of difference to the history of Pandemia."

Shandie giggled at that and looked to the imperor for guidance.

"Let me see!" The Imperial visage was stern. When Shandie stood up, turned, and pulled down his breeches to show the awful welts, stern became menacing.

"Who did that?"

"Ythbane," the boy whispered, making himself decent again and sitting down faster than he had intended. A wince of pain escaped him.

"Boars' blood!" the imperor roared. "Why?"

Shandie cringed. "I was fidgeting at the ceremony last night . . . I didn't know I was, honest! And then I turned around, 'cause I thought I shouldn't have my back to the warlock. But Ythbane said I was wrong." He sniffed.

"God of Mercy!" the old man whispered. "Master Rap, he was quite right. No one must use power on him, but . . . But if you do feel that you can take this risk, also, then I shall be even more in your debt than I am already, and Gods know, I owe you my life!" His eyes were hot with shame, but a hint of challenge burned there also.

Might as well be hanged for a horse as a pony, Rap's mother had always said.

Sorcery! "How does that feel, Shandie?"

The prince gasped and looked at him in wonder. "Thank you, sir!" A tear trickled down his cheek.

"You're quite welcome, and please don't call me 'sir.' What else is worrying you?"

"Nothing, Rap! Nothing. I feel very good now, thank you." He squirmed happily, enjoying the feel of it.

Rain drummed on the roof and streamed across the big windows. Water flew out in sheets from the wheels and flared under the horse's hooves. A platoon of hussars was clearing the road ahead, and another brought up the rear, but the crowds had long since fled in search of shelter, and there was little traffic.

The imperor had sensed Rap's worry and was waiting to hear.

"Shandie," Rap said, "I think there is something else bothering you." Even his occult senses could not explain the strange haze around the boy. It wasn't magic, but it certainly wasn't healthy.

"Well . . . Nothing!" The boy cowered back, fearful.

"Tell me!"

"Well . . . It's just . . . just that I'd like a spoonful of my medicine now. But I can get it as soon as we get to the palace!" he added guiltily.

Rap felt the imperor react to that. The old man seemed even more shocked than before.

"What sort of medicine?" he barked.

Shandie turned even paler. "It makes the pain better. Moms gives it . . . But I can take it myself when I want to."

"God of Slaughter!" the words came out softly, but the skeleton face flamed with anger, like a fever.

"Can you explain, Sire?" Rap asked, still puzzled.

"Some sort of habit-forming elixir. It's been done before." The old man paused, then muttered, "It diminishes the acuity of higher intellectual functions."

Rap didn't know such big words any more than young Shandie did, but he could read the meaning behind them: *It rots the mind!*

Knowing now what he sought, Rap probed gently until his sorcerous instincts found the trouble. Tricky! He reached in and . . . *wiped.*

Shandie jumped. "Oo!" he said. "Ouch! Oh, it's gone! I don't feel scratchy-twitchy anymore!"

"Gods be praised!" Emshandar said. "Shandie, you must never let them give you that medicine, never again. You mustn't take it yourself, either! Can you promise me that, soldier?"

"Yes, sir. I don't like the taste. It just made the hurt go away, and the scratchy-twitchy feeling. And Rap's cured that, too, now. It won't come back, will it?"

"I don't think so," Rap said, gently mopping up the last traces of the addiction.

The old man leaned back with a sigh, looking older than his realm. He smiled gratefully at Rap, but he was clearly running out of strength again, and their private chat would have to wait until he was stronger — and probably until Shandie's sharp young ears were not so close. Rap could grant occult strength, of course, but he was not sure if power used like that would leave a hangover. It might be dangerous.

Besides, Rap had a problem of his own. He could barely remember the last time he had eaten. "Are you hungry, Sire? I'm famished!"

Emshandar IV was probably not accustomed to such audacious questioning, but his thin lips smiled tolerantly. "Yes, I'm famished, too."

Shandie brightened.

The coach was very well sprung, and the roads were smooth. Eating would be no problem.

"Do you both like chicken dumplings?" Rap asked.

6

Not much more than a year ago. King Holindarn of Krasnegar had summoned a certain oddly gifted herdboy to his study for a confidential chat.

210

How grand those royal quarters had seemed to that callow lad! How clumsy and awkward he had felt amid the grandeur of books and soft armchairs and peat fires on sunny days!

All those would seem rustic and quaint to him now. Now he could see that Holindarn had been no more than an independent landowner, ruling a self-styled kingdom smaller than the imperor's Opal Palace on its hill. He had been a good man, though — better than almost anyone Rap had met in his long journeyings since. Few indeed were the inhabitants of Pandemia who had seemed worthy of admiration: Gathmor, in his rough way, and the sailor-folk of Durthing, of course; but who among the leaders and the gentry? The Lady Oothiana in Faerie, of course. Ishist, the filthy little sorcerer, perhaps. Holindarn's sister, certainly. And maybe, just maybe, this Imperor Emshandar himself. Time would tell . . . maybe.

Emshandar had obviously felt safer as soon as he was back in his private quarters and had arranged for them to be guarded by men known to him. His next priority had been a bath.

So Rap had asked Shandie to take him on a tour of the palace, and they had soon discovered a common love of horses. Having begun with the stables, they ended by spending the afternoon there, leaving no time for artwork or ornamental gardens or Architecture of Historical Significance.

Now they had returned to the Imperial chambers, where the ossiferous old man was still being primped and tonsured by teams of fussing valets; all the while grumpily demanding this special servant and that old retainer, and growing ever more furious as he discovered their absence. A big man once, still as tall as Rap; likely a soldier in his youth; strong ruler of a mighty nation for over thirty years, brought down by long sickness until now he could barely stand unaided . . . small wonder he was ill-tempered! Perhaps curing his illness had been a doubtful mercy.

And now three attendants were swathing him with elaborate care in an enormous length of soft purple fabric, adequate to have made a sail for *Stormdancer*. Of course it needed no special tailoring to accommodate his shrunken form, as a doublet and tights would have done, but as far as appearances went, it was quite the silliest garment Rap had ever seen.

Lounging sleepily on a silk-embroidered chair in a corner of the imperor's great bedchamber, he watched the performance tolerantly and was amused at how little he was moved now by genuine grandeur, by brocade and tapestry and priceless works of art. Holindarn's peat fire on a sunny day — now that had been impressive!

Knowing he was about to die helped deaden his emotions, of course. His premonition was a monstrous choking horror that he was finding ever more difficult to ignore. Some terrible danger was bearing down on him, and yet he

could find no escape from it. He considered fleeing on foot, and he even pon
dered the possibility of transporting himself by magic to Dragon Reach, say
or Krasnegar — and those options seemed to make no real difference. Jus
drifting along with events seemed to be the least painful course available to
him, and he was resigned to doing only that.

Perhaps he was suffering from too little sleep or too much stress, but the
jotunn temper still seethed through his veins, threatening to lash out in mad
ness whenever he let the warlocks drift across his thoughts, or brooded on
Gathmor's senseless murder or the abuse inflicted on little Shandie.

The boy was stretched out on the great four-poster bed, chin in hands
occasionally popping a nervous question to his grandfather or the mysterious
sorcerer. By defying the Protocol and working his wonderful cures, Rap had
made himself a very big hero to the boy. However little he felt like a hero, he
knew how boys — especially fatherless boys — needed men to emulate
Shandie would have found few worthy of his admiration in this cesspool of
intrigue.

Poor Shandie. Poor Gathmor. Poor Inos.

Gathmor, why did I not make you stay by the sea?

About this time yesterday, Rap and Darad had delivered the sailor to his
last rites. It had been a very private service, but each of the sequential set had
come in turn to pay his respects. Even Andor had been almost sorry. Sagorn
had spouted philosophy and Thinal had wept, but Jalon had sung a soul-melt-
ing seamen's lament that would echo in Rap's heart until the day he . . .

Don't think about that.

Don't think about Inos, either.

"Grandfather?" Shandie whispered, with a sidelong glance at Rap.

"Uh?" the imperor said, scowling at his teeth in a mirror held for him by a
trembling valet.

"Grandfather . . . Fauns are all right, aren't they?"

"Oh, yes. I suppose that will have to do — bring my sandals. What? Fauns?
Of course they're all right. Why wouldn't they be?"

"Well . . . I mean, I know imps are all right, but Moms says that Jotnar
are murderous brutes, and gnomes are dirty, and goblins are cruel. Thorog
says elves are all right. And fauns are all right, too, aren't they?"

His grandfather twisted around and frowned. "Who's Thorog? Never
mind. I think your mother has been filling your head with some odd ideas.
Master Rap, tell him about fauns."

Shandie turned a worried gaze on Rap.

"I don't know much about fauns," Rap said with a shrug. "I've hardly met
any. My mother was a faun. My father was a jotunn."

"Oh. I'm sorry! I mean I'm sorry I said —"

212

"That's all right. I've met some really horrible jotnar, like that Kalkor I killed today. Killing is bad, but he deserved it. I know some good jotnar, too. And one of the best men I know is a gnome. He smells horrible, but he's a loving father to his children and a very powerful sorcerer. Ythbane is an imp, isn't he?"

"Er . . . yes." Shandie meant *sort of*, so he knew, somehow. How?

"There are good imps and bad imps, Shandie. There are good jotnar and bad jotnar. Same with all of us. Some of us increase the Good and some of us, I'm afraid, seem to increase the Evil. We just try to do our best, most of us."

Shandie nodded solemnly. Rap thought again of last year's herdboy, and what his reaction would have been had he been asked to deliver a lecture on ethics for the heir to the Imperial throne.

By the time Emshandar demanded wine brought and lamps lit, and dismissed his valets, Shandie had laid down his head and fallen asleep, tiny as a doll on the great bed.

Emshandar struggled to his feet and hobbled toward a comfortable chair near Rap. It was only a few paces away, but he swayed and grabbed at a bedpost to steady himself.

"Son of a gnome! Leave me alone, will you?" he shouted, feeling Rap's occult touch on him. Then his anger faded to shame. "My pardon. Sorcerer. I know you meant well." He stood for a moment, studying the sleeping boy, his skull-like features melting into a worried smile. "Were it not for him, I believe I would ask you to put me back as I was before! But I should like to deliver his inheritance to him, if that be possible" He bared his teeth like an aging watchdog, too stiff to fight, too proud not to try.

He lurched over to the chair and sank into it, gasping with weakness. He poured wine with a trembling hand.

"I am sure your Majesty will feel stronger in a few days."

"We don't have a few days! Now you will take wine with me. I have questions."

Already the miserable day was drawing to a close, rain still dribbling over the great windows. Rap accepted a crystal chalice, changed its contents to water, and sat back to be cross-examined.

"How long have you been a sorcerer?" the imperor asked brusquely.

"Since dawn this morning, Sire."

"Burning turds!" The haggard old man stared, then sipped wine thoughtfully. "So we could claim that you were ignorant of the Protocol?"

"Not a chance, your Majesty. I've met Bright Water several times, and Zinixo, and Lith'rian, too."

The old man grunted, raising his white brows in astonishment. "Have you indeed? So they know of you, and you knew the risk. Then I suppose my next question is, why did you do what you did today? No mundane in all Pandemia has more power than an imperor, yet I can offer no reward a sorcerer would need. Why did you heal my sickness?" He pursed his lips over teeth that seemed much too large for the sunken face.

Rap applied a quick magic to smother a blush. "I lost my temper, Sire."

"Gods' bottoms!" The old man began to laugh, a great braying fit of laughter quite out of keeping with his emaciated appearance. "Well, you are an honest man, if not a wise one." Still chuckling, he refilled the goblets. Rap began to talk. He outlined the story as briefly as he could, leaving out only the dread fate he had seen waiting for him in Hub.

The windows were dark when he had finished, and Emshandar was staring at him blearily. Rap wondered if he should have detoxified his wine, also.

"There are no precedents!" the imperor muttered. "We'll have to meet the wardens, and tonight, if the dwarf really predicted the meeting. But I can't deny that you are in grave danger."

Before Rap could bring himself to mention that other awful danger, the old man sighed and went on.

"It is very rare for the Four to appear in public. Decades may go by without even the imperor meeting them all together. For many centuries my predecessors have kept a secret journal of their dealings with the wardens, to guide their heirs. There are shelves and shelves full of these great tomes, and no one ever has time to read them all. I read over the last couple of dynasties and gave up. I'll introduce Shandie to them when he's older, if I'm spared. But I can't recall anyone ever using power on an imperor or his family. That's about the only provision in the Protocol that absolutely everybody is aware of!"

Rap was about to say that it would not matter —

"Of course I'm grateful!" the old man snapped, and yet his face was saying that he hated being indebted to anyone. "What you did may have been foolish, but it was a wondrous thing for me and my grandson. I will do anything in my power to save you."

"That is very —"

"But I may not have any power!"

"Sire?"

The old man scowled at the goblet he held. "If the Senate and the Assembly and the Four all ratified Ythbane as regent . . . I wonder how the sly-handed twister did it, though?"

"A joint resolution," Shandie said sleepily, "based on an Act of Succession passed in the reign of Uggrota III."

The two men turned to look at him in surprise. He was awake, but barely. He smiled without opening his eyes.

His grandfather beamed proudly. "Clever boy! What else has been going on while I was sick?"

"Oh . . . Lots of things. Thane Kalkor came. And there is going to be a campaign against the perverts in Zark in the spring, and the dwarves have agro — abro — broken the Dark River Treaty." Shandie yawned, and then yawned again. "Drought in East Ambel, good harvest in Shimlundok. The goblins are still killing our soldiers. The XIXth Legion won the pennant again, but the IIIrd came second. Marshal Ithy won a lot of money on that, he said. Riots in Pithmot because of the new tax bill."

"Well done, soldier! Good report! You go back to sleep now." Emshandar's fond smile faded away as he turned back to Rap — he had been shaken by the news, especially the war talk. "Ithy?" he murmured. "Olybino?"

He shook his head angrily and swallowed more wine. "That's politics for you, Master Rap!"

"Sire?"

"Ythbane needed support. War? New taxes? He bought it dearly, I fear." For a moment he brooded, then glanced around to see if Shandie was listening. He was, but didn't seem to be. The old man dropped his voice. "I appointed that half-breed consul just before Emthoro died. Afterward —" He gestured in Shandie's direction. "— I could see there would have to be a regent appointed. I hoped it would be my daughter, although she isn't cut out for ruling. I decided Ythbane was smart enough to keep the great families in line and would promote her interests, meaning to manipulate her himself. I did not consider him strong enough to take power personally. Seems I was wrong! He went after . . . " He stopped with a shrug before mentioning Shandie's mother by name, but Rap understood.

The imperor's face was a gray desert, scoured by the ages, but when he looked up, his eyes gleamed like sunlight striking rock-girt pools, "So why am I telling all this to a coachman?"

"Because you don't know who rules the Impire tonight, Sire."

Emshandar nodded bitterly and drained his glass. It clattered as he laid it down with a shaky hand. "Oh, they obeyed me today, but that was mere courtesy. The imperor must be mundane, the Protocol says, and that toad Ythbane stole the throne with bribery and threats and a sure way with women. No sorcery."

"While I used sorcery to bring you back."

How would the wardens judge? But they remained unmentioned.

The old man sighed. "Whom can I trust?" he whispered. "The Assembly goes to the highest bidder. The Senate? The pompous do not easily reverse themselves. Coalitions and compacts and corruption! The army? Ithy?"

"The marshal was a worried man, Sire. I think he will be true to his duty."

"But his duty is to the law! What is the law? That is the question! Well, even my grandson is not worth a civil war. Sorcerer, this is hard for me to say, but I am asking for your help." When Rap would have spoken, he raised a hand like a bundle of dry twigs. "Let me finish! By rights you should have already fled from Hub, hoping to evade the wardens' wrath. That may be possible, if you can evermore resist the temptation to use your powers and remain one more mundane among millions. But without your continued aid, I fear that the recovery you have granted me will be short-lived indeed. If you do nothing but warn me who is lying and who is true . . . that would not be a serious breach of the Protocol, I think."

Was ever pride so humbled? A coachman, a stableboy!

"I shall do anything I can to help, Sire, but my time is very short. Something terrible happens to me today. Tonight."

Rap explained, and the old man looked shocked — and also bewildered.

"You are sure of this foresight?"

Rap shuddered. "Yes."

"It does not sound like the wardens. Their usual punishment for illicit sorcery is to enslave the culprit. If I remember rightly, it is South's turn to get the words. The sinner is merely a container, to be discarded when no longer needed. You know that the words can only be extracted by straight mundane torture?" Emshandar reached for the decanter and frowned at it for being empty. "I can see no need for immolation!"

Perhaps the white glare was not the worst possible future, though.

"I shall do what I can to help, Sire," Rap repeated. Emshandar's problems were his fault. He who wakes the dog must bear the bite, his mother had always said. Besides, he could promise anything now.

"I am grateful!" the old man insisted. It was true, but he hated it. "Is there anything . . . I mean, if I should survive and you do not . . . This Inosolan? What do you want for her?"

"Happiness."

A cynical smile crept over the thin lips and into the hollow eyes, like sunlight trekking a landscape on a cloudy day. "Happiness is rarely within the gift of imperors, Master Rap. Misery is our favored coin. But I promise you I shall try, if I am spared."

He sighed, an old man, and a very weary one. He needed a few weeks to recuperate and he wasn't going to get them. "I told those dolts to wait on me in the Emerald Hall long since. To keep them waiting much longer would be unwise. And after that, I fear, we must adjourn to the Rotunda and meet with the wardens; or some of us must."

Premonition began to prickle along Rap's arms as if the room had suddenly chilled. "Which way is the Emerald Hall?"

He scanned in the direction the old man pointed, but even a sorcerer needed time to explore the great sprawling collection of buildings that was the Opal Palace. "Eight sided, green carpets?"

216

"That's the place." The imperor was looking at him oddly.

A few people were patiently waiting in the Emerald Hall, but not as many as there should have been. The tingling grew urgent as Rap flashed his far-sight around and sought out Emine's Rotunda. He could find that one easily enough, because Shandie had pointed it out to him. It was unmistakable anyway, on the crest of the hill.

"They're starting without you, Sire."

Most of the great dome was filled with night — a menacing sooty evil to Rap's premonition — but a score or more tall candelabra spilled a dappled puddle of light in the center. Within this brightness, twenty or so courtiers were standing in small groups, talking in low voices. Three were in uniform, the rest wore the same sort of foolish wrapping as the imperor wore, most white, a few bright red. Kids in bedsheets, playing at being wraiths! Azak was there, easily identified by his height. Absurd! If his own court could see him now, he would be laughed at all the way to Nordland. The women looked good, though, in loose, many-pleated gowns. Inos at her husband's side . . .

The five thrones were all empty.

"I don't see Ythbane," Rap said. It was hard to make out faces at that range without starting to use real power — enough power to make him conspicuous to the wardens. The Opal Palace was a dead spot within Hub's occult bustle, an oasis of silence like a city garden. Almost any use of magic here was going to ring out in trumpet fanfares. "What color?"

"A consul's toga has a purple border, but I suppose he may have grown too big for that now."

"He wears the purple," Shandie murmured sleepily.

"Then he isn't there yet," Rap said. "But it can't be long."

Even a mundane could have seen the pain on the old imperor's face as he gripped the arms of his chair and tried to rise. He sank back, helpless. He bared his teeth, gathered himself, and tried again, with no more success. Sweat shone on his forehead, his breath was harsh. Then he glanced miserably at Rap in a wordless appeal for aid. The will was there, but the body had been starved and immobile for too long.

"I can give you strength. Sire, but I fear there may be a price to pay later. I have no experience at this."

"I will pay the price!"

Rap poured energy into him, and watched in fascination as color suffused the pale cheeks and the bodily fires blazed up to match the burning will.

"Aha!" he shouted. "Thank you, Sorcerer! The old warhorse will tread a measure yet!" He lurched to his feet.

Premonition! Rap rose, also, aware that every hair on his body seemed to want to stand up — also — on its own. His fate was waiting for him in the Rotunda.

There he would meet whatever it was that had burned out his foresight in white flame. He would have been shaking like a terrified child had he not been using his powers to calm himself. At least he thought he was — at that level it was hard to know what was occult and what was just wishing. But he wasn't going to let the old man see his fear, not after promising he would help. Running away would solve nothing. Back wounds hurt twice, Sergeant Thosolin had liked to say.

"Shandie, my boy? Wake up, soldier!"

"Grandfather?" Shandie seemed to smile in his sleep. He rolled over and sat up. The grin became a yawn, and he stretched his broomstick arms.

Emshandar had paused before a full-length mirror to inspect his appearance. "My shroud has slipped," he muttered disgustedly. "I suppose you could make me look . . . no, never mind." He turned to his grandson. "Come along, lad. We've got to go and meet the wardens."

Already scrambling crabwise toward the edge of the bed, Shandie froze, and his eyes fixed on his grandfather in horror. Suddenly his happiness had vanished and he was petrified. Rap found that curious.

"Hurry!" the imperor said.

"Do you really think he need come, Sire?" Rap said.

He provoked an Imperial glare that could have razed a city. Obviously a chance to see the Four in action would be an important part of the heir's education. Equally obviously, Shandie was a vital element in the cloacal ferment of Imperial politics and should not be left around unguarded at this important moment. Most obvious of all, his grandfather had not noticed the boy's freezing dread.

"Come, soldier! On your feet! Pity we haven't got time to dress you properly."

With a gasp of relief, Shandie came back to life. He slid down off the bed. Now he was beaming again. "All the wardens coming tonight, Grandfather?"

What was going on inside that maltreated little mind? Somehow the question seemed important to Rap's battered premonition, despite that talent's present hysterically overworked condition.

"I could make a toga for him, Sire, if that's what you mean."

Emshandar said, "Of course!" approvingly, but Shandie quailed as if his nightmare had engulfed him again, gazing up at Rap accusingly. Why should togas bother him so? Could his fear be in some way related to the savage beating he had received the previous night?

The imperor had still not noticed. "Excellent! Pray do that, Sorcerer."

218

"What color?" Then Rap wondered if he was just trying to delay the inevitable a little longer. He did not look at the Rotunda.

"Plain white," the imperor said. "Quick!"

"Easy," Rap said. "Stand up straight, tribune,"

The boy's fright was as intense as it was inexplicable, but he was trying very hard not to show it to either his grandfather or his new sorcerer friend. Yet he was shaking.

"Do you want a roll of thunder, or just a quiet sort of sorcery?"

"No thunder please, Rap." The big eyes stayed locked on the sorcerer. Rap's humor had not stopped his chin quivering.

"Very well. White toga . . . " Rap ensorceled the boy's garments to a replica of his grandfather's tunic and toga, in white. He added gold sandals and ran an invisible comb over the short wavy hair. "That looks not bad at all!" he said admiringly, mostly to himself. "If anyone tries to beat you, I'll turn him into a walrus!" he promised.

Shandie tried a shaky smile and a nod. Then he set his jaw and squared his shoulders in an obvious imitation of his grandfather, although he was still almost ill with his inexplicable terror. Rap's promise of protection was not reaching deep enough to soothe it away.

But if a puny child like him could do his duty despite such fear, then Rap should be able to attend to his. Whatever it was.

Aargh! Another quick scan showed him that time was running out. "Ythbane's arrived, Sire! With his wife. He's carrying something."

"A buckler and sword. Quick, Master Sorcerer! We must hurry. Your garb now."

Rap balked like a horse put to the face of a cliff. He was a churl, not a patrician. Besides, those ridiculous wrappings left half the shins uncovered.

"I don't think so!"

The imperor flushed. "Only foreign dignitaries attend the Rotunda without formal court dress!"

"I do."

"You can't go like that!"

"I go like this or not at all!" An imp toga, goblin tattoos, and faun legs?

For a moment he thought Emshandar was going to order his head cut off. Veins swelled under the papery skin.

"Do you know what you're going to look like to them? What they'll think of you?"

"A bumpkin, a yokel."

"Well?" the old man thundered. Shandie's eyes widened in alarm.

"That's what I am," Rap said stubbornly. "You want my help? You take me as I am, or not at all!"

Ythbane had mounted the lower step of the dais. He was one step from the Opal Throne.

"God of Fools!" the imperor muttered angrily. "Well, then, let's go!" He glanced at the silken bell-rope dangling by the bed. "A litter . . . there isn't time for that, is there? Can you magic us there?"

"Yes, Sire. But if the wardens are watching, it'll scorch their eyeballs!"

"Let it!"

Rap shrugged. All very well to say so, but how was this done? He remembered Ishist saying that Lith'rian could move himself around without a magic portal, by means of sheer brute power. Mmm!

Well, he obviously must not lose anyone on the way, so he stepped between his companions to take hold of the imperor's thin elbow and Shandie's clammy little hand. He sharpened his view of the ambience . . . the encircling darkness that was the Opal Palace . . . the twinkling minor magics of Hub beyond . . . beacons shining on high towers in the wardens' lairs . . . occasional flickers beyond the horizon from sorcerers dwelling in distant lands.

He concentrated on the looming threat of the great Rotunda, estimating distance and elevations.

"Ready?" he asked his companions. Then he held the three of them still, and moved the ambience.

Fortune's fool:

> BENVOLIO: The Prince will doom thee death
> If thou art taken. Hence, be gone, away!
> ROMEO: O, I am Fortune's fool!
> BENVOLIO: Why dost thou stay?
> Shakespeare, *Romeo and Juliet*, III i

9

Sacred flame

1

Within the nested darkness of Emine's Rotunda, under the myriad little flames and crystals of two candelabra, the Opal Throne crouched in wisps of many somber hues, dreaming of the evils it had known.

Before the throne, the regent stood on the top step, clad in purple toga and armed with the Imperial regalia. One step down, his wife sat on a chair. An empty chair on the other side was likely intended for Shandie.

Ythbane glanced over his audience, as it counting that no one was missing. Straight ahead of him, at the end of the tapering indigo mosaic, stood South's Blue Throne. Below its single candelabrum, it was a floe of light adrift on a sea of darkness.

And then the imperor came striding out of that darkness with his grandson and a sorcerer. The spectators learned the news first from Ythbane's face. They turned quickly to inspect the newcomers.

Holding his eyes firmly on the usurper, Rap could still scan the company. Inos was there, of course, and the look she was giving him was quite appalling shameless. Her dumpy aunt beamed at her side. The pleated gown rathe suited her, tactfully hiding her bulges. All the women looked chilled. The men were better off, in their heavy togas. Azak was lowering and uncertain — so he should be, wrapped in that sail. Why couldn't he have been given djinn costume? A scarlet-crested helmet located Marshal Ithy, and a man in a purple-hemmed white toga had to be a consul. Three men in red togas and a woman in a red dress must be senators. Bare chested and helmeted Ambassador Krushjor and another jotunn were staying well back on the north side of the illuminated area. Little Chicken was with them, also in jotunn breeches. He was the only person smiling, unless you called that outrageous glazed simper of Inos's a smile.

Rap wished he knew more of the politics. Who ought to be present and was not? Which patiently loyal supporters still waited forgotten in the Emerald Hall? No one of importance, he suspected. Ythbane was depressingly confident.

The warlocks were Emshandar's only hope now. Would they answer the regent's summons? Whose side would they take?

As Rap reached the front of the onlookers, he stopped and laid a hand on Shandie's puny shoulder to stop him, also.

Emshandar went on alone, a gaunt, white-haired wraith of vengeance, a striding skeleton swathed in purple. He halted before the dais and straightened from his usual stoop. For a moment he stared at Uomaya, who hung her head and did not look at her father-in-law. Then he lifted his gaze to Ythbane, who smiled.

Two men in purple, two rulers where there could only be one.

Under Rap's hand, Shandie was rigid — trying to hold himself still, hardly breathing and yet unable to suppress his trembling.

The confrontation seemed to hold for a month . . . and then the imperor broke the silence. "We relieve you now of your temporary responsibilities, Lord Ythbane."

Ythbane shook his head. "We are happy to see that the improvement in your health continues. Consul?"

One of the purple-hemmed politicos cleared his throat meaningfully. The imperor shifted around to glare at him.

"The People's Assembly will be enraptured to hear how your Majesty has rallied and will certainly vote thanks to the Gods, and a public celebration. Plus prayers that the remission continues, I shouldn't wonder."

The speech had omitted much more than it included, and Emshandar hadn't liked it.

"We congratulate you on your unanticipated promotion, *Lord* Humaise. Does anyone know where Consul Uquillpee is?"

Ythbane broke the silence. "Doubtless he had urgent business elsewhere."

Rap scanned. "There is a consul waiting in the Emerald Hall, Sire." He wondered if he should bring the man, for he must be an Emshandar supporter, but he was elderly — the shock might give him a seizure.

The imperor did not suggest it. With the skill of a lifetime of concealing his emotions, he looked over the small gathering without expression. "Epoxague, then? What of the Senate?"

The man addressed was small and venerable, draped in red. He wore a little mustache, which was unusual, and he obviously wished the imperor had picked anyone but him.

"The Senate will concur in those sentiments, of course."

"And rescind the regency?" the old man barked.

"It is never easy to predict what the Senate in its wisdom may decide. But if I had to guess, then I would venture that the noble senators would lean to the view that resolutions cannot be juggled to and fro with every up or down of your Majesty's condition. Of course, if the remission is long-lived . . . If, after six months or so, your Majesty shows no signs of a relapse, then I feel sure that restitution of your former standing would be possible."

His face told Rap that he did not expect the old man to live that long under any circumstances. Inos and her aunt were scowling at him. They would be on the imperor's side, of course, because Rap obviously was. Everyone else had been carefully selected from the Ythbane partisans.

Emshandar's shoulders had sunk a little. He looked around again. "Ithy?" he said quietly.

As if he had expected the summons, the marshal removed his helmet and tucked it under his arm. His hair was short and grizzled, his face leathery and somber. He paced slowly forward to confront the old man at close quarters, as a bull might inspect a scarecrow unexpectedly invading its pasture.

"Em!" he said softly — so softly that many, perhaps, did not hear. "My standing orders say I report to the regent. But I learned my trade from men you taught, Em. My commission bears your signet. You administered my oath of office. What exactly are you asking of me now?"

The regent frowned, and Rap sensed the first tremor in his confidence, but very small — a doubt as insubstantial as a cloud of gnats.

For a long moment the old imperor stared into the soldier's eyes, and the audience held its breath. "To uphold the law, Ithy, as you swore."

The marshal nodded. He replaced his helmet, saluted smartly, and went marching back to his former place.

An invisible corona of triumph seemed to blaze up around the regent, and his friends were exchanging sly smiles. He made an almost imperceptible gesture with the short bronze sword, as if challenging the haggard old man to charge up the steps and take the throne by storm.

Emshandar's shoulders slumped further. He glanced despairingly around at Rap.

"Ah, yes!" Ythbane said. "We thought you'd brought along a gardener, but we remember now. He's a sorcerer, isn't he? How odd that the imperor emeritus would bring a sorcerer into Emine's Rotunda! You will of course have an opportunity to appeal to the Four very shortly. They have been known to overrule the Assembly and the Senate and the Imperial army — but we can not recall exactly when the last time was. And they don't approve of stray sorcerers meddling in their business!"

The old man tried to straighten again, his face flushed. He was almost out of strength.

Ythbane could tell. His smile was a poison stiletto. "Maya, my dear, your father-in-law is weary. Why don't you help him over to the chair we brought for him?" He pointed with his sword to where a plain wooden stool sat far back, barely visible in the dark.

His wife pouted at him and then at her father, her face sour and disagreeable. She did not move.

Rap realized with surprise that his hand on Shandie's shoulder was shaking more than the shoulder was. The boy seemed to sense this at the same moment, and glanced up at him questioningly.

Ythbane noticed the movement. He smiled at his stepson as a snake might smile at a mouse. "And we brought a chair for little Shandie, also! Come and sit here by us, son."

A shiver ran through the prince and the sorcerer both.

"I have a question!" Rap barked. "Did you beat this boy?"

"I always beat him after formal ceremonies," Ythbane said in a toneless voice. "Nearly always."

Rap had spoken on impulse and compelled a reply almost unconsciously. Puzzled by that reply, he pressed harder. "For what reason?"

"I tell him he has been fidgeting, but in fact I want to make him fear and hate formal ceremonies of any kind, so that when he comes to his majority, he will be happy to leave the conduct of state business to me."

The faun in Rap shrank back in horror, and the jotunn part of him clenched like a fist. He said harshly, "You enjoy it?"

"Yes, I do." The words were a stench in the ambience.

"And what was the medicine you gave him?"

"Another precaution, an elvish draft of poppy and narcotic, guaranteed to be habit-forming and debilitating. He is already addicted, and will remain easily controlled by it, even as an adult."

Evil of evils! Rap glanced triumphantly over the audience to see what effect his odious confession had produced.

Almost none. So a boy had been whipped? Every man present had been beaten often enough in his youth; none of them had seen Shandie's injuries. Epoxague was frowning, and a few of the others, but they were not about to change their political views because of something said in the presence of a sorcerer.

Released from his truth trance, Ythbane was flushing furiously.

"We expect the wardens will be interested in what was just done!" he snapped. He raised the sword to strike at the small shield on his left arm. Then he hesitated, eyes glinting. "Come here, Shandie!"

Shandie twitched. Rap tightened his grip to prevent him moving.

"Very well!" Ythbane said. He started to swing the sword.

This was the human reptile who had provoked Rap's foolish outburst of sorcery in the first place, and that stupidity had done no good at all. Indeed the day's events had likely strengthened the regent's position. Now he was glorying in his evil ways, likely to triumph completely, even winning back Shandie, that innocent pawn, prize, puppet . . .

Intolerable! Rap struck magic at Ythbane as a man might swing a stick against a tall weed. The regent passed right over the lower dais and crashed to the floor beyond. The shield clanged, the sword went clattering away into the darkness. Uomaya screamed, and a few others cried out. Shandie whooped and jumped joyfully.

Ythbane tried to rise, and Rap struck him again, knowing he must knock the man unconscious quickly, or in his jotunn madness he would surely kill him.

The regent lay still, blood trickling from his mouth.

Better!

The audience was petrified.

Inos glared furiously at Rap. *Idiot!* said her eyes, *Now you have really done it, my lad.* She definitely had a point there. Striking the ruler from his throne — in three thousand years, there could have been no worse desecration of Emine's Rotunda.

Emshandar was the first to move. He shuffled over to the prostrate Ythbane and bent to tug at the shield until it came loose from the limp arm. Then he headed out into the shadows to retrieve the sword. He came hobbling back, flashing Rap a glance of jubilation.

He climbed the two steps until he stood before the Opal Throne. His daughter-in-law stared up at him in terror, but Shandie was grinning. So were Inos and her aunt. Everyone else was shocked into silence, most of them staring in confusion at the thrones of the wardens, still inexplicably deserted.

The imperor spoke first to Uomaya. "Be gone from my sight!" he sai
hoarsely, pointing with his sword at the outer darkness. She slid sideway
from her chair, gaping at him as if expecting to be cut down. Then she turne
and fled.

The old man sank wearily onto the throne that had been his for a gen
eration. For a moment he just panted quietly, looking over the assemble
witnesses with evident satisfaction, displaying the teeth that seemed s
oversized for his wasted features. Legally nothing had changed, Rap knew
Legally Ythbane still reigned. But men were ruled by their hearts as well a
by laws, and Emshandar seated on the throne of his forefathers and hold
ing the state regalia was not the friendless petitioner who had bee
spurned so lightly a few minutes ago. Now he could rule hearts, and mind
must follow.

If others would obey him, then he was dangerous again, and therefor
worth obeying. It was a circle: Power made fear made obedience made mor
power, and no one understood the recipe better than the old lion himself
These few men and women were the tiller of the Impire, and by turning them
he could set whatever course he willed.

Guessing his next move, Rap forestalled it.

Dropping to one knee, he pointed at the lonely three-legged stool in th
distance. It had been planned as a humiliation, but it would make a goo
refuge. "Shandie," he said, "you go and sit there and watch. And fidget all yo
like, because no one cares any more about that."

"Yes, Rap! Thank you!" Without even a glance to see if his grandfathe
approved, the boy went running off.

Rap's presumption earned a hard stare of Imperial anger as he rose. An
he was not finished yet. His temper had ebbed as fast as it had flowed, leav
ing a scum of disgust behind it. He had attacked an unarmed man! He
would never have used a sword or even a stick like that, so where was the
excuse for using sorcery? As he paced over to Ythbane's still form, he
recalled sour old Mother Unonini, perched on the one good chair in
Hononin's dingy little room and preaching: *Sorcerers are human, too, Master Rap
They are torn between evil and good, as we all are — more so, perhaps, because their powe
to do good or evil is so much greater.*

He'd behaved like a lout. And in front of Inos, too!

Ythbane had a broken shoulder and a fractured skull, together with a daz
zling collection of bruises. By the time Rap reached him, though, they were
all cured and his eyes were open. As an afterthought, Rap changed his purple
toga to plain white. He held out a hand to help the man rise, then left him
standing there and returned to his former place before the Opal Throne,
blandly ignoring the imperor's wrath.

— which sought out a more rewarding target.

"Epoxague!"

"Your Majesty?" The little senator was doing a good job of concealing a very large amount of worry.

"As we recall the Act of Succession," the imperor said, "it decrees that when a regency is needed, sovereignty shall devolve upon the next in line. Did our daughter refuse to serve?"

The little man rubbed his mustache. "With respect, Sire . . . the next in line was a minor. The wording seemed ambiguous as to whether the sequence then continued to the second in line. There was considerable debate."

"Pigs' guts!" Emshandar flushed with fury. "I'll bet there was! Nit splitting! Of course that's what it means!"

The senator seemed to shrink slightly. "That did seem to be the view of the majority, Sire, although a narrow one."

"Then why was Orosea not appointed?"

Epoxague's face shone damply below the golden trellises of the candelabra. "There is provision for bypassing a designated candidate who is unsuitable, Sire, and some honorable senators believed that your daughter's long absence from the capital might have rendered her unfamiliar with present conditions in —"

"Sewage!" the imperor roared. "Unadulterated sewage! What was worrying them was that Leesoft has elvish blood in him, and those two sons of hers have slanty eyes. Isn't that so? They didn't want slanty-eyed princes any nearer the throne than necessary?"

"That view may have . . . That opinion was never expressed in my hearing, Sire, neither in public nor —"

"Cuttlefish! So you accepted a mongrel merman instead! There were no recorded votes, of course?"

"No, Sire."

For a moment the imperor stared threateningly at the wretched senator. "The Ythbane regency is dissolved. Should another be necessary in future, either for us or for our grandson, then our daughter will serve. Is that clear?"

Pause. "Yes, Sire."

"You will promote her interests?"

Longer pause. "Yes, Sire."

"We have your oath, freely given?"

The senator looked uneasily at Rap, who smiled mysteriously; then he glanced at the four empty thrones and finally he yielded to the evident threat. "Yes, Sire. I so swear."

"Hummph! Consul?"

In a few minutes, the old fox had extracted that oath from every imp present, including Marshal Ithy, who was the only one pleased to give it. By then Ythbane had gone. When his followers began deserting him and no occult aid arrived, he walked quietly away into the darkness, heading for the west door. Rap let him go, and Emshandar either did not notice or did not care.

"As for Lord Ythbane," he concluded, "he is hereby banished for life to the city of Wetter, upon pain of death." He scowled at the flicker of reaction. "For assaulting the heir apparent. Consul, see that the Bill of Attainder is passed quickly and sent on to the Senate."

Emshandar would not make the mother of his grandson a widow, but his leniency had surprised the audience, although only a sorcerer could have told so from their hard-schooled faces. The old man leaned back for a moment and rubbed an arm across his eyes. He was exhausted, and close to having to admit it. He looked over the company again.

"Sultan Azak, you are welcome to our court — you, and your so-beautiful sultana, also."

Azak seemed to touch his forehead to his shins as he bowed. Inos curtseyed, flashing Rap a glance of desperation. Miserably Rap pretended not to notice. He had removed the curse and night was at hand.

"The peace proposals you brought are acceptable," the imperor added wryly. Marshal Ithy flinched, and so did a few others. Azak looked startled, then pleased, then suspicious, all in one fast blink. He bowed again. "Your Majesty is most gracious!"

Rap thought of all those stalwart young legionaries he had seen marching boldly eastward. So he had prevented a bloody war that might have dragged on for a generation? That was good news, but it was most certainly a political use of sorcery, even if accidental.

Where were the wardens?

Emshandar's well-trained face was transparent enough to Rap. He thought he had won now. The Four had not stepped in to block him, and Ythbane had been discredited. Inos's problems were irrelevant, for Rap had survived and could look after his own wants.

"That would seem to complete the evening's business!" The old man sighed gratefully. "Marshal, you will attend us in the morning."

Ithy saluted, his face grim as he contemplated all those legions he had moved to Qoble and must now return.

Emshandar laid the sword and buckler at his side and put both hands on the arms of his throne to rise.

Shimmer!

"There are a few matters left on the agenda, your Majesty," said the high, sweet voice of an elf.

2

Lith'rian sat on the Blue Throne under the candelabrum. To mundane view he was a golden-skinned adolescent, slumped back at his ease in a toga of shimmering moonlight blue, a garment that seemed more mirage than substance, although it was opaque enough. The sandals on his outstretched feet shone like pearl. His toenails had been silvered, although he was too far off for anyone but Rap to notice.

In the ambience, he was bewilderingly different. True, the physical likeness was there, and where Kalkor had shown as a transparent wraith, the elf was far more solid. He seemed to be standing right in front of Rap, hands on hips, smiling a welcome and studying Rap as Rap was studying him. His slanted opalescent eyes twinkled with cheeky and tolerant amusement. His limbs were slim, his ribs visible above a juvenile flat belly; yet to occult vision the signs of age were obvious — the tiny traces another elf would look for, in earlobes and fingernails. Lith'rian must be older than the imperor, for he had been South since the year Emshandar's father succeeded.

But the physical likeness was only a tiny part of his spectral presence. Rap reeled before a rainbow chorus of sights and sounds: sunlight singing along crystal forests, flowers schooling like fish, odors of roses and whirling stars, pattern and counterpoint and dance. This was a glimpse of the intricate mind of an elf, and its sheer complexity almost sickened him until he managed to suppress the images and quieten the music. Lith'rian detected the reaction, and his mirth burst up like foam from breaking surf.

The imperor had struggled to his feet and was bowing.

"We meet again, Master Rap!" a private thought from the elf said.

"Yes." Rap braced himself for attack. Yet if attack was what the warlock planned, he could have caught Rap off guard in the first second after he arrived.

Joyous elvish laughter, like birdsong: *"You were only a few minutes late in reaching Arakkaran. I warned you the outcome was too close to call."*

Fury!

Despite the gaiety and boyish charm, Rap knew this man to be an unscrupulous prankster. He had bound his daughter to a gnome. He and his fellow wardens played games with Inos as one of the pieces.

To lose one's temper in any fight was a mistake. To lose one's temper when dealing with an elvish sorcerer would be rank insanity.

Trouble was, Rap's temper had not yet cooled down from Gathmor's death. It simmered still.

Evidently he had masked his feelings, though, for Lith'rian was chuckling. *"I was very much afraid you might arrive in time to stop the wedding. No, do not jump to conclusions! Olybino had reported that Inos was dead, remember."*

229

Meanwhile events were creeping along snailishly in the mundane world. "You honor us with your presence, your Omnipotence," the imperor said. His haggard face was grim at the thought of dealing with the wardens in his present exhausted state.

"Not exactly, your Majesty," Lith'rian said from his throne. "We do not come in answer to your summons. Do all your companions comprehend the significance of that distinction?"

"So East lied?" Rap snarled. "So what?"

In the ambience, summer sky darkened to looming storm. "*Can, you not see! He lied his way out of a pond and into the sea! He had sent her back to Zark once. Had she then set off for the Impire again, he might have taken drastic steps! That ceremony was a protection for her. You should be grateful to me. All is not lost yet, and it might very well have been. Had you succeeded, you would have failed!*"

Trickster! Trickster!

Rap's fury had struck down Kalkor easily enough. This smirking yellow-bellied elf would not be so easy.

It might feel good to try though . . .

Emshandar was scowling, and explaining. "The Council may be summoned at any time by the imperor, or by the warden of the day, which today is his Omnipotence, Warlock Lith'rian."

"And I have chosen to exercise that privilege," the elf added, as the spectators all bowed or curtseyed. "There are some serious matters to discuss, involving unauthorized use of sorcery."

The threat barely penetrated Rap's spinning head as he tried to restrain his rising anger and also follow the writhing skein of images, the conversations proceeding on two levels. He was certain that the elf was about to make the confusion worse.

"*You don't trust me!*" Lith'rian wailed mockingly at Rap. On the throne, the boy waved a languid hand. "Our beloved brother of the west, his Omnipotence, Warlock Zinixo."

"*Watch this one, Master Rap,*" he added privately. "*He is immensely powerful, and very dangerous.*"

The dwarf materialized on the Red Throne and simultaneously in the pale nothingness of the ambience. He was scowling on both planes. On the throne, in a toga like the embers of a stormy sunset, he was too young and too short to be impressive, diminished by the scale of the throne itself, which made him look like a child.

In the ambience, ironically, he did look physically dangerous, his thickness and heavy limbs more than making up for his lack of height. His wide chest glinted with hair like iron filings, and he seemed as indestructible as a granite pillar. Kalkor's image in the ambience had been transparent, while

Lith'rian looked almost as solid there as he did in the mundane. If density of appearance was a measure of occult power, then Zinixo's adamantine mass was very ominous.

His mind . . . Instantly Rap understood why elves and dwarves were so notoriously incompatible. Zinixo brought with him images of vast dark caverns, deep winding labyrinths where dangers lurked around every jagged corner. Paradoxically, these mingled with visions of barricades and beetling fortress walls built of gigantic rocks. How much was racial and how much the warlock's own Rap could not tell, but suspicion blew from those battlements like winter fog.

"We meet again, your Omnipotence," he said, bowing.

His insolence kindled images of enormous millstones grinding noisily. "I knew I should have killed you while I had the chance. The witch deceived me!"

"I bear you no ill will," Rap insisted, knowing he would not be believed.

A prickly hedge of lavender sparks had sprung up between elf and dwarf, seeming to originate about equally from both of them. It wavered as each tried to get Rap on his own side of it. He rejected it, staying neutral, and it withered away. He wondered what he looked like to the warlocks. He did not feel very solid, certainly, and he had no experience at concealing his thoughts.

Imperor and courtiers had turned expectantly to the north.

"Her Omnipotence, Witch Bright Water," the elf said.

On the throne she was small and almost beautiful, clad in flowing draperies that shone like the dazzle of sunshine on fresh snow. Her arms were bare, and not as greenish as a goblin ought to be in this light. The dark hair coiled high on her head was surmounted by a tiara of twinkling diamonds. Little Chicken should be impressed by this vision of goblin maidenhood.

Rap had seen her naked once before, as an ancient crone, and had been appalled. The scrawny little relic that appeared before him in the ambience was immeasurably older, and so little human that he felt no emotion except horror. Almost nothing there was original. He had known that she was centuries old, but now he could see that she must have been patching herself with sorcery all those years as organ after organ wore out. She was tiny as a child, and hideous.

Hideous did not begin to describe the mental baggage that came with her. Boys writhing in torment, sailors drowning, brutal gang rapes . . . death! Galaxies of dying faces, multitudes of rotting corpses. Three centuries of death — plague and rout, bloodshed and sickness and lonely old age. Bright Water was obsessed by the fate she had evaded so long. This was the secret of her madness. How much death could one witness in three hundred years?

Fortunately Rap was rapidly gaining some control over his susceptibility, and he could fade out the nauseating images almost completely.

And even as her youthful public image nodded to acknowledge the homage of the assembly, a shrill goblin cackle rang out for Rap in the ambience. "*And we also meet again, faun! The first time I saw you, I foretold your great destiny, did I not?*"

"*Huh? No, you didn't! You said you couldn't foresee me!*"

The mummified green monkey in the ambience waved arms that seemed too long for her, while the air overhead whirled a blizzard of corpses. "*But we knew why I couldn't, didn't we, eh? Not knowing means knowing if you know why you don't know! Leaves only one explanation, eh?*" She peered closer, so that he recoiled, although there was no real movement or closeness involved. "*And you have retained your tattoos! That surprises me!*"

It also pleased her, and her favor might be much safer than her disapproval in whatever was about to happen. He bowed. "*Goblinhood is no small honor,*" he said, hoping that sounded gracious. "*I am several times in your debt, ma'am.*"

The tiny form sank down and genuflected to him in mockery. "*You certainly are! And you will remember that when the time comes?*" Then she jerked up her head, a shriveled brown coconut. "*And my dear brother of the west, also?*"

If that was intended as a joke, it failed to amuse Zinixo, who scowled even harder, eyes flickering everywhere. His battlements were just as high on Bright Water's side as anywhere else. Claws scratched on rock in the underworld.

"And his Omnipotence, Warlock Olybino," Lith'rian proclaimed to the mundane audience.

The imp who appeared on the eastern throne wore a sumptuous uniform decorated with gold and jewels. Even his cloak and the horsehair crest on his helmet shone like spun gold. He looked young, and handsome, and virile.

His image in the ambience was elderly, bald, and paunchy; and also fainter than any of the others. He was short, even for an imp. Olybino was the only one who had never met Rap, and he pouted disagreeably up at him as if he had never wanted to. Oothiana had called him the weakest of the Four, and Lith'rian despised him — although the elf probably despised a great many people.

He certainly did not look impressive. He might even be pathetic, were he not so dangerous — for the flabby little man stood within scenes of bugles and floating pennants, of godlike warriors clashing swords in noble combat and shining armies locked in battle. This was idealized war, war as a sport for warlocks, with none of the mud and stink and pain of real war. In a way it was even worse than Bright Water's obsession with death, because the people in it were completely unreal. At least the goblin's visions were capable of suffering.

So here were the wardens, revealed at last — four handsome young people on their thrones in Emine's Rotunda and four ogreish nightmares crowding n around Rap in the ambience. He had a strange illusion that they all wanted something from him, although he could not imagine what. He felt as if skeletal fingers were pawing at his arms and digging in his pockets. Remembering the palsied, putrefying beggars of Finrain, he decided he would prefer to be beset by them, or by starving anthropophagi.

"Do sit down, old friend," Lith'rian remarked to the imperor. His kindly tone might be genuine, but it shocked the courtiers. Emshandar sank down stiffly onto his throne.

"Death Bird!" the witch of the north shrieked, springing to her feet and stretching out arms in invitation. The spectators jumped, and Little Chicken actually fell back a pace. Then he squared his thick shoulders and advanced toward the White Throne.

Under an ominous night sky, the giant fortifications to the west had crept much closer to Rap, and now a great boulder came hurtling down from above, aimed to crush him. He stepped aside and let it sweep on past, twirling downward forever through the ambience. He dug fingernails into his palms to restrain his temper. That odious gray runt had sold Rap to the galleys. There were some other scores to settle there, also. Evil take the lot of them!

"West, *behave yourself!*" Olybino snapped petulantly. "*He's just testing,*" he told Rap. "*He isn't using anything like his full strength.*"

Another boulder came bouncing down a hill, straight for East. A thick-limbed warrior stepped forward and smashed it to a shower of gravel with one stroke of his shining sword. Olybino laughed hoarsely. "*You are being childish, West!*"

But some false note in the voice left Rap wondering how much of his resources that pompous imp had needed to parry the dwarf's playful blow.

Little Chicken had reached the witch, and she was embracing and kissing him fondly. In the ambience Rap himself lay screaming on the floor of Raven Lodge. He closed out the image easily now, his control increasing with practice. On a parallel plane, the tiny relic of a goblin woman leered up at him. "*You die good, faun!*"

"*And now he has my promise!*"

She cackled like a startled barnyard. "*So he has!* Your Majesty," said the young woman by the White Throne, "this man is most dear to us. We charge you to make him welcome in your house and to see he is returned unharmed to his people. *You will not deny him his destiny!*" the hag told Rap with a friendly leer. "*And you will remember that I helped?*"

She was mad, totally mad. She did not seem to realize that Rap could detect the writhing horrors of her mind. It seemed strange, in fact, that the warlocks should also be revealing themselves so blatantly. Was it possible that they were not viewing the ambience in the same way he was, as a Jostling confusion of ideas and emotions projected by themselves? It was certainly unfair that he must undergo this contest when he had had so little time to learn the sorcery business.

Little Chicken was heading back toward Krushjor, dazed and aroused by the youthful witch's caresses, while being assured by the puzzled imperor that he was an honored guest of the palace.

"Yesterday," Lith'rian proclaimed, "his Impermanent Highness, Regent Ythbane, tried to summon us here to consider the case of Sultan Azak. He also planned to inquire if Thane Kalkor had used power on him — which he had, of course. My colleagues and I, aware that another sorcerer was in the vicinity, decided that events might best be allowed to continue for another day."

A giant stone pillar toppled . . . Rap stepped back and let it shatter at his feet. That one had been closer. The young dwarf glared resentfully at him under his craggy brows. Rap frowned back warningly.

Lith'rian piped on: "Now it may be that that same sorcerer has solved the Kalkor problem permanently for us — perhaps occultly, although the thane was a Nordland emissary — and has also cured a grave sickness inside the crowned head of the imperor. Furthermore, he possibly laid a truth trance upon the regent and thereafter smote the poor fellow from the throne. We must consider, Sister and Brothers: first if any of these alleged acts was real and second, if so, whether it constituted political use of occult power; and third, if so, then what punishment is fitting. Are there any other charges?"

The Rotunda fell silent. Rap had not moved on that plane at all, but the nearer spectators had been edging away from him, leaving him even more isolated than before. Emshandar stared miserably at him, eyes bleary with weakness, face crumpled like old paper. On his stool out in the darkness, Shandie was hugging himself and jiggling his feet in an agony of apprehension for his new friend Rap. Inos and Kade were holding hands and biting their lips in mirror image.

"Very well," the elf said. "The defendant known as Rap is present — such a demotic, nondescript name! Our dear brother of the west? How say you? Did the alleged acts occur? *Speak to the nice people, Shorty. In sentences if you can.*"

But the dwarf answered occultly, and even that was a growl. "*Who gets his words?*"

"*That's irrelevant just now, Stone Head.* What say you to the evidence, Brother?"

The youth on the Red Throne was chewing a fingernail. Then he spoke mundanely for the first time, in a voice like falling rocks. "I reserve judgment."

Wasps buzzed in the ambience, but the other seeming youth, the elf, just shrugged. He looked across at Bright Water. "Our sister of the north, what say you?"

"There is no truth in the allegations," the young woman said promptly. The mundane witnesses gasped with surprise. Inos beamed, and Shandie pulled his feet up on his stool so he could hug his knees — but Rap saw the ancient crone simpering mawkishly at him and heard the shrieks of his own dying corpse.

Olybino did not wait to be asked. "Of course he's guilty!" he snapped. On dusty plains in the ambience, legion after legion was marching onward to battle. The warlock of the east wanted Ythbane restored, and the Zaridan war, also.

"Brother West, do you wish to judge now?" Lith'rian trilled. "*Last chance, Ugly!*"

"Yes, he did all those things," the dwarf admitted grumpily.

"And I concur," Lith'rian said, with an occult sound of retching. "Defendant, by vote of three to one, we find that you committed certain suspicious acts. Now we must consider whether any one of those constituted an illicit use of occult power — that is to say, for political ends."

He beamed at the company in the Rotunda, but in the ambience he scowled at the dwarf beside him, amid a strong stench of barnyard. "Perhaps we'll go round the other way this time, *and give stone-wits a chance to think about the question.* Brother East?"

Hooves thundered and banners snapped in the wind. "Guilty!"

"Sister North, how say you?"

"Not guilty," the goblin maiden said. The hag leered at Rap. She had another fate in mind for him, but she seemed to think he ought to be grateful for the opportunity.

If all this was designed to confuse him, it was succeeding admirably; his mind reeled between conflicting existences.

"Dear brother of the west?" Lith'rian cooed.

"*Who gets his words?*" the dwarf demanded again.

"*If you must know, it's my turn. The last one was that imp in Drishmab, and East got her, nine years ago.*"

"There was no illicit use of power!" the dwarf rumbled.

In the ambience, Lith'rian winked an opal eye at Rap. "And I regretfully say there was. Your Majesty, the wardens are evenly divided. North and West are for acquittal, East and South for conviction. How says our mundane brother of the center?"

A great horror came over the imperor's face. He knew what had been done, by whom, and who had gained from it. Now his honor was thrown into conflict with his gratitude. The spectators seemed likewise appalled, holding their breath, waiting for his reply.

A rock the size of a melon whistled out of nowhere, aimed straight at Rap's head. He ducked and let it go past. He was sure he could have swung at it with an occult bat and hurled it right back at the dwarf, but he was also sure now that such a response would reveal more of his power than simple avoidance did. If Zinixo wanted to know his strength so badly, then that was good enough reason to keep it secret.

Furthermore, Rap was beginning to suspect that he lacked all the spectral paraphernalia that accompanied the others' projections within the ambience. Its absence might not be a weakness but a sign of strength, an ability to see more clearly or manipulate power more directly.

Fool! Did he think he could be stronger than a warlock?

But if that dwarf pulled any more tricks, it might be fun to find out!

"I find no truth in the allegations," Emshandar said harshly. Sweat was running down his ribs below his toga as he uttered this blatant lie.

"Then we find the defendant not guilty!" Lith'rian proclaimed. His youthful smile was a blizzard of blossom petals lifted by a summer breeze in the south.

Drums rumbled defiance from the east and armed multitudes clashed in fury; men and horses screamed.

Something gurgled in agony to the north and more claws scrabbled in dark crypts to the west.

The mundane spectators broke into applause. Little Shandie jumped to his feet and cheered. Inos released Kade's hand, ducked around Azak before he could block her, and raced through the forest of candelabra to Rap, obviously intending to throw her arms around him. He dodged her, as he had been dodging the dwarfs attacks, and held up a hand to ward off any second attempt. He knew Lith'rian by now. There was more to come.

"*Master Rap,*" said the elf. "*You could read the ambience when you were a mere adept, could you not?*"

Rap nodded, bracing himself as he sensed the danger closing in.

"Inosolan!" Azak roared. Inos gave Rap a hurt look and reluctantly walked back to her husband's side, her head bent low.

"*Faugh!*" Bright Water shrilled. "*You should have felt the mastery he had when he only knew one word of power! I guessed then what his destiny was!*"

"*Master Rap,*" Lith'rian said, caution like a fence of crystal spears bristling around him, "*I think you would make an excellent warden. If you wish to contend for the Red Throne, I for one would have no objection.*"

Bright Water screamed an objection, a bugle rang out joyfully in the east. But Zinixo did not wait for argument or discussion, nor even for Rap's own reply. He struck instantly, as the elf must have known he would. The great mass of fortifications tipped, split, and crashed down in a landslide toward Rap.

Rap used the direct physical simulation that had worked on Kalkor. The dwarf's spectral image was right beside him in the ambience. Spurning any pretense of subtlety, he hurled himself on it with all the occult weight he could summon. That version of Zinixo toppled over backward with Rap on top of him, grappling for his throat. The two ghostly presences rolled and struggled as if locked in mundane combat, and there was nothing transparent or unreal about it that Rap could sense. The dwarf's breath was hot on his face, and his thick body slick with sweat.

They squirmed and twisted on a shadowy ground, directly in the path of the hurtling mass of rocks.

The spectators in the mundane Rotunda would see nothing at all happening. In the ambience, the torrent of rock divided and roared past on either side. Rap tightened his grip on the massive neck, and saw panic and madness in the agate eyes staring up into his. Ironically, he knew that in the real world the dwarf's great strength could have easily torn him off and smashed him. In terms of occult power, though, he thought he was holding his own.

Above them, a cavern roof shattered and began to fall.

Without releasing his grip, Rap twisted and rolled, hauling the dead weight of the dwarf on top of him as a shield. Two massive rocks struck on either side of them and fell together, forming a canopy to deflect the rest of the crashing debris. Rap stared up at the hate-filled gray face and continued to squeeze with his thumbs. Huge hands seized his wrists and tried to wrest them away. And failed.

The dwarf seemed to grow impossibly heavy, crushing Rap down against jagged rock. He ignored the pain, squeezing, squeezing, and watching the bulging face of his opponent. They were both panting and straining, but Zinixo seemed to have run out of tricks. He flailed punches at Rap's ribs, but they were nothing like the blows he could have landed in a mundane struggle. Then his great hands clawed for Rap's neck, meeting the challenge directly.

"I've got you!" Rap gasped. "I'm stronger! Yield, damn you!"

In the Rotunda the spectators had guessed that something was happening between these two. The faun and the dwarf were standing rigidly and staring at each other. In the ambience they thrashed and rolled, straining strength against strength, pouring sweat, panting harshly.

The other wardens were intent and silent, watching but seemingly not taking sides. Yet, in the corner of his mind, Rap caught a faint image of a fiery fence encircling the battle and luminous angry shapes dancing around, trying to penetrate and being blocked. If that was not mere hallucination brought on by an overtaxed, pounding brain, then it might represent Zinixo's votaries being denied a chance to intervene.

"I don't want your throne!" Rap said. He was on top again, trembling with the effort of keeping his grip, very near to the limit of his strength.

But the dwarf was in worse shape, with his tongue lolling and his eye bulging almost out of his head. He uttered meaningless croaks of fear.

For a moment nothing more seemed to happen. Then Rap realized that in the Rotunda the corporeal Zinixo had lurched down from his throne and was staggering across the floor to attack the corporeal Rap. Rap had no reserve left to deflect a mundane assault. If the dwarf could bring real-world muscle and strength into the battle, he might win yet.

Somehow Rap dragged up a last feverish effort and dug his thumbs in even harder, squeezing relentlessly until he thought they were about to meet inside the great neck. Will! It was all will, and endurance, and stubborn purpose.

"Yield or I kill you!"

The spectral Zinixo uttered a choking rattle and went limp, like a sack of sand.

It was no trick — the warlock was dying. Revenge! Revenge for Yodello and Oothiana and being sold as a thrall and for the murderous attack itself   . . .

Do what is good, not what seems good! One of his mother's sayings. Rap fought back against his seething fury. Bind the dwarf, then? Make him votary, a slave sorcerer, to serve his every wish and be loyal unto death?

Where was the moral high ground in that? Revolted by his own black hate, Rap released his occult grip.

Below the lights of the branching candelabra, the real Zinixo stood swaying before him, eyes glazed. Rap also felt spent, shaking and mentally battered. It was impossible to believe that he had no wounds, no bruises, that his back had not been shredded or his gullet crushed. He gulped great gasps of life-giving air.

The mundane spectators were staring in complete lack of understanding. The other three wardens smiled contentedly.

"Hail to our new warlock of the west!" Lith'rian said.

"I am no warlock!" Rap shouted, appalled at the mad hatred staring at him in the dwarf's stricken eyes. *"I don't want your throne, West! This wasn't my idea."*

Zinixo bared his monstrous crusher teeth. His huge fists were clenched and trembling.

"I mean you no harm!" Rap insisted.

But, for all his occult power and physical might, Zinixo was still a timorous boy. He had been the strongest of the wardens, yet always unsure of himself. A stronger sorcerer than himself was an unbearable threat to him. He saw treachery everywhere; he could trust no one. He stared at Rap in dread and hate.

"I won't change my mind," Rap insisted. He held out a hand, *"No hard feelings?"*

It wasn't going to work, he saw. Nothing could ever reconcile Zinixo to the existence of a stronger sorcerer than himself.

238

"*Well, if you won't make friends willingly,*" Rap said, "*then I suppose I'll have to put a
)yalty spell on you, but I don't really want to have to —*"

Zinixo grabbed the proffered hand, and jerked.

Rap stumbled forward. The dwarf grabbed his head and pulled it down to
iis own level . . .

And whispered a word of power into Rap's ear . . .

A *fifth* word of power.

3

For Princess Kadolan, it had been a day of extremes. She could not recall
iny day in her life that had veered so often between the Good and the Evil.

It had begun with the astonishing realization that she was awakening on
i lumpy bed in the Opal Palace. To have arrived in Hub at all after a life-
ime of longing should have been a wonderful experience, but at first it had
)een marred by the need to remain incognito. Furthermore, Doctor
;agorn's house, while comfortable enough, had been in a shameful state of
ieglect. Captain Gathmor had done a wonderful job of making her quar-
.ers *shipshape,* as he liked to call it, but two nights there had been more than
)lenty. A smelly backstreet tenement was no more inspiring for being
ocated in Hub than it would be in any other city. Then, yesterday, she had
)een reunited with Inosolan, and together they had become guests of the
mperial regent himself.

Or possibly his prisoners. Their status had unquestionably been interro-
;ated, because Azak was a prince of a land that the Impire was about to
nvade, and Inosolan still had a claim to Krasnegar, over which the
Nordlanders were rattling their swords. She had even been questioned about
Proconsul Yggingi and the way he had roused the goblins. Kadolan had
never much cared for the seamy art of politics, and she felt that her present
advanced age ought to excuse her from becoming involved in not just one
but *three* possible wars. As she had told Eigaze, the only bright spot she could
see was that no one could possibly blame her for the Dwanishian border dispute, as she had never met a dwarf in her life. Inosolan had told her glumly
just to wait.

And, of course, that night she had indeed met a dwarf, or at least been in
the presence of one. A warlock! So great an honor! Very few people ever
knowingly met a sorcerer in their lives, let alone one of the Four. Yet,
although she would never say so, had the young man in question not been
sitting on a throne, Kadolan might easily have mistaken him for a surly
young churl escaped from a workgang somewhere. Warlock Zinixo was sadly
lacking in polish.

From the history lessons of her childhood until sorcery entered her life in the person of Queen Rasha, Kadolan had hardly spared a thought for the Four. Had she needed to think about them, she would likely have imagined four benevolent, elderly sages sitting around a table somewhere, probably wearing funny hats. Inosolan's account of meeting Warlock Olybino had begun a revision in her thinking, and the dwarf had completed it.

The wardens were a sad disappointment!

She had thought yesterday hectic. Today had certainly been worse; up and down like a thresher's wrist, all day long.

Having wakened to the memory that she was staying in the Opal Palace, she had then been sobered by the sight of peeling wallpaper and cracked plaster. Her room was not located in one of the more prestigious wings.

Breakfast had lifted her spirits — excellent food on magnificent silver plate, very well served.

Then Inosolan and Azak had joined her, and she had seen at once that Inosolan had some bad news to impart. Unfortunately Azak was quite the most suspicious man in Pandemia, and had been determined not to let Inosolan out of his sight, or hearing.

Right after breakfast, her day had brightened again as Eigaze arrived with four other old friends from Kinvale days. That had meant four more joyful reunions, although saddened perhaps by the awareness of time passed. Eigaze herself had once been graceful as an elf and thin as a willow. Now she had a son in the Praetorian Hussars taller than a pine tree, while she herself . . . well, who was Kadolan to criticize?

Up and down — Inosolan had dragged Kadolan away to go and visit the unfortunate Duke Angilki, and that had been a sad duty. The poor man had not moved an eyelash in two days, and the doctors were in their most somber mode. But the palace infirmary did have certain rooms where no man, even a sultan, was allowed to go, and those had probably been Inosolan's objective all along. She had hauled Kadolan into the first one she saw, and there imparted her dread news.

Master Rap had visited her in the night. Kalkor was a sorcerer; the result of the duel between them was not preordained as the magic casement had suggested. They had been assuming that he would win the Reckoning and could then worry about staying away from goblins in future, but apparently that was not so. And finally Inosolan had described her efforts to share her word of power with Rap, and his discovery that she did not know one. Disaster!

They had been a doleful party when they drove out to the Campus Abnila to view the second Reckoning, and the unending rain had not helped to raise anyone's spirits.

Up again . . . Despite his forebodings in the night, Master Rap had somehow found the occult strength he needed, and he had ended the notorious career of the infamous Kalkor very sharply. Kadolan had felt very pleased by that, even if the man had been a relative of sorts.

Down . . . The worst yet: Master Rap had lifted Azak's curse. Kadolan blamed herself for that. For weeks she had tried so hard to explain to the lad that he was the subject of the God's command and Inosolan's destined mate. He had never quite admitted that he returned her love, but why else would he have followed her all the way to Zark? Obviously Kadolan's entreaties had been inadequate, and the foolish boy had cleared the way for his rival to claim his unwilling bride.

She had always believed that honor was the finest attribute a man could possess, but now she saw that even honor could be carried too far. Excess was always on the side of the Evil.

And then he had also cured the old imperor! In some ways that had seemed like a wonderful blessing, and a most charitable thing to do, but it was very obviously a forbidden use of sorcery. At one stroke, Holindarn's former stableboy had upset the whole political structure of the Impire.

That was when Kadolan had decided that this day was going to live in her memory as the worst she had ever known. Battered and bewildered by so many changes of fortune, she had given up trying to keep track, and had concentrated on merely remaining sane.

However, she had been careful to stay close to her niece. The sultan had been eyeing his wife with blatantly lustful glances, which Inosolan had been ignoring while cheerfully dragging Kadolan around the Opal Palace as if determined to view every one of its sculptures and innumerable points of interest in a few brief hours. Meanwhile the day had been drawing relentlessly to its close. Kadolan could hardly chaperon a married woman in her bedchamber.

Since Master Rap had gone off with the imperor, there had been no word of him. His sorcery had cured the sultan's curse, but it had left the Krasnegar situation unresolved. She had not been too surprised, therefore, when the regent had summoned them to the meeting with the wardens. That was not the sort of summons she enjoyed, but it had at least offered the possibility of some answers to some of the problems. Trying very hard to hold fast to her faith in the Gods, Kadolan had accompanied Inosolan and Azak to the Rotunda.

The start had been inauspicious — the regent in command, and no sign of the imperor. But then Emshandar had appeared, apparently in good health, and Rap still with him, like a court sorcerer. She had begun to think that her prayers might yet be answered.

Down again . . . With no warning. Rap had used very obvious sorcery to reveal the regent's questionable tactics and displace him from the throne Kadolan had watched in rising apprehension, while Inosolan's fingernails dug into her hand. The boy was ignorant, of course; he had probably received no schooling at all, but she had come to know him a little during their journey from Arakkaran, and she knew he was well informed about the occult. How therefore, could he possibly expect the wardens to allow such open use of sorcery around the Opal Throne itself?

But for a heart-stopping moment, it had seemed that the faun's temerity had escaped notice. Visibly exhausted but yet jubilant, Emshandar had been about to end the meeting and send them all off to bed — that being one of the problems that had not been solved.

And then the wardens had come.

Disappointing . . . the Four were definitely not what Kadolan had expected. Warlock Lith'rian looked barely old enough to shave — although she had a vague idea that perhaps elves didn't — and Warlock Zinixo still resembled an escaped quarry worker. Witch Bright Water was young and about as close to beautiful as a goblin could ever be. Warlock Olybino was the handsome young soldier Inosolan had described. None of them looked old, or especially benevolent.

Fair enough, appearances were unimportant. It was the way the Four behaved that really upset Kadolan. True, they granted Master Rap a trial. They did not follow normal courtroom procedure, for the judges called themselves as witnesses, but she supposed that was reasonable enough when the judges were omniscient. She could not disagree with the testimony, because she had witnessed the events herself. But thereafter justice seemed to go sadly awry. The dispassionate, disinterested guardians of her childhood lessons dissolved like mist.

The verdict was quite obviously skewed by political self-interest. Of course an elf and a dwarf could proverbially never be on the same side of anything, but Bright Water's vote for acquittal seemed to have no logical explanation at all, unless it involved Master Rap dying horribly at the hands of the young goblin the witch had embraced so shamelessly.

And the old imperor! Emshandar had always been spoken of as a man of honor. He had been a good imperor, ruling as a man of peace although he had soldiered well in his youth. A man of law and justice. The elf had been very cruel in forcing him to cast the deciding vote and put his heart before his head.

Of course Kadolan had wanted Master Rap acquitted, and she had joined in the applause with everyone else, probably much more sincerely than most of the spectators. Yet somehow she had felt a *wrongness*, and almost a feeling of *guilt*. She elt like an accomplice to something shameful. Perhaps it was to be expected of o turbulent a day that the best news it could produce would be so flawed.

Inosolan had no such scruples. With a yell of delight she released Kadolan's hand and pulled loose from Azak's arm — for the sultan was being quite shamelessly attentive to her, like a love-sick boy — and went tearing over to embrace Master Rap. Kadolan was left standing between a gold candelabrum on one side and an almost equally tall sultan on the other, and she was not sure which was putting out more heat. She thought for a moment he was going to pursue his errant wife and drag her away bodily, but he restrained himself when he saw Master Rap evade the hug.

"Inosolan!" Azak bellowed, and Inos slunk back to him like a beaten dog.

Kadolan cringed. She was certain that Inos was going to refuse to share a room with her husband that night. There was going to be a most frightful scene. Azak was probably capable of using force, and even Imperial law was on his side there. Gods knew what Zarkian law would have to say on the matter. Why, oh, why had Master Rap been so pigheadedly honorable?

Frightful scene or not, surely the trial had ended and everyone could leave? Her feet and ankles were complaining bitterly that every day must end at last, even a day like this one. She peered around at the company — the wardens on their thrones, the haggard old imperor, gentlemen in red or white togas, or uniform, ladies in their white chitons. They all looked exhausted. What were they all waiting for?

Then she saw that everyone was studying either Rap or the warlock of the west. Both of them, in fact — they seemed to be glaring very hard at each other.

What was the wayward faun up to now? Cheeking a warlock?

If the God of Love Themselves had not decreed it, Kadolan would never have seen this boy as a suitable partner for Inos. He seemed to do the wrong thing so often. It wasn't that he was headstrong — the Powers knew that Inosolan needed no tutoring or assistance in that direction! No, Master Rap so often seemed to act deliberately, and for the best possible reasons, and then commit the worst possible blunder. Disaster followed him like a black dog.

The staring match continued. That was the sort of silly game very small boys played, not young men. Not sorcerers, surely?

Then why did everyone seem to be holding their breath?

Abruptly the dwarf lurched down from his throne and reeled across the floor toward Rap. The warlock seemed to be drunk, or ill, and Master Rap remained paralyzed, the audience still spellbound. Kadolan glanced at Inos, and she obviously did not understand what was happening either. But this was no childish matter, clearly,

243

About two paces from Rap, the dwarf halted and raised great killer hands as if about to attack him. But then he just stood for a moment, swaying on his feet, and suddenly the game seemed to be over. Both contestants started from the trance; both breathing heavily. Rap wiped an arm across his forehead. What *had* all that been about?

Then the elf explained. "Hail to our new warlock of the west!" he sang.

Inosolan Jumped. So did Kade, despite her sore feet. Warlock?

Apparently not. Rap shouted out that he was no warlock. Now everyone seemed completely confused, even the wardens. Rap and Zinixo were back watching each other, but Rap at least was trying to make friends. He smiled. He held out a hand.

Then West accepted the handshake, vigorously. And not just a handshake — an abrazo as well? How disconcerting! She knew that in some times and places it was permissible for men to embrace one another, but she had thought that it was an elvish custom, not a dwarvish one.

Kadolan relaxed with a sigh of relief. Well, perhaps now the show was over and they could all go off to bed, please?

No — suddenly the day made another of its mad plunges into disaster.

Warlock Zinixo vanished, totally. Master Rap staggered back, clutching his head. The other three wardens all leaped to their feet, and Warlock Lith'rian clapped his hands over his ears.

That gesture . . .

Rap had done that just after Rasha had made him tell her a word of power, as if he had heard something mundanes could not.

Not a kiss. A whisper!

Rap spun around, looking at the imperor — who had fallen back in his seat, aghast — and then at the other three wardens in turn. And finally he turned to stare across at Inos, as if in farewell. His face was a mask of despair and his eyes were already glowing with a pearly gray light.

It was a judgment — a judgment on the perverted judgment! The Gods had spoken!

Kadolan heard herself cry out. The Rotunda swayed and the rushing sound of rain was suddenly impossibly loud . . . Inosolan caught her and Azak helped, and they lowered her to a sitting position on the floor, but then she resisted, refusing to lie down despite the spinning howl in her head.

Rap screamed.

So did several other people. His clothes were smoldering, smoking . . . fire trickled out from his collar. And suddenly he was engulfed in searing white flame.

Inosolan released Kade's arm, and a second time she raced across the oor of the Rotunda to Rap. "Tell me!" she yelled as she went. "Share them! Dilute them!"

Impetuous as ever, she threw her arms around him and was enveloped in re also. Her dress vanished in one flash. For a moment the pair of them ere visible, two bodies locked in terrible embrace, blazing together, filling the Rotunda with light so noontime-brilliant that the candles seemed xtinguished.

Spectators raised hands to shield their eyes from the glare; the floor was triped black with their shadows and the shadows of the candelabra. The seats nd distant walls sprang into view; the great stone ribs of the ceiling shone verhead, with every crystal pane reflecting back the incandescent lovers' yre through a gathering haze of white smoke.

Consumed, the bodies vanished, and the fire, also, and the Rotunda was lunged into Stygian dark.

Sacred flame:
>All thoughts, all passions, all delights,
>>Whatever stirs this mortal frame,
>Are all but ministers of Love,
>>And feed his sacred flame.
>>>>>>>>>>>>Coleridge, *Love*

10

Bold lover

1

The midnight sky was dusted with a myriad of bright stars. Slowly they grew brighter and larger, becoming candleflames and crystal droplets on the candelabra. A dull, faint light returned as eyes adjusted, although a greenish afterimage of the immolation still ached on the retinas. Shapes of gentlemen in togas materialized in the gloom and two ladies came hurrying to Kadolan's assistance.

"No, please!" she protested. " . . . standing a little too long. Quite all right . . . If you'll just help me up . . . "

Marshal Ithy himself was at her side then, bringing the chair vacated by Princess Uomaya, and willing hands helped her into it. She felt a fool.

The Rotunda seemed very dark, still. The warlocks had vanished. The imperor was slumped on the Opal Throne, elbows on knees, face in hands. Dismay and fear ruled the court.

Gone? Inosolan gone? Rap gone?

Kadolan's mind could not comprehend the tragedy. Surely the Gods could not be so cruel?

Voices began to rise as people demanded explanations. Azak's harsh tones broke in, explaining what had happened.

Plop! Heads turned. Sudden silence.

Inosolan was back.

She was standing exactly where she had been when she vanished, before the throne. The golden hair that had scorched away in flames was restored to its former glory; her sheer chiton hung again in soft folds, clinging daringly to her figure. Kadolan had watched that garment sear away to nothing, and the sandals, also.

Not a burn, not a scar . . .

Inosolan smiled vaguely and said, "Hello?"

The imperor looked up, incredulous. Others just stared.

Azak recovered first. He moved forward a few paces and then halted, peering at the apparition from a safe distance. "Inos?"

She blinked over at him as if still bewildered, her smile a trifle unfocused. "Who else?"

"What happened there?" he demanded.

"Where? Oh, there! Well, it's a little hard to explain . . . " She pondered for a moment. "Very hard to explain, actually."

"Where is Rap?" the imperor asked harshly.

Inosolan turned and looked at him wonderingly. "Rap? Oh, Rap. Yes, he'll be along in a moment, Sire. Had some business to attend to, he said."

Kadolan tried to rise, and someone laid a hand on her shoulder to restrain her. "Inos!" she cried. "Are you all right?"

Inosolan turned more, until she had gone all the way around. "Aunt? There you are. Yes. Yes, I'm fine. A little dazed, maybe."

"Will you please tell us what happened?" the imperor asked behind her.

This time she merely twisted her head to look at him. "It isn't easy to describe, your Majesty. Not easy at all. Maybe Rap can tell you, when he gets here. I don't think I can. But I'm all right. And he's all right."

Then Azak lurched into motion. He strode over to Inos and grabbed her shoulder. "*What is the meaning of this?*" he roared.

Inos blinked again and peered up at him. "Meaning of what?" she asked, her voice a little firmer.

"*How dare you disappear with that man like that?*"

"Take your hands off me!"

"*Slut!*" The sultan gripped her other shoulder also and shook her. The spectators gasped and bristled.

The imperor straightened. "Sultan!"

But Azak did not seem to hear. He released Inos. "*Whore!*" He swung a hand at her face.

Somehow Inos dodged the blow, stepping back with extraordinary agility in a swirl of fabric. "How dare you!"

"Dare? You are my wife, and I —" Again he tried to strike her.

The imperor roared an objection, and several of the men in uniform stepped forward. But again the blow had missed, and now Inos shouted back apparently recovered from her confusion, her face flushed with anger.

"Brute! You odious brute! Hit me, would you? Well, I've had quite enough of your tantrums, Azak ak'Azakar." She spun around to face the imperor. "Sire You are chief magistrate of the realm, and high priest, also, are you not?"

The old man started, then nodded. "And what of it?" He seemed to have forgotten his weariness for the moment.

"My marriage to this man has never been consummated. I ask that it be annulled."

Azak howled like a frustrated tiger and reached for her. At the touch of his fingers, Inos slipped away from him and moved nimbly to the base of the dais, as if seeking protection from the imperor. When the sultan tried to follow, a tribune stepped in front of him. He was unarmed, but his uniform made Azak hesitate.

Emshandar snapped, "Silence!" and the players seemed to freeze. "How long since the ceremony, my dear?"

Inos hesitated. "Two months. No! Longer . . . "

The old man smiled, and although it was doubtless intended as a kindly expression, his smile made Kadolan think of a skull. "One month is adequate A bridegroom who does not consummate a marriage within one month after the wedding is deemed to be impotent, and the marriage is henceforth null and —"

"Impotent!" Azak bellowed. He tried to move, and the tribune blocked him again. "There is no such law in Arakkaran!"

"It is the law here!" Emshandar said, showing his teeth once more. "You have our permission to withdraw, your Majesty!"

Azak was speechless.

"Good-bye, Azak," Inos said. Her voice was soft, but there was a smile hovering around her face. "Thank you for what you did to help."

"You are my wife!"

"No longer." She walked forward to him and looked up sadly. "It would not have worked. I could never have been happy."

"You swore —"

"Yes, and I am sorry. I did not know. But I could not have been happy, and I think you would not have been happy, either. You did care that much, I am sure. You would have tried. I'm sure you would have tried. It is better this way."

The big man clenched his fists, glaring down at her. Then he raised his gaze to the imperor on his throne. "I understood you wished peace between my land and yours?" he said threateningly.

The spectators stiffened, Emshandar flinched. Kade reflected that wars had been started for much less cause than the theft of a monarch's wife . . .

Inos put her head on one side and regarded the sultan thoughtfully. "You don't like sorcery, Azak, do you? I'm an adept now."

"Adept?" He fell back a step.

"An adept. Rap told me two words of his words. He had too much power, you see? Burns out the mundane vector . . . " She paused, wrinkling her nose. "Perhaps I haven't got that quite right! Rap can explain, when he gets here. But he told me two of them, and then everything was all right. I'm an adept now, Azak."

"Sorcery!" he muttered, as if it were an obscenity.

Inos's smile became feline. "Of course you might not be too bad as a husband — not now that I have ways to control you if you get out of hand."

Shaking his head vigorously, Azak backed away another step.

"No? Well, then — good-bye, Azak!"

She moved as if about to kiss him, and again he retreated.

"You may withdraw, your Majesty!" the imperor repeated firmly.

Azak snarled, as if planning a warlike retort.

"I know you loved me," Inos whispered. "No one doubts that."

Pause . . . The company seemed to hold its breath. "Love!" he muttered angrily. "I brought this on myself, you mean?" Then he bowed stiffly to the throne, spun on his heel, and stalked swiftly away, a haughty giant with his pride bleeding. The sound of his boots faded into the darkness. The spectators relaxed.

Inosolan came floating through the copse of candelabra as if dancing, heading for Kadolan, and other people moved nervously out of her path.

"It's all right," she said softly. "Everything's all right."

Kadolan rose, and this time a hand assisted her instead of stopping her.

"I'm glad, dear. Very glad."

They hugged, and certainly Inosolan felt quite solid, and normal. There was a faint smell of burned cloth about her, that was all. Kadolan sent a secret prayer of thanks to the Gods, with a promise of many more to come — later, when she had more time.

Conversation was stirring again. Marshal Ithy bowed to Inosolan and kissed her hand. A lady senator murmured congratulations. The imperor's head had drooped as it he was almost asleep, and some of the candles had guttered out already. Visions of a soft, warm bed floated through

Kadolan's mind like temptations of the Evil, but obviously the imperor wa waiting for his sorcerer, and no one would leave before he did. Weary weary!

"Sire?" That was Senator Epoxague, bowing before the throne.

The imperor rubbed his eyes, and then said, "Your Eminence?"

"May I be so bold as to ask whether the Impire will now recognize my cousin as Queen of Krasnegar?"

Emshandar blinked, then smiled faintly. "She does appear to have relin quished any claim to Arakkaran. The wardens . . . " He glanced around a the empty thrones in their isolated bubbles of light. "Yes! We recognize he royal state. We see no obstacle."

Inosolan sniggered playfully. Putting an arm around Kade, she dragged he over to the throne, and they both curtseyed.

The senator bowed. "Inos, you are confident that Master Rap is all right That he will return?"

"Oh yes," Inos said airily, as if immolation and resurrection were ordinary everyday affairs. "He said he would. You can always trust Rap's word. He'll be along shortly, I'm sure."

Epoxague's eyes twinkled, and he turned again to the throne. "Sire? This has been a most memorable evening. If nothing else, it has surely witnessed the first divorce to be performed by a reigning imperor in . . . a very long time, shall we say? But why stop there? Why not a wedding, also?"

"Wedding?" Kadolan said, startled.

Inos clapped her hands. "Yes! Yes! Can you? I mean, would you?"

The gaunt old imperor seemed to be quite as startled as Kadolan. He studied the senator darkly for a moment, and Inos also, as if suspecting mockery. Then he shrugged and bared big teeth in a smile. "If I say I car conduct a wedding, I don't know who will argue. And if that is what your sorcerer wants, then I shall be happy to oblige him, for I am deeply in his debt."

"Inos!" Kadolan whispered. "Not tonight! Surely this is not necessary?"

"I hope it will be!" Inos said, full of glee.

The senator coughed discreetly. "It is not a rare custom, Kade, here in Hub. Big, formal, temple weddings take time to prepare. A brief civil cere mony in advance . . . not uncommon. Not usually advertised, of course — but often thought advisable."

Kadolan said, "Oh!" doubtfully. Of course young blood ran hot, and she could understand the logic. It just did not seem quite, er, *seemly*, but if that was how it was done in Hub . . .

"It discourages anyone from backing out of the contract is what he means," the imperor said. "But it is not improper, Highness."

And if the imperor said so, then it was so.

"And it is the Gods' command!" Inos beamed triumphantly. "Trust in love, Aunt!"

The spectators were beyond being surprised by anything now, but Kadolan sensed a bright mood of amusement and jubilation rippling out from that blissful smile on Inos's face. It showed in the answering smiles and quiet shrugs, overriding the chill and fatigue. The imperium was restored, the war canceled, the raider dead, the succession secure . . . Why not a wedding?

"If your Majesty says so, then I certainly have no objection," Kadolan said. She had no right to object anyway. Inos was of age now, and a queen. Suddenly Kade felt discouragingly old. Her task was finished. With Inosolan married to a sorcerer . . .

"Very well!" Emshandar said. He chuckled and heaved himself more upright on his throne. "From what Master Rap told me earlier this evening, I do not think he will have any objections whatsoever. But I do wish you would produce the bridegroom!"

Plop!

Everyone jumped as Master Rap appeared in their midst, but he was only what he had been before, a tangle-haired, oversized faun in leather work clothes. Whatever he had been doing had taken a toll, though; for a moment he just stood, slumped, dejected. Then with an obvious effort, he turned and peered blearily up at the imperor.

"If you know of any out-of-work sorcerers. Sire," he muttered, "there is a vacant palace to the west."

The onlookers flinched, but Emshandar nodded approvingly. "You have done noble work this day. Sorcerer. For me, and for all Pandemia. I think few will mourn Zinixo."

Rap had discovered Inos standing beside him. He smiled wanly at her. He murmured, "Thanks!" almost inaudibly.

"I only wish," Emshandar said, a little more loudly, "that you would accept the Red Throne yourself!"

"Me?" Rap rubbed his eyes. "No, not me." He went back to studying Inos's radiant smile, almost as if it puzzled him. The imperor frowned at being so peremptorily refused.

"Sire?" Inos said impatiently.

"Mm? Oh . . . Very well!" The old man rose unsteadily, leaving the sword and buckler on the throne. He stepped down to join the others, wavering a little; but when he straightened he was taller than anyone there except Rap. "How does it go? Are there any here among you present who know cause why this man and this woman — Shandie!"

The little prince had hurtled in from the darkness and wrapped himsel around Master Rap's legs like a blanket. "Rap! Rap! You're all right, Rap?"

The sorcerer laughed and patted his shoulder. "Yes, I'm fine! You're al right?"

The prince nodded vigorously. "Yes! Yes, I'm all right!"

The imperor said, "Shandie!" again, menacingly.

Rap tousled the boy's hair. "Sorry, Sire! You were saying?"

They were all so weary, Kadolan thought. They should all be in bed, and especially that exhausted old imperor. Master Rap also was as limp and hag gard as if he had not slept in days. Only Inos seemed to have recovered com pletely, and she looked as if she were floating.

"Anyone who knows cause . . . " The imperor scowled. "Oh, never min that bit. Do you, Rap, take this . . . "

"You like horses, Shandie," Rap said. "Maybe you an' me can go for a rid tomorrow, huh?"

The boy's reply was drowned in a cry of objection from Inos and a roa from the imperor: "*as your wife?*"

"Wife?" Rap said faintly. "*Wife?*" Then he seemed to register the grouping — Inos at his side, and Senator Epoxague beyond her, as honorary father o the bride . . . Kade at her back and the imperor in front. Marshal Ithy ha appointed himself best man, beside Rap.

He stared at Inos as if he had never seen her before. Certainly he coul have never seen her look happier.

Kadolan sensed that this awful day was about to produce another of it sickening reversals.

"Wife?" he whispered. He paled. "Wife? Oh, Inos! No! Not now!"

She started as though he had slapped her. "What? But, Rap, Azak's gone I'm free now! I love you, and I know you love —"

"No! Inos! I can't!" He recoiled in horror, bumping into Marshal Ithy with out seeming even to notice him. "We mustn't!"

"Why not?" she cried angrily.

He was shaking his head. "Because . . . because . . . The words . . .

"I don't care if you're a sorcerer, you dummy!"

"But . . . that's it! I'm not! I'm . . . I'm . . . *Oh, Gods!* No! No! No!"

Master Rap spun on his heel and raced off into the darkness, following the path Azak had taken. The sound of his footsteps faded into silence.

Inos turned to Kadolan with a wail. "Aunt? What happened? What's wrong?"

"I don't know, dear! I don't know!"

Obviously something was wrong, though. Very wrong. It had to be more than Master Rap's obvious dislike of weddings.

2

I loved a young man,
       Young man, Oh . . .
I loved a young man,
        Long ago . . .
I gave him gold, and rubies, too,
I gave my all, his heart to woo.
Young man, young man, young man. Oh . . .
        Long ago . . .

The weather had changed, as if to acknowledge the imperor's return. Late-afternoon sunshine made a brave effort to gladden the palace gardens, where a last few battered roses were a lament to lost summer. The branches above them were bare, and sodden heaps of yellow leaves lay on the damp earth by the little boxwood hedges. It was not winter yet.

Inos's voice floated out through the windows of the music room. Her fingers raced over the keys of the spinet, wringing skeins of melody from them in complex arpeggios and glissades and counterpoint.

Jalon, weep your eyes out!

She stopped with an ear-stabbing discord and spun around on the stool. An audience of about thirty men stood there with their stupid mouths agape — secretaries, flunkies, even legionaries. She slammed down the lid and jumped to her feet. Quailing before her anger, they started to back away, then all turned tail and stampeded out of the room.

Idiots!

It was two days since she had become an adept.

It was already beginning to pall. She could ride anything in the palace stables. Sketching had always been one of her talents, and now she could dash off a likeness in half a dozen strokes. Poetry, needlework . . . no problem. She had even attempted a little archery, and there was certainly nothing to *that* anymore. She had extracted a bushel-basketful of military secrets out of Marshal Ithy without him even realizing, and the previous night she had danced that brainless (but rather cute) young Tiny to utter exhaustion.

There was nothing to *anything* any more!

But where in the names of all the Gods was Rap?

Slipping her feet back into the shoes she had recently kicked off, Inos set her jaw firmly and departed in search of the imperor.

Finding the antechamber was easy. Getting past it was not, even for an adept — there were just too many heralds and footmen and chamberlains. By the time she had reduced the sixth or eighth to sweating, blushing, stammering cooperation, the first was starting to recover. Trouble was, they might lose their heads if they admitted her without permission, and the fear of death was a powerful antidote to charm.

Eventually she yielded to their terror-filled pleas, and sat down alongside the other forty or so men and women patiently waiting. She started up a conversation with the mousy bureaucrat next to her and discovered he knew nothing at all that she would ever wish to know. He was concerned about a problem with public water supply in some Gods-forgotten little town in North Pithmot, and that was about the extent of his existence. He expected to linger in the antechamber for another month at least before being admitted to the Imperial presence.

Inos certainly did not. She had a kingdom to rescue. She had a lover to find. After all that she had endured since leaving Arakkaran, she was not going to settle for being an ornament in a waiting room.

However, a senior herald soon appeared in a tabard so laden with gold thread that it must have weighed a hundredweight.

"His Imperial Majesty regrets that he can receive no more of you today, and bids you return on the morrow . . . "

Nobody moved.

The herald consulted his slate. "Except for the following . . . "

He pursed his lips, turned the slate over, then lowered it. " . . . her Majesty Queen Insolan, her Highness Princess Kadolan, or Doctor Sagorn."

Inos rose and glanced around, but she would certainly have noticed either of the others, had they been there. She advanced to the door as everyone else began gathering up briefs and petitions and reports, preparing to depart.

She had expected the emperor to be in the next chamber, but she was conducted through several grand rooms and passages. There were other doors, too, and probably important personages entered through those, bypassing the rabble.

However, when she finally reached the Presence, the surroundings were flattering enough — a small private sitting room, with big windows looking out at soggy, depressing winter garden scenery, but a small fire burning, and only four chairs. Emshandar shook his head as she was about to perform a formal court curtsy, waving her to a chair. The flunkies departed, closing the door, and he moved to a table bearing crystal and wine.

Despite her impatience, she must observe the formalities — Inos sat down and tried to compose herself.

The portraits on the wall would be his children, Orosea and Emthoro, and Inos recognized the work of Jio'sys, who was well represented in the palace. Even from her seat, she could scan the names of the many books stacked on the high shelves: law, history, economics, dull stuff. Two words of power had greatly increased the acuity of her senses, although she had uncovered no occult abilities in herself so far. The rugs were authentic Zogonian wool and the smaller porcelain figurines on the mantel were authentic Kerithian. The big one was a fake, though.

The imperor looked weary, but he must have had a busy day, and he was visibly stronger than he had been when she had last seen him, in the Rotunda. He was swathed in a bulky robe with ermine trim, and she could guess that he had just changed out of something much more formal. His white hair was sparse, his face still a vellum-upholstered skull, but his glance was steady and very penetrating. As he settled into a chair and raised a crystal goblet to her in a toast, she suddenly recalled Sagorn in her father's study, so long ago. He did look a tiny bit like Sagorn, as much as imp, even an emaciated, raw-boned imp, could ever resemble a jotunn. Perhaps the memory came also from the song she had been singing, or the bouquet of the wine.

"Magnificent, Sire! Elvish, of course?"

He raised a frosty eyebrow. "You can't do better than that?"

She sniffed again, and held it to the light. "Valdoquiff. The fifty-three?"

He chuckled. "The forty-seven."

She felt herself blush at his amusement. "I don't think I have met the forty-seven before!"

"So you couldn't know it. But Valdoquiff, certainly. You have been exercising your talents, young lady! I have had reports of some of your exploits."

Of course the palace was always a warren of rumors, and she would be a source of wonder. Her recent impromptu concert was probably the talk of the court already.

The old man's eyes twinkled. "And your dear aunt is recovered?"

"Oh, quite recovered, thank you. She is socializing to excess. You may anticipate a severe tea famine in the capital shortly. And your Majesty's honored self, if I may presume to ask?"

"Oh, I'm well! I grow stronger with every meal. I'm also having a marvelous time shifting my last ten years' mistakes onto Ythbane's reputation. The damage that man did in a few short weeks!" He chuckled and sipped his wine, regarding her acutely. "Beautiful young maidens do not come calling on old men from choice. How may I help you?"

"Sire . . . Have you seen Rap?"

He nodded. "He's been spending quite a bit of time with my grandson. He's done wonders for the boy already."

Inos bit her lip. Shandie indeed!

"Do you happen to know where I might find him? Rap, I mean."

The long Imperial upper lip stretched to forestall a smile. "Oh, yes. He said he was going to Faerie."

"*Faerie?*"

Now the smile broke free. "He had some urgent business there, he said."

He had some urgent business right here in Hub that he should have attended to first! She set her teeth.

The imperor coughed discreetly. "That is confidential, though. He asked me not to mention it to anyone, except you when you came."

Worse! If Rap had been foreseeing her movements, then it was no wonder he could avoid her. How dare he! How could he? *Why?*

"Have you seen your distant cousin, the duke?" Emshandar inquired.

Inos shivered. "This morning. He was awake . . . but he isn't really there. I gather Rap had seen him before I did. He's like a child — Angilki is. The doctors seem puzzled."

"Rap isn't. He repaired the damage, he said, and it was definitely a sorcerous wound. But he can't replace the memories that were lost."

Why had Rap not reported this to Inos before he told the imperor? Sorcerer or not, when she got hold of that young man, she was going to pin his ears back so fast his tattoos would pop off.

"I have some more sad news for you," the old man said. "I sent a note to your quarters, but since you are here . . . The duke's mother, the dowager duchess, has passed away."

"That is not sad news!" Inos snapped. "She was responsible for all of my troubles. A lot of them, anyhow."

"Oh? Well, she was not a close relative, I know, but a little seemly grief might be good politics."

Inos apologized, angry at her clumsiness. The cavernous old eyes were never leaving her face, and she realized that Emshandar's reputation as a shrewd mover of men might be well deserved.

"It leaves Kinvale in a strange position," he said, and let her work out the implications. The duke was now incompetent, his daughters underage.

"Daughters!"

"Yes. However, Kinvale happens to be one of a very few dower fiefdoms — the title can pass through the female line. The only question, therefore, is whom I appoint as guardian for our mutual cousins until the new duchess can succeed."

Inos parried the hidden question, because she felt that Kade should answer it herself; it had also brought her mind back to her own future.

But the imperor was still 'way out in front of her. "We have had some word of Krasnegar." He waved sadly at a high-piled table that probably represented his evening.

256

"The road is open again?"

"No, indeed! We are holding the pass itself, but even the XIIth Legion has failed to retake Pondague, or where Pondague used to be. The little greenies fight for every tree." The old soldier shook his head disbelievingly. "Even the XIIth! My old outfit!"

If not by road . . . But of course it was only in Krasnegar itself that harbors closed a few weeks after midsummer. The ships then must sail back to the Impire, and reports extracted from the captains would take more weeks to reach Hub. The timing was reasonable.

"And how is Krasnegar, Sire?"

"Bad." He heaved himself out of his chair and went to search the heaped table. "Right after I pulled the troops out, a jotunn by the name of Greastax arrived with a longship full of the usual scoundrels. He claims to be Kalkor's brother, holding the realm in his name. Half brother, I expect. Ah, here it is. This is a summary of what we know."

He handed her a booklet of eight or ten sheets in a leather binding. The hand was neat and professional, but behind the bloodless bureaucratic prose was tragedy. She scanned through it swiftly and passed it back, shocked to the depths of her soul. "Thank you . . . Sire?"

The imperor was chuckling as he returned to his chair. "You're not quite as speedy as Master Rap, but then he didn't need to turn the pages."

Now she was in no mood to be teased, nor even to humor old imperors. "That news is months old! How many more deaths and rapes since then?"

Emshandar stared at her over the rim of his wineglass for several bleak seconds. "The Gods know. The raping may have been reduced by the time element. Last spring . . . Those troops were the worst in our army. I would never use trash like that Pondague detachment for anything but garrison duty. The killing . . . likewise! Those who might resist have already done so, and only the cowed remain. But what about food supply?"

"It is always touch and go," she muttered, mulling over what she had just read. The trade had been poor. At least two ships had returned with their cargoes intact, rather than deal with the bullying jotnar overlords, and the imps had already looted all the money and valuables from the city. She wondered if Foronod would have managed to accomplish his usual harvest miracle with a demoralized or depleted workforce. Anything that impaired the harvest threatened famine by spring, in any year.

"I must go!" she said. "Soon!"

The skeletal old man shook his head sadly. He did not need to speak, because a moment's thought reduced what she had said to obvious nonsense. She could do nothing. Even the Impire's crack troops could not penetrate the taiga now, and the seas were frozen until summer.

Only Rap.

"He read all that?" she asked.

"Yes. Plus some earlier reports on Krasnegar, which will interest you also Do you know, there, was not one reference to Krasnegar in the Imperia archives? Inisso did a fine job of making it immemorable." A gentle smil eased the severity of the wasted face, but she realized that he was hiding great weariness. She should go and let him rest.

"Inisso died centuries ago!"

"I know. But when the news broke, I had no recollection of ever havin; heard of a place called Krasnegar. I demanded files, reports . . . any thing! There was nothing. So I did what imperors usually do in emergen cies — I asked the appropriate warden. Needless to say, her ravings tol me very little."

Inos evaded the unspoken invitation to comment. Bright Water woul have been on the side of the goblins, not the rampaging imp army that ha started the troubles.

"I got more from Olybino — he was concerned about the troops . . . Bu basically the secretariat had to start from scratch. They did some analyses o Krasnegar's economics and social structure that will be of interest to its queen I am sure."

"Will I be its queen?" She spoke more to herself than to him.

It would all depend on Rap. He could evict the jotnar. He could make th people accept her, although she doubted there would be much fight left in th town now. If she arrived with a sorcerer, she would be accepted. If she didn't then there might not be any town left by summer.

Where was Rap?

If he would make her queen, then she would gladly make him king.

She looked up with eyes suddenly misting. The old man in the bulky rob . . . It was not Sagorn he had been reminding her of, but the last King o Krasnegar, and that was stupid because Emshandar emphatically did not look like Holindarn. Just something about the way he held his glass, and lounge in the chair . . . Something fatherly . . .

She sniffed. "Excuse me. Sire! I have presumed upon your time long enough . . . "

"You stay! You will have another glass of wine with me and we shall drag all your troubles out into the open."

She tried to protest and again he overruled her — imperors of the XVIIth Dynasty were not noted for their meekness. He had nothing to do with his time except work and more work, he said. Her company was welcome. He refilled the goblets, then he settled back into his big chair as if ready to spend the night there.

"Sultan Azak has gone. I expect you know."

"He came around to say good-bye," she agreed. "That was good of him! But I had gone riding. Kade saw him, and Char was there. Rap cured him, too!"

Then she had to explain how Char had been beaten by the legionaries. Frowning, the imperor lifted a slate from alongside his chair and made a note on it.

Life without Azak would be easier, certainly. "Rap has been busy," she remarked, and was surprised at the edge to her voice. "Sorcering here, sorcering there . . . All work and no play!"

Emshandar sighed and steepled his fingers. He stared at the windows for a moment; the lawns were darkening as the winter day faded in pinks and orange.

"Inos . . . if I may call you that . . . I have more experience of dealing with sorcerers than any other mundane in the world — four wardens, and oftentimes their votaries. When we learned about the goblin problem, for example, and I could get nothing out of Bright Water, I appealed to East, and he transported a man to Krasnegar. Next day he was back and I talked with him for an hour. I knew all about you and your kingdom months before the official word arrived. It's not part of the Protocol, it's just a favor wardens do for imperors, once in a while . . .

"So what I'm leading up to is that I do know sorcerers, and no one else can say that. And they are not like other people!"

She shivered. "How not like other people?"

Even an imperor tended to drop his voice when he talked of sorcerers. "They don't seem to think like us."

"Sorcery makes people 'unhuman'? That's what Rap told me."

The imperor nodded. "When Master Rap wakened me from my sickness — then he seemed quite ordinary. Melancholy, perhaps; he was brooding about something. Naive. But a very pleasant young man, I thought; unschooled, but well above average. Yet I was not too surprised to learn that he'd only been a sorcerer for a few hours. Since that night, when you and he . . . Since he came back, he is sadly changed!"

As Inos had not met him since then, she could hardly be expected to comment on that. But the bald statement worried her: changed? She was changed herself, of course — she was an adept now.

Emshandar was regarding her with an intimidating Imperial curiosity. "Will you tell me what happened that night?"

So in spite of all his jolly little chats with Master Sorcerer Rap, the old fox had not managed to learn that? If Rap wouldn't tell, why should she? Well, for one thing, she really had nothing to tell.

"I wish I could, Sire! It's still not at all clear in my mind. Rap moved us both to . . . he called it the ambience. It's another world, sort of. Beside this world and yet not part of it."

"You obviously went somewhere. Can you describe it?"

She shook her head. "No words fit. Not light nor dark. Not silent nor noisy. No up or down. A world of mind? As hard to describe as a dream." He did not comment, so she forced herself to continue. "Once he'd shared two of his five words with me, then he managed to wrest the power under control. He cured our burns, dressed us . . . sent me back." It should have been the greatest experience of her life, and it was all just infuriatingly vague, and fuzzy. "I think he blocked my memory. I can remember the fire hurting, but not what the pain was like."

Emshandar nodded solemnly, studying her face as she spoke.

"That's odd, though!" Inos said. "I just realized . . . Zinixo told Rap a fifth word, expecting to kill him with a burnout. Then he would have got back the power he'd given away. But Rap shared two with me, and that reduced his overload so that he could control it. But when he killed Zinixo afterward, then he must have received all the power of the word they both knew?"

Emshandar took a sip of his wine, as if considering what to say, and when he did speak, he was obviously being cautious. "I gather that he didn't actually kill West. He wouldn't say precisely what he had done with him, just that the dwarf would not be bothering any of us again."

Inos shuddered. One thing she did remember from those lost minutes was that Rap had been angry as she had never suspected he could be. He had frightened her.

"One other thing I must know," the imperor said quietly. "Rap was a human furnace. How did you ever find the courage to rush over and hug him like that?"

"My aunt is always accusing me of being impetuous."

"*Impetuous?* Plague of lawyers, woman! That was more than just impetuous!"

"Well, Sire, I met a God once."

She expected surprise, but he said, "Yes, I've heard." He heard everything, obviously.

"And, seeing Rap about to die like that, I suddenly remembered what They told me — to trust in love. The warning seemed to fit. The man I loved needed help. It felt like what I was supposed to do."

He shook his head wonderingly and raised his glass to her. "I admire you beyond words for doing it. Had my legionaries a tenth your courage, I would rule the whole world."

Even adepts could blush all the way to their ears. "But Rap would not explain what happened?"

Emshandar shook his bony head. The room was growing dim, the fire
ighter. "No. And whatever it was, it seems to have scared the wardens spit-
ss. Bright Water babbles. Lith'rian has disappeared altogether; he's probably
iding down in Ilrane. And Olybino won't talk at all. He just says that what
appened is impossible. Which is not exactly helpful."

"And Rap? Do you know why he's avoiding me?"

"No. Some things he won't discuss, and you're one of them. But he's
hanged, Inos. I didn't know him very well before, but he is certainly not the
ame as he was."

He stared at the coals for a moment. "If it didn't sound so absurd, I would
ay he's in deep trouble and needs help."

3

The unseasonably fine weather continued. A couple of days after Inos's
rivate chat with the imperor, an elegant brougham made a long trip south-
vard through the winding thickets of Hubban urban sprawl, until it came to
. rattling halt on a narrow street in a nondescript district somewhere on the
rosperous side of slum. A few spectators watched from the street, and more
rom behind window drapes. Fine carriages came by often enough, but never
arriages escorted by four Praetorian Hussars, with their fine horses and
hiny plumed helmets. Those splendid young men seldom strayed so far
rom the palace.

Their tall but rather chinless leader doubled over in the saddle to peer in
he brougham's window.

"This is the place, I think." He pointed at a plain, weathered door at the
op of a short flight of steps.

Kade had never used that door, but her bedroom window had looked out
n this street. She recognized the mismatched buildings opposite. "Very
ikely."

The hussar swung a long leg and dropped nimbly to the road. "I'll
nnounce you."

"Wait!" Kadolan said. "That would be a great honor, Tiffy, but I think I'd
etter come with you."

Frowning, he opened the door to hand her down. "Why?"

"Well, there might not be anyone home if just you went. You are rather
ntimidating, you know."

Tiffy blushed scarlet with pleasure. "Oh, I say! Do you really think so?
Intimidating?"

Beaming proudly, he guarded her from perils unspecified as she mounted
he stoop. Then he yanked the bellrope hard enough to bring every firecart in

the city, although Kadolan had already seen a drape twitch. For a few minute
nothing happened, then the door opened.

"Doctor Sagorn!" she chirruped.

The old man looked both heated and bothered. His hair was awry, his ga
ments disheveled. He nodded sourly to Kadolan and blinked at the shin
breastplate beside her, the ferociously scowling boyish face above it.

"My house is honored, your Highness." Sagorn stepped aside to admit he
not disguising his reluctance.

Tiffy eyed the lintel and began removing his helmet. Kadolan laid a han
on his arm. "This will be rather a private meeting, Tiffy."

"Oh?" He peered distrustfully at Sagorn.

"A medical matter, Tiffy."

"Ah!" With a final warning pout at the discomfited physician, the hussa
refastened his chinstrap and went clattering down the steps to the street to wai

Kadolan did not recognize the room to which she was shown, but sh
had seen its like elsewhere — a typical medico's sanctum, dread and drea
although this one could have been brightened considerably by cleaning it
leaden-paned casements. It came complete with chairs and desk and omi
nously stained table. The shelves lining its walls bore many impressivel
weighty books, plus hundreds of bottles labeled in illegibly cursive scrip
racks of butcher implements of all sizes, and more complex instruments o
unguessably horrible purpose. The obligatory skeleton hung in a corne
grinning through a shroud of cobwebs. Anonymous nasty things floate
inside jars.

Much less to be expected were two large trunks, one already roped closed
the other open and half filled with books, clothes, and more medical equip
ment.

Kade chose the better of the two chairs. Sagorn settled on the other. H
ran a hand through his hair, smearing his forehead with grime. He was sulk
ing.

"You are planning to leave town." Kade found she could not make a state
ment so obvious sound like a question.

"How did you guess?"

"May I ask why?"

He glared. "That should be even more obvious."

She shook her head. "It seems illogical when the emperor himself wishes t
consult you. Your prosperity will be guaranteed for life, I should think."

"Prosperity? Bah!"

He rose, tall and grim, and began pacing the office, his slippers making
unpleasant gritty noises. "You know well enough how we have guarded ou
secret, and for how long! Now we are unmasked! Our curse will become com

ion knowledge. We shall be the laughingstock of mundanes and the prey of
orcerers! The imperor may reveal us to the wardens. And all this disaster has
efallen us because we answered Holindarn's plea and went to Krasnegar!"

"You are being quite ridiculous," Kadolan said calmly. "Nobody is revealing
our secret. The imperor merely seeks your counsel regarding the Duke of
Kinvale. Master Rap has done all he can with sorcery, but he suggested your
kills would still be valuable. As for sorcerers and wardens — if you have any
rouble with them, then I suggest you mention that you are a friend of his.
rom what I've heard, that will stop any of them."

Sagorn shot her a startled glance as he shuffled by. He did not speak. Kade
et out her annoyance one more notch.

"What is even more surprising is that you are doing your own packing. I
hould have thought you would have delegated that to younger hands. Or is
our decision subject to argument?"

"God of Pity, Kade! You know I can't control what the others may do!"

"But they usually accept your decisions, don't they? Your judgment?"

The old man snorted. "Tell me what you want of me and then go."

"Have you seen Master Rap?"

"Not since Gathmor's funeral." He stopped his aimless pacing and stared
lown bleakly at the open trunk for a moment. "Ah . . . you did not know?
My apologies, ma'am."

"I suspected," Kade said sadly. On the journey from Arakkaran, she had
leveloped a curious admiration for the rough sailor. He had possessed many
idmirable qualities. "Did his death have anything to do with Master Rap's
lecision to fight Kalkor?"

"Everything."

She sighed. She had known that the faun did not change his mind lightly.
I am sorry. And glad that he is now avenged. And I wish you knew where
Master Rap was! Well, perhaps you can guess why he's avoiding Inos?"

Sagorn stopped by the second-best chair and sat down again. "Avoiding
her?" he repeated incredulously.

"Definitely. You know that he is now a full sorcerer? You have heard what
he did, and that the wardens acquitted him?"

"There are more stories about the faun sorcerer running around Hub than
there are rats in the sewers, but I think I have the gist, yes. West challenged
him to duel, or vice versa. He vanished in flames and then returned victorious.
He is the new warlock of the west."

"No, he refused the honor."

"Typical!" Sagorn muttered in disgust.

"It was Inos who saved him, but he has not spoken to her since that
night. He healed Angilki as well as he was able, and Azak's crippled retainer,

also. He has been spending time with the prince and also with that young goblin. He reportedly went out of town, but he's back. Yet he does not go near Inos!"

Sagorn leaned back without taking his eyes off Kadolan. He crossed his legs and then smiled his sinister smile. "And when did you see him?"

"This morning," she admitted. "I was on my way to my room, and suddenly he came around a corner. He spoke to me, very briefly, and then he just wasn't there!" She was trying not to show how upset she felt, but the old sage could read her well enough.

"What words did he speak very briefly?"

When she hesitated, Sagorn said, "I can't advise you if you withhold information!"

"He said. 'Tell her I do love her!' That was all."

The old man frowned, very dark. "How did he seem?"

"Upset. Wild, even."

"Mad as a shampooed cat, I expect," Rap said, closing the door behind him. Kadolan started and looked accusingly at Sagorn, but he was obviously even more surprised than she was — frightened, even.

Rap put his hands on his hips and regarded Kadolan sourly. "Isn't nice to repeat private conversations!"

"It isn't nice to eavesdrop, either!"

He might be a powerful sorcerer, but he *looked* like a stablehand. And he still had a wild, jumpy look about him.

"Furthermore," she snapped, "you may say you love her, but you are being extremely unkind to her. She is very upset."

He scowled.

"At least you owe her an explanation!" Kade said. She wondered if he was ill. His face was drawn; he seemed feverish.

"Well, she isn't going to get one." Rap turned his gaze on Sagorn's baggage and then on the scholar himself. "I came to keep my promise."

The old man licked his thin, pale lips. His knuckles were white on the arms of his chair.

Rap chuckled meanly. "See? It isn't the imperor he's running from. Nor the wardens, either."

It's you," Kadolan said.

"Because he knew I would come. He knew I would keep my word. Suddenly he can get what he's always wanted. And now he's too old, aren't you. Doctor? You've had a hundred years, and you could have had another hundred — on and off." He laughed and turned to Kadolan. "And he dare not trust the others, because they're all younger than him."

"I think I should leave." She began to rise.

"No, stay and watch!" Rap said. "This should be entertaining. I'm ready to perate, Doctor Sagorn." He put his head on one side and seemed to squint or a moment. "Who left the sorcerer's house?"

The old man had cowered down in his seat. "I did," he said hoarsely.

"Stand up, please," Rap said.

Sagorn rose stiffly, his face pale. He backed away as Rap approached, ut the faun merely sat down on the roped trunk and stared at him as if he vere a public notice. The old sage moved to the window and then turned t bay.

Rap shook his head sadly. "A beautiful piece of work! Rasha was right; it's shame to spoil it. Who disappeared last?"

Sagorn muttered, "Thinal," as if his mouth hurt.

"Close your eyes, Princess," Rap said.

"I thought you told me to watch?"

"It'll take me a moment to put some clothes on him."

Kadolan said, "Oh!" and closed her eyes.

"You can look now."

She opened her eyes again. Thinal stood beside Sagorn, staring up at him vide-eyed. For once the little thief wore garments not too large for him. The old man was returning his gaze like a mirror. Almost a century since they had parted: Thinal the leader, and Sagorn the youngest boy in the gang.

Rap chuckled. "And how do you feel about this?"

"Fine, Rap." Thinal pulled a sickly sort of smile. "Fine. Thank you."

Again Rap chuckled. "No, you don't!"

A sudden glint of hope came into Sagorn's haggard face. Thinal's teeth began to chatter, and he stuffed a knuckle in his mouth.

"The fairy asked you," Rap said. "She wanted to know your greatest wish. But she didn't believe what you said."

Kadolan didn't understand that, or know who the fairy was, but she did now that Rap was playing with the men, and the knowledge made her uncomfortable. It was not like him.

"Who went before you, Thinal?"

"Jalon, Rap."

"Close your eyes, Princess . . ."

And then there were three. The little minstrel was pale as a corpse, gaping at Rap in horror.

Next came Andor. He hid his feelings better, holding a calm smile on his handsome face. "Hello, big brother!"

Thinal said, "Oh, bleeding offal!" He seemed ten years younger than Andor. He was shorter and ugly, yet somehow there was a ludicrous trace of family likeness.

And then the room was crowded. Darad glanced down at the other for and guffawed in triumph. His nose was still crooked and he still wore gobli tattoos like Rap's, but he had all his teeth back. "I knew you'd do it, sir! I knew you'd free us!"

Rap snorted in disgust. "There they are, Highness. The whole gang together at last. What do you think of them?"

She studied the five ill-assorted men. They were all staring at one another, ignoring both her and the sorcerer. "I think you should take a vote Master Rap."

He laughed coarsely. "They've gotten what they wanted, haven't they A hundred years, almost, they've been searching for release. And now look at them!"

She wondered where his anger was coming from. Rap had not been lik this on the journey from Zark.

The five men were still gaping at one another, tongue-tied.

"I don't need to take a vote," Rap sneered. "They've got what they though they wanted — and they don't want it! They had the best of five worlds, each of them, and they didn't know it!

"Well," he added, "I've kept my promise." He rose and began walking to the door.

Darad's wits had been churning along in their tortoise fashion. Now it was he who shouted, "Wait!"

"Something wrong?" Rap asked, halting.

Darad frowned hideously. "Sir . . . Sir, can we talk about this?"

"Talk about what?" Rap looked puzzled.

"You've made your point," Sagorn said acidly. "All these years we've been deceiving ourselves. It wasn't a curse, it was a blessing . . . "

" . . . at least," Andor said, "once we gained a word of power it was."

Jalon shouted, "Now you have shown us. We don't want to be separated!" The others were nodding.

"So you want me to put you back together again, I suppose?"

"We share memories," Sagorn said . . .

" . . . it means we've almost become . . . " Thinal added.

" . . . like one man," Darad finished.

None of them seemed to realize how they had spoken; they were not trying to be funny.

"It wasn't me who showed you," Rap said. "I'm right, aren't I, when I say that lately you've been switching back and forth a lot more than you used to?"

The five nodded in unison, without looking at him, still unable to take their eyes off one another. Their voices blended in a babble.

"That's so," Sagorn said, apparently to Andor.

"Since we got caught up in his adventures, at least," Jalon told both of
1em.

"In Arakkaran," Darad informed Thinal.

"The night we rescued'm from the jail, 'specially," the thief agreed, watch-
1g his brother.

"But now our word of power is diluted!" Andor complained to Jalon . . .

"All it takes is a little cooperation," Rap said. "A little consideration."

"Put us back, please, Rap?" Thinal said, whining.

"I gave you what I promised!" The sorcerer frowned. Kadolan held her
reath.

"Please, Rap?" Jalon's ice-blue eyes glistened with tears. "We'll remember!
We'll cooperate!"

"Just a minute, though," Darad rumbled. "You've got to stop the rest of
hem from keeping me away for years and years. That old Sagorn 'specially.
He burrows down into those books of his and forgets all the rest of us!"

Sagorn flushed. "Cognizant now of my advancing years —"

"He's not the one I don't trust!" Andor broke in. "It's him!" He jabbed a fin-
ber at his weedy brother. Thinal flinched and looked guilty — but then
Thinal would almost always look guilty, Kadolan thought. He almost always
was guilty, of something.

"What's he done?" asked Jalon, surprised.

"Nothing!" Andor retorted. "That's what I mean! Why do you suppose he
lever hangs around? Why does he always call one of us back right away? He's
vaiting us out, see? In a couple of centuries or less, we'll all be older than
Sagorn is now, and then who's going to inherit all our memories and experi-
nce? That young guttersnipe, that's who! He's robbing us blind!"

Thinal started to protest. The others interrupted, and in a moment they
vere all shouting at once. Kadolan looked to Rap and was relieved to see a
brief hint of his old half grin flicker wistfully over his mouth as he watched
he argument. Then he coughed, and silence tell instantly.

"Well?" he said.

"Please, Rap," Jalon said. "Don't leave us like this! I feel like a turtle out of
ts shell. We helped you get what you wanted, didn't we, and —"

"*What I wanted?*" Rap jumped up, blazing anger, and everyone recoiled. "*You
hink this is what* . . . " He cooled his fury as slickly as a man might close a
book, and Kadolan found that inhuman control even more scary than the
nexplicable rage itself.

"Very well," he said quietly. "I can put a time limit on each of you. Would
you prefer that?" He glanced around at nodding heads. "You all want to be
out back?"

Five heads nodded again.

Darad's clothes collapsed on the floor. Then Andor's . . . Jalon's . .
Only Sagorn was left.

"There you are, Doctor," Rap said harshly. "Operation a success?" Withou
waiting for a reply, he spun around to Kadolan. "When do you want to go
Kinvale — and Krasnegar?"

"Why don't you ask Inos?" she asked.

"I'm asking you."

She was wary of him in this feverish, bitter mood. She said, "Is there ar
great hurry?"

He hesitated, his eyes suddenly distant. "No. No, the time is not yet rip
A week or two more won't hurt much anyway. You want to stay here fc
Winterfest, don't you?"

"Yes," she admitted. "Inos doesn't, but I do." Eigaze had been raving abou
Winterfest in Hub. Kinvale's celebrations were nothing by comparison, sh
said. And there would be no celebration in Kinvale this year, anyway.

"Parties?" Rap said scathingly. "Balls and banquets? Inos always like
parties. Tell her to enjoy them, then! Krasnegar is not much of a place fc
fine balls."

"They don't matter! We can go anytime."

"Stay for Winterfest! But Inos does want to go home after that?"

"Why don't you ask her?"

"I'm asking you."

"Yes. If you'll help."

He stared at her as if she had suggested something shocking. "Of cours
I'll help!" he snapped. "It was my home, too, you know!"

Then he spun on his heel, marched across the room, and disappeared ou
through the door.

Without opening it.

The room seemed very quiet with only two people there.

"Well, Doctor?" Kadolan asked.

The jotunn rubbed his big jaw with a long-fingered hand. "Well wha
ma'am?"

"Diagnose our sorcerer for me."

"I am an expert in mundane medicine only."

She gave him her best royal glare. "You can speculate."

"Inos is in good health?"

"Perfect health."

"And what exactly happened when she and Rap vanished in flames?"

"Her recollection seems rather muddled."

"Ah!" Sagorn turned away, and began picking up the clothes left behind by
the sorcerer. "I should need more facts."

Kade rose, exasperated. "One reason I came here was to reassure you that the imperor's invitation was an opportunity for you, Doctor, not a trap. But if you continue to misbehave, then I shall call in my hussars to take you to the palace by force — and don't think they won't!"

Sagorn glared. Then he shrugged. "What do you want to know?"

"Your opinion of Master Rap."

"No question. A very obvious hypothesis, at least. He shows all the symptoms of a man enduring severe pain."

4

The rivalry between the great families of the Impire was a bitter and never-ending business, but it peaked every year at Winterfest, when they clashed headlong in an ostentation contest. For months the preparations had proceeded in darkest secrecy — the gowns, the orchestras, the food, the wine, the entertainment. No expense had been spared, no menial unexhausted.

Rap had told Kade that Inos was to attend the parties. Despite her worries, she trusted him, and she obeyed. As an honored guest of the imperor, a state visitor, she had very little choice anyway. To refuse would have been an insult.

Last year's foolish flirtation with bustles was but a shameful memory. Sanity had returned, bringing laces and ruffles and flounces spread so wide by hoops and panniers that a lady must turn sideways to pass through a door. The favored colors were claret and hyacinth, or salmon for those whose complexions could stand it. Lace and jewels, bows and embroidery, beads and seashells, bouquets and frills — nothing must be omitted in the decoration. Hair likewise must be gemmed and teased, coiled high on a framework until it overtopped even the plumed helmets of the tall hussars.

For men, hose and doublets were out, white silk tights were in. The cutaway coats in bright velvets hung low at the back, but rose high in front to better display the tights, and especially this year's outstanding absurdity, a bejeweled and embroidered codpiece. The exact amount of padding a gentleman employed — on his calves, for example — was a question of taste for him, a matter of concern for his tailor, and a topic for speculation by the ladies.

Life became a continuous procession of balls. The scented invitations drifted into Inos's dressing table like snowflakes. She dragged herself from bed at noon, spent the rest of the daylight hours preparing, and was off to dance the night away again. Who exactly was paying for all this she dared not ask — she had a recurring nightmare that the imperor might play innkeeper and present the slate when she departed, a bill whose final total would amount to more than the gross value of her kingdom.

Queen Inosolan of Krasnegar was unquestioned Belle of the Season. No ball was worth a pinch of parsley if Inosolan did not attend. She was a celebrity because of the events in Emine's Rotunda, and she had an intriguing aura of the occult about her. Rumor linked her with the mysterious faun sorcerer who had rescued the dynasty.

But in addition Inos's dancing was miraculous, her beauty unmatched, her wit devastating. The debutantes spoke darkly of witchcraft.

Few of them could see that it was not wit or grace or beauty that drew the young men to her, but rather her wistful air of tragedy, her romantic melancholy, the haunting echo of a breaking heart.

She received an average of four proposals of marriage a day. At least two of them were always from Tiffy, but she noted five or six young men of quality, almost any of whom might now be ruling in Krasnegar had he chanced to drop by Kinvale a year ago. Too late! Too late!

Every night flew by in a whirl of candlelight and music and handsome soldiers. And when each new winter day dawned, she crept back to the palace and soaked another pillow.

Of Rap she had seen nothing at all. Shandie seemed to be the only person who ever met him now. She sent a message by the boy: "Tell Rap I love him very much."

Next day came the answer: "Rap said he knew that."

Then — "Tell Rap I want to help him."

But — "He laughed and said you were the last one to help him."

And that, inexplicably, was that.

She had two opposing dreads. One was her vague memory of the ambience, that sinister half-world of shadowless nonbeing. She suspected that Rap must be spending much time in it — for he did not seem to be anywhere else — and she had nightmares of his becoming trapped in it, fading away forever from the mundane.

Her other, contradictory, fear came from the magic casement's vision of him dying in the goblin lodge. Was that awful fate now inevitable? Was that what kept him from her? Her great-grandfather had reputedly been driven mad by something he had seen in the casement. Was Rap to suffer the same cruel fate? Why, though, must he shun her? The days flew by and left no answers.

Two nights before Winterfest came the grand finale, the imperor's ball. The guest list ran to thousands, although there were several categories of invitation and the festivities covered many precincts of varying opulence. The main affair alone included twelve ballrooms, seventeen orchestras, a continuing circus of performers, enough fine food to feed all Zark, and a hundred thousand candles. Eigaze had been absolutely right — the Kinvale affair was a child's birthday party compared to this.

Guests and strayed sheep had been pouring in to the capital for days, and they included Princess Imperial Orosea and her husband, the Duke of Leesoft. Shandie vanished squealing into a scrimmage of cousins and stayed there, so that even he saw nothing of Rap anymore.

The great night came, and when his Imperial Majesty took a partner on his arm for the opening promenade, the only lady in the realm he could have chosen was the Queen of Krasnegar. Leesoft and Orosea fell into step behind them.

The tall old man was almost unrecognizable as the invalid Inos had first seen being carried around like a trophy of war. Now his color was back, his face had filled in and become more human. He was stronger than he had been for years, he insisted, and no one doubted that his grip on the Impire was as firm as it had ever been. The Dwanishian dispute was already settled; the legions would be vacating Qoble as soon as the passes opened. The Senate could not have passed the new Succession Act any faster on wheels.

His hair was trimmed short in military style, and he wore a uniform, although it was a designer uniform of kidskin and gold foil, not bullhide and bronze. As was her custom, Inos wore green, and tonight a very talkative sea-green satin that hissed and whispered all the time. The cut of her bodice was as daring as any in the hall — well, almost — and she was perfectly aware that no one outshone her. This was the culmination of the Hubban social season, and of her year. In a brief three weeks she had conquered the capital of the Impire, and tonight was her night. She might go on to establish herself as Queen of Krasnegar, but even if she stayed in Hub she could never hope to retain her present rule as queen of the capital. In another month someone else would reign.

Honors were transitory, youth was fleeting, but this was her night.

Half the young men of the Impire were ready to fall at her feet, and the only man she wanted was not there.

Emshandar smiled approvingly at her as they began the procession. "It never ceases to amaze me," he said whimsically, "how feminine beauty always manages to triumph over the worst outrages that dressmakers can commit!"

Inos granted him a maidenly blush — she was quite good at those now. "Your Majesty is most gracious." She murmured an appreciation of the surroundings.

They paraded forward, acknowledging the smiles and salutes of the company, all of whom would in turn join on the end of the promenade. Emshandar made polite conversation about nothing . . .

"Any sign of Rap?" he asked quietly, his expression not changing.

Inos did not let her reaction reach the hand she rested on his jeweled vambrace. "None, Sire."

The withered old lips smiled sadly. "I commanded his presence! So we se
who rules this Impire, don't we?"

More smiles. Nod to the new consul and his pretty wife.

"Do you know Death Bird?" Emshandar muttered. Confidential remarks i
Hub were usually made with minimum lip movement.

"No, Sire, I don't think so."

"A goblin, the one Kalkor brought. He has some other name, but the war
dens call him Death Bird, for some reason."

Inos beamed at Kade, being squired by Senator Epoxague. "Then I de
know him. Rap called him Little Chicken and said he was his slave."

Emshandar was still looking everywhere but at Inos. "Olybino i
enraged. He says the goblin has been spying on military training camps, dis
guised as an imp."

She barely contained an unseemly snigger. "How do you disguise a goblin
as an imp? Boil him in strong tea?" She acknowledged Marshal Ithy with on
of her larger smiles.

"With sorcery."

"Oh!" She apologized. Then a few implications registered and she broke the
rules by looking straight at the imperor and speaking plainly. "That's no behav
ior for a guest!" Spying, when there was a war on? Goblins and winter togethe
had driven the XIIth Legion back from the pass, the most humiliating setback
the Impire had suffered in years. She knew that reinforcements were being sent

Emshandar's eyes twinkled, even as he nodded respectfully to the widow
of a famous senator. "Rap asked permission, and I said he could do anything
he wanted. That was my big mistake, you see! I should have excluded this
evening from that sufferance." They had reached the orchestra. As lead cou
ple they veered to the right . . .

He chuckled. "I also told Olybino to complain directly to Rap about it i
he had worries. That son of a mule went chalky pale and disappeared!"

The first real dance of the evening she had promised to Tiffy, and it was a
brisk fandango, designed to clear the floor of older folk. It was also brisk
enough to produce a marked list in Inos's coiffure. With a hasty apology to the
next promised partner, she headed for the powder room to put things to rights

As she was returning, sweeping along a dim corridor, she suddenly sensed
that he was there.

Rap!

She wasn't sure how she knew, but she was certain.

She stopped and stood still, keeping her eyes lowered. Somehow she
located him, in the shadows of a doorway. Minutes seeped by. No one else

ame, there was no sound except the muffled beat of the orchestra, and her
eart was louder than that. But she knew he was there, watching.

Very slowly she raised her head. At first, she dared not look straight at
im. It was like meeting a wild animal, a deer or a fox. If she made a sudden
love she would scare him away. He would be gone in an instant.

He was as well dressed as any man in the palace, better than she had
ver imagined him. Silver-buckled shoes, snowy tights — including a frilly
odpiece as outrageous as any young gallant's — ruffled cravat and cutaway
elvet coat . . .

And by all the Gods his hair was flat!

Finally she met his eyes — wild, tortured eyes, staring at her with a mute,
nbearable longing that twisted her heart. The tattoos were missing.

He had done all this for her, she knew. She could never have conceived
Rap dressing up like this, even if he had done it with sorcery.

Still moving very gently, raising a hand as she might coax a squirrel to a
rust . . . "Don't speak," she said softly. "Just come and dance."

He nodded and swallowed hard. He came forward timorously, as if she
vere a soap bubble vision that might vanish if he touched her, or as if he
eared to waken himself with any sudden move. She shook her head when he
eemed about to say something.

She took out her dance card and ripped it in two, dropping the pieces. She
grinned at him invitingly, and he managed a small quirk of a smile in response,
nd then she knew that she had won — it was going to be all right.

She felt the callouses on his fingers as he took her hand.

He led her to the ballroom.

Her promised partner was waiting. He blanched when he saw her with a
aun, and Inos ignored him.

Rap was going to dance with her!

Sorcerers made wonderful dance partners, graceful and flawless. He never
ook his eyes off Inos. No matter how complex the pattern, or who else he
night be whirling or leading, his gaze was always on her. He never spoke. He
did not smile, he just stared, with that same mute longing.

He danced like an elf. Fingers touched fingers, hand touched shoulder,
arm around waist . . . the night flew away, and she danced with Rap.
Minuets and sarabands, and she danced with Rap. Polonaise, tarantella,
danced with Rap. Gavottes and courantes and mazurkas. *Rap!*

She hardly spoke, either, all night long. She smiled to wide-eyed acquaintances, she spun around with men she knew or didn't know, but always she
was dancing with Rap. And she knew that whatever else the Gods might do,
They could not call back this night.

Hub did nothing except by ritual and tradition. The imperor's partner wa
expected to reserve certain especial dances for each of the consuls, an
Marshal Ithy, and some others. Inos danced with Rap and no one intruded o
a sorcerer.

But even a sorcerer could not stop the sunrise. Unbelieving, she saw can
dles guttering in the chandeliers and weary footmen hauling back drapes t
let the sickly light of morn seep through high windows. The floor was almo
empty. Red-eyed musicians held the last fading chord of the final danc
Where had the time gone? She could have danced forever.

All over the hall, the couples were closing the evening with the tradition
embrace. She held out her arms to Rap and lifted her lips to be kissed.

He backed off.

"Rap!"

He shook his head wildly.

"Rap, kiss me!"

"No!" he shouted. "No!" Then he lowered his voice to a sob. "Oh, Inos! D
you think I wouldn't if I dared?"

"Tell me!" she said, moving toward him. "You're a sorcerer! You overcam
the strongest of the warlocks! *Who are you afraid of?*"

He gulped. "You!"

"No!"

"No. Me!"

And he was gone, vanished. Plop.

Rap! How could he be so callous? Stunned, Inos walked to the door alone
and there found Kade. Kade, haggard with exhaustion. Kade who should hav
gone off to bed hours ago.

Kade who held her as she started to weep.

5

She met him again on Winterfest Day.

The bells were ringing, and she was accompanying the imperor to church
The morning was all faded to gray, sky and earth grown old together, and th
towers of the White Palace in the distance were pearly-white ghosts. Fros
flakes hung glinting everywhere, as if the air had frozen around them to hol
them up. Stones and the stark, bare trees were pale with rime.

The only color left in the world was in the long procession winding acros
the cobbled court, ladies and gentlemen in their high-collared cloaks and sof
plumed hats. Reds and greens and gold shimmered when everything else wa
white. The spectators were few, drab and muffled. Most folk were already a
worship, or else home with their families this day, preparing whatever feas

heir means could supply. Anyone who chose to hang around the palace and watch the gentry on Winterfest had something missing from his life.

Inos was well back in the parade, being squired by the adoring Tiffy. His spurs clinked softly with every step. Kade and Senator Epoxague walked just ahead, and the royal family at the front had already passed through a columned arcade and entered the church. The bells pealed joyously, the frosty air sparkled, and sometimes tiny snowflakes tickled her eyelashes. In her mind she was rehearsing all the prayers she would make. For Rap. For Krasnegar. For wisdom and courage and dedication to make a good ruler. For the strength to trust in love. But especially for Rap, whatever troubled him so.

As she drew near the ancient arches, she knew he was there. Two words of power had brought her no occult abilities that she knew of, so what she felt was a sending from Rap.

She peered, this way and that, and finally located the solitary figure by one of the great weathered pillars.

She murmured an apology to Tiffy and reinforced it with the most beguiling smile she could muster. On him her smiles were hot coals on butter. Then she scurried away from the procession, holding her cloak tight against the cold, clasping its high collar up to protect her ears. She rounded the pillar.

Rap was leaning against it, arms folded, watching her with no expression that she could read. He was back to artisan work clothes, but spurning both coat and hat — a sorcerer's ears would never freeze. His hair had recovered its moorland look, and the stupid goblin tattoos disfigured his eyes again.

"You called me!"

He nodded, looking surly. "Wondered what you thought you were doing."

"I was going to go and worship the Gods."

"That's what I was afraid of." His voice was bitter as alum.

Oh, Rap! "I think you should explain that remark."

He curled his lip. "Sorcerers play games with mundanes. The wardens play games with nations. What do you think the Gods do for amusement?"

She had never heard such rank blasphemy in her life, and for a moment it took her breath away.

"You met a God!" Rap said, his voice rising.

The church doors thumped closed . . . one! . . . two! The bells had stopped ringing. The knots of spectators were wandering away from the gray and white yard.

"They told me to trust in love," she said.

"And what did that mean? You didn't know, did you? Andor, you thought. Then Azak, you thought. Now Rap, you think. 'Yes, he is only a common coachman, but the Gods have given me special dispensation —'"

"It meant that I must rescue you from the fire, my lad."

He shrugged. "Did it? You're still not sure. Not certain. You don't thin
an ambiguous command may reflect on the competence of the commander
Or reflect on Their sincerity, maybe? Cause a little confusion and watch th
fun, perhaps?"

"Rap, you stop this! I won't listen!"

He shrugged again. She spoke quickly, before he could. "You told me yo
were only a mage, but the next morning you were a sorcerer. Where did yo
get that fourth word, Rap?"

"Can't tell that."

"Kade told me where you got the third word, and I saw you get a fifth, bu
where did you get your fourth? You begged a word from me, but I didn't hav
one. Who else had a word to share. Rap? *What did you pay for that word?*"

He flinched, and her suspicions swelled to horror.

"Bright Water!" she whispered.

"Nonsense!"

"I think so! Maybe not one of her own, but she made sure you got one
She's very fond of that goblin monster, and —"

Rap shook his head and her tongue stopped like a balking horse.

"She had nothing to do with it! Not that I know of. Yes, Little Chicke
did. But don't worry about that."

"Tell me what you paid for that word!" she shouted, banging her fis
against the frosted stone of the pillar. There was no one else in sight now
"How can a goblin torture a sorcerer unless the sorcerer agrees to be —"

"That's true." For the first time a faint hint of a smile touched Rap's eyes
"And probably not even then. I'd find it awfully hard not to lose my tempe
when he began breaking things."

Relief! That nightmare had haunted her for weeks. "It isn't going to happe
then? The third prophecy?"

"Not prophecies — I told you. But, no, I don't think it is. It isn't quite
absolutely, completely certain, and you mustn't talk about it with Littl
Chicken if you see him. But no, I don't think he's going to insist. Never min
that! When do you want to go to Krasnegar?"

"'Insist?'" she queried.

"Forget Little Square-Eyes! When do you want to go to Krasnegar, and
what are you going to do when you get there?"

"What do you advise?"

"You want to be queen, then you've got to learn to make your ow
decisions."

"Rap!" Inos said crossly. "Stop playing silly games. You've been there?"

He nodded, looking just a tiny bit shamefaced. "I've glanced around. N
one saw me."

"Then report. You can't expect me to decide when I don't know the situation."

He pulled a face. "It's worse than I thought at first. This Greastax is just a young lout — he even looks like a younger version of Kalkor. His 'men' are mostly not much more than boys. Greastax is no thane, and the whole thing was an irregular prank. He heard about the inheritance, took a ship, and came to claim it in his brother's name."

"What would Kalkor have said?"

"Said?" Rap scoffed. "He'd have slaughtered the lot of them for impudence."

"How many?" she asked, trying to remember Krasnegar in winter dark, when the streets were choked by drifts and peat was precious as gold, when fresh air was deadly and white bears might roam the harbor.

"Greastax and forty."

"Holding the whole town?" What sort of sheep did she have for subjects? Boys, you said? And only forty-one of them?"

Rap shook his head. "It's easy to laugh, Inos. But you're not there. You have no wife and children, no sisters and parents. Some of the Nordlanders have died, yes. Just youths, but they're big, and they're armed, and they are ruthless! The imps took away all the weapons, and these young brutes came sailing in the next day. They kill any man who talks back. Six or seven of them stirred up more than they could handle and died, but then the others slew babies and burned houses in retribution."

It seemed all wrong that so few could tyrannize so many, but Krasnegar had no history of any warfare worse than barroom brawling. As long as the invaders were armed and united and the citizens were neither, then resistance would mean suicide or the massacre of innocents. She could see that when she remembered how Kade had been used against her in Arakkaran.

Rap was watching her intently. "He rules in Kalkor's name, so who dares oppose him? No one can leave. Some tried, and the goblins sent back their eyes in bags. The imps wouldn't let anyone on the ships, because no one had money."

She shivered, and not from the cold. "I think I understand. And what can you do to help?"

For a moment the cold, ironic mask slipped, and he looked puzzled. "Me? Anything you want. Court sorcerer. I'll melt down the castle if you tell me to."

"That seems a little extreme."

"You decide what you want. Load your coach when you're ready to leave."

"Rap!" she said hastily, frightened that he was about to vanish. "Give me a clue?"

He frowned. "If you give someone something for nothing, that's how he'll value it."

"I do value —"

"I didn't mean you. That's your clue. Go talk to your Gods about it!" H
stare became icy. "And one more thing — forget about us, Inos! There's n
you-and-me in your future! If you want a man to share your throne and warr
your bed, you'll have to pick some other strong lad. Not me!" Muscle
clenched at the corner of his jaw. His neck was corded.

"But, Rap, why —"

"No why!" he shouted. "I'm just telling you a fact. That's a prophecy, if yo
like, a real prophecy."

"I love you, Rap."

He shrugged. "And I love you! That's the problem!" He was fading, th
brown of his clothes becoming gray, and fainter. She thought she could se
love and pain and longing in his eyes, but he was leaving.

"Rap, wait!"

He shook his head, and spoke in a faint, distant voice. "Another clue
When do Nordlanders celebrate Winterfest?"

He had gone. She was alone in the cloister, and the yard was bare an
naked under the frost of the winter morning. She began to move to th
church door and then changed her mind. Shivering, she tugged her cloa
tight about her and headed back to the palace.

6

Two days after Winterfest, the farewells began. The first to go wa
Shandie, heading off to stay with his aunt until spring came. His mother wa
rarely seen and he never spoke of her, but he was a much healthier, happie
little boy than he had been during the regency. The Leesofts departed in ;
caravan of coaches. Others followed.

Kade and Inos began their own good-byes. There were many good-bye
A dozen young men swore they would come to Krasnegar on the first shi
of spring. It would be heavy laden, Inos thought, and just as burdened whe
it returned.

Eigaze wept and ate chocolates. Her father was more restrained, but hi
political standing had not suffered by befriending Inos. He was heavil
favored for the next consulship, and she was glad of that. Tiffy swore his hear
was broken and he would resign from the hussars to become a priest. Ino
made him promise to wait at least a week, confident that by then soft arm
would have cushioned his fall.

Kadolan had a strange farewell with Sagorn and his companions. Ino
skipped that one, as she knew neither the sage nor Jalon well. She had me
Thinal not at all, and retained unhappy memories of the other two.

278

The imperor was gracious, and he had not presented a bill. What he had
ffered instead was a treaty between Krasnegar and the Impire, a pact of non-
ggression. Inos found the idea amusing, but she also saw what the sly old
aan had seen sooner — however meaningless it might be in practice, such a
ocument would give her authority if any of her subjects wanted to argue her
laim. The text was brief and seemed harmless. Sagorn approved it for her;
mshandar chuckled and claimed that it was the only honest treaty he had
ver signed.

Nor would he even accept thanks. "I am far more deeply in your debt than
ou are in mine, Queen Inos," he said. "Had it not been for you, Master Rap
vould hot have come to Hub. I owe you my life and my Impire."

"You owe them to Rap's folly, Sire, if I may say so."

"Blessed are fools, for they have no doubts. But most of all, I owe my
randson to him, and to you."

"You will miss him greatly."

The foxy old eyes misted. "That is what grandchildren are for — so that
he old may also dream, a promise of a future in return for the lost past. Did I
ell you what Master Rap told me?"

"No, Sire." Of course he knew that.

"Greatness! He said he foresaw greatness in Shandie!" Then the ruthless
ld rogue sniffled quietly and changed the subject.

*   *   *

Clutching her cloak tight about her, Inos came down the steps with Kade,
nd the coach was waiting. Tiny snowflakes drifted down from a pewter sky.
he was not at all surprised that the solitary footman grinned at her with teeth
hat could have graced a cart horse, nor that his face had a faintly greenish
inge. The cold would not bother him.

She walked over to the coachman, who was petting the lead right horse
nd whispering in its ear.

"Nordlanders celebrate Winterfest at the time of the nearest full
noon," she said softly. It had taken her much trouble to discover that sim-
le fact in Hub.

He nodded and granted her a small smile. "Logical that they would, isn't
t? Three nights from now."

"They will be feasting?"

"And drinking."

"Rap . . . I am so grateful. If there is anything —"

He lost the smile. Business was all right, apparently, but personal affairs
vere not. "Think hard, Inos!" he said grimly, "This is the start of a lifetime. A

kingdom will suck you in and bind you forever. You may never hear a wor
of thanks."

"Will the people accept me?"

He eyed her for a moment. "After what they have been through? And
can add a few tricks. But is it what you want?"

"Yes. It is my second greatest wish."

He scowled and turned his back on her to speak to the horse.

There were four of them in the big coach as it rumbled off along th
Avenue Agraine in search of the Great West Way. Bundled in fur robes, wit
hot bricks at their feet, they were an oddly assorted bunch.

Duke Angilki was indifferent, smiling faintly at nothing. He did tha
for hours at a time, rarely speaking except when he asked for food or bath
room in a childish monotone. Sagorn's skills had achieved nothing fo
him, and he would live out his days as one more monument to the ev
known as Kalkor.

Kade was engrossed. From her capacious purse she had produced
lengthy scroll entirely covered in a crabbed, spidery writing. She bega
studying it intently. Last summer she could not have read a word of it, an
certainly not in a bouncing coach.

Locked in a strange medley of emotions, Inos gazed out the windows a
the great buildings gliding past. She had come to Hub and conquered; sh
would never return. The strange adventure was drawing to its close —
Kinvale, and Zark, and Thume, and Ilrane, and Hub, and ultimately Krasnega
again. The butterfly would return to its cocoon. Now she must create a new
life there for herself, heal wounds, forge new friendships or recast old ones
learn the lonely life of a ruler. With the overland road closed, perhaps fo
years to come, Krasnegar's lot would be harder than ever, and all the problem
of that tiny make-believe kingdom would come to roost on her thin shoul
ders. She would not even have Kade to lean on.

With a sorcerer it would be possible. Nothing might be possible without him

She could not bear to live with Rap around and not love him.

She could not bear to think of living without him around.

And yet, ultimately, her royal duty included producing an heir.

"Some other strong lad," he had said, but he was the only strong lad sh
wanted.

Trust in love? Was that a divine admonition as she had believed for s
long, or was it, as Rap had said, merely mockery?

The fourth passenger was Master Odlepare, the duke's secretary. He was
balding, angular man of sour disposition, prematurely middle aged. He had a
infuriatingly condescending manner.

Shortly after the coach passed by the sinister Red Palace on its hill, and ong before the interesting architecture stopped, he had become bored vith silence.

"I brought some *thali* tiles, ladies," he remarked. "If either of you cares ɔ play?"

"It is not one of my favorite games," Inos said, thinking of the Oasis of Tall ˥ranes with inexplicable nostalgia.

He sighed odiously. "Well, perhaps some other day. We have many days ɔ pass. Many weeks."

"Weeks?" Kade said, looking up innocently. "Days? Oh, I hardly think so. ∕laster Rap," she continued without raising her voice, "it is a trifle chilly in ιere. Would you be so kind as to provide a little warmth?"

There was no reply, but the windows silently misted over.

Kade removed her lap robe. "Thank you. That is much better."

Master Odlepare had turned milk white. His mouth hung open.

"A faun?" He gurgled. Coachmen were often fauns, but the worthy secre-ary should have realized that a team of eight could not normally be driven ɼom the perch, with no postilion.

"A faun," Kade remarked calmly. "You were the duke's secretary, were you ιot? I have here a copy of the accounts submitted with the latest tax remit-ance from Kinvale, and some of the figures strike me as a trifle odd. Did you ιave any part in preparing this?"

He gurgled again, nodding.

"Assuming," Kade said, "that further building activity is curtailed or even ɗiscontinued, how many retainers do you estimate could be struck from the :state workforce?"

Stifling an unbearable desire to snigger, Inos turned to the window and wiped a small viewing area clear. Kade had run Kinvale before, periodically, when Ekka had been sick or bearing children. If Master Odlepare had :xpected the new imperial protector to be as addle-headed as she normally ɔretended, then he was in for a harrowing awakening.

The carriage picked up speed, the snow became thicker. The coachman ιever stopped to change horses. Shortly before lunchtime, he slowed to turn ɔff the highway. Inos took another peek through a fogged-up, rain-washed windowκ and recognized the gates of Kinvale.

7

Kinvale was strange and eerie. No guests graced its lofty halls, no orches-ɯras played for afternoon tea or evening banquets. Much of the furniture hud-ɗled under dustcovers, and the grates were dark.

Rap and the goblin bedded down the horses and then were seen no mor
The servants and the duke's daughters greeted Kade with cries of joy an
great relief that the long suspense was over. The imperor could not possibl
have found a guardian more welcome, nor more efficient. She took charg
easily, calming fears and issuing polite requests that sent men and wome
running to obey.

Inos wandered the damp and empty rooms like a ghost, the last of th
great army of unmarried ladies of quality who had come there over the yea
to find matches suited to their station. Had her father taken Sagorn's advic
and consulted the magic casement, she would never have been one of them
She had a heart-stopping vision of herself holding a brownish, wide-nose
baby with unruly hair . . .

No, that would not have happened, but with his daughter at his side
surely Holindarn would have recognized his own failing health and taker
proper steps to groom her and ensure her succession? Perhaps not. She ha
been a wayward, ignorant child in those days. Foronod and the other jotna
might still have balked at a juvenile female ruler. They would certainly hav
vetoed Rap as consort.

"Might have been" was a useless exercise.

What would the people say now? Was Foronod still alive? The bishop
Mother Unonini?

On the following morning, Inos summoned a carriage and went int
Kinford to shop. Hubban clothes would be useless in Krasnegar; none o
them would be warm enough and many would be thought indecent. Sh
bought wools and furs, in simple, practical styles.

That afternoon she began to pack a trunk, but for the rest of the day, an
for the two following days, she had little to do except pace the echoing corri
dors in an agony of apprehension.

How dare he desert her like this? A few times she went into the steamy
pungent stables and yelled, "Rap! Come here at once! I need you." She tried i
in some others places, also, but it never worked.

The servants began to look at her oddly.

On the third day Kade emerged from her bookkeeping waving a gues
list she had prepared for spring. Six months of mourning were plenty, sh
said brightly, and the duke might benefit from genteel company. Nonsense
Kade wanted company for Kade, but Inos saw that Kinvale would soon b
its cheerful self again, and her heart fluttered with fears for its own strengt
of purpose.

Then she wondered if Rap had planned this ordeal to test her nerve. Tha
thought stiffened her will as nothing else could have done — doubting her
was he? How dare he!

The third evening arrived with no sign that Rap still existed, or Little Chicken, either. A full moon rose in the twilight, huge and orange and ominous in the northeastern sky. Inos shut the drapes on it. She joined Kade in a private supper made horrible by their nervous efforts to cheer each other up.

But Inos did not doubt that he would come. Whatever else he was — and she had an extensive list of his shortcomings on the tip of her tongue at the moment — Master Rap was a man of his word.

She retired to her room and dressed for Krasnegar, in a long wool gown of cypress green. She could expect to find the town cool even indoors, but her thick dress and thicker underwear felt unbearably hot in Kinvale. She rang for footman to rope up her baggage. Then she was ready.

Carrying a fur coat and thick mitts, and sweltering even in the unheated dankness of the deserted mansion, she went down to the library to wait. There was a cheerful fire burning there, and he could find her when he was ready.

As she opened the door, she heard voices.

The library was a big room, gracious and comfortable — usually. Tonight it was filled with shadow and a strange sense of something uncanny that prickled the back of her neck. White-shrouded furniture made eerie humped shapes like ghosts of bison. At the far end, by the light of the fire and a single jumping candleflame. Rap lounged at his ease in a big armchair. Facing him in another was the goblin.

Automatically Inos turned to leave. Then she remembered her father saying that no one could eavesdrop on a sorcerer. She decided she had been summoned, so she stood and listened, her hand still on the handle.

" . . . as queen," Rap said. "That will be tonight. I'd like a couple of days to see her settled."

A couple of days?

The goblin grunted and mumbled something at his big fists, which were clenched together on his knees.

"No," Rap answered. "You can stay here and wait, if you like. Or come with us. It makes no difference. Just a couple of days, and then I'll be ready to keep my promise."

Inos's hands began to shake.

Little Chicken sat back and stared stonily at Rap. "You tell me now? Tell me what the big secret is? What you wouldn't say?"

"I'll tell you after we get to Raven Totem. We'll have time, won't we? You'll need a few days to invite the neighbors to the barbecue." Rap chuckled at his own black humor, and shivers ran all over Inos.

"No!"

"No what, Death Bird?"

"Don't want to be Death Bird. Don't want your promise anymore."

Inos thought a silent prayer to the Gods — all the Gods!

"You must become Death Bird!"

"Don't want to kill you."

"You must!" Rap sighed. "I suppose I do have to tell you. Remember th witch and the warlock used foresight on you? They saw your future. You hav a destiny, and now I can see it, too. It's mind-boggling! There's no escaping destiny like that one."

"Tell!"

"The imp with the fancy helmet? Yggingi. He did what no imp had eve done — he attacked your people in force. He marched through the taig looting and burning. The Impire has never done that before, Little Chicke never! The legions go where there's loot to pay for their upkeep, and th north never had anything worth looting."

His companion laughed, a heavy, brutal noise. "Goblins got mad?"

"Did they ever!" Rap chuckled softly. "But it was a turning point. Th Impire won't forget. This time they'll settle for holding the pass at Pondagu and be happy with that. There will be peace, then — for a while. But th legions never forget a slight. *They will be back!*"

"Goblins don't forget either. Be ready for them!"

Rap rose and turned to stand with his back to the fire. He did not look a Inos, but of course he must know she was there. He was telling this to he also. His face was shadowed, but it wouldn't show anything, anyway.

"Yes, the goblins will be ready for them. The goblins may even move firs — I haven't bothered to check exactly. But the goblins have got to star preparing soon, Little Chicken, my friend!"

There was a thoughtful silence, then the harsh goblin voice said, "Prepar how?"

"You're going to need all the men you can get. Warfare is a wastefu business."

Grunt! from Little Chicken.

"The goblins will have to change their ways, and soon, so that those boy can live and grow up to bear arms. They'll have to practice archery, and disci pline, and marching. Above all, the tribes must be unified."

There was a longer silence, then, before Rap went on, his voice hyp notic in the shadows. "The goblins need a leader, and that is the destiny that waits for you, Death Bird. You are the first goblin in years, perhaps th first in all history, to see the world beyond the taiga. No goblin has eve traveled as you have. Imps and jotnar and fairies and anthropophagi — you know them, and their ways. You've watched the legions training, you've seen their weapons."

"Others have been fighting."

"Throwing spears from behind trees. We're talking invasion over the pass
ow. We're talking a goblin kingdom."

"Won't work," Little Chicken said flatly. "No tattoos! If paint tattoos on
e, Sorcerer, won't work, either. Are like sailors, goblins . . . don't like sor-
ery. Magic tattoos fake!"

"This is what I'm trying to tell you! You must earn your tattoos. Any man
·ho wants to change old ways to new ways and make men follow him in new
·ays — that man has first got to show that he's mastered the old ways, so that
·eople will listen. Not just goblins. That's true of all races, everywhere. So you
iust take me back to Raven Totem as a prisoner. You must win back your honor
nd earn your tattoos by putting me to death. You've got to make a good show
— a fabulous show, one people will talk about for years, a fabled torturing."

Inos fought down dizzying surges of nausea. She wanted to run, she
·anted to scream, and she dared not move at all. She forced herself to listen,
·ooted by the sheer cold-blooded horror.

"I promised you a good show," Rap added quietly. "And I'll keep my word.
)ays and days. They'll follow you then! You'll be chief of Raven Totem in a
·ear. After that you can start preparing. You'll have to go slowly, and it'll take
. long, long time. But one day you'll lead your nation over the pass and carry
he war to the Impire."

"Wanting that?" the goblin demanded, and Inos was wondering the same.

"No, I don't, but I have no say in the matter. It's your destiny, and the way
he world works. It's as unchangeable as past history. The Gods decide such
hings, not me."

The goblin squirmed in his chair. "Won't! Don't want to kill you, Rap."

"I thought I was Flat Nose?"

"Use any Evil-begotten name you want!" Little Chicken barked, unexpect-
·dly switching from goblin dialect to impish with a Nordland accent. "You're
ny friend now! I like you, Rap, admire you . . . Love you, I suppose! I can
·ee where our ways were wrong. They're bad — not just for the victim, but
·or the whole goblin culture. I wish it could be stopped. I've given up torture,
.nd there is absolutely no way I'd do those things to a friend! Never!"

Inos released an audible gasp of relief and wiped her forehead with her
·leeve. Her legs wobbled. The men had not heard her cry out.

"You must do it!" Rap insisted. Who could resist a sorcerer? "It is your
·destiny!"

The goblin snarled something Inos missed, which was probably a nautical
·obscenity.

"The Gods have given you a destiny, and I gave you my promise!"

"God of Pus! Rot my destiny! I give you back your promise . . . don't
·even talk about it. You're making me ill!"

Suddenly Rap laughed, and Inos marveled that his laughter sounded s
familiar to her. She would have recognized it anywhere, but she could no
remember the last time she had heard Rap laugh.

"You big dumb green monster!" he said. "For weeks and weeks I tore m
heart out to get one kind word out of you. Now you defy the God
Themselves for my sake?"

"For weeks and weeks," the goblin responded, "I could barely keep m
thumbs out of your eyeballs! The only thing keeping me sane was the though
of all the lovely things I was going to do with your tripes eventually . . . bu
I've reconsidered, and decided to leave them where they are. For a nongoblir
you're quite likable trash, Rap."

"You don't want to be king of the goblins?"

Pause . . . "Not on those terms."

"This is awful!" Rap said. "The innocent savage has been perverted b
the vices of civilization. But here . . . if I'm Rap now, then this must b
Flat Nose."

The newcomer merged silently from the shadows behind the goblin
chair, although Inos was certain there had been no one there a moment ear
lier. Even so, she had more warning than Little Chicken, who sniffed suspi
ciously, looked over his shoulder, and then hurtled from his chair in a leap
that carried him to the far side of the fireplace. He yelled, "Arrk!" as he went

There were two Raps present. The new one was a little shorter and slighte
than the old, garbed in soiled buckskins. His filthy face was marred by a
patchy beard. Inos could guess what he smelted like for she had met that Rap
near Pondague in the spring. He stopped at the edge of the fire rug and jus
stood, wearing the same faint good-natured, vacant smile that she saw every
day now on Angilki.

"Sorcery!" the goblin hissed.

"Yes," Rap said, studying the apparition. "It's not a real person — only the
Gods can make those. But it's close enough for what you need. It will bleed
and writhe, and near the end it will start to scream. The only words it know
are 'Thank you.'"

"Evil sorcery!" Little Chicken advanced a step or two and poked the simu
lacrum with a stubby finger. He peered into its unworried eyes.

"Not evil from my point of view," Rap said. "Nor yours. There's no *person* ir
there, Death Bird. It will seem to suffer and die, but there's no mind, no soul
It'll last a long time."

"I told you — I don't approve of torture anymore. Beside, it would be
cheating!" He sounded tempted, though.

"This is how you can put an end to the custom! You still remember all
those wonderful ideas you had?"

"Yes," Little Chicken admitted. "And I learned some really innovative stuff from Kalkor." He sounded almost wistful.

"Then use them! A historic torment! It's necessary for your destiny. It's this for me, and I'd be grateful if you chose this one. And besides . . . it would probably be safer. I might get angry."

Rap held out a hand. Little Chicken hesitated, then chuckled and took it. Inos was not quick enough to make out exactly what happened next, but Rap flew over the goblin's shoulder and landed on his back with an impact that shook the house. Little Chicken went down hard on top of him. Inos heard a few brief grunts and thumps, a small table went over loudly, and then it was the goblin who went spinning through the air, arching up from the floor like an arrow, passing completely over an armchair. He came down heavily, fortunately breaking his fall on the surrogate Rap, which had been standing immobile through all this, smiling emptily. Goblin and counterfeit crashed in a heap, and a muffled voice from underneath said, "Thank you!"

The real Rap stood up, panting and straightening his clothes. "Want some more, Stalwart?"

"Not fair!" a growl from the floor said. "Used magic!"

"So did you — well, you used occult muscle, anyway. Now you've started breaking up my double there already. Get up and let me fix his leg."

Something knotted in Inos's throat. This nonsense was probably a masculine way of dealing with emotion, but why could Rap laugh with Little Chicken when he could not laugh with her?

The goblin guffawed and switched back to goblin dialect. "Was last chance for exercise." He bounced nimbly to his feet. "Start throwing my brothers around like that, will scream *Sorcery!* and use me for wall hangings . . . much as the little green savages deserve it. And you have no idea how I'm going to miss that good impish beer!"

"That explains it, then," Rap said absently, peering down at the prostrate simulacrum. "I couldn't understand why your destiny was completely mundane, but it is. It seemed odd . . . I suppose it makes sense. You'll have to hide your strength. Men might hesitate to follow a superhuman into battle."

He reached down a hand and helped the false Rap to its feet, where it stood in dutiful silence. The real men faced each other, amid a pause that swiftly became too long for comfort.

"Full moon," Rap said softly. "Good traveling in the northlands."

"Summon neighbors," Little Chicken agreed, but he still seemed indecisive.

Again Rap held out a hand, then changed the gesture to a hug. The two men embraced.

"Gods bless, Flat Nose."

"The Good go with you," Rap said softly. "Buckskins? Grease? Phew! A
right — I'll put you at the door to Raven Totem."

Goblin and counterfeit faded and were gone.

The casement's third prophecy would be fulfilled.

Rap turned to the fire and leaned an arm along the mantel. For a momer
he seemed to slump, but whether it was from relief or despair, Inos could no
tell. Then he straightened and looked around for her. He bowed.

"Good evening, your Majesty."

Keep it formal.

She strolled forward and tossed her heavy coat on a chair. The air bore
lingering stench of rancid bear grease. "Good evening, Court Sorcerer. An
where have you been these last few days?"

"Running in the woods with a goblin." Rap's face was between her and th
light on the mantelpiece, and unreadable.

"That helped him to the right choice?"

"Undoubtedly."

"You wouldn't have let me listen if you hadn't been sure."

"But it was only this afternoon that I was sure."

"Most sorcerers would just adjust his mind to suit themselves."

"Perhaps." His voice was giving nothing away. "That might have upset hi
destiny, though."

"Why did you let me see all that?"

He shrugged. "I won't be staying long in Krasnegar, Inos. I didn't want yo
. . . wondering."

"Thank you," she said, thinking of Krasnegar without him.

"You are most welcome. And what are your Majesty's commands fo
this evening?"

She perched on the arm of the chair the goblin had occupied. "If I turn u
with a court sorcerer and he blasts the jotnar to fritters, then the people wil
cheer loudly, hail him as Inisso II, and put him on the throne."

"Which would be fine by you," Rap agreed, an ironic smile crinklin
his tattoos.

She nodded — very fine!

He wrinkled his nose. "But not by me."

"So we have to let the citizens free themselves, which means givin
them weapons."

"And leadership. But then they will have bought their freedom, and wil
value it accordingly." He smiled faintly. He would smile as long as she kep
the talk on business. If she tried to tell him how empty life in Krasnegar wa
going to be without him, then he would just vanish, or tell her she didn't
know her own mind.

There was nothing else to discuss, then.

He was gazing at her quizzically, saying that it was time now. Her heart
ad speeded up as if it expected her to flap her arms and fly all the way to
Krasnegar. But Rap would magic her there, and Rap would protect her — for a
ouple of days, he had told the goblin. After that she would be on her own.

Sink or swim. Win or lose. Live or die.

That was her choice, and now, irrevocably, she must decide: to be a but-
erfly in Kinvale or an ant in Krasnegar. Now! Speak!

She thought of the goblin. He also had been caught up between two
worlds like corn in the mill, seduced by the easy life of the Impire and summoned home by duty. That might be the real reason Rap had summoned her
o watch Little Chicken's departure . . .

Who was she to start a war? By what right did she ask men to die so she
could reign?

There was nothing left to say except either "Let's go!" or else "I'm too
frightened."

She had promised her father. Choose!

The door clicked. An elderly lady came wandering along the room —
hort and plump, immaculately dressed and begemmed, not a hair misplaced.

"There you are," Kade said sternly. "Master Rap, I have a complaint."

He bowed to her. "Your Highness, I am distressed to hear it."

Kade nodded vaguely to Inos and then addressed Rap again. "I have
been rather looking forward to having Kinvale the way it used to be,
peaceful and settled. For the last ten or fifteen years, Angilki has been con-
tantly tearing it apart and putting it back together again, but he won't be
doing that anymore."

"Aunt!" Inos said testily. "Just what are you getting it?"

"My little sitting room. You know how fond I am of that room!"

"Yes, Aunt, I know how fond you are of that room. So *what?*"

"There is a door in the north wall, and I'm quite certain it was not there an
hour ago."

Inos turned to stare at the sorcerer. "Rap?"

His teeth showed in his shadowed face. "I thought you might appreciate a
little company once in a while. Drop in for tea, maybe."

Inos gaped wonderingly at him for a long moment. "Oh, Rap! You mean
that this new door leads to Krasnegar?"

"Magic portal. Useful for tea parties, famines, invasions."

"Rap! Oh, Rap!" Suddenly the prospect had changed. She would have
Kade's shoulder to weep on. She would have an escape hatch. Now there was
absolutely no reason not to go ahead. Her doubts of a moment ago now
seemed completely absurd. Why had she hesitated?

"Rap!" she cried again, and she jumped up from the side of the chair and tried to throw her arms around him.

She ran into invisible molasses that brought her to a stop about a handsbreadth away from him. She saw something close to panic in his eyes, and although their faces were so near, he shouted at her.

"Idiot! How often must I tell you? We can't!"

"Rap!"

"Never! Not even once. Not even to say good-bye."

Bold Lover:

> Bold Lover, never, never canst thou kiss,
> Though winning near the goal —
> > Keats, *Ode on a Grecian Urn*

11

Alteration find

1

Rap's taste in interior decorating was no match for Angilki's. Kade's private parlor room was a small room, but it had been beautifully proportioned. The walls were papered in pink roses, and the original woodwork was smooth and shiny white. The new door was an odd-sized excrescence in one corner — mahogany red, thickly embellished with carvings, spangled in eye-twisting runes of gold and copper. It just did not go.

"I could move it to the back of a closet somewhere," Rap mumbled, scratching his head and apparently recognizing for the first time the monstrosity he had created.

"I love it!" Kade insisted. "Now that I know what it does, I just love it! I did try the handle," she confessed guiltily, "but it seems to be bolted on the other side."

"It's only a dummy, actually," Rap said. "Unless you also say the magic word, which is 'Holindarn.' Are you ready, your Majesty?"

There was no need to worry about baggage now. Inos swallowed a sum merful of butterflies and said, "One more minute, Court Sorcerer." She bega buttoning her coat.

"I'll be with you," he said quietly. "But you don't want to show up with horsethief, so nobody's going to notice me. I'll be immemorable, Like this."

Glancing up from a particularly awkward button, Inos found herself look ing at a man-at-arms. Ear flaps dangled from a conical iron helmet, framing face that was typically imp — swarthy, poxy, and pudgy. Nothing much els was visible except furs and a breastplate. He wore a short sword and padde leggings. And boots. There was nothing especial to notice, except that he wa a man-at-arms dressed for winter. She remembered how once before she ha seen Rap clad somewhat like that and had failed to recognize him even wit his own face on.

Then he was himself again. Smiling warily, he stepped by her and haule a chintz-covered chair out of the way. "Go ahead, try it!"

Inos turned to Kade for a farewell hug and kiss. "If I'm not fighting any wars tomorrow afternoon, I'll stop by for tea and tell you all about it," she promised, surprised how husky her voice sounded.

"That will be lovely, dear. If you can." For a moment Kade clung to Inos and her cornflower-blue eyes were unusually misty. "Inos . . . " She bit he lip. "I'm not going to start being maudlin at my age, but . . . I do want you to know that your father would be very proud of you now!"

Gulp! "Well, let's wait and see how he would feel tomorrow, shall we?"

"Your courage, dear, I mean. What you try is always lots more importan than what you achieve."

"Goodness, Aunt! I have never heard you moralize like this before."

"That's because you always refused to listen, dear. But I am serious! You father would have approved of you. Your sense of duty, and your courage."

If this farewell was protracted any further, it was going to become a rathe obvious cowardice. "And he certainly would not disapprove of his sister, o what she has done for me and for Krasnegar. Now I really must dash off, or shall be late for the massacre."

With that, Inos broke free and turned quickly to try the magic portal "Holindarn!" she proclaimed. The door shivered but did not budge.

"Here, put some muscle into it!" Rap leaned an arm over her to push. He was closer than he'd been since she tried to tell him her word of power weeks ago. Then she'd kissed his cheek. If she turned her head quickly, could she manage that again? The door began to move, and wind shrieked. Torrents of icy air whirled into Kade's sitting room. Drapes leaped, papers flew. Coals tumbled and smoke vomited from the fireplace. Kade squealed in alarm.

"Sorry!" Rap shouted over the gale. "Have to work on this a bit!" He heaved harder, and the opening was large enough for Inos to slip through, into frigid darkness.

The door thumped closed behind her. She hadn't heard Rap follow. She had forgotten how intensely cold air could be, like ice water on her face.

"Akk!" she said. "Light?"

Then her eyes adjusted, and she saw moonlight beyond a window on her right and a fainter one straight ahead.

"Recognize it?" Rap's voice inquired sardonically at her back.

"Inisso's chamber!"

She turned, and the magic portal was a blackness filling the central arch. The side arches framing it were simple casements of clear glass. She stared out in wonder. Far below her, the snowcapped roofs and battlements of the castle, and of Krasnegar itself beyond them, fell white and steep to the distant harbor, a snowy plain glowing silver under the moon. Every chimney sported a plume of smoke, rising slowly in the crystal-still air. Her heart thumped in her throat and she felt tears that were only partly due to the cold.

Home! Home at last!

"The casement! What have you done with it?"

"I got rid of it. They're nasty things. You're better off without it. But we sorcerers have strange ideas of humor — on this side, the portal's a real door, always. Don't forget the magic word, or that first step will get you. Ah! There's the trouble!"

Vague in the darkness, he moved off to where the western casement had blown open. "Faulty clasp!" he said, shutting it. "There!"

Inos could see her breath now, like a white cloud. She could feel the cold aching in her lungs. She had returned to Krasnegar as she had left it, by sorcery, and in the exact same spot.

"Rap? What did you mean when you said the magic casement didn't prophesy?"

"Well, it did in a way. But its prophecies tended to be rather nastily self-fulfilling."

"Doctor Sagorn said . . . "

"Sagorn doesn't know half as much as he thinks he does," Rap said firmly. "And he had magic casements wrong! A casement does not advise what's best for the person opening it. It doesn't care a poop for his welfare, not the way a preflecting pool advises a person. Casements are fixed things and care only for the welfare of the house. Inisso's house in this case."

"I'm not sure I follow that. How did the vision of the goblins killing you help anyone?"

293

"It made me see that he was important, and help him when he was in Hub. The goblins will have a king. Raven Totem is one of the most northerly lodges and Little Chicken won't attack Krasnegar, for my sake. He'll direct the tribes southward. Another king might not."

"Oh!" Inos said doubtfully.

"Magic casements are evil!" Rap insisted. "It made me cheat Sagorn out of a word of power, and it made Kalkor kill Gathmor. Rasha made a magic casement — not a very good one, I admit — but it led her to you and that brought me, and then look what happened! It put the welfare of Arakkaran ahead of hers. No gratitude at all."

Inos did not argue, but it seemed that the casement had effectively arranged events to bring her back here with a sorcerer in attendance so she could claim her throne, and in that case . . .

"Watch your step here." A flicker of light burst forth and strengthened. Rap was holding a lantern. The room was a shambles of bedding and discarded clothes. She saw empty bottles, too, and the remains of meals.

"I didn't have time to tidy up," he explained as she began picking her way through the mess. "The imps must have boarded men up here."

The thick door had been repaired, most likely by Rap. It opened silently and he led the way down the curving stair. Her heart was thumping painfully, and there was a horrid dryness in her throat.

He paused partway down. "All clear," he said after a moment. "The whole tower's deserted. And it's all a mess!"

"Rap! I just thought of something! I came up this tower months ago and disappeared. Now I reappear and come down again . . . What do I say if they ask where I've been?"

"Ignore them!" Rap said sarcastically. "Tell them you're starving and ask what's for breakfast."

"Rap!"

He continued to walk down the steps, with her following. "They're not going to ask," he said. "You're a queen, and monarchs don't get questioned. Just glare at them, like the imperor does."

Easy for him to say — he was a sorcerer. She would have to practice glaring.

They emerged into her father's bedchamber. The mattress lay on the floor, amid some dirty straw pallets. A few fragments of furniture remained, but most of the rest must have gone for firewood. The two portraits above the mantel had been defaced with charcoal and used for knife-throwing targets. Rags and bottles and dishes lay everywhere. A fierce anger began to warm her.

The next room was as bad. The withdrawing room was worse, although admittedly it had been bad when she saw it last, with charred rugs and broken china littering the floor. There was an ominous stain near the fireplace.

294

Down and down . . .

The Presence Chamber showed signs of recent occupancy — lingering warmth, embers still smoldering in the grate, rumpled bedding. Four or five men were living here, she deduced. Her home had been denied, and her tunnish blood boiled in her veins.

On the last stair Rap halted, and she heard faint sounds of music and shouting. The beat of her heart was almost as loud. The lantern faded and disappeared. Then Rap's strong hand gripped her wrist.

"Invisibility spell," he whispered.

They picked their way down, step by step. Faint light showed ahead, seeping around the curve of the stone, and then she began to stumble — not only was there no Rap ahead of her to explain that tight grip, but she could not see her own feet. He steadied her, and they came cautiously into the Throne Room, and into noise.

Here also lay bedding, and peat glowed hot in the grate. The throne itself had been removed, but when she raised her eyes to look through the arch into the Great Hall, she saw it out there, in the middle. A young man was sitting on it, with a girl on his lap.

Tables defined a central arena like a dance floor. Other men sprawled at those tables, with other girls, and they were laughing and jeering as they watched two more girls dancing clumsily in the center. Off to one side somewhere, a small orchestra battered away discordantly at a jig tune. Flames leaped in the big fireplaces.

Girls. Not women. They all looked younger than herself, and most of them had no clothes on. She tasted bile in her throat. More than the increasing warmth was making her sweat inside her wrappings. Azak! Pixies . . .

The men were all jotnar, roughly dressed, most of them. A few had begun to strip. They were big. She had forgotten how big jotnar could be. These fairskinned youths were intimidatingly huge . . . . just youths, most of them. A few were older, but she could see none without some trace of beard. The one on the throne must be Greastax. He wasn't much more than a boy, and he certainly did look like a young Kalkor. He was going to die if she had to kill him herself.

But Nordland raiders never parted from their weapons, even when celebrating Winterfest.

Here and there she recognized palace servants, scurrying to and fro with bottles and plates. She knew some of the girls, too. Friends, a few of them, and younger sisters of friends. Children!

Perhaps there were no older women available now for such sport?

"Gods!" she muttered under her breath. "Gods, Gods, Gods!"

"Forty-one!" Rap whispered with satisfaction. "All accounted for. Got any scruples left now?"

"None!" she said. "They die! All of them!"

"Good. Let's go a little faster, all right?"

"Oh, yes!" She saw another dress being ripped off, and she could gues
what sort of entertainment was about to follow. She almost commanded he
court sorcerer to strike down these brutes as he had blasted Kalkor. But tha
would be too simple. If she hoped to hold her realm by mundane means, the
she must win it by mundane means . . . or seem to, at least.

Rap's invisible hand tightened on her wrist. "Steady now!"

Shock!

She was plunged back into darkness and arctic cold, and snow underfoot
The impact disoriented her and she cried out, shivering already.

"Sorry. I can't zap us out of the castle. Here — through here."

He put her hand on a vertical edge. Her dazzled eyes had begun to pick
up the moonlight again, and an opening. She recognized the postern gate
and clambered through with a visible Rap close behind her, out into the yard
before the castle, silvered by the high moon.

The sky was an iron bowl, with only a few stars showing through the
moonlight. The deadly cold prickled in her nostrils and made her eyes water
Her breath was a rainbow-tinted fog, but there was no wind, and the smoke
from the houses rose in soft pillars the color of the moon.

"Why can't you —"

"Shielded." He took her wrist again. "Indoors again."

Shock! She stumbled, and he put an arm around her, just for a moment
Her ears popped. A torch spluttered in a sconce ahead of her, and she looked
around, seeing rough wooden walls and stone floor and a few closed doors
They were in one of the innumerable covered alleyways that were
Krasnegar's winter arteries. The temperature was much higher — around
freezing, likely.

"Ready for your big reappearance scene?" Rap's tone was jovial, but he was
eyeing her carefully.

She nodded. "Let me get my breath back. It's all a bit much."

"Fine," he said. "No one will disturb us. Open your hood."

She fumbled with lacing, hearing now a muffled rumble of conversation
nearby. A sign on the nearest door proclaimed it to be the Beached Whale
and she could smell fish amid the odor of people and tallow. Now she knew
where she was, down near the docks. How small it all was! How cramped
and shabby!

"We'll pick up some jotnar here, and then go on and collect some imps,"
Rap said.

"Suppose they don't want to come?"

"That's up to you. Here, let me."

Brusquely he pushed back her hood as she began unfastening the coat. She as very conscious of his closeness, but he was being businesslike and did not em to notice. Something ghostly stirred her hair.

"Now look!" Rap held up a mirror. There was her face — pale, but stern, ot terrified and bewildered as she felt it should be. Her honey-blond hair sat n waves that might have come straight from the hands of one of Hub's expert oiffeuses, and an emerald tiara sparkled on it. The gown showing through er open coat was much more ornate than it been when she put it on, glitter-ng with scrolls of seed pearls and sequins. Obviously Rap had his own ideas f how a Queen of Krasnegar should look, but he might be able to judge the ocal thinking better than she could. Yes, not bad!

And something else . . . Not *majesty*, surely? Regality? She could not lace it, but she could believe at she was looking at a queen. Was she doing hat, or was he?

"Rap! This tiara belongs to Eigaze! I borrowed it for the imperor's ball —"

"No, you've got one just like hers now." The mirror disappeared as inexplic-bly as it had come. "Coronation present from me. I've got the weapons when ou ask for them. Now go in there, Queen Inosolan, *and claim your inheritance!*"

She nodded dumbly. Then their eyes met.

"Give me one little kiss? Just one?"

His efficient, businesslike expression faded to one of agony. "Oh, Inos!" he vhispered. "Not even your fingers."

She closed her eyes. "You're going to explain this to me, you know," she aid. "What you're afraid of. I won't stand for it!" When she looked again, he ad turned to open the door. She took a deep breath and raised her chin.

As the door swung open, she was assaulted by heat, and tumult, and a reek f cheap beer. The big room was dim, yet fogged by smoke from the oil amps. Below the rough-plank ceiling, dozens of men were standing in groups or slouched at tables, yammering away in rowdy voices.

She strode past Rap and headed for the brightest spot she could see. A nan jumped up from his seat as she approached and wandered off without noticing her. Rap's arm was there when she reached for it; she raised her skirts vith her other hand and stepped nimbly up onto the stool.

The racket spiraled down into sudden stunned silence. All eyes were on ner. Pale faces staring, golden heads and silver. This was a jotunn watering hole, but there were imps present there, also, and perhaps that was a good ign. She must unite the factions, but surely adversity would have already drawn them closer than before?

Men at the back scrambled to their feet to see better.

"The princess!" a voice said in awe, and others picked it up: "The princess! The princess! . . . "

"The queen!" shouted another in the far corner, and again there were som
echoes. A few fists banged on tables. Then silence. She thought the light w
brightening around her and dimming elsewhere. Her mouth was parched. N
it wasn't —

"I am Queen Inosolan. I have returned to claim my realm!" She dared no
pause there in case someone started to scoff. "I bring weapons and I call fc
you to take up arms in my name and wreak vengeance on the jotn . . . o
the invaders!"

Rap threw a massive bundle onto the table with a mighty metallic crash. A
sudden tug at her waist told Inos that she now wore a sword. She reache
under her coat and drew it.

She flourished it overhead and the blade struck the ceiling so hard that th
hilt almost slipped from her fingers.

"Who is with me?"

The longest two seconds of her life . . .

"By the Powers, I am!" a high-pitched voice cried. A young jotunn spran
to his feet a couple of tables away. He was very lanky, his blond hair almos
brushing the ceiling, his face bright pink from too much beer.

Kratharkran, the smith, prompted a voice inside her ear, but she knew Kratl
How he had grown!

"Mastersmith Kratharkran, you are welcome! I appoint you leader here
Issue these weapons, and bring your squad to the bailey. I shall meet you ther
with others. The raiders are all gathered in the Great Hall, and we are goin,
to kill them!"

"Aye!" Kratharkran roared in a squeak absurdly ill suited to his size. Other
jumped up, also, and then stools were falling all over the room, boots clumping

"Gods save the queen!" Kratharkran piped, and a chorus echoed him
"Gods save the queen!"

Rap had gripped her wrist again. She jumped down, and her sword mirac
ulously — and fortunately — vanished as she did so. Invisible hands steadie
her when her coat caught on the stool. Rap pulled, and she headed for th
door as a great drunken clamor of shouting and falling furniture filled th
room behind her.

She was out in the passageway and running, being towed by Rap.

"Beautifully done! Oh, beautiful!" he shouted back at her.

"You did it, not me!" She laughed aloud, and he turned his head to smil
at her.

Then he flung open the door of the Southern Dream and dragged her insid
before she could draw breath. The ceiling was even lower, the light even dim
mer, and most of the clustered heads around the tables were dark. Well, imp:
should be even more willing to kill jotnar, although it might take more of them

Again she was up on a stool; again the light seemed to draw in around
er. She had her speech ready — too ready, for she began almost before
here was silence. "I am Queen Inosolan. I have returned to claim my
ealm . . . "

The same crash of weapons from Rap, the same shocked silence . . .

Longer . . .

Freezing, horrible silence!

Impish Krasnegarians were less easily aroused than their paler-skinned
countrymen. Her new euphoria sank into dread. She saw her tiny amateur
rebellion being stomped to bloody pulp by those ruthless young professionals
p in the castle. She saw her own armed jotnar victorious but turning on the
mps in civil war. She saw all kinds of disaster.

"What, cowards?" she shouted. "I have fifty jotnar behind me. Will none of
ou come also to avenge your sisters and your daughters?"

Muttering . . .

Hononin the hostler, to your right, said the invisible guide.

"Master Hononin? Where is your loyalty?"

The wizened old man clambered to his feet, more bent and wrinkled even
han she remembered. His eyes glinted angrily at being thus singled out. "I am
10 fighter, Princess."

"Queen!"

"Queen, then." He looked unconvinced.

"And neither am I, but I am Holindarn's daughter, and I am not a coward!
Sometimes we must all stand up for the Good."

"You bring another army like the last one?"

"I brought no one, but I offer you blades. Now, do the imps hide under
beds and let the jotnar have all the swords?"

"No!" a few timorous souls somewhere said uncertainly.

"Well, then . . . " Hononin's angry old eyes settled momentarily on Rap,
and paused. Inos wondered what message might be passing there, or what sorcery in use. Then his gaze flickered around the room, and the bent shoulders
straightened. "When you put it like that, ma'am, I wouldn't mind spitting a
couple of those young brutes myself."

Inos's head swam with sudden relief. She swayed on her perch and felt her
shoulders being steadied. "I appoint you leader, then. Bring your men to the
bailey with the others! Revenge!"

A shout of "Revenge!" sprang up, but she thought she heard a few of "Gods
save the queen!" also. Then she was on her way to the door again.

"Even better!" Rap crowed, hauling her along the alley. She was breathless,
soaking wet inside all her cumbersome garments. He almost dragged her up a
long flight of stairs to the Sailor's Head.

That was where she first noticed women present, and she added a new command: "Women come, also, and attend to the girls those animals stol. They must be rescued unharmed!" And there it was the women who starte the shouting.

The Golden Ship   . . .

The King's Men   . . .

The Three Bears   . . .

She had never realized how many saloons Krasnegar had. She made a not to tease Rap about his experience with them all. And they were not a third of the way up the hill yet.

Then he pulled her into a side corridor and stopped. "Listen!"

She listened — a deep roar, far away, like surf or continuous thunder. was all around them. The town had come alive like a stirred anthill.

"The men of Krasnegar!"

"Rap! We've done it! We've done it! No, you did it."

"It was you," he said softly.

It was the weapons, mostly. Even an adept should not be this effective and she suspected he'd put a sorcery on her, a *majesty*. But he gave her n time to ask.

"Fasten your coat! Some of them are ahead of us. We've got plenty already and they'll collect more. Ready?"

Shock!

Again, cold and dark like hammerblows . . . She gasped and clutche her coat over her chest. "Rap! You didn't give me time!"

"No time!"

They were standing at the postern gate again, and he was staring back across the drift-filled yard, awash with moonlight. A narrow track across i had been trampled clear by many feet, leading from the mouth of Roya Wynd, the covered way that connected castle and town. A wider opening i the walls marked the start of the wagon road, but that would be filled with snow, abandoned until springtime. Yet now it showed a flicker of light, the same yellow glow that shone on the undersides of the drifting vapor cloud rising from every chimney.

"Gods!" Rap said. "The whole town's coming!"

And Inos could hear the singing — there was an army fighting its way up the street, and probably another coming up the covered walks. She tried no to think of the dangers, of people being crushed. She had started a revolution and must pay the price, whatever it turned out to be.

Her teeth started to chatter.

"Sorry!" Rap murmured absentmindedly, and at once she was cozy warm all over, from ears to toes. He was still clad in only the simple pants and

alf-unbuttoned tunic he had worn indoors in Kinvale. His boots and shirt
ere thin, southern wear, his head was bare.

It was the postern that was bothering him. For eight months of the year
1e castle gates stood closed, drifted shut by thick snow. Only the little
ostern gate stayed open always, just wide enough for a man or a horse. An
rmy could not pass through such a slot.

Rap stuck his head inside and peered around, then came out again. "Evil-
egotten nuisance, this shielding," he mumbled. Again he studied the far side
f the court. "If the raiders wake up in time and can get here to hold this door,
hen I'll have to show my hand. I think I'd rather do it this way. Come on!"

He pulled her back along the snowy track a few paces. Even as he did so,
he heard the gates creak. Slowly, noisily, and occultly, the two great flaps
egan to swing forward, crunching mountains of snow ahead of them. When
hey stood about halfway open, Rap released them.

"That should be enough," he said. "I wonder if anyone will ever think to
sk who opened the castle?"

The noise of singing was louder now, the chimney smoke was glowing
rightly overhead. A line of lights came into sight up the hill — men bearing
orches, twenty or more abreast, floundering through the snow, cursing and
tumbling. They were being propelled by the rank behind them as inexorably
s Rap had moved the gates, and that rank by more behind it. The steaming
nass advanced up the hill as irresistible as moving pack ice. Any man who fell
vas going to be trampled, but those first brave leaders were having the worst
f it. The rest were finding easier going, and the singing came from them.
Another mob suddenly erupted from Royal Wynd, a darker company against
he snow, men without torches. They continued to pour into the courtyard,
ind now the main mass was at the top of the road.

"Come on!" Rap took Inos's wrist again, and they ran before the advancing
norde — through the barbican, past the guardroom door, into the bailey. Her
ather had fought a losing battle every winter to keep the bailey as clear of
now as was practical, but this year no one seemed to have tried very hard.
She floundered through drifts as Rap pulled her over to the armory steps.

"Stand up here!" he said. He was not even panting; his stupid boots were
orobably full of snow. "Here they come — hold this!"

Somehow Inos found herself teetering on top of a wall and clutching a
nonstrous torch, hissing and spluttering, with leaping flames as long as her
arms. It was so heavy she almost dropped it.

Before she could complain, the archway flickered and rumbled. With
swords shining in the light of their torches, with their feet crunching on the
hard-frozen snow, with voices raised in defiant song, the men of Krasnegar
stormed into the bailey.

Inos felt her heart swell and tears prickle at her eyes. She had summoned her people, and they had rallied to their queen! Her speech was ready on the tip of her tongue as the vanguard reached her perch. She raised her flaming brand in a heroic gesture and cried out, "My loyal subjects —"

The army went right by her without an upward glance. Nothing she could say was going to be heard anyway. Echoes boomed from the walls as the bailey filled up with roaring men, their leaders already past the kitchen quarters and the stables and the wagon sheds, advancing remorselessly on the Great Hall. More and more poured past Inos, the forgotten leader.

She peered around for Rap and found him below her, in the corner between the steps and the armory wall. He was doubled over, helpless with laughter. She could not recall ever having seen Rap laugh like that. She hurled her torch down at him in fury.

"Idiot! There are people being killed in there! Do something!"

He sprang up beside her as nimbly as a grasshopper. He had stopped laughing, but the old familiar half grin curled around the corners of his mouth. "You want me to call them back to listen to your harangue?"

"No — of course I was wrong! But let's get in there!"

"Right," he said cheerfully, and moved them both to the Throne Room. *Shock!*

It was a good vantage point. The revelers in the Great Hall had just awakened to their peril. There was shouting and confusion. The jotnar were pulling on helmets and sword belts — even clothes in some cases. The orchestra wailed into silence. Then the great doors crashed open and a foam of swords and smoking torches rolled into the hall, the crest of a tidal wave of men.

Inos hauled off her thick coat, discarding mitts and boots in the same flurry of movement. "Shoes!" she demanded.

"Just like that? How about some proper respect?" But Rap ensorceled shoes onto her feet. They pinched her toes.

The young jotnar were no cowards and as trained fighters they knew how to deal with a trap. Hastily forming a wedge, they charged the invasion, but they were too late to take the door. Servants, musicians, and girls all fled screaming from the developing battle, and the only place that offered even temporary shelter was the Throne Boom. Behind them the Great Hall rang with clashing swords. Men howled curses and roared defiance. Tables and benches went over, dishes rolled and smashed; bodies were falling on top of them.

The first naked girl to arrive was Uki, the miller's youngest. Inos threw her coat to her and scrambled up on a chair, raising her arms in welcome to the rest. The panicking mob stumbled to a halt, staring in disbelief.

Voices cried, "Inos!" and "The princess!"

"I am your queen, and Krasnegar is liberated!"

Their replies were hardly audible over the hubbub of battle out in the hall. ios waved an arm at the door to the stairs. "The room above here is warm!" ie yelled, hoping Rap would take the hint. "Women upstairs!" The closer irls heard her and raced that way. The rest followed, piling up in the ntrance in a squirming mass of bare flesh. The men, including Rap, watched ie performance with interest.

Inos was more concerned with the fight beyond the arch. She could see lood, shockingly bright in the flickering torchlight, and men were going own. No one had armor. But sheer weight of numbers was starting to carry he day, and the citizens were roused now, even imps screaming jotunn war ries back at the retreating brigands. In a moment it would all be over.

She lifted her skirt and leaped from the chair. She ran for the throne, trust-ng her court sorcerer to follow. As she jumped up on the scarlet cushion, she vondered what her father would have thought of all this. She hoped that (ade was right, and he would have been just a little bit proud of her now.

The tide of battle died out as one last half-naked jotunn was hacked down lmost at her feet by three imps simultaneously. The shouting in the hall was ading, although a huge multitude outside still bellowed its eagerness enter.

Rap was with her, standing alongside the throne. She reached out and tou-led his hair. There was frost on it. "Bell?"

At once the great bell of the castle *boomed*.

"Gods save the queen!" a voice cried. Others began to pick it up in refrain: Gods save the queen!" *Boom!* "Gods save the queen!"

Boom! went the bell in the distance.

Bloody swords were being waved overhead — dangerously. Pale faces ınd brown faces were grinning at her in a dazzling sea of faces. But her trou-bles were only beginning. Somehow she must gain control over this beast nob she had roused. They had swords. Most of them were reeling drunk — f not from beer, then from excitement. There had been few weapons in her ather's kingdom. If imp and jotunn fell out now, there would be a much greater bloodbath.

She held up both arms for silence, and the noise began to dwindle.

But not fast enough. "Quieten them, please," she said softly, and a hush fell.

"If there's a body near you, and it's one of the Nordlanders, please drag it ɔut and throw it over the north battlements!" That command brought a brief cheer and some turbulent movement within the throng. "Help the wounded ɔver to the fireplace!" She wondered how many of her followers had died in the last few minutes, and decided not to mention those. "I am Queen Inosolan, and I claim this throne by right of inheritance!"

Another cheer, not quite so loud.

"Money!" she whispered.

"Money?" Rap echoed, looking up at her in astonishment.

He had told her himself that there was no money left in the town. She could not guess how the people were surviving without it — by some form of barter, presumably.

She peered over the nearby faces, and the only one she recognized was the old hostler. He was small and stooped, with both hands in his pockets, but his gnarled old face was grinning at her. Evidently he had given his sword to some younger man, but he was honest and respected.

"Master Hononin! Set up a table by the door. I have brought money. Buy back the swords — five crowns per blade."

His jaw dropped. "Five?"

Boom!

"Five crowns per blade! Here, Sergeant, give this man the coin."

Rap snorted, but he held out two huge leather bags. The old man pushed forward grumpily, tried to take one in both hands, and dropped it. It fell with a metallic crash that silenced the returning tumult.

Boom!

"All surviving members of my father's council pray attend me!" Inos shouted. "Help him, Rap!" she whispered.

But Hononin was already snarling orders to recruit assistants, and in a moment the money was heading for the door. Now the important thing was to clear the hall while she still had control.

She saw another familiar face. "Mistress Meolorne! The girls we rescued are upstairs in the Presence Chamber. Will you please take care of them — see they are clothed and returned to their families?"

Boom!

Quietly: "You can stop that accursed bell now, thank you."

Louder: "Tonight the beer is free! Tell every tavernmaster in town that when you toast your queen tonight, the crown will pick up the tab!"

The resulting cheer shook the castle, and a whirlpool developed near the door as eager subjects began hurrying off to drink to her health before the supplies ran out — as they surely would, unless Rap chose to intervene.

Inos paused to consider her next move, rubbing her throat.

Then she saw a tall man being helped through the crowd toward her, and her heart jumped into her mouth.

It was the factor, Foronod. His silver helmet of hair was unmistakable, and yet she thought that it was now more white than ash blond. He was ten years older than he had been in the spring. He was stooped, leaning on a cane, and ragging one foot. A patch hid one eye; his nose was misshapen. Who had one this — imp or jotunn?

The faces closest around her were aging rapidly. The young bloods had een trusted to handle the fighting, but now the elders of the town were arriv ng to oversee the political consequences. The burghers, the merchants, the enior craftmasters — these men she must win over, and they would be her pponents. All the cheering, blood-splattered, baby-faced smiths in the king om would count for nothing compared to the factor or a rich fishmonger.)ne thing had not changed since the last time. Foronod was still the key.

"Factor Foronod!" she cried out as he drew near. "You are a sight for sore yes! No, do not kneel!"

The single ice-blue eye blinked angrily. Kneeling had likely been the last hing on his mind. Inos held out her hand to be kissed.

He ignored it. "No Imperial army this time?" he barked. His sufferings had ot broken his spirit, obviously, nor improved his manners.

"The imperor has recognized me as Queen of Krasnegar! I bring a signed reaty of nonaggression between his realm and mine." She saw the imps mong them react to that.

"And Thane Kalkor? What happens when he hears of this?"

She had been expecting the question and could barely restrain a smile of riumph. She was much better equipped this time than last, when Andor had een newly exposed and her father not yet in his grave.

"Thane Kalkor is dead. I saw him struck down by the Gods."

The jotnar recoiled. The imps beamed.

Foronod recovered quickly. "And who is his successor?"

Senator Epoxague had put that very question to Ambassador Krushjor or her.

"That is very uncertain. There will be many claimants, and it may take /ears for them to kill one another off. Forget the Kalkor line, Factor. I am queen here by right of inheritance — or by right of conquest, if you prefer. I ›ring peace with our neighbors and peace among ourselves. I demand . . . ")emand what? She could not recall any ceremony of homage or oath of fealty in rustic little Krasnegar. "I require your duty, Master Foronod."

She watched him wrestle with his heritage. Yet what alternative did he have? He must have been praying every day for months that Kalkor would arrive and turn out to be better than his odious young brother. Vain hope that had been, had the factor only realized! But now she had taken away even that thin chance. Unless he wanted to raise up a local king, such as himself, then she was the only claimant. And the young men were with her.

Foronod thumped his cane forward one pace. Leaning heavily on it, he reached for her hand and raised it to his dry lips. "I am your Majesty's loyal and obedient servant, and welcome your return with all my heart." Then he straightened and stepped back. "Gods save your Majesty," he added as an afterthought, pouting as if the words hurt.

It was a fair surrender. "As you were for my . . . our . . . father, so for me you will always be one of our . . . er . . . my most trusted and honored counselors, Factor." A little muddled; she needed practice.

She recognized one of the senior imps nearby, a merchant whose name she had forgotten. He was something important in the import business, she knew, and had also been a member of the council. She scrambled down and settled herself on the scarlet cushion. Rap reached out and laid a small hassock at her feet.

Inos glanced expectantly at the merchant.

He shuffled forward and went down on his knees before her.

2

There was almost no daylight in Krasnegar in midwinter, but the full moon rolled all around the sky. Clocks were rare in that easygoing town, and Inos lost all track of time. There was so much to do that she forgot to eat or sleep or even sit down.

She hardly saw Rap at all, but occasionally he would appear and order her to the table. Then she would gulp down whatever repast was there without noticing it. Even at those moments, the turmoil left her no peace. So many had gone — she was appalled. The bishop, dead of a fit. Mother Unonini, slain by a jotunn while trying to prevent a rape, and Sergeant Thosolin under similar circumstances. Chancellor Yaultari had died in a dungeon, Seneschal Kondoral of a broken heart, they said.

Mistress Aganimi the housekeeper had survived, though, and she set to work restoring order in the pigpen that the jotnar had made of the castle.

With her unending supply of gold, Inos hired men and women by the hundreds. There was normally little to do in winter, but she put the idle hands to work. Her money began to surge through the town, and that helped, also. Clothiers and carpenters and tradesmen of all descriptions suddenly found themselves doing business on a scale they had never dreamed of. Prices soared and she had to issue decrees against profiteering.

She named a new council, expanding it from the eight or so her father had preferred to twenty-four, bringing in some women and even including a few youngsters of her own generation, like Kratharkran, the high-pitched, exuberant smith. The elders scowled at her innovations and she faced them down with the assurance of an adept and with the queenly glamour that Rap even-ally admitted having cast on her. Her deadly green stare became legendary, eflecting query or argument like a steel shield.

She demanded an inventory of food supplies, and the records were found o be in a hopeless muddle.

That was partly due to Rap, who was quietly going around filling warehouses and storerooms when no one was looking. Foronod was driven almost o distraction, and Inos was very happy to have the old factor distracted; at east he could not then be stirring up trouble. Apparently the beating that had amed him had been done by the jotnar, not by imps, but he was obviously ot the man he had been, and she began to ponder a replacement for him.

No one knew how many had died, nor how many mouths remained to onsume the feedstocks, so she ordered a census taken, the first in the history f Krasnegar.

Jotnar could always be counted on to let celebrations get out of hand. Inos vas delighted to discover that Corporal Oopari had repented of his desertion — or wearied of his fiancée, perhaps — and had returned by ship during the ummer. She promoted him to sergeant and put him in charge of the guard nd the militia. He moved fast, but the aftermath of a riot was a full jail. King Holindarn had acted as his own chief justice. Unable to see herself in that ole, Inos appointed an independent judiciary.

Many houses had been deliberately burned in the Terror, and often the lames had spread to adjoining buildings. Timber was almost nonexistent, because in the past it had always been imported.

At her first council meeting, the queen pointed out that there was unlimited wood a few days' trek to the south.

But no way to transport it, Foronod told her snappily.

Why couldn't we bring it in on sledges?

Goblins . . . causeway . . . weather . . . horse   fodder . . . Objections rolled out from the elders like smoke from wet peat. Inos looked at the grinning younger faces around the table and put the matter to a vote. The council promptly decreed that the Royal Krasnegarian Militia be expanded from eighteen to eighty, armed with Inos's swords, and trained as soon as possible in ways of defending lumberjacks from goblin attacks.

The expedition would need horses, and moving them across the causeway n winter had never even been attempted before. She ordered it done, and stabling made ready on the mainland.

She wanted a special service of thanksgiving, and there must be funerals for the eight men who had died in the ephemeral war of liberation. Her former tutor, dull old Master Poraganu, was horrified when she appointed him acting bishop. She knew he was conscientious and would do a good job, but she wondered guiltily how much she was spiting him for uncounted hour of boredom.

Almost every woman of bearing years in Krasnegar was pregnant, either by an imp legionary or a jotunn raider, and many were near their time. The medical facilities were hopelessly inadequate, so Inos ordered a whole wing of the castle converted to a maternity ward. That led her thoughts to a midwifery school and also a public child care organization for the summer, when the women would be needed to work.

Half the fishing fleet had fled during the troubles, so she had to think about boat building and manpower.

All these things pretty well took care of the first three days of her reign.

3

"And now you're going to go and have a good night's rest," Mistress Aganimi said firmly.

"Oh, I'd love to, but —"

"No buts. Your bedroom's ready at least, and I've had a good fire going in there to take the chill off. Off with you now! Can't have our dear queen working herself to death . . . "

As a child, Inos had disliked the bleak old housekeeper, who had often stolen her friends away to put them to work, while laying down laws that came from no statute book Inos had ever discovered. These last three days, though, the formidable Aganimi had been almost as indispensable as Rap.

She tried to find some better arguments in her fatigue-softened head, and saw that there weren't any. Gods, if the kingdom couldn't last a night without her, what good was it?

Was this really bedtime? The sky was a bright smear above the hills to the south, and that meant either sunrise or sunset, but noon for certain. There was enough light dribbling in the windows that she didn't even need lantern, for once.

As she began dragging her feet up the stairs from the Throne Room, she wondered if she had the strength even to reach her bed. The kings of Krasnegar had always slept at the top of Inisso's Tower. That was holy writ, although no one had known that the reason was to guard the other chamber above the bedroom. Well, everyone must know about that now.

She crossed the Presence Chamber, smiling at the boys there trying to bow to her while encumbered with shovels and buckets. The cleaning up was going well now.

She crossed the Robing Room, and here girls were working with mops and
ʀgs. Why would Aganimi have kept boys and girls apart? Efficiency, proba-
Iy. Less fun, though. Remember to change it.

She crossed the empty Antechamber. Timber needed sledges and sledges
ʀeeded runners and runners needed iron; so she had been informed. Iron
as in short supply. To melt down dwarvish steel swords for such a purpose
ʀas unthinkable, the smiths had told her. Don't think, then, just do it, she
ad replied.

She crossed the Withdrawing Room, also barren now. If they could build
ʀoats, they ought to be able to make furniture that didn't look as if it had been
ʀrown away by trolls. Of course she could always slip down to Kinford through
.ap's magic portal, then order what she wanted shipped north in the spring.

She crossed the Dressing Room, slowly, puffing hard. She could steal timber
ʀom the goblins, but nails didn't grow on trees. Rap could make nails, but she
ʀould rather not ask Rap for help, except when she had to. It felt like cheating.
ʀhe wondered how many nails she could smuggle in through the magic portal
ʀefore people became suspicious, and why that didn't feel like cheating.

She dragged herself up the last stair and into her bedroom, and shot the
ʀolt. Peace!

As the housekeeper had said, there was a cheerful fire glowing in the grate.
ʀhe temperature was almost comfortable close to the fireplace. The only fur-
ʀishings were a faded old rug and a small bed that Inos had not seen before. It
ʀas piled high with furs and quilts and Rap.

He was lying on top with his hands behind his head, watching her with-
ʀut expression. He was still wearing the same garments as before, but he was
lean and fresh shaven and his goblin tattoos had disappeared. She wondered
ʀhen that had happened.

She went over to him, and he raised eyebrows in welcome.

"Not tonight, I'm too tired," she said.

He pulled a face at such off-color humor.

"Of course you could fix that," she added hopefully.

"I want to show you something — upstairs."

Inos shook her head quickly. "No! Not now!" She was so tired that even
he thought of . . .

Rap nodded. "Good, it works!"

"What does?"

"The aversion spell. I restored it."

Inos looked at the sinister, forbidding door. "I don't care. I'm not going up
ʀhere right now. Maybe tomorrow, when I'm not so tired."

"Use the same password."

"Holindarn? Oh . . . see what you mean." Her apprehension and dislike vanished, being replaced by normal curiosity as to what a sorcerer might have to show.

Rap swung his legs down from the bed. "Come on! I've also repaired the shielding round the castle, so no one can spy on you from outside except when you're in the topmost chamber." He opened the door for her and she began dragging her feet up yet another narrow staircase.

His voice echoed behind her. "I've even raised the causeway a little — think it's subsided since Inisso's time. And now it's goblin repellent, just in case. And I've restored the inattention spell on the whole kingdom. I made as strong as I dared. Any stronger, and the ships would forget to come."

"You've been busy."

"You haven't exactly been lazing around yourself."

Then she had reached the chamber of puissance. It was astonishingly warm. Rap's doing, no doubt. It had been cleaned out. Again, Rap's doing — only sorcery could have removed every trace of dust like this, and even put shine on the floor.

Southward, the magic portal was a darkness where the magic casement had been, flanked by windows in the two smaller side arches. Sunrise or sunset was streaming in through those.

The only furniture was a massive chest, so that must be what she had been brought to see. She crossed to it and tried the lid.

"Different password," Rap said. "Shandie."

"Why Shandie?" The lid came free in her hand.

"Just easy to remember, hard to guess."

She looked at the contents — hundreds of wash-leather bags.

"Gold," Rap said at her elbow. "Never knew a woman go through money like you do, but that lot ought to keep you in pins for a while. The big bag there is your crown. I can't find the original, so I expect the imps took it, but that's an exact duplicate."

Crown? Who cared? She dropped the heavy lid and turned to him with tears starting in her eyes. "Rap, if this means —"

"Yes, it does. Now come along." He put an arm around her waist and led her over to the portal. He said, "Holindarn!" and opened it and they both recoiled at the bright afternoon sunshine in Kade's private parlor. Smoke puffed from the fireplace, but not so vigorously as last time.

And Kade, who had been sitting reading a book, jumped to her feet in alarm.

"She's all right," Rap said. "Just about out on her feet though. She's hardly slept."

"Everything's fine," Inos said. Sharp guilt pangs reminded her that she had not been keeping Kade informed.

"Yes, dear, I know," Kade said. "Well done! Now sit here."

Between them, they guided Inos to a rose-patterned chair. Old age was .ally making her legs shaky these days. Her joints had forgotten how to .end. Someone put her feet up on a footstool, and someone else tucked a pil- .w behind her.

"She just ate," Rap said. "A hot bath and about ten hours in bed should do . No one will go looking for her in the castle, but she'll relax better here."

Inos stared up with bleary, resentful eyes while Kade went hurrying out to .rganize and Rap perched on the back of a chair, one foot on the floor, one .angling. No tattoos now. Hair a bird's nest. Stupid face with wistful expres- .on. That was her man and he was leaving her.

"I'm going, Inos."

"I can tell." She was too weary to argue, and that was why he had chosen .his moment. Arguing with Rap was never productive, anyway. Pigheaded idiot!

"You'll do all right," he said. "You've been doing all right."

"I couldn't have done anything without you."

It wasn't fair. It just wasn't fair!

"That's true, but I've haven't done much since the first night except throw .ut money. I gave you no advice, you know — none! You knew what to do by .nstinct. I'll keep an eye on you . . . "

"I love you. You love me. But you're going away."

"And you want to know why. And I can't tell you. Oh, Inos, dearest, I'd tell .ou if I could!" He stared at her in dismay. "Listen — the words are more than .ust words, obviously. They may be the names of demons or elementals. I .on't know that, but it seems reasonable. The elemental is bound by its name .nd must serve whoever knows it. Makes sense, sort of. Then when you share . word of power, you give the poor old elemental one more person to serve, .o its power is . . . Well, you get the idea."

With her head back on the cushion like this it was hard to keep his face in .ocus. Hard to keep anything in focus. The warmth was drugging her.

"And the words are more than just words in other ways, like not showing .p to magic." He rubbed his forehead as if it hurt. "They don't even like to be .alked about."

She didn't want his lecture. She wanted him to hold her and stay with her .lways.

"And of course they are hard to say." Rap rose to his feet and straightened. .Except that they don't want to be lost. When I thought I was dying in Azak's .ail, one of my words got very agitated in case it was going to be forgotten. I .hink I would have found it easy to tell that word to someone then."

Inos was going to ask a question and she had forgotten what it was and she .wasn't sure her mouth would work very well just now.

"So sometimes the words behave almost as if they're alive themselves." R₄ took a deep breath, and she realized foggily that he was having trouble tellir her all this.

Pain? Painful to talk? Painful to tell a word?

"What about five words?" she murmured. "Explain what happened ₄ Rasha, and almost happened to you."

Rap opened and closed his mouth a few times, then shook his hea₄ "Sorry!" He turned to stare out the window at the winter sunshine. "Someor told me once that Zinixo was the most powerful sorcerer since Thraine. bested him! But I can't . . . "

"Olybino said that what happened was impossible."

"It damned nearly was. The dwarf was a pushover compared to that. But was mad then. I couldn't have . . . done what I did . . . if I hadn't been s mad at the dwarf. I hated him so much . . . "

She gave up. "And you won't tell me why you're going away."

He spoke to the window pane. "Inos . . . When two people are in love . . They like to hold hands, and hug each other, and kiss, and . . . Well, ₂ affectionate in all sort of intimate ways."

"You astonish me." She yawned enormously. Very vulgar.

"One thing leads to another. I'm sorry if this shocks you, but I'm a sorcere and I can see through walls, and, well, I'm afraid I've seen what happens . . .

"I've been told all about it."

"You have?" He sounded surprised. "Well . . . that's why I'm going awa₄ I don't trust myself not to go totally out of control."

For a moment the absurdity cut through her fog. "Rap! Oh, Rap! I war you to go totally out of control! The sooner the better!"

He turned and stared at her, shaking his head. "I don't mean that exactl₄ Well, I do. Of course I do. But I might not be able to control what else . . .

Again she wondered why he was having so much trouble in saying wha he wanted to say.

"Sorcerers can marry," she protested weakly.

"They don't marry sorceresses."

"Inisso was married. Olliola was his wife's name."

"But they didn't know more than . . . " He groaned and stopped.

"You'll come back, though? Soon?"

He hesitated and she said, "Promise!"

"All right. I promise. Before winter."

"Sooner!"

"No. Oh, Inos! It isn't you, love!" he said huskily. "Believe me, it isn't you And it isn't Krasnegar. We've seen a lot of the world, haven't we, between us And I know I haven't found anywhere I like better than dowdy littl₄

rasnegar. It's dull, but it's honest and it's friendly. It has no wars or injustice
r oppression. You must feel that way, too, don't you?"

She nodded wearily.

He had moved. He was kneeling by her chair, but his whisper came from
long way off. "Inos . . . If I said you could come with me; if I said we
ould go and live together always in a wonderful place and never have any
orries ever again . . . What would you say to that, Inos?" "Duty?" she
murmured. Silly question! She felt a very soft touch on her forehead . . .
hen Kade was shaking her shoulder and saying her bath was ready, and Rap
ad gone.

4

Slowly the days began to lengthen. Slowly Inos's life shaped itself into a
outine. Slowly her reforms began to show results.

The lumber expedition was successful beyond her dreams, and three oth-
rs followed. Apparently no one had ever thought of sledges before. The
ood was green, of course, but there was plenty of it. Either the goblins did
ot notice this new activity, or they did not care, and the only injuries were a
ew toes lost to a combination of frostbite and inexperience. The wear and
ear on the horses was more worrisome, but Inos had shown even the elders
hat new ways could be better, and her reputation suffered no harm.

Babies began arriving, and most of them were accepted and loved as they
xpected to be. Neither they nor their mothers could be blamed for their exis-
ence, and life was a precious thing in the bleak north. Krasnegarians rallied
ogether to welcome and cherish the smelly little darlings.

Tea parties with Kade became a regular part of Inos's life, and a wonder-
ul relaxation. Kade, having organized Kinvale to her satisfaction, was avail-
ble to help in other ways, also. Her shrewd common sense was worth a
lozen councils.

"This," Inos explained one sunny afternoon in her aunt's parlor, "is List
Number One."

Elegant in a rose cambric tea gown, Kade accepted the scroll with a well-
manicured hand. "Adzes, awls, bishop . . . A *bishop?* Really, Inos! A *bishop* in
a shopping list?"

"And at least two chaplains. That's just the repair-and-restore list, to get us
back to where we were. Now here's List Number Two, stuff we need to
eplace the land traffic the goblins have blocked. It's mostly salt and some
oodstuffs, but we do need fresh livestock to build up the herds, and the
ailors won't like that."

Kade pursed her lips, and then tried List Number Three.

"That's an Inos-innovation list," Inos said airily, waving a hand that w
decidedly not manicured. "Books and teachers and things, and furniture f
the palace."

"Musical instruments? Five hundred pairs of dancing shoes?"

"Well, they're not all necessities, I admit. And of course all three lists con
after the usual trade that comes every year, like grain and medicine and spic
and dyes and sponge iron —"

"What's sponge iron? Well, never mind, dear. I don't suppose I should t
any happier for knowing. Have some of this sponge cake instead."

Bored by lack of respectable company during the official mourning f
Ekka, Kade was delighted to act as Krasnegar's business agent. She calle
in the merchants and collected bids, she chartered the ships, and finall
she insisted on paying for everything out of Kinvale's ample revenue
Ekka had caused much of Krasnegar's troubles, she said, and her estat
should make recompense. Rap's gold would not last forever. Besides, ho
was Krasnegar going to survive in future if the goblins stopped tradin
their furs?

Inos had not even thought of that problem. She inquired and learned th
the goblins had not shown up the previous summer. No one seemed very wo
ried, but she asked Foronod to work out the figures for her, and he soon di
covered that Krasnegar depended on goblin trade even more than on trad
with Nordland. The Queen and factor agreed to suppress that worrying info
mation, keeping it even from the council — queen and factor were develop
ing a reluctant respect for each other.

Spring came early, and the causeway cleared sooner than expected. Th
herds departed, the boats were made ready. Life went on.

Slowly Inos reestablished friendships and made new ones. Her crown se
her apart, though, and she had to accept that subjects, no matter how loya
could never be true intimates. Even at parties, she was alone. The old storie
of Inisso had been revived, and it was generally assumed that she had inher
ited his magical powers. Odd packages of things like nails and medicines turn
ing up from time to time around the castle did nothing to dispel such rumor
She guarded the secret of the portal to Kinvale; she thought that without tha
magical escape, she would have gone mad.

The ice cleared the harbor and the southern fleet arrived. The citizen
were astonished by the number of ships that came that year, and how man
needed items were suddenly available.

Foronod continued as factor, but he was no longer capable of the infinitel
detailed supervision for which he had been renowned. Inos herself spen
weeks on the mainland, looking over his shoulder, watching, studying, an
eventually almost superseding him. An adept could learn to do anything.

314

The goblins did come, although they now inexplicably refused to cross
e causeway and insisted on doing their bartering on the mainland. Queen
d factor were very relieved to see the first party arrive, and the bundles of
inking skins the women carried. On impulse, Inos offered swords in trade,
d the male goblins were overjoyed to accept. She had plenty of swords and
o use for them.

Only after that first party had gone did it occur to her to read over her
eaty with the Impire. She discovered that it forbade her to sell arms to gob-
ns. Dear Emshandar!

The nights grew longer. The harvest was gathered into the town, and that
reat task was completed earlier than anyone could recall.

Every day now Inos hoped for Rap. He had promised to return before win-
er, and she knew he would keep his word.

He had not faded in her memory, and no other strong lad had taken his
lace — or, rather, the place that should have been his. She had spent long
ours pondering the inexplicable change that sorcery had produced in him,
he hints he had dropped, the curious glimpses she had caught once or twice
f something in him maddeningly just out of reach of understanding. Now
he had a theory. It was far-fetched, but it matched her skimpy evidence.

She also had a plan.

Inosolan was not yet ready to admit defeat.

5

A full moon was creeping over the horizon as Rap rode down to the shore.
he air was nippy and the ground hard, but there was no snow lying around
et. The God of Winter had been neglecting Their duties. The tang of weed
nd fish, the strident gull calls — it was all heart-rendingly familiar to him.
hree wagons were waiting on the tide, anonymous black shapes below the
vercast sky. With a broad border of ruddy sunset on one side and the silver
tain of moonrise on the other, earth and sea were melding into gray. The
aves, though, bore heraldic trim of gules-on-argent.

Few people still lingered amid the shoreline cottages, and they paid
mall heed to the stranger on the big black horse. One or two nodded in a
riendly fashion and then went about their business. He was being immem-
rable, and they would barely recall seeing him, nor notice that he rode
vithout bit or bridle.

Little remained to be transported: some hides, bones, and a few casks of
alted horsemeat to feed the dogs. In bad years the people ate the horsemeat,
f course, and sometimes the dogs, also, but this would be a good year.
oronod was missing, which was proof in itself that the town was stocked up

for the winter. There was still plenty of peat heaped around. Krasnegar cou
never have enough of that. As long as the weather permitted, the wago
would continue to haul peat.

Inos had done well. Rap had checked on her progress — often at th
beginning, less frequently as he saw that she was coping. She herself had us
ally been inside the castle, and hence shielded from him, but he had seen th
happiness in the streets. Krasnegar was going to survive. He would not hav
come back had he not promised. He need not stay long. This would be th
last time.

He noted the new winter stables with surprise, and casually made the
goblin-proof as he rode by. Times were achanging, even in Krasnegar.

He trotted past the lead wagon with a nod to Jik, who returned the no
then frowned to himself as if annoyed by a failing memory.

Evil flickered his ears at the ripples washing the shingle; occultly rea
sured, he ventured to splash his big hooves into the water. Fleabag sniffed su
piciously and tried a taste of this unfamiliar, restless fluid. He took mor
persuading than Evil, but he followed, growling briefly.

The gaps were narrow, now that the tide was near the ebb and the caus
way higher than it used to be. Soon Evil was trotting over Big Island and th
big dog loping ahead again. The road was curving in to shore, and Rap final
allowed himself a scan of the docks ahead. It was all heartbreakingly as he ha
expected — humble folk going cheerfully about their business, fishing net
hanging on their racks, many of the boats already out of the water and bein
made ready for their long rest. Peace and friendly dullness and security. A
empty wagon was just starting its outward journey, its driver having seen
horseman crossing.

And Inos! She was riding Lightning along the dock road; coming to watc
the crossing, doubtless. Not much would escape Inos, Rap thought. Sh
would be as good a ruler as Krasnegar had ever had. But he had always know
that. He blinked away a tear and laughed aloud at the thought of a sorcere
weeping. What reason could a sorcerer ever have to weep?

He saw that she was peering at the lone rider, shielding her eyes from th
sunset. He lifted his occult veil for her. Her instant reaction made her mou
shy, but Inos brought it under control at once and kicked it into a gallop. Ev
splashed through the last traces of Big Damp, and the two horses met on th
slope beyond.

"Rap! Oh, Rap!"

God of Fools! The stupid child had tears streaming down her cheeks. H
would never have come had he not promised.

"Hello, Inos." He was glad he had farsight, because his eyes were goin
blurry in sympathy. Not a child. Beautiful, gorgeous woman.

"That's Evil! And Fleabag? You've been to Arak-karan?"

"I've been all over the place. Good to be home." *Liar!*

She choked back a question — about Azak, of course — and then took a arder look at Rap himself. He cursed under his breath; he should have done omething about his appearance.

"Rap! What's wrong? Are you ill?"

"No, no. Just a little tired, is all." *You're breaking my heart, girl. That's what's rong.*

"You look terrible! What's the matter? Gods!"

Of course! "You look great, Inos. And I know you've been doing a great job 1 the monarching business."

She gave him the sort of suspicious stare his mother had given him any me he hadn't wanted seconds. Then she faked a smile over it. "And you've ome for the Harvesthome Dance!"

He had quite forgotten the Harvesthome Dance. "Of course," he said.

He stayed three days and he almost went crazy.

At times he wished he'd just turned up as his old self, but then he'd ave had to answer the same questions over and over, and people would ave seen the way Inos looked at him and tried to hang on to him, and he would have had difficult explanations to make when he disappeared gain.

So he stayed immemorable, but that meant he couldn't talk with his old riends. He would nod to them and they would react as Jik had — familiar ace, can't place it. Boyhood pals had become tall men. Gith, and Krath, and in. Some had beards. All the girls were mothers now. Ufio, Fan . . . He net them all at one time or another, mostly while Inos was dragging him round the town, showing him what had been accomplished and what was eft to do, talking excitedly all the time and pretending her heart wasn't as ore and sick as his. He saw how the people smiled when they saw her, and ow eagerly they saluted and hoped for her answering smile. They were roud of their young queen. Imps had always cherished romantic ideas about eautiful princesses and impresses, but here in Krasnegar the feeling had ecome universal. To tease one of the local jotnar about having a female ruler vould be very unhealthy.

Just once Rap saw Inos meet resistance. An aged carpenter began disputing er newfangled ideas on furniture. Green eyes flashed, the ambience shivered 'ery slightly, and the old man's feet and tongue began stumbling in unison as e tried to bow and apologize and flee, all at the same time. Apart from that ne occasion, Rap never detected her regal glamour in use or even being eeded. It was a lovely piece of work, though, almost undetectable; best spell e'd ever made.

He met just about everyone again at the Harvesthome Dance, but no or met him. The Great Hall was strung with ribbons and jammed with peopl and filled with noise and laughter and music.

It was sort-of music, for Krasnegar was not Hub; nobody cared abou beat or key too much, as long as it was loud and cheerful. He dance twice with Inos, but the rest of the time he insisted she dance with som of those loyal subjects hovering hopefully around her. She hadn't found lover yet, that was obvious. She could have had hundreds, that wa equally obvious. They all loved her, and every young man in town wa crazy over her.

He could make her fall in love with one of them if he wanted. Then sh would be happy, wouldn't she? He stood in the shadows and wrestled with h conscience. He'd once told the imperor that he just wanted Inos to be happy He could make her happy with sorcery. So why didn't he? He must think har about that before he departed.

They talked a lot, or at least Inos did. She was proud of what she'd accom plished, and with good reason, and he let her explain everything over an over, although he'd seen it all within the first few minutes. Much of it he' seen from far away, too.

He talked less, but he told her how he'd gone to Arakkaran to fetch h dog, and how terrified Azak and Kar had been when he showed up. When h described the feast they had put on for him, with jugglers and belly dance and goats' eyes, and the tricks he'd played when they took him hunting, the she laughed till she cried.

"So you rescued Fleabag? How about the panther?" she asked.

"I left the panther. I never was a cat person."

"And Azak gave you Evil?"

"I took Evil. I thought Azak owed me that much." And he told her a littl of his other travels — in Faerie and Dragon Reach, and Durthing.

"Not Thume?" she asked.

No, he said, he had not been to Thume.

They talked all around their private problem, and never mentioned it He had tried to tell her once, and the words had not let him. Or perhap that compulsion had come from higher authority than the words — h wasn't sure.

Inos was plotting something. He'd known that from the moment they me on the shore. He could have worked it out, or pried it out, but he didn't. H turned off his insight so he couldn't read her face at all; which was unpleasan for him, but then the whole visit was one unbearable agony.

At night he left the palace so he couldn't watch her. Near the harbor h found a comfortable garret that no one was using, and he fitted it out with a ɔmfortable bed to lie on. He never slept now; he'd almost forgotten what eep felt like.

6

On the fourth morning, Rap joined Inos for breakfast in the Great Hall. he was sitting alone at the high table, and he came in by the door and alked over and took a chair beside her. The sun was just rising, promis-ıg another astonishingly fine day. She was wearing a very simple pale-ꞃeen dress, and her hair hung loose with just a band around it, and she was ; beautiful as he had ever seen her. The smoothness of her cheek was a ıiracle in itself.

He was back in riding clothes.

"You're not leaving already!" Her voice was accusing, her face paler than it ꞁould be.

"Might as well catch the weather while it lasts," he said, not looking at her. Jot with his eyes, anyway.

"Morning your Majesty." A decrepit old waiter shuffled up to Inos and laid mug of chocolate and a silver bowl of sticky porridge in front of her. He adn't noticed she had company.

Before she could say anything, Rap made a bowl of porridge appear in ꞃont of himself — a golden bowl. She tried to laugh, without much success. ʰhe old man went hobbling off, having missed all that.

"I thought I might take Firedragon," Rap said between mouthfuls. "He and have always been good friends, and I think he's getting a little old for his ꞁsponsibilities."

"Of course."

"And I'll leave Evil. I thought you'd like having him looking after things ﹖nstead; an appropriate memento of Azak."

"Oh, very funny!"

He hadn't told her how well Azak had been making up for lost time since ﹖e got home to Arakkaran. Terrible man!

They ate in slurping silence for a while. Krasnegarian porridge was vile tuff, really, Rap thought, and wondered why he was enjoying it so much. It ꞁas strange to eat up here at the high table, a visiting sorcerer. Always, when ﹖e'd eaten in the Great Hall he'd been down near the hearths, with the ser-ꞁants. There were a lot of them there now, dawdling over a hot breakfast. He ﹖new how they felt. Most of them would be newly back from the mainland, ﹖atching up on the summer's gossip, reveling in real beds and dry lodgings, ﹖enewing old friendships, happily sliding into the slower pace of winter. Why ꞁad he been such a fool as to come?

319

Inos kept staring at him, crumpling a napkin in her free hand. Yes, she wa
plotting something, and he stubbornly refused to let himself peek and find ou
what it was.

"Not Master of Horse?" she said at last wistfully.

"You ought to let Hononin have the title. He's good for another ten yea
at least." The pains in the hostler's joints had cleared up miraculously since th
night the queen returned. He would die very suddenly, fourteen years fro
now, near Winterfest.

"And not Sergeant-at-Arms?"

Their eyes met and exchanged moist smiles.

"Not really my sort of work," Rap said. "Oopari's much better at it than
would ever be."

"King, then?" she whispered. "It's the only job vacancy I have to offer a
the moment."

"I don't think I'm qualified."

"You're better qualified than any other man in the world."

Rap sighed. Why did people torture themselves by longing for the impos
sible? He changed the subject.

"Everyone must know you came back by sorcery. How do they feel abou
sorcery now?"

Inos shrugged and abandoned all pretense of eating. "They find sorcery i
everything I do. If I smile at a baby, I've blessed it. My frowns bring on asthm
attacks. But they seem to be getting accustomed to the idea."

"They shunned me!" That still rankled.

She laid a hand on his. "I think they're wiser now, dear. Magic has it
advantages, and they've learned that. Besides, people can get used to any
thing, given time."

Yes. He created a mug of hot chocolate and removed his hand to pick it up

"They would accept you, love."

"They won't get the chance."

"You are definitely going?"

"Definitely."

"For how long this time?"

He looked squarely at her and she bit her lip.

"Forever," he said.

"You're in pain!"

Now, how had she guessed that? "Being near you just makes it worse," he
said. "Much worse. And worse for you, too. I've told you it can never be, Inos.

"Not that sort of pain. Real pain. Sagorn noticed. He told Kade. And the
I began to see it, too."

Rap ate more porridge.

"Ever since that night Zinixo told you a fifth word. You put out the fire, ap — but you didn't get rid of all of it, did you? You've been burning ever nce, haven't you?"

"Not burning." That was a fair description of it, though.

"Hurting? That's why you look so awful."

"I do not look awful!"

"You did when I first met you on the road. When I said so, you made your-lf seem all right again. But those first moments you looked about as old as mshandar. You're hurting!"

He didn't want to lie to her, and he wasn't allowed to explain the problem her, so he said nothing. He expected her to get angry, then, but she didn't. he was giving that napkin a terrible time with both hands under the table.

"I am happy to accept the horse, Rap," she said eventually. "Is there any-ing I can give you in return?"

"Just Firedragon."

She tensed even more. "I would like to ask a favor."

"Anything, of course." He waited. It couldn't be gold, because he'd refilled e chest for her, and she had plenty. Raise the causeway above high-water ark? Alterations to the castle? Well, he wasn't going to pry.

"I want to be a sorceress."

A hot glob of porridge landed unnoticed on his lap. "Inos, no! You don't now what it's like!"

"Tell me, then."

"It's horrible! You stop seeing people as people. They're slow, and stupid, nd *unimportant!* You can have anything you want, so nothing's worth having, r doing, anymore. And nobody else's wants or opinions matter. No, it's awful. ou don't want that!"

She was frightened, and determined not to show it. "You said 'Anything'!"

"You have everything you need, and I didn't mean —"

"I'm sorry I'm so *slow* and *unimportant*, but I could swear I heard you say Anything.' "

He put his face in his hands. Pure, rending desire . . . it was worse than ny carnal lust imaginable. It was a fanfare of silver trumpets. It lit up his heart ke dawn. Escape!

After all, he had told her two words once and managed to stop. The mem-ry of that effort was terrifying, but he had managed it once.

Of course — Common Sense retorted — that time he'd had Zinixo wait-ng to settle. Hatred can be stronger than love. He didn't have his jotunn tem->er stoked and burning now as a distraction.

Pain . . . That was what she was thinking! By telling her two words that ight, he had reduced his power and been able to bring the overload under

control. If he shared two more he would be weaker still, and she was guessir
then that he might not be in so much pain. Maybe she was right!

Try it! whispered Temptation. *Try it!*

For months and months he had fought to suppress the agony. It wa
killing him, day by day, hour by hour. He was fading — he knew that. Ju
maybe she was right, and he wouldn't hurt so much if he shared two mo
words with her.

He would be putting himself at risk from the wardens, of course. They ha
never stopped watching him: where he was, what he was doing. They were a
scared of him. Rightly so, because he was pretty sure he could take on all fou
of them together if he needed to; the new West was nothing much. So th
Four had left him alone, even when he'd gone meddling in their backyards –
rescuing the fairies still in Milflor to hide them and others away where the
would never be found . . . curing an outbreak of plague that Olybino ha
started among the goblins . . . turning back a blaze of dragons that ha
come to investigate what he was doing for Nagg and her little tribe . . .

Rap the stableboy had trampled all over the Protocol, and the Four ha
looked the other way. But if they ever sensed that he'd slipped back to mer
sorcerer power, then they might be tempted to try something.

He discovered that he really didn't care.

And he wouldn't be very much weaker, anyway. He'd still be in comman
of five words, however much they had been reduced by sharing, and not on
of the present Four would dare try that. His mastery of power was a freakis
thing. Maybe that was how some of the great fabled sorcerers of the past ha
gained their power, but most people were destroyed by five. Like Rasha.

Share his words?

Normally sharing a word was a very painful experience, except when o
the brink of death. The act had virtually killed Sagorn, and the pain had fas
cinated Little Chicken. But not in this case. It wouldn't hurt this time. Tel
Inos? Yes! Yes!

But the danger! She didn't know the danger!

He looked into her pale, scared face.

"You're sure?"

She nodded dumbly and passed a pink tongue over her lips — lips t
haunt a man's memory until the day he died.

"It's a terrible risk!"

"I trust you. Just two."

Clever girl!

"That's why you're afraid to get close, isn't it?" she said. "Why you don'
want to be intimate? Losing control . . . you talked about losing contro
You're afraid you'd tell me them all!"

He nodded, astonished that she'd worked that out. Mundanes weren't ways stupid, if you could just give them enough time. She was an adept, of ourse. That would help.

"Three little words," he said. "Easy to say in a moment of . . . er . . . assion."

"And then what? I burn, and I don't have your knack for controlling agic?"

He shook his head. He hurt if he even tried to think about it. To explain as . . . forbidden.

"But you can tell me two!"

"You don't know what you're asking. And it won't make any difference to s, Inos. It'll be worse, because there'll only be one word between us and . . . nd . . . " His tongue began tripping all over his mouth again. "Only one ord left," he finished.

"You said 'Anything'!"

"No! I won't risk it."

She sighed, but her green eyes glinted like sunlight through breakers. "Oh, ap! Just for once . . . If this is the last time we'll ever see each other, just for nce couldn't you let me talk you into something?"

He pushed back his chair. "It's too risky, Inos."

She wadded the napkin smaller than ever. "I'm prepared to take that risk. I sked for a favor and you said 'Anything'! Now, are you, or are you not, a man f your word?"

Why was she pursuing this madness? To aid her kingdom? If she only new what she would be taking on by becoming a sorceress, she wouldn't e so insanely eager to mother that dimwitted brood of yokels. They ould never appreciate what she was doing for them anyway, and she must now that.

To aid Rap? She thought she could do him a favor and ease the constant gony of controlling five words of power. But he suspected she had some ther motive as well. He resisted the temptation to use insight on her; he was ightened of finding himself in there in compromising concepts.

But she'd trapped him. He had said "Anything."

"It's not fair to others, Inos," he protested, knowing he was on his last xcuse. "Those two words you know already . . . one was the one Zinixo old me. The other I got from my mother. I didn't plan it that way, they ere just the first that came to mind." He cringed at the memory of that iery ordeal in Emine's Rotunda, and then cringed even more as he remem- ered who had saved him from it. "I don't know if anyone else knows hose words, too. But the words I haven't shared — those belong to Kade, and Little Chicken, and Sagorn. I'll weaken their powers if I tell thos words to you."

Green eyes flashed again. "Leave Sagorn and his buddies out of this by a means! But I heard you warn Little Chicken not to use his occult strength . . didn't I? And Kade's talent is chaperoning young ladies. She isn't going to hav any time for that from now on if she's running Kinvale. It's time she started tal ing things easy anyhow!"

He glanced despairingly around the hall. The servants were still hard their blathering. The officials and senior staff had vaguely noticed that th queen had a visitor and had chosen to cluster at one of the side tables instea of joining her. There was no one within earshot.

"You're quite sure?"

She nodded. She wasn't quite sure, but Inos had acquired a regal serenity, confidence that came from more than the glamour he had cast on her. It wa not all adepthood, either. Some of it was just Inos being a good queen.

Almost before he realized, he had leaned close to whisper Kadolan's wor into her ear. Relief! The second one was even easier, and the third —

He bit his own tongue and managed to stop it halfway through the thir word. That was the hardest thing he'd ever done in his life — it was pain, was nausea, it was sorrow and fear; and self-contempt, and everything horr ble. It tore at his mind and trampled his soul and racked his body with terrib spasms. It was death and destruction, and more than he could bear. He top pled from his chair, howling. He rolled and thrashed on the floor, hearing th Gods' mocking laughter.

But he'd stopped and his mouth was full of blood.

Then he saw Inos before him in the ambience — transparent, frightenec her hands over her ears. But a sorceress, a glorious, beautiful, desirable sorcer ess. He couldn't bear it.

"*Inos, I love you!*" He reached for her.

"*No, Rap!*" her specter cried, backing away from him in an aura of conflict ing reds and pinks. He went after her, to grasp her and pull her close an force his mouth to her ears, or lips, or cheek, or anything.

In the mundane Great Hall his hand caught the hem of her gown as sh turned to flee. He hauled her back. She stumbled against her chair and the fell, struggling and screaming, and he clasped her in his arms.

He was going to kiss her and tell her he loved her and then share the fift word with her.

In the mundane world, she magicked right out of his embrace, so that h sprawled hard against chair legs, clutching an empty gown. The mundane had noticed the racket and were starting to turn, sluggish as old cabbages.

In the ambience she fled, racing away across a polished plain, a naked girl nning bright and sweet against a somber, discordant sky.

He scanned and found her at the top of Inisso's Tower, in her bedroom, renching open the door to the upper staircase. She was heading for the por- l and escape to Kinvale.

She mustn't escape! He must take her, and tell her, and share everything ith her, and release the awful, burning compulsion. Howling, he vanished om the Great Hall, and everything had happened so fast that the mundanes ere still bringing their eyes around to locate all the disturbance. A final chair t the floor, right by the queen's discarded dress.

Rap stumbled as he arrived in the narrow, curving stairwell, and that gave er an extra second or two. Then he hurtled up the stairs like a bat, without a oot touching the treads.

In the ambience his fingers touched her arm.

Just ahead of Rap's mundane grasp, Inos reached the top of the stairs and anished from ambience and farsight both. Rap, moving occultly, rico- heted off the shielding and sprawled on the steps, pounding his fists in tor- ıent. He forced down the pain, the anger, the maddening love, the nbearable compulsion.

Somehow he brought himself under control, shaking and sweating and eeping like a stupid mundane. Maybe the agony was a little easier to sup- ress now, a little easier than before.

But, Oh, Gods, girl, that had been a narrow escape!

He gave himself no chance to change his mind. He moved instantly to the able and saddled Firedragon in half a second. Fleabag, who had been dozing ı an empty stall, rose at his master's summons. A knot of gossiping hands arely noticed as dog and tack and horse all vanished from their places.

Out in the bailey, one or two looked around in surprise at a mounted man ney had not noticed earlier. He rode out through the shielding of the gate.

Inos was visible in the ambience then, wide-eyed, hair streaming, staring t him in fright. He could reach out and touch her . . .

Physically, she was standing in the chamber of puissance with her hand on he portal.

"It's all right, love," he said, fighting down another surge of agony and long- 1g. "I think I can handle it now. But stay out of my sight! Stay in the castle until I'm gone."

She nodded and ran across the chamber to the stair. He was still riding in he castle yard and he dare not wait on the tide. He moved man and dog and orse to the hills.

The rock of Krasnegar was a mere speck, then, far away against the pale ndless blue of the Winter Ocean. Its castle was barely visible at all.

7

In low, chill sunshine, he rode southward over the hills. The yellow gra
was crisp with frost, crunching below Firedragon's hooves, and the wind c
with a sinister edge. Now and then he would give the ambience a gent
nudge, moving himself across a valley to the far crest, gaining time. He wan
ed to put a great distance between himself and Inos as soon as possible, b
from habit he preferred not to alert the wardens any more than he had t
They probably all kept votaries watching for him all the time anyway.

Once he thought he felt Inos searching, and he blasted out a warning
"Go away!"

"Rap?"

"Yes, but I'm still too close!" He caught a faint image of her in the ambience, a
echo, a scent. Prickles of sweat broke out all over him, and he trembled fro
sheer longing. Would he feel any different when he reached the far ends
the earth? She would be just as visible, just as close in the ambience. Ho
could he ever escape?

"I just wanted to say I love you!"

"Likewise! Now, please, Inos! Go!"

"All right." There were tears in her eyes. *"And now I know what you were doin
and why. Thank you, Rap!"*

His heart twisted. *"You agree? This is what you want?"*

"Oh, yes!" She choked back a sob. *"Good-bye, Rap!"*

Then she was gone, and he could relax again.

Almost. He kept having visions of Inos plunging into the flames to rescu
him — crazy, impulsive Inos. And then he would remember Rasha's fearf
solitary immolation, and her final despairing howl to Azak: *Love!*

A sorcerer could marry, but only a mundane. A mage might love a geniu
or an adept another adept. Four words was the limit. Only mortals with h
freakish control over power would not be destroyed by five.

But two people and five words of power *plus love* . . .

He put the terrible recipe out of his mind and rode on.

He decided to visit Death Bird on his way by. As he had foreseen, th
goblin was chief of Raven Totem now. He'd challenged his father and wo
the hunters' vote that resulted. Then he'd disappointed everyone by letting th
old man live instead of making an entertainment of him. It had been the firs
step in his revolution, and in his way Little Chicken was doing as well as Inos

After that . . .

Rap didn't know what came after that. Endless wandering? More littl
good deeds here and there — minuscule, futile attempts to make the cru
world a little kinder? He had kept his promise to return to Krasnegar. Now h

could see how that promise had been a lantern in the dark all the past year. There was no light ahead now.

Sharing more words with Inos had reduced his pain somewhat, but it was still there, and his craving for her was more intense than ever. How long before he went as mad as Kalkor or Bright Water?

He was a fool. He'd been a fool to heal the imperor. He'd been a fool to spare Zinixo in the Rotunda. And he'd been a paramount fool to make Inos a sorceress, for now only a single word separated them, and she was in great danger. Anywhere, anytime — a moment's distraction and he might find himself at her side, whispering.

So where could he go, what could he do? Power? Even if his words had been weakened, with five of them he was still a supersorcerer. He could do anything he wanted. Riches? Women? He could have all the women in the world, in unlimited numbers, make Andor look like an ascetic. The only one he wanted was out of reach.

He would never be in danger from any mundane peril, nor from sorcery, either, for the Four had obviously decided to leave him well alone. He had many empty centuries to look forward to, until he grew older than Bright Water.

Before noon he was riding through a narrow valley, following a dry streambed, with sere brown slopes rising gently on either hand to the drab hills. Horse and dog were thirsty, and he was hungry. He decided to take a break, conjure up some water and a meal.

Before he could act on that resolution, he felt an eerie awareness, an imminent sense of the numinous. He reined in Firedragon with a mental command and glanced around uneasily. Premonition burned hotter, the ambience began to writhe and shimmer, and finally blazed.

A God stood athwart his path, brighter than the sun.

Rap cursed silently. Stiff from riding, he slid from his saddle and sank to his knees before the towering figure. He bent his head in submission. He had already closed down his occult senses, for the power lashing the ambience was more than mortal mind could stand. Even his mundane eyes could not bear to look at that coruscating glory, although its light cast no shadows, nor brightened the hills.

Firedragon wandered off to graze.

"You must go back!" The voice was male, and thunderous.

"I do not wish to go back," Rap said, staring at the yellow grass.

"You are defying the Gods?"

Yes he was, so there was no point in saying anything.

"You are a fool!"

Yes again.

"You love her!"

"I do."

"And she loves you!"

Undoubtedly. And undoubtedly this was the God Who had appeared to Inos once, long ago, on that eventful day that ended their childhood.

"You are defying Us and spurning the destiny We chose for you both. Go back!"

Rap said, "No."

Risking a tiny glimmer of farsight, he saw the God put Their fists on Their hips in an oddly trivial gesture. A wave of divine fury washed the valley. Strange that the very grass did not burst into flame!

"You are a stubborn fool! You know the formula! You know why the casement could not prophesy for you? You know why the sorcerers could not foresee you?"

"I do." And he knew now what Bright Water had guessed from the inexplicable blocking.

"So you know why a God is always described as 'They'?"

"I do."

"We have promised you this, and you are defying Us!"

To be a sorcerer was bad enough. To be a God would be infinitely worse. Rap set his teeth and said nothing.

Apparently They decided that blustering was not going to work, for suddenly the God became soft, and feminine. The sunlike glare became suffused with pearl, the strident call to duty yielded to the appeal of love. They moved closer, until Their toes were within Rap's field of mundane vision. They made his eyes hurt, but he had never seen anything lovelier.

"Oh, Rap, Rap!" the voice said, gentle now, and coaxing. They sounded like his mother, and he felt tears of sudden anger start. *"Is this fair to Inos?"*

"She agreed. It is what she wants also."

"Maybe she agrees now, to humor you. How will she feel when she is old, when her beauty is gone and age begins to gnaw at her flesh? How will you feel when your manly strength fails you and your eyes water and your back aches? Will you both start patching yourselves with sorcery, like Bright Water, to load a few more years onto your brief span? Repent, Rap! Go back to Inos, Rap, so you can put on immortality together!"

Rap said, "No."

"Five words, Rap! Five words destroy, but when two people who love each other are armed with the strength of five words shared — those make a God. Few are the mortals given this chance."

Again he said nothing. There was evil in every good, and good in every evil. Bright Water had guessed, and tried to help him in her muddled way, tried to bribe a future God so she would have a friend at her weighing.

Suddenly there were more Gods, uncounted Gods, male and female both, blazing beauty all around, filling the dusty little valley with glory, so

at the air rang with music and purity and love. The very sunlight seemed
ab by contrast.

"Join us, Rap!" They chorused. "Your coming was ordained at the birth of the world. For
*nturies we have waited on you. Now the time is ripe, the prophecy fulfilled — be one with
os and join us in glory for eternity!"*

Rap said, "No!"

A great wail filled the whole world. "You can be any of Us, Rap. God of Love,
*od of War, God of Healing. Any of Us will step aside for you. Or be a new God. God of
orses, Rap?"*

Rap said, "No."

Anger shook the hills, bringing maleness, stern and deadly, so that the
ompany of Gods assumed a presence like a horde of armed warriors all
round him, vast and mighty in Their wrath. Pearly glow became metallic
lint, song became fanfare and beat of drum.

"We all must seek to aid the Good, Rap! Think of how a God can aid the Good, and how
*uch They can accomplish; set that beside the trivial powers of a sorcerer. If you and Inos ded-
ate your whole mortal lives to serving mankind, you can hope to achieve nothing compared
what a God can achieve throughout eternity. Repent, and come!"*

"What a God can achieve?" Rap yelled, wishing he could bear to look
pon Them so he could pull faces. "Healing babies, relieving famines, stop-
ing wars? Oh, very worthy! But who made the babies sick in the first place?
Who blighted the crops and started the wars? When prayers are answered
ou expect thanks. When things go wrong anyway, that is because we mortals
re wicked. You have the game stacked so You can score in both goals, can't
ou? The nice things are Your blessings, and the bad things are our sins. What
o You do the rest of the time, when You're not answering prayers? You go
round making trouble, and I don't know whether it's just for Your own amuse-
ent or to humble us so You can —"

"SILENCE!"

He waited for the lightning, but instead he felt a great loneliness and
eariness.

"We love you, Rap. We have been waiting for you. Your troubles are over now. Join with
os and come to us and never again will you —"

Rap said, "No!"

He felt terror . . .

"Gods are not mocked, Rap! Fear what judgment will come upon you if you deny Us now!"

Rap said, "No! I will not go back to Inos. Slay me if You choose, but I am
ot going back. I do not wish to be more than human. I shall live and die a
mortal, and Inos also."

He felt fury — and then sudden despair.

"No more time!" one of the Gods cried. "Look, Rap! Look at what Inosolan is doing!"

Rap sought out Krasnegar with farsight. He saw the castle as a gre
shielded blank, except for the chamber of puissance at the very top. He sa
the steep little town all spread out below it, with every corner visible to hir
He saw the people like ants, scurrying up the streets and alleys, and then h
heard the great bell booming, summoning them to the castle.

Inos! What was she planning?

"Hurry, Rap! Go back and stop her before it is too late!"

She would kill herself! For a moment his resolution wavered, and he fe
the rising surge of joy and triumph from the Gods assembled.

No! "I won't!" he said.

For a moment he really thought They were going to slay him. He fell fo
ward to the ground as Their rage roared and buzzed around him; but then
slowly sharpened to a howling dirge of farewell, fading away in echoes o
eternal sorrow for his folly.

So much for immortality.

He was alone in the valley, lying on the grass. Firedragon was peace
ably munching. Fleabag had lain down to lick his paws, and the Gods ha
gone.

And Inos, crazy Inos! . . . She would kill herself. It was impossible!

He staggered to his feet, and just for a moment he hesitated. He coul
move himself to the castle yard. He could run in through the gate; he coul
flash instantly to the Great Hall.

He could stop her.

No!

It was her decision. This was why she had demanded two more words. Sh
had guessed why a God was called "They."

Two people and five words, plus love . . . She felt as he did. But wha
she planned was humanly impossible! To tell a word of power to one perso
was an agonizing experience. To tell it to more than one was unbearable — h
recalled how he had been unable to share a word with Rasha when Azak ha
been close enough to hear.

Then why had the Gods been worried?

No! He would not interfere.

The world shimmered around him and seemed to darken. He cried ou
with a rending sense of loss. Inos!

She was doing it! She would kill herself.

Frantically he ran to his horse and scrambled into the saddle. He turne
Firedragon's head to the north and dug in his heels. And even as he did so, th
world shimmered again, and shrank, and darkened about him. He groped fo
the ambience and it had gone.

Inos knew four of the five words he knew — and she was destroying them

8

A mundane could not travel as a sorcerer did, and his return took many hours. Long before dark he saw the storm clouds gathering; snow began to fall at nset, out of a lurid, blood-soaked sky. He wondered if the Gods were about level punishment for his defiance. He rode on without a pause, into the ry of an arctic storm.

Inos had done what she planned. Four of his words of power were gone, d he was thrown back to where he had been before he became an adept.

He still had farsight, a poor mockery of a sorcerer's vision, but enough to llow the trail through the hills and lead him on to Krasnegar, even in dri- ng snow and dense dark. That morning the world had been spread before m, all Pandemia; now his range was less than a league, a tiny patch of ass and scrub surrounded by nothing. He could not see what was happen- g in the town, and that was torture. He knew Inos had survived the estruction of three words, because he had felt them all go, but had she anaged to survive the fourth? Even if she lived, what might such torment ave done to her mind?

He still had his mastery for animals, and he used it to coax every possible oofbeat out of poor old Firedragon. The stallion was game and stout- earted. His breath froze around his nostrils, his hooves thumped the hard arth, and he strained his utmost for his friend Rap. The younger, stronger vil could have done no more.

Somewhere on that long mad ride, Fleabag was lost. Probably the dog had st fallen from exhaustion, for Rap would have seen a wild pack pull him own. If so, he would recover. He would follow later if he chose, or else head outh to the forest and survive in wolfish ways.

Rap had no idea how far he must travel, but he knew he must catch the ight ebb tide or die before dawn. He drove his mount as he had never elieved he could treat a horse, but his plight was desperate. Now he had no ower to keep himself warm, or shorten his journey, or deflect hunger and atigue. He was not dressed for the climate; he had brought no food.

Mostly he rode almost prone, leaning his face against his horse's lathered eck, with one hand wrapped in his mane for warmth and the other covering is exposed ear. Every few minutes he would change sides. This was an ordeal o test a goblin, and it would have quickly killed a purebred faun. He espe- ially cursed his inadequate boots, fearing he would lose his toes.

Caked with snow, man and horse pressed onward.

He was so battered and weary that he failed to register the shore cottages hen they came within his range. At first his dulled wits tried to interpret

them as strange rock formations. Then he recognized the sea beyond and sa
that the flood was well underway. He was too late to cross the causew
before morning.

He let Firedragon slow to a walk and headed numbly for shelter. Th
workers would have fled to town when they saw the storm coming, an
there would be nothing there to sustain him. Then his farsight detected
fire, and a man dozing beside it. Furthermore, there were horses in one o
the new stables.

At the cottage door, Rap fell from the saddle and just lay. He could no
rise, but the man inside had heard the hooves even over the noise of the win
The door swung open in a blaze of firelight, and he came shuffling out t
help. He dragged Rap inside and swathed him in a blanket by the hearth.

Rap's head spun giddily with the aftereffects of cold. His heart pumpe
nausea through every vein, and pain besides. He shivered so hard he coul
barely sip at the steaming mug the old hostler thrust into his hand.

Hononin took Firedragon to the stable to rub him down and bed him wit
the other horses. One of those others was Evil, but he was well tethered, an
Firedragon himself was much too weary to make trouble.

Shadows leaped over the rough stone walls and the dirt floor. The win
howled around the slates, and blew puffs of eye-watering smoke into the littl
cottage. In the distance surf pounded the shingle.

Then the old man returned to kneel at Rap's feet and rub his toes wit
horny hands in exquisite torture. By then Rap was just able to speak.

"How is she?" he croaked.

"Don't know," the hostler said in his usual grumpy fashion. "I been her
since afternoon. But she wasn't in good shape when I left." He took th
mug from Rap's shaking hand and refilled it with more soup from the po
on the hob.

"She said you'd be coming," he muttered. "Called me in while the bell wa
still ringing. Said you might be coming soon." He shook his head wonder
ingly. "She's got quite a way to her, for such a slip of a girl. She looks at a ma
with those green eyes! Suddenly whatever else he wants to do just don't see
important any more. After, I wondered if she'd just gone crazy. Decided I'
better come see, anyhows. There was only one road you could come, and
figured you'd need a change of mount at the least."

"You're a good m-m-man. Master Hononin!" Rap said through his insanel
chattering teeth. "How long t-t-till the t-tide?" His farsight showed the cause
way, but the ink-dark sea ran swiftly over it, driven by the rising wind.

"Near to noon. You've got lots of time to sleep. I ought to go check agai
on that old plug you were riding."

332

"He's d-d-done me p-p-proud!" Rap agreed, his words almost lost in the attering of ivory.

" 'Stonishingly like a stallion we've got up in the castle."

"That's j-just your imagination. How's that big black to ride?"

"Murder. Just brought him along for the outing. Think you could handle im?"

"Likely. Tell me about Inos."

"Well, she's queen now. You know that?" The old man peered sourly at Rap ith rheumy eyes. "Met a fellow once, couple a' years ago, near enough. ame to my door one morning. Looked just like you, 'cept he had goblin tat-os around his eyes. Was running with a goblin, too."

"We fauns get around," Rap said uneasily. The explanations he was going need!

Hononin grunted. "Sailors last summer . . . brought some odd tales of oings-on in Hub. Seems there was a faun sorcerer —"

"I'm not a sorcerer!" Rap sniggered. Joy! The burden had gone. "*I am not a rcerer!*" He grinned at the old man and caught a faint answering smile.

"You don't dress well for the climate, you know that? Meet many other ravelers in the forest?"

"I'll tell you everything tomorrow, I swear!" Rap mumbled. "Tell me about nos!"

The old man left off torturing Rap's feet and threw more driftwood on the ire. "Today . . . No, yesterday. It's morning now. She had the great bell ung, so everyone went running up to the castle to see . . . "

It had happened much as Rap had feared. Typically, Inos must have acted t once, as soon as he had departed. Having summoned as many of her sub-ects as she could assemble in one place — not in the Great Hall, though, but ut in the bailey which was larger — she had climbed on the wall by the rmory steps and had shouted out her words of power for all to hear. She had ainted after the third and been rushed indoors by the housekeeper and the eneschal. But she had rallied before the people could disperse and had nsisted on going out to them again and destroying her fourth word, as well. o one knew what gibberish she had been trying to say. Krasnegarians in eneral had no knowledge of the words of power, and if any of those present ad any inkling, they had not explained to the others. She was assumed to ave had a brainstorm.

To tell a word weakened it. To broadcast it to hundreds or thousands of isteners would reduce it to nothing at all.

Rap would not have believed it was physically possible. He was not sur-rised that Inos had collapsed completely at the end. The council had been

summoned, but then Hononin had gone off to gather some horses and bed
ding; he had caught the morning tide with minutes to spare.

And that was why there had been a fire and food and dry blankets waiting
for the exhausted traveler. And until the tide allowed him to go to Inos, Rap
had nothing better to do than enjoy them.

As his eyelids began to droop, he realized that he was free of pain at last;
he was actually going to sleep, for the first time since before Winterfest.

He would never taste his mother's chicken dumplings again.

Hononin had undoubtedly saved Rap's life by being at the cottages in the
night; in the morning Rap returned the favor. A full winter blizzard howled
over Krasnegar, and only his farsight let the two men find their way across the
causeway. Rap's mastery kept the horses under control, but as soon as the trav
elers reached the dock, Rap left his companion and rode hard to the castle.

The first person he met in the stable was Lin. He had grown taller, but
mostly plumper. Behind a misty mustache, Lin was a very typical imp.

"Rap!" He stared as if seeing a ghost.

Rap sprang from Evil's saddle. "Where's Inos?"

"She's not well. But, Rap, where in the world —"

Rap took him by the throat. *"Where's Inos?"*

"In the P-p-presence Chamber," Lin stuttered, eyes bulging.

"Look after my horse!" Rap roared, and sprinted out the door.

Now he dared not even try to cross the bailey on foot; he raced around
the long way, staying indoors. He met dozens of people, in twos and threes.
They backed out of his way with startling eyes. Shouts of "Rap!" pursued
him. One or two tried to stop him, and he pushed them aside and kept on
running.

He crossed the Great Hall while many of the staff were sitting down to
their lunch. Snow had coated the windows, the fires burned bright in the
gloom, fogging the air with a haze of fragrant peat smoke. Nevertheless he
was recognized, for he had been the only faun in the kingdom. Cheerful chat
ter died away, and heads turned. He ran to the Throne Room, heading for the
stair. And there his way was blocked by Kratharkran, just descending. Tall and
barley-haired, he was so like the young raider Vurjuk that Rap recoiled.

"Krath!"

"Rap!"

Krath, Rap recalled, had been appointed a member of the Council — Inos
had told him. "How is Inos?"

A dark frown came over the big man's boyish face. "Not good. Where did
you come from, Rap?"

"Never mind! I must see Inos!"

The smith shifted his feet so that he blocked the doorway — all of the doorway. He folded his arms. Yesterday Rap could have blasted him to Zark. Today he could not force his way past Krath with a sledgehammer.

"She's resting!" the jotunn said, regarding the stranger with deep suspicion.

"But is she conscious?"

"No, she's not. The doctors are planning to bleed her, if you must know."

"*Bleed* her?" God of Fools! Krasnegar had never been renowned for the quality of its medicine. Holindarn had sent to Hub for a doctor when he fell sick.

There would be much better doctors in Kinvale.

Rap took a deep breath and forced his wits to work. Guile was what was needed here. Fortunately, Krath had always been a trusting sort of fellow.

"Krath," he said, "she's my wife."

9

"He says he's her husband," Krath squeaked.

Inos lay on a makeshift bed in the Presence Chamber, one floor above the Throne Room. Her face was pale, her eyes closed, her hair a flood of golden honey on the snowdrift pillow. Tall candelabra had been gathered around the bed to give light, and the medics were hunched around her like vultures. Six or eight others stood around watching, making the room dark and crowded, and the only one Rap recognized was Foronod — the strangely aged Foronod with the eye-patch, leaning stoop-shouldered on his cane.

The covers were up to Inos's chin, so the leeches had not started yet. Kinvale was beyond the magic portal, six floors higher up the tower.

Foronod made a scoffing noise. "That's the first I've heard of a husband. Can you prove it?"

"Yes," Rap said brashly, and strode forward with all the swagger and confidence he could muster. Why, oh, why had Inos not settled for nullifying three words and left him an adept?

A portly black-clad doctor backed away reluctantly, and Rap went down on his knees by the bed.

"Inos! It's me. Rap!"

No reaction.

"We are waiting for your evidence, Master Rap," Foronod snapped.

Wits churning, Rap rose to his feet and glanced around. "If you will ask the others to leave for a moment, Factor, I shall be happy to explain."

The old man's lip curled in a faint smile of contempt. "I don't see why a certificate of marriage need be so private. Produce it."

335

"I liked you better in the blue doublet you wore at the Harvesthom
Dance, Factor." Rap turned to Krath. "You drink a lot for a member of council
lad. You were the one who threw up behind the awards table."

He had not made any friends with those remarks, but he had obviously
sown some doubts. Their faces were infuriatingly opaque to him now, but
even without insight he could see the hesitation and the old fear of sorcery
He had transformed Andor into Darad, he had guided wagons, he had myste
riously vanished from a locked room — now he had mysteriously reappeared
He had an uncanny reputation.

A sudden odor of scorched hair caused him to move away from the near
est candlestick. He would not be a very convincing sorcerer if he set himself
on fire.

"The last time we met, you were all marked up as a goblin," Foronod said
his one eye glinting angrily. He thumped his cane on the floor.

"And you accused me of stealing horses. I made some improbable state
ments on that occasion also, did I not? And I delivered my evidence. I showed
you what Andor really was." Rap put on the most stubborn expression he
could manage.

Foronod glanced around the group, but he evidently decided that there
was no one there he wished to consult. "Very well, I shall humor you." He
limped to the stair that led up to the Robing Room and opened the door
"Come with me and I shall listen to whatever weird tale you have to recoun
this time. Mastersmith, you had better accompany —"

"I am staying here," Rap said stolidly, "with my wife. You and Krath may
remain. Everybody else — out!"

"You have no authority —"

"I have every authority. I am the queen's husband!"

"A clerk? A herdboy?"

"Krath," Rap said without turning, "who was Inos's closest friend?"

A pause, and then Krath's high voice said, "You were, Rap. Always."

"Close friend does not mean king!" Foronod snarled.

"It does now."

For a moment the issue swung like a weathercock. Perhaps it was because
the factor had only one eye to glare with, or perhaps Rap still retained traces
of a sorcerer's self-confidence, but he won the confrontation.

"Excuse us a moment, ladies and gentlemen, please," the old man said
scowling mightily.

The doctors scowled back, then trooped obediently to the door. The oth
ers reluctantly followed — most of them. One plump lady folded her arm
and set her chins obstinately.

"I do not leave her Majesty unchaperoned!" she proclaimed.

336

"Mistress Meolorne," Rap said, gripping her elbow. "You did a splendid job
ɔ here on the night Inos returned to claim her kingdom. I saw how you com-
ɔrted all those unfortunate girls, finding clothes and —"

"You *saw?*" The haberdasher reluctantly moved her feet as Rap urged her to
ɹe door.

"I saw. Now allow us a moment here and everything will be explained,
promise."

She stopped and would budge no farther. "I shall not leave her Majesty
ith three men!"

"Even when one of them is her husband?"

"Prove it!" The flabby face stiffened, the deep-set eyes glowered at him.

It would have to do, but he hoped she would not join in the violence. "All
ght," he said. He closed the door, surreptitiously sliding the bolt. "Now,
ɔme and see this, gentlemen."

He moved back to the bed and lifted candelabra aside to make room. He
ɪent over Inos, as if looking for something. Foronod hobbled forward on his
ɑne, Krath lurched over with long strides, coming close.

To fight any jotunn was foolhardy, and a jotunn blacksmith was a night-
ɪare opponent. The matter must be settled with the first blow, for there
ɪould be no second. It was a despicable thing to do to a friend.

"I love her, Krath," Rap said sadly. "I wouldn't do this for anyone else."

"Do what, Rap?"

Rap swung around and put his fist with all the strength he could muster
ɪto the young giant's most vulnerable spot. Doubled over, Krath hit the floor
ɹith a howl of agony and a clamor of many candlesticks, even as Rap turned
ɹe other way and slammed a blow on the factor's jaw, pulling the punch more
ɪan he had intended — to strike a cripple was even worse. Foronod went
ɔwn over a table, in a shattering of glasses. Mistress Meolorne's scream shat-
ɹred others. Rap ripped the bedclothes away from Inos and stooped.

He had lifted her and was heading for the far door before Meolorne
ɹacted. She charged at him, claws out, and he rammed into her with Inos.
ʼhe fat woman recoiled and sat down heavily on the rug. Foronod was yelling
ɪd struggling to rise. Krath was retching.

Rap staggered up the stairs with Inos a dead weight in his arms. He fum-
ɪled awkwardly with the handle and stumbled into the Robing Room. He
ɪcked the door shut, reeled off balance for a moment, then managed to turn
ɹound and grope for the bolt with hands he could not see below his burden.
ɪ slid with a satisfying click.

Thereafter he felt as if he were enacting a bizarre replay of another flight
ɪp this same tower, when he and Inos and the others had been pursued by the
ɪmpish army. He was dismayed at how weak he felt and how heavy Inos soon

became. He could feel the warmth of her through her nightgown; shoul
have brought blankets in this cold. His heart was pounding as if about t
explode, his breath was coming in harsh gasps, making white clouds in the ic
air. His body streamed with sweat and there was a bitter taste in his mouth.

Antechamber   . . .

All the doors had long since been repaired and fitted with shiny new bolt
The metal was so cold it stuck to his sweaty fingers. He had time, though
because it would take a while for the pursuers to find axes and enough stror
men — Krath at least would not be participating.

Rap's next meeting with friend Kratharkran was going to be a painfu
experience.

Well, it was worth it if he could save Inos — and he felt tremendous sati
faction in pulling this off without the aid of any despicable sorcery at all!

The stairs were dark, the rooms gloomy, all the casements caked wit
snow.

Withdrawing Room . . . more stairs . . .

He still had his farsight. He could watch the pursuit. Oh, Gods! The ne
doors were flimsy, shoddy affairs compared to the old. And jotnar were no
imps. Two enraged young giants had just shattered the first one with benche

Dressing Room . . .

Another door collapsed into splinters without a struggle. They had throw
away the benches and taken to using feet and shoulders. Would even a ston
wall stop a really mad jotunn? *They were gaining on him!*

The Royal Bedchamber . . .

He was at the limits of his strength. His head throbbed and dark patche
swam before his eyes. He must rest or he would faint. With legs like strips o
hot dough, he wobbled over to the bed and dumped Inos down on it.

He sprawled unexpectedly on top of her, his breath rasping like a saw.

There was an arm around his neck.

He raised his head and peered into the only truly green eyes in Krasnega

"You stink like a stable," she said quietly.

Rap said, "Awrrk," or thereabouts.

"I do think you might have washed or something first."

"Inos! Oh, Inos!"

"Husband!" she murmured. Her eyes had closed again.

Rap made another incoherent noise. "You were awake?"

"I heard some of it," she said sleepily. "That was a very romantic way t
carry me to my bridal bed, but was it wise?"

He tried to get up, and the arm tightened like a saddle girth.

"Kiss me."

"I smell like a horse."

"Kiss like a horse, then. But kiss me."

He kissed her — gently, tentatively, excitedly, joyfully, wildly, passionately
. . *prolongedly.*

Joy! Inos! Love!

"My!" she said at last. "I didn't know you cared." Then she opened her eyes
astonishment. "You're weeping!"

"Of course I'm weeping, you crazy, idiotic, headstrong nincompoop!"

"Oh, you do care!" Sudden anxiety . . . "You don't mind what I did?"

"No, no! It's wonderful. I never wanted to be a sorcerer, darling!"

Relief! "Darling! To hear you say . . . What is that confounded racket?"
os was no longer an adept, but the royal glamour was still there, and the
een eyes flashed with regal annoyance.

"Foronod and the rest of your loyal subjects. They think you're being
ped. They're just breaking into the Dressing Room."

She smiled contentedly and closed her eyes again. "Then we just have
me for another kiss before I send them all away and it happens."

"You're all right?"

"One more kiss should do it."

"But —"

"I suppose we shall have to slip down to Kinvale in a day or two and make
is wedding official," she mused. "But that can be our little secret."

A stableboy? A wagon driver? A horsethief?

A flat-nosed, ugly faun?

The royal glare was switched on again as she looked at him. "I distinctly
emember ordering you to kiss me."

"But —"

But she was queen. The glamour was still there.

He obeyed.

They would all obey, always. She was the queen.

Alteration find:
>   Let me not to the marriage of true minds
>   Admit impediments. Love is not love
>   Which alters when it alteration finds,
>   Or bends with the remover to remove.
>
>   . . .
>
>   If this be error, and upon me proved,
>   I never writ, nor no man ever loved.
>   Shakespeare, *Sonnet CXVI*

Epilogu

Irksome word:

"C harming!" Kadolan said. "No, you look much more tha
charming! Beautiful! Ravishing!"

"Gods, Aunt! Is that an appropriate expression for a brid
on her wedding day?" Without turning, Inos grinned mischie
vously from the dressing-table mirror.

"You know what I mean! You look absolutely divine!"

Inos's happy smile faltered slightly; she shivered. "Not that, either!" The
she laughed. "But I accept the compliment. In fact, I agree wholeheartedly
Considering the short notice, I think I've done not badly. Even Eigaze woul
approve. And it's fortunate Tiffy isn't here — he'd certainly find a well t
jump into."

"Tiffy's married, dear. And expecting. Didn't I tell you about Eigaze
letter?"

"Mm? Perhaps you did. The marriage doesn't surprise me, and I think I now what you mean otherwise." Inos poked thoughtfully at the heap of arls before her. "One string, do you think? Or two?"

"None. You make them look dull and lusterless."

"My!" Inos murmured, pleased. "That sounds like one of Andor's lines. Just e tiara, then? After all, it was a present from Rap." She chuckled softly. "The ly present he's given me since a nest of quail eggs he found on . . . no, at's not true! He gave me my kingdom."

Kadolan muttered agreement. Truth be told, she was seeing her gorgeous ece as a blur of emerald silk. It had been common knowledge for years ound Kinvale that one infallible cure for drought was to invite Princess adolan to a wedding; she invariably wept enough at a wedding to irrigate ery farm for leagues. Already she needed her handkerchief, and soon.

"It's almost sunset," she said hastily. "Why don't I go and see if the other alf of the ceremony has arrived?" She headed for the door.

Dabbing her eyes, she proceeded along the corridor. The groom and the est man were supposed to come at sunset, and she realized that she had completely forgotten to ask who was going to be best man. Probably some castle unky she had never met. She sighed wistfully, thinking that the most appropriate choice would have been Captain Gathmor. Or Minstrel Jalon, maybe.

At least it would not be that terrible goblin!

Planning a wedding had always been one of her favorite occupations, and he felt cheated at having been allowed only three days to arrange this one. et that was not so surprising. Of all the young ladies she had introduced to atrimony in her years at Kinvale, none had proved so difficult to bring to e altar as her niece.

Because of Rap's lie to Foronod, this must be a very intimate affair; a secret edding, really. And that was a shame, too. Kadolan had many happy memo- es of Holindarn's wedding, when all Krasnegar had rejoiced and partied for ays. Still, it was fortunate that Marshal Ithy happened to be visiting Kinvale the moment, returning from his inspection of the Pondague lines. He had appily agreed to give away the bride.

And Inos had decided to hold a full-scale coronation in the summer. he had never been formally crowned, and now Krasnegar had a king to rown also. Kadolan certainly intended to be present for that. She would neak in through the magic portal, which still remained a close-guarded tate secret, and pretend that she had come by ship. She reminded herself hat Rap knew nothing of those plans yet, so she must be careful not to nention them this evening.

But a formal wedding would have been nice. The imperor would have sent representative, and royal gifts. And what was the use of having so many rel-

atives if you couldn't summon them all to lavish affairs like weddings? Eve
Eigaze and Epoxague might have come to a Kinvale wedding, but they cou
hardly be invited to Krasnegar. Some distant relatives were just *too* distant!

She paused to catch her breath at her parlor door, then tapped discreet
and went in. Pink light shone through the lace curtains, candles had been l
already, but there was no one there.

Tutting quietly to herself, she went over to inspect the flowers. The rose
were well past their best now, but Kinvale's chrysanthemums had a well
deserved fame in the district. Then a rush of smoke from the fireplace warne
her, and she turned around as the magic portal swung open, admitting an ic
blast from Krasnegar.

A short man stood framed in the entrance, his leathery, weatherbeate
face a mask of shock. Cutaway coat and tights, a rapier at his belt and a tr
corn hat clutched nervously in front of him . . . for a moment Kadolan di
not recognize him in such finery. Then her eyes misted again. Oh, well don
Master Rap! How very appropriate!

The best man spun around and attempted to return to Krasnegar. He wa
obviously blocked. "Good preserve me!" he shouted. "You told me there wa
to be no Evil-begotten sorcery!"

Rap laughed from the darkness beyond him. "I did warn you about this bi
No more, I promise! Go on with you! Oh, your Highness! You kno
Krasnegar's Master of Horse, I'm sure?"

"Certainly I know Master Hononin!" Kadolan advanced with her han
out. "You are a sight for sore eyes, you old rascal!"

A sight for weepy, sentimental old eyes, too.

Hononin glanced around to make sure there was no one else present. "I'
never have agreed to this nonsense if I'd known I was going to be decked o
like a one-man carnival!"

"Then Rap was right not to tell you!" She kissed his cheek.

He grunted. Then he chuckled softly. "How are you, Kade?"

"Wonderful! And you?"

"Not bad."

"The years are kind to you, old man. Better than you deserve, I'm sure!"

"Well, now, that takes royal impudence! I'm three months younger tha
you are, as I recall."

"I see you two know each other quite well!" Rap commented, coming i
and closing the door.

"First boy who ever kissed me!" Kadolan said archly, just to see if she coul
still make Honi blush. She could.

"As I remember, it was you who kissed me! And if your mother hadn
come looking for you, you'd have —"

"Well, it was a long time ago," Kadolan said quickly. She dabbed her eyes
ain with her lace handkerchief and turned to inspect the bridegroom. "Your
aj — *Oh, no!*"

Rap bowed, managing his rapier quite skillfully. But then he kept his face
wn and fumbled with the hat he was holding.

"Let me see!" Kadolan said, in a voice much sharper than her normal tone
r addressing kings.

He raised his head ashamedly. His lower lip was puffed and cut, and he
d two very generous black eyes. He could not have looked worse had his
blin tattoos been restored.

For a moment no one said anything.

Then Hononin cackled. "Told you you'd be in trouble, King!"

"*Don't* call me that!" Rap said angrily. "Sorry, your Highness," he added
mbly. "You think Inos will be upset?"

"Upset?" Oh, dear! Kadolan sighed. "Well, I suppose she will just have to
 upset, won't she?" Old fears stirred momentarily. This was what happened
hen royalty married beneath them . . . Then she chided herself for
nseemly pride. The Gods had approved this match, and the boy had excel-
nt qualities, as she well knew. Even if he was no longer a sorcerer, he was a
ood man.

He would just have to learn that a king should not go brawling.

He had done his best, she supposed, but there was lint on his collar, his
ravat looked like a collapsed soufflé, and whatever he had used to plaster his
air had left it in plates and spikes. And Inos was looking so *radiant!*

Anxious not to show her disappointment, Kadolan turned to the sideboard
here the best crystal waited. "Inos is almost ready," she said bravely, "and the
haplain has arrived. Will you join me in a glass of wine, gentlemen?"

Without waiting for a reply, she unstoppered the decanter. A royal bride-
room with black eyes! "Do be seated. Wine, your Majesty?"

Rap winced. "*Please,* ma'am! I keep telling Inos — I really don't want to be
alled that! She's the queen. I'm just her husband." He blushed scarlet, all
round his bruises, and said quickly, "Am about to become her husband, that
. Everyone in Krasnegar remembers me as a stableboy. I feel such a *fool* when
hey bow and call me 'king' and 'sire'! I'm sure they're laughing at me. There
ust be some better title I could have."

That was something else he would have to get used to, Kadolan decided.
here *was* no other title, and Inos wouldn't agree to it if there was.

Rap made another appeal for sympathy. "You know what she's planning
ext? A *coronation!*" He shuddered. "But I'm not supposed to know, so please
on't mention I mentioned it."

"I promise. I did know, and I'm looking forward to it!"

He sat down with a groan.

Winning a brief struggle with his sword, the hostler perched on the lip a chair. He sipped the wine and raised his grizzled eyebrows approving Kadolan settled on the pink brocade sofa opposite.

"I trust that no one will notice your absence this evening, Honi?"

"Of course not. Except the horses, and they don't talk to no one but Rap He leered. "And no one will intrude on their Majesties, either! Not with th wolf on guard!"

Kadolan almost spilled her wine. "Wolf?"

"You remember Fleabag!" Rap said, beaming happily. "He introduced yo to Darad, remember?"

"And to Sultan Azak!"

"Well, then! I thought I'd lost him in the forest, but he came trotting acro the causeway this morning, wagging his tail." Rap hesitated and adde vaguely, "Lucky I happened to be down at the docks."

Kadolan wondered why anyone would be down at the docks in Krasneg now that they were all snowed in. Still, Master Rap was the king now, so sh wouldn't ask. Obviously Hononin was wondering the same thing, for he wa scowling. As a boy, Honi had been fearfully shy, but he'd concluded that peo ple didn't notice that if he scowled. He'd been scowling ever since.

There was an awkward pause.

"Talking of Master Darad," she said brightly, "I must remember to sho you the letter I received last week from Doctor Sagorn and his friends."

"Yes?" Rap said politely, sipping wine. "I didn't know Darad could write."

"I'm sure he can't. Doctor Sagorn passed on his regards, and he made h mark. Doctor Sagorn's own part was rather *dry*, I admit, but Sir Andor adde some very witty comments, and Jalon sent a beautiful sonnet."

"And Thinal?"

"He made his mark, also. He is thinking of going into business, appar ently. He feels he is getting too old for climbing walls, the doctor says." Fo a moment Kadolan reflected on all the curious friends she had made on he adventures — Sultan Azak, Mage Elkarath, little Prince Shandie, the lior slayers and their wives, and the wardens, although of course they wer never friends . . .

"What sort of business?" Rap asked.

"Jewelry, of course."

He chuckled. "Of course. May the Gods defend his customers!"

Again an awkward pause . . . Rap caught Kadolan studying his face, an he colored again.

"It was Krath, you see," he muttered.

"Krath?"

"Inos did mention him, I think . . . When she was telling you how I, er .
. rescued her? I struck a jotunn. I know that's a stupid thing to do, but I did-
: have any choice."

"Oh! Of course! She did tell me." Kadolan felt a little better — not a vul-
r brawl, but a royal rescue. "No ordinary jotunn, either. A blacksmith! Yes,
at was very brave of you."

"It was very dumb of me! Of course he's been hunting me ever since. And
:sterday he brought some friends to help, and then I couldn't avoid him,
en with farsight."

Kadolan sighed and finished her wine. "Well, I see that under the circum-
ances you had no choice. And I thank the Gods that you're well enough to
me to the wedding at all."

Rap stiffened, and Hononin uttered one of his raucous chuckles.

"You don't know the half of it!" he said. "It was a fabulous match! If Krath
ad laid a fist on him, he'd have been a human pancake, but Rap used some
rcery or other —"

"That was *not* sorcery!" Rap said crossly. "Little Chicken taught me some
rows." He pouted lopsidedly around his swollen lip. "I was doing all right,
o, but then —"

"You were wrecking the castle!" Hononin said. "Slam a jotunn into a
one wall often enough and the wall must break eventually. Krath wasn't
ver going to give up! But then the queen arrived." He chortled. "With the
uard! Furious! Royal tantrum! She ordered Sergeant Oopari to arrest the
nith for treason!"

"It took all six of them to do it," Rap said, with obvious satisfaction.

"Well, he'd lost his temper by then," Hononin observed solemnly.

"You see, ma'am . . . " Rap hesitated, and then drained his glass. "As
on as she left this afternoon, to come here, I went down to the cells and
sued a royal pardon. Ma'am, I had to! I mean, I can't hide behind Inos's skirts
l the time! Not if she really wants me to be . . . " he scowled, and said,
ing!" as if it were an obscenity.

"So where did your, er, injuries come from?"

Rap shrugged. "Krath and I went off to the Beached Whale to celebrate,
f course."

Hononin cackled. "They're renaming it the Sunken Whale. Some sailor
ade a joke about fauns, so Krath put his head through a plank table. His
hipmates didn't approve, but Krath's three uncles were there. Soon everyone
ined in, and things began to get violent . . . Haven't seen such a free-for-
ll in years!" Surreptitiously he winked at Kadolan.

For a moment she was startled, then she understood and carefully sup-
ressed a smile. This was Krasnegar they were discussing, not Hub. If Master

Rap was ever to be more than the queen's husband, he would have to establi
his credentials, and the hostler was implying that he had made a good start.

"Then I am sure that Inos will understand," she said. "But don't expe
instant forgiveness! Perhaps we should go now . . . "

Rap fidgeted and stared down at his hands. "She's going to be upset?"

"I'm afraid so."

"Very upset?"

"Extremely upset."

He looked up with dismay. "I don't want to upset her."

She felt puzzled. "Then you should have waited until after the wedding.

He nodded miserably. "Then . . . Will you promise not to tell her . .
both of you?"

Quite perplexed now, Kadolan said, "She can see for herself."

Rap groaned. "I mean this."

Black eyes and split lip disappeared.

Kadolan jumped. "Oh!"

Hononin uttered a low growl. "You told me you weren't a sorcer
anymore!"

Rap nodded, looking completely dejected. "That was true when I said i
Ma'am . . . can you remember your word of power?"

"No . . . no, I can't!" Kadolan had sensed something inexplicable whe
Inos was destroying the words. She'd attributed the feeling to mild dyspeps
until Rap and Inos had come bursting through the magic portal that evenin
to tell her that the magic was destroyed and they wanted a quick wedding an
everything was wonderful. And now she could not even remember what he
word had been.

Rap glanced at the hostler. "They're great long, gibberish things, yo
see. The only reason people can remember them at all, when they've onl
heard them once, is that they're magic in themselves. They're magicall
memorable."

Now Kadolan began to understand and was hard put to hide a sudde
excitement. "So when Inos destroyed them . . . "

"She just stunned them!" Rap said crossly. "Or some of them. All thos
hundreds of people who heard them three days ago . . . now they're start
ing to forget what they heard."

"The words are coming back, you mean?"

He nodded glumly. "Seems so. Some. And because I have this natural tal
ent for sorcery . . . I think that's what it is. I seem to be the one they'r
coming back to."

"Well, I don't see why you're so miserable! I still don't understand why Ino
tried to destroy them in the first place."

346

"Because the G-G-Gods . . . " He stuttered, and gave up. "It's hard to
plain. But it doesn't matter now. I asked Inos if she could remember what
·e words were, and she said no. So, as long as she doesn't remember, we're all
;ht. I don't think I'm going to get all my power back, anyway." He waved a
ind to indicate his eyes. "This . . . it's just an illusion. I'll need to show my
·ce tomorrow, back in Krasnegar . . . You won't tell Inos, though?"

Nor had Kadolan ever understood why he didn't like being a sorcerer,
it that was not her business. A little magic had always come in handy for
·ling Krasnegar.

She rose, and Rap sprang up also.

"I shan't tell her — if you do something about the lint on your collar!"

This obvious blackmail made him scowl as ferociously as Hononin ever
id. Then the lint vanished, as did the wrinkles in his coat. The lace of his
·avat stiffened and began to shine like fresh snow. The buckle of his belt
·arkled and his hair settled into shiny waves.

"Much better!" she said. "Oh, much!" Suddenly he was an astonishingly
·andsome royal bridegroom. How romantic! "Inos will be delighted!"
·npulsively she kissed him. He looked startled, and then grinned bashfully.
·he was astonished to discover that he was shaking. Rap, nervous? Rap who
·ad faced down pirates and sultans . . .

"Thank you," she said. "And you do promise to behave yourself this time,
·on't you?"

"Behave myself?"

Rap, who had overcome goblins and dragons . . .

"Not disrupt the ceremony by brandishing swords?"

"Of course not!"

Rap, who had challenged warlocks and — she suspected — even the Gods
·hemselves . . .

"Or coming in on a horse . . . backward?"

"Certainly not backward."

"Or running away?"

"Ah!" Rap said darkly. "Now that *is* beginning to seem like a good idea."

"Don't worry, Kade," Hononin said cheerfully. "I'll keep him there if I have
·o run him through with my sword."

Rap, who would be a faithful, loving husband and a solid, honorable
·ing . . .

Suddenly Kadolan's eyes started to do what they always did at weddings.
·he turned away quickly and headed for the door. Rap strode by her and
·hrew it open.

She curtseyed. "After you, your Majesty!"

"*No!* Please, ma'am! I *don't* want to be called that!"

347

"Surely that is for the queen to decide? Or do you intend to overrule h
all the time?"

Rap turned scarlet. "*Overrule* her? Of course not! Never! Inos is the quee
I'm just . . . just . . . Oh, *God of Fools!* . . . " With a muffled noise th
sounded vaguely nautical, he strode out into the corridor, where he continue
to mutter angrily.

Hononin leered like a gargoyle and offered Kadolan his arm.

"Sorcerer or not," he whispered, "any man who falls in love that dee
hasn't got much hope, has he?"

"None whatsoever!" she agreed quietly.

They chuckled in unison and followed Rap out.

And the door closed behind them.

Irksome words:

The play is done; the curtain drops, Slow falling to the prompter's bell:
A moment yet the actor stops,
And looks around, to say farewell.
It is an irksome word and task . . .
Thackeray, The End of the Play

About the Author

DAVE DUNCAN, born in Scotland in 1933, is a Canadian citizen. He received his diploma from Dundee High School and got his college education at the University of Saint Andrews. He moved to Canada in 1955, where he still lives with his wife. He has three grown children and spent twenty-five years as a petroleum geologist. He has had dozens of fantasy and science fiction novels published, among them A ROSE-RED CITY, MAGIC CASEMENT and THE REAVER ROAD, as well as a highly praised historical novel under a pseudonym.

9 780759 239586